KYLA STONE

THE LAST SANCTUARY

The Last Sanctuary

This book is a work of fiction. Any references to historical events, real people, or real places are fictitious. Other names, characters, places, and events are products of the author's imagination, and any resemblances to actual events or places or persons, living or dead, are entirely coincidental.

Printed in the United States of America

Cover design by Damonza

Book formatting by Vellum

First Printed in 2025

ISBN 978-1-962251-44-0

Paper Moon Press

 Formatted with Vellum

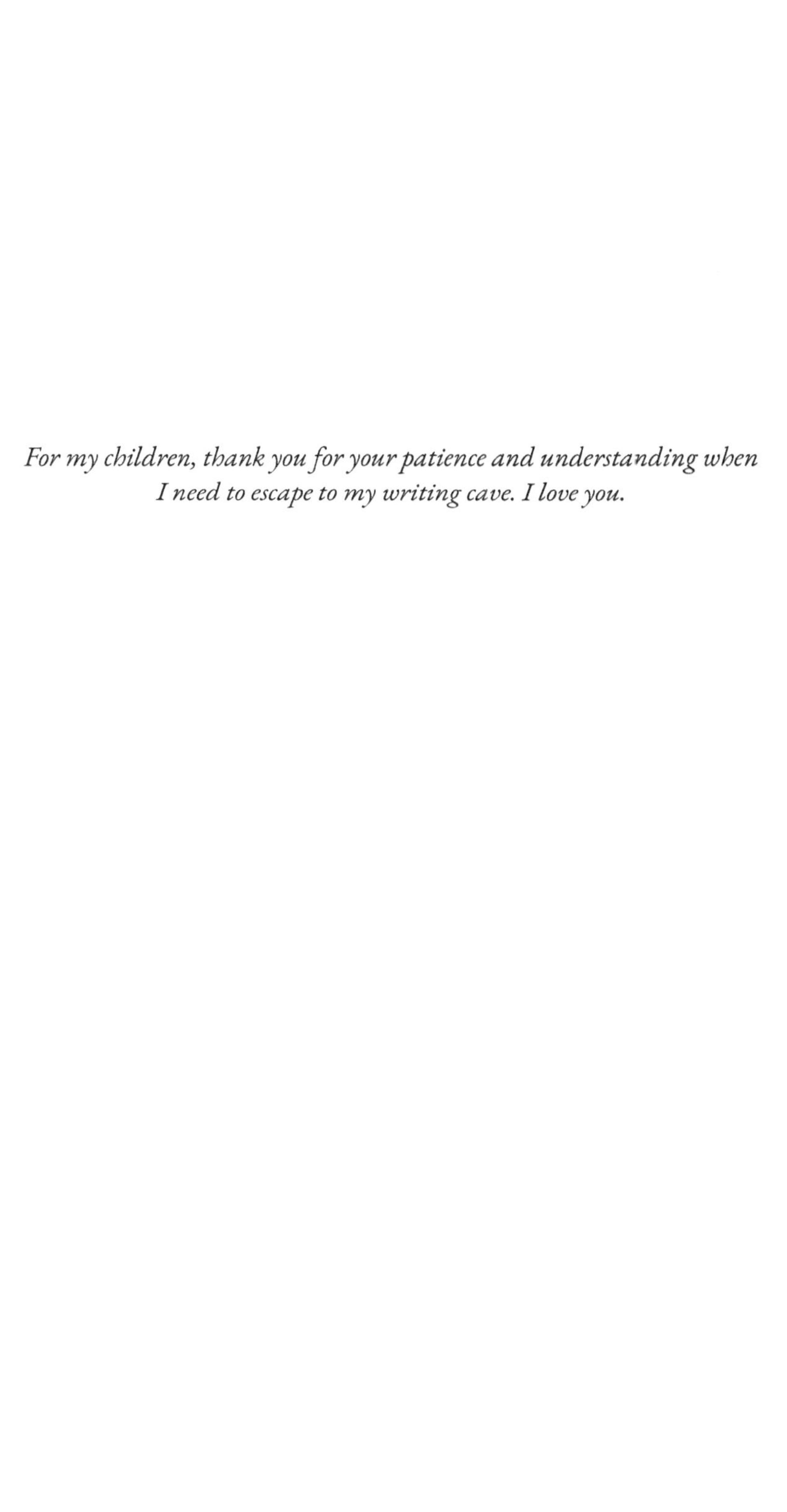

For my children, thank you for your patience and understanding when I need to escape to my writing cave. I love you.

Just as despair can come to one only from other human
beings, hope, too, can be given to one only by other human
beings.

— ELIE WIESEL

Chapter One

Silence could drown a person.

At least, that's what Raven Nakamura's mother had said three years ago, the day she left home for good.

Raven's mother hadn't been correct, though. It wasn't silence.

There were more sounds than Raven could count—the whirring of insects, the breeze rustling the elm and maple trees lining the flagstone paths, the constant calls, screeches, hoots, bellows, grunts, and growls of the numerous and varied exotic animals that lived here in the wildlife sanctuary Raven called home.

It was isolation that could drown a person. Solitary confinement. Loneliness like a great bottomless sea, sucking you under.

Her mom had been full of crap. She'd told herself whatever would justify abandoning her husband and her home, leaving her whole life behind, including her daughter, discarded like a grubby candy wrapper, a piece of trash to sweep away, to ignore and forget.

Raven rubbed her eyes with the back of her arm and forced herself to focus on the swishing tail of the enormous cat sprawled in the enclosure a mere twenty feet below her.

The Siberian tiger tilted his great head and blinked lazily up at her, yellow eyes shining with a vicious, uncanny intelligence. A seven-year-old male, Vlad weighed over five hundred pounds and stretched nine feet from nose to tail.

A creature of incredible power and beauty, his thick orange fur, was stippled with inky-black and rippled across his muscular torso and powerful forelegs.

His majestic head was larger than a basketball and ringed with a thick white ruff. Sharp fangs glinted from impressive jaws. He flexed enormous paws that could rip off a man's face.

Every inch of him was formidable, exquisite, and lethal. Raven utterly adored him.

The tiger was just fine with isolation. They were solitary creatures by nature, nomads of the jungle. Or, in this case, of Haven Wildlife Refuge, the family zoo Raven's father had owned and operated for over a decade.

The private zoo was nestled along the perimeter of the Piedmont National Wildlife Refuge, a 35,000-acre nature preserve located twenty-five miles north of Macon and about sixty miles southeast of downtown Atlanta.

Not too far from civilization, but the nearby sanctuary of the Piedmont wilderness made it feel isolated, remote, a million miles from the loudness and chaos of the cities. That, and her father barely allowed her to leave the grounds.

Raven wasn't afraid of being alone. She vastly preferred solitude to any kind of human contact. She'd inherited that trait from her father.

Her mother had been the one who couldn't stand the loneliness, the isolation, the long hours with wolves, bears, and a tiger for company. Her mother had loathed this place so much she'd chosen her freedom over her daughter.

Raven gritted her teeth at the swell of uncomfortable emotions squeezing her chest: anger, shame, and loss. Too many emotions to count or name.

Usually, she was successful at keeping thoughts of her mother buried in a dark corner of her brain, shoved somewhere down deep, so deep she couldn't feel the sting of betrayal, the grief of rejection.

Out of sight, out of mind.

Except for today. October sixteenth. Raven's eighteenth birthday.

It was a beautiful fall day—too lovely for the dark tangle of emotions knotted inside her, for the awful things happening outside the safety of the fenced walls of the sanctuary, the disturbing reports coming from the nearby towns and cities of Georgia and beyond.

Scraps of clouds drifted across the sun, shining brilliantly in the cobalt sky. It was a pleasant sixty-five degrees. Nature hadn't changed. The sun still shone. The breeze still kissed her cheeks and ruffled her ink-black hair.

Raven wore her usual cargo pants, scuffed work boots, and a loose *Nirvana* T-shirt. Her N95 mask was stuffed into the cargo pocket of her pants, just in case.

Not that there were many visitors left to worry about. Or any. Not anymore.

Her fingers tightened around the small parcel she held in her lap. Her mother had sent her something, after all. It had arrived two weeks ago, the day before the postal service had stopped delivering the mail. A hiatus, they'd called it.

She didn't want to know what was inside the box. At the same time, she did. She considered chucking it into the tiger enclosure so Vlad could rip it to shreds as part of his daily enrichment activities.

And yet, if she threw it away unopened, that niggle of curiosity tugging at the back of her mind would remain unassuaged.

This was the last birthday she'd have here. Which meant this was the last present from her mother she'd ever receive, whether the mail came back or not. Likely, not.

Raven shifted her weight, stretched out her legs, and leaned over the edge of the tiger house roof to catch a glimpse of her hiking backpack slumped against the outer wall of the enclosure.

She'd spent the last week stealthily scrounging supplies: binoculars, fishing wire and lure, snare wire for small animal traps, a single-person tent, a sleeping bag, a LifeStraw and water filtration tablets, a tin cup, plate, and pan, flint and spare lighter, compass, toiletries, granola bars, dried venison strips, and several self-heating meal pouches.

She'd packed in secret, but she needn't have worried. Her father noticed little unless it had to do with the exotic animals, the maintenance of the refuge, or instructing her in one of his favorite subjects: survival skills, zoology, and how to scrub bear urine from concrete.

And now, with the keepers failing to show for the third week in a row, her father had to pull sixteen-hour shifts to keep the place running. She was right there with him, working from dawn to dusk to feed the animals and clean out the cages until her fingers blistered, until her bones ached with exhaustion.

Even after weeks of working nonstop side by side, they were like strangers. He'd shut down after her mother left—hell, he'd been a stranger for years, if she were honest.

An aching pang stabbed between her ribs. A person could be loneliest around other people. Living, working, and breathing right next to someone else—a stranger who wasn't supposed to be a stranger. That's what hurt the most.

It was a loneliness that hurt more than actually being alone. Maybe her mother had been talking about *that.*

She pushed the ache down somewhere deep. It was just as well. It didn't matter. None of it mattered. She was leaving.

She'd had enough. Enough of people who only hurt her. Enough of this place that had once seemed magical but now only held dark memories of disappointment, pain, and regret.

Her grandfather owned a hunting cabin one hundred and fifty miles northwest of Haven Wildlife Refuge. It was remote, fully stocked, and off the grid, with a hand-pumped well and solar power.

Located in the Blue Ridge Mountains, deep within the Chattahoochee National Forest, it was far from humans and the besieged cities, accessible only by an unmarked trail barely wide enough for an ATV.

The map detailing the directions and specific location of the cabin was tucked into her backpack. She didn't remember its exact location, only that it was somewhere north of a tiny town called Scorpion Hollow.

The cabin was far from here, from her dad, and the bitter memories of her mother. Far from the distressing news reports, the alarming death tolls, the itchy masks, the constant, unrelenting fear.

It was time to strike out on her own.

It would take a few weeks to get there. She knew how to survive in the woods. Knew what berries were poisonous, which plants and nuts and mushrooms were edible, how to track game and set snares, how to construct a shelter and start a fire in the rain.

Beneath her perch on the tiger house roof, Vlad grunted and stretched his big paws, flexing his claws into the red rubber ball that served as one of his enrichment toys.

Almost against her will, her gaze was drawn back to the box in her hands. No matter how much she wanted to, she couldn't leave the gift unopened. She had to know.

Raven set aside the attached letter and slid her fingernails between the cardboard flaps of the box, slicing through the tape. She dug through the balls of Styrofoam and pulled out a small knife.

The off-white handle was made of polymer, an imitation of ivory, and carved in the shape of a wolf, its tiny mouth opened in a snarl. The blade was short, slightly curved, and sharp. It was a whittling knife, like the one Raven used to carve the animals she displayed on her bedroom windowsill, back when she was a kid.

She hadn't carved anything in three years. Not since the day her mother left.

Raven sighed, disappointed despite herself. What had she expected? Last year, her mother had sent a ridiculous hoverboard as a gift. As if she'd forgotten Raven was no longer ten. She'd stuffed it into her closet and forgotten about it.

Her mother didn't know her anymore.

Raven flicked the blade closed and shoved the whittling knife into her pocket. She didn't want it, but she couldn't leave it on top of the tiger house. A strong wind might blow it into the enclosure, and Vlad, who ate everything, would swallow it whole.

Her gaze landed on the white square of the envelope. Only her mother wrote physical letters by hand instead of messaging on WhatsApp, Snapchat, or social media.

However, the internet had gone sketchy a couple of weeks ago. Same with cell service. Nothing was working anymore, and hadn't for awhile.

The lack of communication was disconcerting, amplifying her sense of isolation. Even doomscrolling or watching hours of mind-numbing fake videos of dancing kittens was better than the nothingness, of being completely cut off from whatever horrors were taking place outside these walls.

Maybe her mother was smarter than Raven gave her credit for.

With a sigh, she opened the letter and skimmed her mom's familiar, precise, neat script. There were the usual miss-yous and love-yous, each one like a stab to Raven's gut.

A few lines toward the end caught her eye. *I'm coming to get you,* her mom had written. *With everything that's happened, it's too dangerous for you there.*

Her heart lurched in her chest. Fumbling for the envelope, she rechecked the date stamped on the front. Almost three weeks ago. Her mom said she was coming, for the first time in three years.

So where was she?

I've tried to call and message, but the connection has been spotty this last week. Things are bad. Everything is falling apart out there. I'm worried this is it. The end.

The Settlement is a safe place for us. There are good people here. It is well-fortified. Until I come, wear your mask. Be careful. If, for some reason, I'm prevented from reaching you, then come here. Find good people you can trust. Whatever you do, don't be alone.

I love you.

The Settlement, where her mother had found refuge, was a self-sustaining New Age commune located near Elijay in the Blue Ridge Mountains of northern Georgia, a hundred miles or so northwest as the crow flew.

It was dangerous for a woman to travel alone, especially through gang-controlled Atlanta, but now? With all this? Millions of people spreading sickness, disease, death to anyone who got too close.

The world had gone mad again. And things were so much worse than the last time, and the time before that.

Raven balled the letter in her fist and crumpled it between her fingers. Her hands trembled, her knuckles whitening.

Had her mom already tried to come for her? If so, she hadn't made it. Had something happened to her?

Her jaw clenched. Old pain sprouted in her gut, tangling her stomach into knots. What did her mom know? She thought she could ride in on a white horse and save everyone, yet she hadn't bothered to visit in all this time.

Raven could handle things just fine on her own. She'd been taking care of herself for years, since long before her mother had left, always seeking something else, something better, always searching for the perfect life she'd never been able to find here at home.

Steeling herself, Raven stuffed the letter in her pocket next to the whittling knife. She was far too busy to worry about her mother right now.

She took a deep breath, then slipped to the edge of the roof, crouched, and leaped to the ground. It was a long drop, but she softened her legs and curled into a roll before scrambling to her feet.

She brushed twigs, pine needles, and mulch from her pant legs, then whistled one long note, then two short ones—Vlad's signal for food.

Behind the tiger house, in a fenced area off-limits to visitors, she could draw close to the eighteen-foot-tall fence. The rest of the enclosure was circled by a deep ditch, surrounding a six-foot-high perimeter wall on the tiger's side, with a four-foot-tall wall on the visitors' side, which provided the illusion of unobscured proximity.

Vlad typically lounged on a rock shelf beside his shallow bathing pool. A thin trickling waterfall streamed above him. The rocks were a polymer replica airbrushed to look authentically aged and weathered, while the waterfall poured from a hidden PVC pipe.

At her approach, Vlad rose lightly to his feet and sauntered up to the fence. He eyed her, his ears pricked, waiting impatiently. She pulled a piece of dried venison from her cargo pocket and held it in front of him.

Vlad chuffed in approval. Normally, tigers ate raw meat. In particular, Vlad enjoyed beef, cow femurs, and horse meat, along with turkey and chicken necks, which aided his dental hygiene.

Lately, Vlad had developed a taste for jerky, specifically deer jerky. She took several steps back and hurled a few pieces over the fence.

Vlad's head snapped toward them. He pounced, snapped his jaws shut, and inhaled the venison in the blink of an eye.

Vlad prowled back to the fence and pressed his enormous body against it, chuffing eagerly for a good petting like some hugely over-grown house cat.

Tigers didn't purr when they were happy or content. Instead, they chuffed, which sounded a lot like a cough.

Carefully, Raven pushed her fingers between the metal bars and scratched his thick fur along his flank, far from his sharp teeth.

He chuffed encouragingly. She felt the solid bulk of him, his muscles taut as cables beneath the lushness of his fur.

No matter how tame he acted, she could never let her guard down, not for a second. Vlad was a magnificent creature; he was also a voracious and efficient predator.

Once, she'd seen him leap into the air and take down a hawk in mid-flight, a full twelve feet off the ground. The poor hawk had made the unfortunate decision to fly over Vlad's enclosure.

This particular tiger had an appetite for his human keepers. At his last home in Dubai, Vlad's uber-rich owner would parade him before his aristocratic friends on a gold chain during decadent parties —until the aggrieved tiger had had enough and attacked two people, killing one and maiming the other in the seconds it took a security guard to raise his tranquilizer gun and dart him.

Maybe that's what they deserved for forcing an obstinate tiger to socialize. More likely, they'd taunted and abused him to the point of desperation, until he finally struck back.

She withdrew her hand. The tiger turned his great head, ears flicking, and gave her a lazy stare, as if affronted. His tail twitched rhythmically behind him.

"Don't look at me like that," she said.

His ears flicked.

"That's what I thought. I'm the only one who feeds you treats, remember? What would you do without me?"

Vlad blinked one yellow eye.

"That's right. No more attitude from you, big boy."

He chuffed again. It almost sounded like he was chuckling, like he was as amused by her as she was by him.

She lowered her voice. "I'm going to miss you most of all. Don't you dare tell anyone—"

A loud shout splintered the air.

Raven jerked her head up, stiffening, expecting a lecture from her father for shirking her responsibilities for ten minutes to play with the tiger again.

But the shout hadn't come from her father. In the distance, the head zookeeper, Zachariah Harris, approached from the stone pathway that circled the perimeter of Haven Wildlife Refuge.

Zachariah was hunched over. He stumbled along the path near the bobcat enclosure, about one hundred yards from where she stood next to the tiger house.

Raven hadn't seen him in days, not since he first started coughing. He'd immediately quarantined himself, holing up in his loft above the Grizzly Grill, Haven Wildlife Refuge's only restaurant.

Her father had claimed it was only the flu. Not the other kind of sickness. The kind he didn't want to talk about or acknowledge. He'd insisted the refuge was still safe, that everything was fine.

Everything was about as far from fine as one could get.

Shielding her eyes with her hand, she watched in alarm as Zachariah moved toward her. He faltered, regained his footing. Kept moving.

Instinctively, she took a step backward, off the path, toward the fence line. She yanked the wrinkled mask from her cargo pocket and slipped it over her nose and mouth, hooking the straps behind her ears. It felt incredibly flimsy. She cursed herself for leaving her latex gloves in her room.

"Zachariah, you're sick! You need to stay away—" Her voice broke off, her throat closing like a fist.

Zachariah had worked at Haven as head zookeeper for fifteen years, as much a fixture as Vlad the tiger or Electra, the park's old arthritic bobcat. The Zachariah she knew was a spry and cheerful white-haired man in his late sixties, his face scored with deep wrinkles, his eyes always sparkling with good humor.

This Zachariah was something different.

His bloodshot eyes bulged. The veins in his eyes had burst; his eyeballs glistened crimson. Blood smeared below his eyes and marred his slack mouth. His skin was gray.

Raven took another step back. A small part of her registered that she was too near the fence, Vlad pacing in his cage at her back. The horror of Zachariah's condition blotted out everything else.

Zachariah shuffled closer. Fifteen feet away now.

"Stay back!" Her spine bumped against the fence. Frantic, she glanced to the right and left for an escape route.

Behind her, Vlad stalked angrily, his tail twitching. He gave a low uneasy growl. To her left was the deep moat where Alex, the twelve-foot alligator, lounged in his large pond. Only his prehistoric predator eyes and broad snout appeared above the waterline.

To her right, Zachariah blocked her path to the rest of the refuge. She glanced back at the tiger house, at the tree she used to scale the roof—surely, an old man couldn't climb up after her—but he moved too quickly and cut off that avenue of escape, too.

She was effectively trapped.

And he was coming straight for her.

She shrank back. "Stay away!"

Zachariah lunged at her.

For an old, sick man, he was impossibly fast. Before she could react, he seized her arms with an iron grip.

"Help me!" Zachariah shouted inches from her face. Blood-flecked spittle struck her cheeks, landing on her eyelashes. "Please! Help!"

His hot hands burned her bare arms. His whole body radiated a terrible heat, as if his insides had burst into flame. She tried to wrench from his grasp. He was strong, impossibly strong.

Terror spiked through her. The face mask was a flimsy safeguard, practically useless with Zachariah this close. If a single microscopic droplet entered her system through any orifice—her mouth, nose, eyes, or ears—she knew what would happen.

She'd watched the news reporting the overrun hospitals, the suffering people left to perish in their homes, the millions of sick and infected—then hundreds of millions, then billions. All of them, dying in the throes of agony.

"Help me—please!" he cried.

"Let me go—!" Raven struggled to break free, to no avail. Zachariah coughed again, splattering bloodied phlegm onto her ear and the side of her neck. His cheeks were spidered with swollen, pulsing, purple-black veins, as if there were worms inside him, rotten worms squirming beneath his skin, his diseased flesh.

In the enclosure behind her, Vlad was working himself into a frenzy. Snarling, he slammed against the fence, the metal rattling against her spine.

"Raven!" Her father ran up the path from the direction of the park entrance. He was dressed in grungy white overalls, a gray T-shirt, and tall black boots, with a work belt around his waist. He held a tranquilizer gun in his right hand. He waved his arms wildly. "Get away from him!"

"I'm trying!"

"Zachariah!" her father ordered. "Stop! Now!"

For an instant, the force of his command startled Zachariah from his sickened fugue. His grip slackened. Raven pulled away and dashed to the right along the fence perimeter.

Vlad snarled and hurled himself against his cage. The fence shuddered from his considerable weight. The tiger's claws scraped the metal fencing mere inches from where her head had been a moment before.

Zachariah stood in confusion, swaying unsteadily on his feet. She pushed past him and fled past the waist-high fence ringing the alligator moat to the stone path before pausing at the tiger house, which she could climb to safety if Zachariah came after her again.

Frantic breaths tore from her chest. "Dad, be careful!"

Her father circled the old man until he stood between her and Zachariah, the tranquilizer gun gripped in both hands.

"He has it," he said, his voice bleak. "The virus. It's here."

Chapter Two

"Go home, Zachariah," Raven's father ordered, steel in his voice. He spoke calmly, but the tranquilizer gun pointed at Zachariah's chest told a different story. "You don't belong out here."

Zachariah stared toward him, but not quite at him, with eyes red as blood. "You have to help! It's inside me! I can't get it out! I can't!"

"Go back to your room right now. Lock yourself inside. I'll take care of you, Zachariah, I swear it. But you need to go—now."

Zachariah swayed. Blood-speckled foam glistened at the corners of his mouth. A fetid stench emanated from his pores, a smell with which she was well-acquainted from living among carnivores—the rancid odor of rot. Of decomposing, maggot-riddled flesh.

Raven tensed, unsure what her dad was prepared to do if Zachariah defied him, if he came at them again. The old man was delirious, too sick to be coherent, to recognize or control his aggression.

Vlad paced and snarled at the fence line, his black lips pulled back from his gleaming fangs. He reared onto his hind legs and lunged repeatedly against the fence. He growled low and fierce.

Vlad despised guns. The sight of one regularly worked him into a frenzy. This was something else. The tiger wasn't focused on her father or the tranquilizer gun; his yellow gaze was fixed on Zachariah.

His ears flattened, tail lashing in alarm. His behavior was clearly distressed, as if he sensed danger in Zachariah's sickly odor and odd behavior. She felt as unsettled by Zachariah as the tiger did.

She stared at her old friend in growing horror. He was barely recognizable as Zachariah, let alone a human. His eyes, reddened and rimmed in blood, filled with an all-too-human emotion—terror.

"Please," she whispered. Her gut churned with dread, with that palpable sense of *wrongness*. "You're hurting yourself. Please go home so you can rest."

"Home," Zachariah mumbled. He shook his head violently, as if he were shaking off fleas or gnats. He took an unsteady step backward, then another.

Raven's father tracked him with the tranquilizer gun. "That's it. Keep moving. Nice and slow, now."

The zookeeper coughed again, a harsh, retching sound. "I have to go... I have to... get away... before... before..."

"Before what, Zachariah?" Raven asked.

He never finished his thought. His jittery, disjointed gaze roamed back and forth, his eyeballs rolling in a strange, frenetic pattern. With a sudden intensity of focus, his eyes fixed upon Raven. He blinked rapidly. For an instant, he was lucid. He *saw* her.

"I'm sorry." He spoke in a choked, jagged voice. Something wet and thick gurgled in his throat. "I didn't mean to—I didn't want to hurt anyone... I'm so sorry..."

"Zachariah—"

"Forgive me. Please, forgive me..."

Raven stood on the path, her entire body trembling. She could feel every fleck of spittle stuck to her cheeks, her neck. Panic bit at the back of her throat, the same panic she saw reflected in his tortured gaze. Whatever he'd done to her, he hadn't meant to do it. She understood that. "I forgive you."

The old man turned and lurched away. He staggered up the path toward the foxes, the zebra, and the bobcat, in the opposite direction of the park entrance, where the lodge, the restaurant, and the loft he called home were located.

Neither Raven nor her father stopped him. Relief flooded through her. He was gone. For the moment at least, the threat had passed. Except it hadn't. Heart thudding in her throat, she tentatively touched her face. Her fingers came away wet with speckled phlegm and blood.

"He coughed on you," her father said in a hoarse, stricken voice. "Did it get in your eyes or mouth?"

Her pulse roared in her ears. "I... I don't know."

Her skin crawled. Every hair on the back of her neck stood on end. Zachariah had coughed in her face. His infected, bloodied spittle had landed on her skin. Had microscopic droplets infiltrated her eye sockets? Her ears? Her nostrils?

She felt contaminated as if the virus was splitting and spreading inside her right now, right this second, like thousands of tainted spiders crawling through her insides, invading her organs, infiltrating her bone marrow, burrowing deep and invisible beneath her skin.

"Don't touch anything." From ten feet away, her father dug in his pocket with his free hand, keeping the tranquilizer gun in his right hand as he tugged out a spare pair of plastic gloves and a bottle of disinfectant spray, and tossed them to her.

"You need to wash yourself thoroughly, right now." He gestured to the coiled hose hooked to the side of the tiger house, used to scrub the walls and floor of the tiger den. "Hurry."

She pulled on the gloves. Carefully, she unhooked her blood-tinged mask and threw it on the ground. She'd dispose of it properly later, but for now, she just wanted it off.

She sprayed her face and hands with the disinfectant spray and scrubbed her skin until it felt raw, then used the hose to wash her face, hands, arms, and torso thoroughly. The freezing water soaked her clothes, but she barely felt it.

The scrub down wouldn't do anything, not if the virus was already inside her, but she scoured her skin as hard as she could anyway. She had to do *something*.

After several minutes that felt like an eternity, she carefully peeled off the gloves and dropped them onto the sidewalk beside the mask.

Raven offered her father the disinfectant spray, but he just shook his head. "Keep it. You need it more than I do. Reapply it every hour."

It wouldn't do any good, but she nodded to put him at ease as much as she could, to comfort him. There was nothing to feel comforted about.

She stuffed the bottle in her pocket. Her fingers trembled. Images from social media feeds flooded her mind: the jerky phone videos posted to TikTok and Insta and YouTube of people vomiting in restaurants, their eyeballs bleeding in ER waiting rooms, the body bags piling up in the morgues.

She'd listened to the statistics and watched the talking heads repeat the mind-numbing numbers, so large they hadn't seemed real. Neither had the footage of the rioting outside government buildings, or the soldiers with guns at checkpoints, enforcing curfews and travel bans in cities she'd never visited.

Like some terrible movie or collective nightmare she couldn't awaken from, it somehow hadn't seemed real. Not until Zachariah got sick.

Even then, her father had insisted it was nothing. And she'd only heard wheezy coughs through a door when she dropped off meals. She hadn't witnessed the virus up close and personal—until now.

"How could you?" Her father stared at her, his jaw working, a vein in his temple throbbing. He was upset. "How could you be so careless?"

She flinched. "I had my mask."

"But no gloves." There was blame in his voice, and recrimination. "You let him get too close."

"He trapped me."

"You should have tried harder. Pushed him down if you had to."

"What did you want me to do, jump into the moat with Alex the giant sharp-toothed alligator? Scale Vlad's cage and have tea and crumpets with a tiger?"

"Either option would have been preferable."

She went rigid. He wasn't entirely wrong. She'd allowed herself to be distracted by other things—her birthday, the letter, her mother. She'd let her guard down. And it had cost her. "You said it was the flu."

"I was wrong." His expression was shell-shocked. "You don't put yourself in danger for anyone. Do you understand me?"

"Yeah, I get it. Message received." She forced herself to think of something other than the microscopic virus particles that might be percolating through her blood at that very moment. "Zachariah is suffering. He needs medicine."

Her father lowered the tranq gun. Wearily, he rubbed sweat from his forehead with the back of his arm. His skin was sallow. Bruises circled his eyes from weeks of stress, lack of sleep, and overwork. "No."

He turned away from her, likely to head to the rear of the park, to the wolves, where he spent his free time after the animals had been fed and cared for. Her father was a man of few words—quiet, intense, and contemplative. Her mother had hated it. Raven had grown used to his taciturn nature, to his long silences. Today, his reticence was unacceptable.

"No? What do you mean, no?" She repeated the same thing she'd said eight days ago, when Zachariah first started coughing, when he'd quarantined himself inside his loft. "There must be something we can do. We should call Dr. El-Hashem in town—"

"No doctors left to call. I told you." His accent thickened. He'd moved to the States from Tokyo when he was a kid, and he barely had an accent anymore unless he was angry or upset.

Her mind filled with the images of the overrun hospitals and medical centers, guarded by soldiers refusing the sick at gunpoint. The screaming children, the weeping parents. The bleak news reports of thousands of body bags piling up in the morgues.

"What about Dr. Carter?" she asked, grasping at straws.

Dr. Carter was the exotic animal vet who cared for the wild animals that called the refuge home. He hadn't come to treat Electra the bobcat's abscess three weeks ago.

On vet days, Dr. Carter used to let Raven assist with fecal screening programs, routine vaccinations, and other issues that cropped up. Kodiak, a two-hundred-and-sixty-pound black bear, needed a claw cutting for an ingrown toenail; Gizmo, a bonobo, suffered a toothache that required an extraction under anesthesia.

When he'd failed to show, her dad had called him. After multiple messages, the vet's wife had finally answered, coughing violently and raw with grief. Dr. Carter had died two days before, another casualty of the Hydra Virus. Three days after that, the phones stopped working.

"Then the pharmacy in town—"

Her father's gaze hardened. His eyes were black as onyx and mirrors of her own. He glowered at her. "Too dangerous. Absolutely not."

"Zachariah is our friend. He's worked here forever. He stayed to help even after everything went to hell. We can't just—"

"He's dying," her father said flatly. His fingers tightened on the tranquilizer gun. "He's a dead man walking. Nothing we can do at this point."

She gestured helplessly. "He's also suffering. He's in pain. Some meds can ease—"

"I said no." Her dad coughed into his mask. He had asthma. He was always coughing. The stress—and the mask—made it worse. A bead of sweat rolled down the side of his face.

"But—"

"How do you think he got infected? He went into town to look for more fuel for the generators and to get meat from the renderer. I warned him to be careful. He wasn't careful enough. He tried to help someone, and look where that got him? Got us?" He winced, as if speaking the words physically pained him. "You will not risk yourself for him, not for anyone."

She gave a sharp jerk of her head, capitulating as she always did.

It made her feel selfish and helpless and impotent. She longed to grab her pack and run as far away from this place as she could.

"We don't risk the living for the dead."

"I know that." She hated it, but she did know. Her father was right, as always, as much as she resented it—and resented him for it, at this moment.

Vlad snarled his discontent. He hurled himself at the fence. He wouldn't stop until her father holstered his tranquilizer gun. He didn't put it away, though Vlad was obviously agitated. Deeper in the park, several of the wolves started to howl.

A cool breeze rustled through the oak trees interspersed throughout the wildlife refuge. Fall had transformed the leaves into rich shades of fiery red, burnt orange, and plum purple. Fallen leaves littered the pathways and enclosures.

Her dad coughed again into the crook of his arm. He wiped beads of sweat from his forehead. His face had hardened into his usual expression—flat, closed, and impassive. "The hybrids need to be fed. The bonobos need fresh hay in their night house. And when you're finished with that, Vlad's house needs scrubbing out."

"Yes, sir," she said through gritted teeth, though it was the last thing she wanted to do today.

A part of her loved the refuge and the animals within it—this place had been her home for as long as she could remember. But a darker, bitter part of her resented it.

The needs of the animal refuge had taken over her life. After her mother left, her father enrolled her in online high school classes. He said she was safest at home, because even three years ago, the world was a dangerous place, with the crop blights and food shortages, the riots and domestic terrorist attacks, and school shootings growing more common every day.

Everything was falling apart slowly and then all at once.

After graduating from high school last spring, there was nothing to keep her from working all day. She couldn't afford the incredible expense of college. Instead, she'd stayed at the refuge and helped the keepers rake droppings and shovel fresh straw, fed and watered the animals, and ensured the foxes weren't digging escape tunnels in their pens.

During operating hours, she'd waitressed at the restaurant or managed the guests, kept idiots from leaning on the wolves' fences or throwing French Fries at the bears.

For the last month, it had been Raven, her father, and Zachariah. Now, she and her father had to do it all, just the two of them.

Dread settled in her stomach like a block of ice. "What about Zachariah? Do we just leave him out here, then? What about when night falls? How are we going to get him back in his room?"

Her father's grip tightened on the tranquilizer gun. "I'll take care of it."

"But how—"

Her father didn't answer. Without another word, he strode up the path, deeper into the refuge, headed the way that Zachariah had departed a few minutes earlier. He'd already dismissed her from his mind as he turned to his myriad other tasks.

He'd always cared about this place and the animals more than people.

More than her mom, more than Zachariah, more than her.

It figured he wouldn't remember. She might have forgiven him with everything going on, except that he never remembered. Not once. She told herself it didn't hurt anymore, that she was too strong to care.

Raven turned back to the tiger house. Her limbs felt heavy as lead. No matter what horrific atrocities were happening in the outside world, her dad kept order in his domain. While Zachariah was wandering around out there somewhere, suffering, and dying, Raven would spend the afternoon mopping up tiger scat the size of her head.

It didn't feel right. None of this felt right. She glanced up at the large tree in Vlad's enclosure. No cow heads were hanging from the branches today, not since Zachariah had fallen ill.

When she had been a little girl, she used to watch in terrible fascination as Zachariah hung the bull heads he'd procured from the renderer on several branches eight to twelve feet above the ground. It was for the tiger's enrichment.

Raven never squealed or allowed herself to appear squeamish as Zachariah nonchalantly wedged horns attached to a bull's head in the fork between two branches, or hung a disembodied head upside down, the ghastly purple tongue poking from the thing's maw.

Afterward, Zachariah had squeezed her shoulder in silent reward for her bravery, then pointed at Vlad, who repeatedly sprang high in the air, batting at the heads eagerly, intent on bringing them down for his next meal.

"He's working for his dinner like the rest of us, right?" Zachariah grinned at her. "They look gruesome, but they're nothing to fear. Simply the way he likes to eat, little bird."

Zachariah faced everything with a jovial fearlessness. He'd made Raven want to be brave, too. Because of his kindness, she hadn't suffered a single nightmare.

As for her father, the concept that his young daughter might be frightened of bloodied, severed animal heads hadn't entered his mind.

She sucked in her breath, fighting the wave of sorrow flooding her system. For a moment, she couldn't move from the grief rolling through her body.

And that persistent fear niggling at the back of her mind—that she, too, was now infected.

If a single pathogenic particle slipped through the fibers of the N95 mask and invaded her body, she was done for. In ten days, she'd be the one choking on her blood, her organs melting into a toxic, insidious stew.

She shoved the thought down deep. There was nothing she could do about that now. What was done was done. She was so deeply sorry for Zachariah. She grieved for him. But she had too much work to do to feel sorry for herself.

Raven straightened, took a breath, then pressed her hand to the bioscanner beside the locked, steel-reinforced door and pushed the button to lower the drop gate on the other side of the tiger house, which opened to Vlad's enclosure.

The scanner beeped. The service door swung open with a hiss. Before she went inside, she peeked around the corner at her backpack, still ready and waiting next to the wall.

The tiger house dens were six feet by twelve feet, with steel sheeting lining the walls, a welded mesh floor, and a steel-barred sliding drop gate. There were two chambers, though they had only one tiger.

Gristle, shredded fur, and the curved bones of horse ribs covered the concrete floor of Vlad's den. This would take a while. She picked up the mop in the corner and took a shallow breath through her mouth. No matter how often it was scrubbed clean, the tiger house always stank of raw meat, of death.

"You're disgusting, you know that?" she muttered, though the tiger couldn't hear her. "The things I do for love."

A loud yell filtered down the hill, followed by a high-pitched scream.

Raven dropped the mop.

Zachariah.

Chapter Three

Raven dashed outside, her heart thundering. She shielded her eyes against the sun. At the top of the hill beside the wolf enclosure, the figure of her father stood several feet back from something lying in the pathway.

She sprinted up the hill, knowing what she would find, dread like cement filling her chest. Her father glanced up as she approached and came to a halt beside him. He looked like he'd aged ten years in the last ten days.

Zachariah lay sprawled on the sidewalk. His limbs were bent awkwardly beneath him, his features contorted in a mask of pain. Tears of blood stained his gaunt cheeks. His eyes were open, staring in frozen horror. He didn't move. His chest didn't rise or fall.

She swallowed hard. "Is he—is he dead?"

"He will be." Her father holstered the tranquilizer gun. "Stay back."

She didn't point out that she'd already been contaminated from less than a foot away. If the mask hadn't protected her, there was little point in taking precautions now. That horse had already left the barn.

Her father coughed and cleared his throat.

She knelt on the paved path beside the body. He no longer

looked like the Zachariah she'd known and loved, the one who always grinned at her, his weathered skin splitting into a hundred grooves and wrinkles, who loved to ruffle her hair, who'd nicknamed her 'Little Bird' with great affection.

Something was on Zachariah's torso. A small gray tube with an orange top stuck out from the man's concave chest. Her stomach sank like a stone. "What did you do?"

"He's no longer suffering." His voice was flat, expressionless.

She jerked out the dart and stared at the syringe, the needle. Reeling, she stumbled to her feet. "You gave him a dose intended for a five-hundred-pound tiger. You stopped his heart. You... you killed him."

"He was dying anyway."

It was true. She knew it was true. Still, the thought of pointing a gun, even a tranquilizer gun, at a friend and pulling the trigger set bile roiling in her stomach. She took a steadying breath, then another. "I didn't say goodbye."

"He wasn't himself anymore," her father said brusquely. "He could barely speak."

Revulsion filled her, sour acid stinging the back of her throat. It was horrible, too horrible. She felt sick, her whole body going hot, then cold, then hot again. She thought of the virus, possibly inside her, the same virus that had done this to Zachariah.

"I should have kicked him out the moment he coughed."

She looked sharply at her father. "And abandon him when he most needed us? Where would he go? Who would feed him or bring him water? Who would take care of him?"

"He promised me he'd stay in the loft. He swore to me."

"He was sick! Crazed with pain."

"It was a mistake to allow him to stay."

"He is—was—family."

"No, he wasn't. He wasn't family, and he shouldn't have been here. I should've kicked him out like I wanted to." His harsh gaze, glittering with anger, slanted toward Raven.

She was the one who'd begged to allow Zachariah to stay, who'd suggested the quarantine in the loft. It was her fault. Her father blamed her for this.

She shook her head, incredulous. Did her father even have a heart? Did he care about anyone else? He hadn't shed a single tear when her mother left. He would've abandoned Zachariah without a backward glance or a second thought.

"We aren't animals."

"Aren't we? It's survival of the fittest, it always has been. Just now, everyone knows it."

Anger boiled up inside her, pressing against her ribs, but she shoved it down. It was useless. Her father didn't care about her outrage. Arguing with him was a waste of precious energy. And she felt tired, so tired.

Tears stung her eyes every time she looked at Zachariah. She wanted to sit on the back patio with him the way they used to, with steaming mugs of hot cocoa. She also wanted to tell him a corny joke, like the ones he'd told her when she was little. *Why did the cookie go to the doctor? Because he was feeling crumby.*

He was the grandfather she'd never had. Now, he was dead.

"What now?" she asked dully. "We have to bury him. We have to... do something."

"I'll take care of it."

"We have to bury him," she repeated.

Her father glanced down at Zachariah's body, his eyes narrowing. "I said I'll take care of it."

"That's not the same thing." Her father was extremely unsentimental. Who knew what his idea of 'taking care of it' meant. "He needs to be buried. We have to show our respect."

"Fine." Her father expelled a sharp breath. "I will bury him."

"I'll help you."

"No, you won't."

"He was my friend, too—"

"I said no!" He coughed again, a deep horrible hacking that shook his shoulders. Taking a step back to keep several feet between himself and Raven, he pulled down his mask to wipe his mouth with the back of his arm.

Raven stared at the mask, aghast. It wasn't white like it was supposed to be. It was tinged with a sickly, pinkish hue. Her gaze dropped to his right arm. His faded plaid shirtsleeve was speckled with red droplets.

The realization struck her, sharp and swift as an axe blade. She saw suddenly what she hadn't noticed before, what she'd refused to notice, choosing to focus instead on her stupid birthday, the stupid gift from her mother, and her ridiculous plans for escape, which seemed suddenly empty and selfish.

Sweat leaked down her father's face, beaded on his forehead, and stained the underarms of his shirt. Sweat on a cool day. The bruised circles beneath his eyes, which she'd assumed were from lack of sleep. The coughing wasn't from his asthma.

And the smell. She'd barely noticed before now, but Vlad had. Vlad, who frantically paced behind the iron bars at the bottom of the hill, his lips pulled back from his two-inch teeth.

He snarled and shook his head back and forth repeatedly, unable to rid himself of the pungent stench. The sour, noxious scent turned her stomach. Dread sank in her gut like a stone.

The stink of sickness.

Her father was infected.

Chapter Four

Raven slumped in a metal chair six feet from her father's bed. Afternoon light slanted through the windows. It bathed the room in warm shadows. Her father groaned, tossing and turning in misery. His limbs were slick with sweat, his face gaunt, and his eyes hollowed.

"Ten feet," he'd growled when she tried to come closer. The CDC broadcasts had recommended maintaining a six-foot distance from any suspected infected persons. Her father thought it was best to extend that number. After all, social distancing hadn't saved the masses.

They were dead. Almost everyone was dead. It was too horrific to contemplate for longer than a few seconds at a time.

To distract herself, she brought him a damp washcloth to press against his fevered forehead, and a pitcher of water for his aching throat and rasping cough. Without power, the water was lukewarm. She couldn't give him ice for his parched throat.

It wasn't enough. How could it possibly be enough?

She stared dully at the bare log walls. Zachariah had died yesterday. This morning, her father had collapsed at the breakfast table. Whatever her plans had been, she couldn't leave her father now.

She knew what the bloggers, newscasters, and influencers had repeated on social media, on podcasts, and in the news: the parade of scientists and virologists and CDC experts, their technical terms masking the true horror: the Hydra Virus destroyed the human body from the inside out.

There was a seventy-two-hour incubation period after infection. Initially, there was coughing and sneezing during the first week, sufficient to spread the contagion.

As the disease advanced through the later stages, the high fevers, breathing difficulties, chronic coughing, and hemorrhaging from the mouth, eyes, and ears started on days ten through twelve. Between days twelve and fourteen came the respiratory failure, followed by an agonizing death. Some infected experienced what Zachariah had—an adrenaline surge during the last stage, coupled with memory loss and aggression, much like dementia—the last-ditch effort of the virus to spread itself.

A small percentage of the population was immune. For the rest, the mortality rate was 100%. There was no cure. No escape once you were infected. No reprieve. No hope.

Which meant she was watching her father die.

Raven hunched over a pine log she'd chosen from the stack of firewood next to the fireplace and placed in her lap. With her new whittling knife, she scraped at the wood with trembling fingers, barely seeing the object taking shape in her hands. Several times, her fingers slipped. The blade nicked her thumb, cutting into her knuckle.

She wiped the blood on her pants and kept working, carving deep into the soft wood, wood shavings tinged with red falling into her lap, drifting to the floor like shriveled petals.

Her legs were shaking, aching to run, to flee, to escape this grotesque stench of sickness and her father's awful rattling breaths. The darkness closed in on her, seeping into her skin, her pores, her cells.

The sight of him lying there, quivering and helpless, his body wracked in pain, sent a hot spike of panic through her gut. She'd never seen him anything but capable, self-contained, strong and stoic, needing nothing and no one. Now he was weak, suffering, a stranger with her father's face.

He may not have been the father she'd wanted—but he was the father she had.

He was dying. And she was helpless.

She closed her hands over the wooden bird she'd carved—a raven. One rough-hewn wing was stained pale red from the nick in her finger. When she had been small, only four or five, she used to collect things—stray buttons, ribbons, pretty stones, bottle caps, magnets, anything shiny and bright and lovely.

Her father had called her a little *karasu*, a raven. Her mother had laughed merrily—back when she still laughed—and the name had stuck.

Her real name was Emiko, but no one had called her that in years. She loved that her father had given her a nickname. As a girl, she'd adored it, clung to it like one of the bright little pebbles she'd tucked under her pillow, hoping with all her heart that the bestowing of a special name meant he truly loved her.

Raven blinked away the burning in her eyes, shoved the knife and the bird carving into her cargo pocket, and stood abruptly, nearly knocking over her chair. "I'm going into town. I'll find a doctor."

Her father opened his eyes slowly. His jaw muscles clenched and unclenched like it took an incredible effort to unhinge his jaw to speak. "There are... none."

Of course, he was right. Millions of people were dead. Tens of millions. Billions. A number too large for her brain to process. Those who weren't dead were taking care of themselves and their families. The hospitals were turning away patients.

Even if doctors and hospitals were functioning somewhere, they wouldn't be able to save her father. The best hospitals in the world hadn't been able to save anyone.

Yet her fear was an irrational thing. A part of her mind clung to the reality of the old world with desperation.

After all, she hadn't seen this new bizarre world with her own eyes. Worse than anything the world had dealt with before. Worse than the other pandemics. Worse than the Black Death.

She hadn't left Haven in weeks, since before the Hydra Virus reared its ugly head.

First, she hadn't had a reason to do so.

Then her father hadn't allowed it.

Her mind didn't want to believe it. Surely, it wasn't that bad. There were still people going to work and coming home, and kids riding hoverboards and playing virtual reality games all day, and stores still open, their shelves stocked with Doritos, Little Debbie snacks, and Mountain Dew.

"Let me get you some medicine. Something to ease the pain," she choked out.

"It's not safe." He turned his head with great effort to look at her. His dark eyes were glassy. His sweat-damp hair was slick against his forehead. "I'll be fine."

She let out a bitter laugh at the irony of his words. "I'll be back before nightfall. I'll make sure the animals are taken care of."

"Don't take stupid risks," he said. "Not for anyone. Not for me. You will not do this. It's too dangerous."

She'd heard that argument a hundred times. *Keep to yourself. Keep your head down. Don't make waves. Take care of yourself, first and only.*

That may be the way her father lived, but it didn't mean she had to live the same way. Not now. Not like this.

She'd obeyed him, only to watch her mother leave and Zachariah die.

She'd been dead set on leaving this place for good—for months, maybe years. But that was by choice. That was leaving someone healthy and alive, someone you knew would continue to move and breathe and do all the things they'd always done while you were gone.

This was different. This was a giant hand reaching inside the cage of her ribs and wrenching her heart out, squeezing the blood from her veins while she watched. This was a weeping wound in her soul that would never heal.

"It won't take long, I promise. I'll come right back."

"I said no."

Raven stood. Some dark thing twisted inside her. "You can't stop me this time."

"I forbid it," he croaked.

"I'm sorry," she said. "I'm going."

His fingers scraped the bed sheets like claws. Tendons bulged in his neck as a wave of agony pulsed through his body. She watched, frozen and helpless, sickened and horrified, but unable to look away.

Looking away felt like a betrayal of both herself and her father. She would watch his suffering because that was the only thing she could do. To bear witness. To be present and unflinching.

The pain released him. He sagged against the mattress, panting. She retrieved the damp washcloth from the nightstand and approached him, intending to press the washcloth to his forehead, but he waved her away.

He pointed a frail finger at something across the room. The tranquilizer gun lay atop the dresser beneath the window, steeped in golden sunlight. "You want to ease my suffering? That'll do it."

She recoiled in horror. "No!"

"I want you to do it." He took several ragged, rasping breaths. "I'm asking you to do it."

"I—I can't."

He worked his jaw, like he sometimes did when he was chewing on words he'd rather keep to himself. The kind of words that cost something, that took something in return. "Let me go out on my terms. Not like... that."

Revulsion settled in her stomach like a block of ice. She shook her head, tasting acid in the back of her throat. "I'll be back. With medicine."

"Raven!" he shouted at her back. "Don't you go!"

She unhooked one of the solar lanterns from the hook on the

wall by the door, brought it to the nightstand, and placed it next to the water pitcher. He'd have light even if she came back after dark.

They saved the generator for critical items, like the electrified fences, to keep the carnivores inside where they belonged.

"Don't you dare leave!"

She headed for the door. Her throat tightened, frantic to escape that claustrophobic room rancid with sickness, shadowed with grief and bitterness and regret. Once she brought the painkillers back and eased his torment, he would forgive her. He would.

"Raven."

She stilled, one hand on the door handle.

"Take the tranq," he said behind her, defeat in his voice. "For protection."

She stiffened. Then she pivoted, seized the gun from the dresser, and fled her father's bedroom.

Rushing through the shadow-darkened living room, she paused to grab her dad's key fob on the shabby coffee table so she could use the battered Camry. It was a hybrid. Her father used the precious generator to keep it charged for emergencies.

Frantic thoughts churned through her mind. Her father was dying. He'd begged her to kill him. She hated thinking about his suffering; she hated thinking of aiming a gun and pulling the trigger even more.

That it was a dart and not a bullet didn't mean much. The result was the same: death.

She pushed those thoughts out of her mind. She needed to focus. Step A led to Step B, which led to Step C.

If she found strong enough painkillers, he wouldn't need the tranquilizer. She would get medication to ease her father's pain. Then she would tackle the myriad chores of feeding and caring for the wild animals at the sanctuary. One task at a time.

Key fob in hand, Raven hurried out the front door.

Chapter Five

Raven drove her father's ancient vomit-green Toyota Camry. The Camry was as old as molasses, leaked oil, and the A/C didn't work, but it ran. Faded stickers advertising Haven Wildlife Refuge covered the scuffed bumper.

She headed west along Juliette Road, over the bridge spanning the Ocmulgee River, which traced the length of the Piedmont National Wildlife Preserve north to south.

Her hands clenched the steering wheel. To the south lay Plant Sherer, the largest coal-powered power plant in Georgia. No smoke belched from the smokestacks, darkening the sky. She didn't want to think about what that might mean.

She drove straight through Juliette, population 250, best known for the Whistle Stop Café, where *Fried Green Tomatoes* was filmed, an old movie she'd never seen and now never would. There were no vehicles in front of the café, nor the vintage clothing shop, or the Honey Comb or Moon Pies Collectibles gift shop.

About fifteen miles southwest of the town was the slightly larger town of Forsyth, with a population of 4,000. Used to be 4,000, she reminded herself grimly.

Several dozen abandoned vehicles clogged both sides of the road. A Ford F150 stood with both its doors hanging open; a gray minivan had been parked at a stop sign and left where it had likely run out of gas.

Even on its best days, no one could say downtown was busy. Today, it was a ghost town. Only a few people hurried along the sidewalks, heads down, masks covering their faces, gloved hands shoved deep into the pockets of their jackets to ward off the afternoon chill.

Most of the sagging storefronts were closed, many with two-by-fours barring their front doors. The windows of Dewie's Barber and Shave were boarded. The ancient red-and-white-striped barber pole was knocked off its base and lay on the weed-infested sidewalk.

Driving cautiously, Raven went to the doctor's office first, a two-story brick building on the corner of Main Street where she'd had every shot and check-up she could remember.

It too had been vandalized. Every window was shattered. The front door had been removed from its hinges and was nowhere to be seen.

By the time she pulled into the parking lot of Maxwell Pharmaceuticals, the hairs on the back of her neck stood on end.

The pharmacy boasted zero broken windows and no graffiti on the brick exterior walls. The sidewalk was swept. A hand-scrawled sign taped to the front door said: "Still Open, 12-4 Tue-Thurs- Sat."

She sat in the front seat for a moment as the engine ticked. Her pulse thudded against her throat. Her mouth was dry and chalky.

Forsyth was a small rural town. A safe town. Nothing like the chaotic, rioting cities. The best thing was to get in and out as quickly as possible.

She glanced at the tranquilizer gun resting on the passenger seat. She knew how to handle guns. She'd gone hunting dozens of times, but the idea of using one against another person turned her stomach.

Could she do it, if she had to? She thought she could. She believed she could.

Part of her wanted to leave the gun inside the car, but the primitive part of her brain reminded her that her father was right. She didn't know what awaited her out in the world. She needed to be prepared.

Raven pushed her mask up over her nose and tugged on a fresh pair of disposable gloves her dad kept in the glove compartment. Tucking the tranquilizer gun into her oversized cargo pocket along with her phone, she exited the car.

Shutting the door, she locked the car and hurried past several motorcycles parked outside the pharmacy, chain-locked to a light pole so they couldn't be stolen.

The bell above the door tinkled as she opened the door and slipped inside. The shadows were deep, but watery daylight streamed through the windows. The shop smelled like pine air freshener and aftershave. She went straight to the back counter.

Phil Maxwell, the owner, stood behind the pharmacy counter. His son, Carl, a stocky bearded man in his mid-thirties, stood next to him. They wore masks and gloves.

"I don't have much left," Phil said, barely glancing at her. His gaze was fixed on the four bikers who were crowded around the vending machine against the far corner. They were big, burly, tattooed, and loud, and stuck out like bulls in a China shop.

Raven scanned the nearly empty shelves. She licked her dry lips beneath her mask. "My dad is sick. He needs something that can help him."

A flash of pity shone in Phil's eyes. "Kioko Nakamura was a good man. I'm sorry to hear that."

"He's not dead yet." Her heart constricted. It was a stupid thing to say, but she couldn't help it.

"He will be," Carl said. He was a short, toady man with a snub nose, flattened face, and dull eyes. He always stared suspiciously at everyone under twenty, like he longed to accuse them of shoplifting or some other nefarious activity. Raven disliked him intensely. "Dead as everyone else. Deader than a doornail."

She forced her voice to remain calm. "I know that. But he's in pain. He's suffering. I don't have a prescription, but..."

Phil sighed and ran his hands through the halo of white hair ringing his balding head. "I've been keeping this place open for just that reason. Carl, go back and grab some oxycodone."

Carl scowled. "That's our last bottle. Our livelihood. All that's left—"

Phil's expression darkened. "Just do it."

Carl obeyed with a huff. He stomped off toward the rear of the store.

Phil dragged his gaze back to Raven. "When's the last time you had power?"

"A few weeks."

He sighed heavily. "Same. Your generator's holding up okay?"

Raven nodded. In the back room behind the counter, a fridge hummed. It contained the medications that needed to remain cold. The doors were wrapped in chains and a large padlock. "And yours?"

"It's lasting, so far. Things'll get worse before they get better, mark my words."

Carl returned and plunked the bottle down on the counter between them. "You hear about all the rioting in Atlanta, Indianapolis, and Chicago?" His eyes glittered with something Raven couldn't quite read. Was it smug satisfaction? Morbid excitement?

"I've heard."

Carl continued as if he hadn't heard her. "They don't have enough workers to clean up all the dead bodies in the cities. They're just leaving the dead in people's homes, only cleaning up the ones who die in the streets—if they're lucky. Ones still living are forced to fight tooth and nail over whatever little bit of food and water's left. The police and National Guard are fallin' apart at the seams, literally. Either all dead or leavin' to protect their families. That's what I would do. Let the government try to clean up its own damn mess for once."

Raven stared at him, aghast. Carl was one of the many reasons she preferred an isolated cabin in the woods to the cruel, indifferent, idiotic world of people. "I think it's a tragedy."

Carl shrugged. "Their fault for living in cities, ain't it? We warned 'em, we did. But they looked down their noses at us country folk, thought they were better than us. Well, who's laughing now, huh?"

"No one's laughing," Raven said, incredulous. "No one's winning. Look around, why don't you? You think this virus cares about your stupid politics and grudges? It kills everyone. Everyone." Her throat thickened. She pressed her lips together, furious at herself for wanting to cry in front of a cretin like Carl.

Carl shot her a gleeful grin. "Don't get your panties in a wad, girly. No need to get all hysterical. I was just making conversation."

"Yeah, well, your 'conversation' leaves much to be desired." If she'd had a tad less self-control, she would've used the tranquilizer gun on this moron. Shoot him right in the ass and see how he liked that.

Phil gave her a sharp look, his eyes pleading. She needed him to help her. Or more precisely, what he could offer her. She shut her trap and smiled her best fake smile. "No hysteria here. See? Perfectly calm."

Phil stuffed the bottle inside a small white paper bag and handed it to her. "Find yourself a safe place and stay there, you hear me?"

"Thanks." She took the bag and shoved it inside the wide cargo pocket of her pants. "How much for this?"

"For you? No charge. Just remember this and pay it forward, however you can. I have a feeling folks are going to need all the help they can get."

"What the hell are you doing?" Carl's froggy eyes bulged, and his face went red as a tomato. "You can't just give it to her—what the hell—"

"I just did," Phil said softly, but in a firm voice. "Your father did a big favor for me once. You tell him this is me making things right. Hell, we might not have much time left to do that kind of thing anymore."

"Do what, sir?" she asked.

"Make things right." He made a shooing gesture at her, his gaze flicking over her head toward the unruly group of bikers, who were growing louder and more boisterous. "Go on. Get back to your father."

Gratitude filled her. She blinked back a wave of tears and

managed a smile. A genuine one this time. "Thank you, Phil. Truly. Thank you."

She turned for the front door. Two more motorcycles pulled up outside. Their riders wore semi-automatic rifles strapped to their chests over their jackets. They were both tall and olive-skinned, maybe in their late twenties.

The tallest one had black hair yanked back in a ponytail. He was gaunt, his body long and sharp as a knife. The other moved with liquid grace, like a dancer—a dancer armed to the teeth. Their faces were lean and hard, their eyes glinted dangerously.

Unease shivered up her spine. Her gut tightened. She'd grown up around predators. She knew one when she saw one. In this case, two.

Instinctively, she sidestepped into the closest aisle and shrank behind a row of shelves containing a few conditioners, shampoos, razors, and shaving cream. She peered around the corner.

The bikers slammed open the door, the glass quivering in the frame, and swaggered inside. The bell jangled in warning. The four bikers gave up on the empty vending machine and sauntered to the counter.

"How can I help you, gentlemen?" Phil asked.

"Give us all the painkillers and antibiotics you got, Pops," said the thin, pony-tailed one. He wore a leather vest with a skull emblazoned on the back.

"*Please*," said the second guy, the lithe one that moved like liquid mercury. His coal-black hair framed an angular face. He gave a languid, mocking smile. He scratched his goateed chin and perused the empty shelves with a disinterested, heavy-lidded gaze.

"We're happy to give you a few," Phil said, still polite, his voice tight. There were six bikers now, all big and intimidating, all armed. Phil tried unsuccessfully not to let them see his fear. "We're rationing the supply to last as long as possible so more people get what they need. With the hospitals closed, this is the only medical care people can get."

"You mistake our graciousness," said a third man. He was blond with hair shorn close to his skull. A scorpion tattoo snaked up his neck. His squinty eyes were set deep in his fleshy, shovel-shaped face. Several empty backpacks were slung across his shoulders.

He placed the backpacks on the counter. He lifted his rifle and set it down beside the backpacks. The barrel faced Phil and Carl. He stroked it fondly. His lips peeled back from his teeth in a sinister smile. "As you can see, we aren't asking."

Chapter Six

Raven crouched lower. Her pulse throbbed against her neck. Her brain screamed at her to flee. There was nowhere to go, no way to sneak out without drawing attention to herself. The tranq gun pressed against her thigh, reminding her that she wasn't completely helpless. Still, one dart gun against six rifles and several big-ass dudes with fists as large as her head wouldn't do much.

Her best bet was to stay small and hidden, using the gun as a last resort.

"Now, let's try this again," the biker with the scorpion tattoo said. "Fill these backpacks with everything you've got." He paused, a sly grin playing across his lips. "*Please* and *thank you*."

"You can't just come in here making demands and steal our stuff!" Carl scowled, his voice rising in fury. "That's against the law!"

Ponytail half-turned, his hand shielding his eyes as if he were looking for something. "I don't see any law here, do you, Scorpio?"

"There are no laws now," said the biker with the scorpion tattoo. "No police, no judges, no courts. Nothing. It's all gone to hell."

"This is a civilized society!" Carl whined.

"Oh, I assure you we are quite civilized," Ponytail said. Slowly, with exaggerated movements, he turned and hocked a massive loogie onto the floor. Scorpio laughed darkly.

Raven tensed. They were baiting him to entertain themselves, but Carl was too stupid and thick-headed to see it. They were cats playing with a meal before they bit the mouse's head clean off.

Carl's face purpled, his jaw pulsing. "You can't go around stealing because you feel like it, taking a man's livelihood right out from under him. It's thugs like you who ruined this country in the first place!"

Several of the bikers stiffened. The lithe one's smile dissolved. "Shut your fat ugly mouth and give us what we want."

"I suggest you listen to Dekker," Ponytail drawled.

Phil shot his son a warning look. "Carl."

Carl ignored it. He pointed his finger at dancer-guy—Dekker's—face. "You won't get away with this, you filthy son of a—"

In one fluid movement, Dekker pulled a pistol from a holster at his hip and aimed it at Carl's flat nose. No surprise flickered in the bikers' faces, no hatred or even anger. Dekker's expression was smooth, his black eyes dull and flinty. "I'm hungry, tired, and I've had a long day. Test me one more time—"

Phil stuck both hands in the air. "We mean no harm. We'll get you what you've asked for."

"No, we won't." Carl was shaking, his eyes bulging, but he would not shut his stupid mouth. "We're not letting you thieving scumbags steal what's rightfully ours."

He didn't get that they were the predators, and he was the prey. He didn't get that they wouldn't have bothered with him if he'd stayed still and small, if he hadn't turned aggressive himself, challenging their dominance—the one thing men like these would not let slide.

Scorpio sneered. "You little pissant."

"You think you scare me?" Carl snarled. He started to reach for something beneath the counter—a baseball bat, maybe. Or maybe a rifle. "You come in here with your big guns and you think you can tell me what to do? Well, you've got another think coming, buddy, if you think—"

"Don't do it," Scorpio warned him.

"Carl—" Phil begged.

Carl reached for the hidden weapon.

Dekker shot Carl point-blank in the face.

The blast of the gunshot exploded against Raven's ears. She clasped both hands over her mouth to keep from screaming.

Carl's face disappeared in a mist of red. His body dropped to the floor behind the counter and hit the tile with a thud. Blood splattered across the counter, nearby shelves, and the sunglasses rack. Red droplets sprayed Phil's pristine white lab coat, his face mask, and his white puff of hair.

Phil stood frozen beside his son's body, his arms still raised in supplication, his eyes wide and startled.

A gasp escaped Raven's lips. Shock went through her like an electric charge. They'd just killed someone. They'd murdered Carl for no good reason at all. Her pulse thumped loud in her ears. Acid burned the back of her throat. She'd watched a man die while she hid. Did that make her a coward? Hot tears stung her eyes.

Covering her mouth with one hand, Raven shrank back against the shelves, accidentally bumping the lowest one with her knee. A shampoo bottle wavered, about to crash onto the tile. She managed to grab it before it fell.

She held her breath, her heart thumping, but no one turned around. No one but Phil knew she was there. The bikers had their backs turned when she'd walked in. They'd been busy emptying the vending machine, so loud they likely hadn't heard her, either.

Scorpio grunted. He wiped a faint spray of blood off his face with the flap of his shirt. He looked at Dekker with a disgruntled scowl. "Did you have to do that?"

"I did," Dekker said, his face impassive. "He offended my... honor."

Scorpio shook his head. "There will be talk about this. Vaughn won't be pleased."

Dekker swiveled and pointed the gun at Phil. He sneered, his features twisting in derision. Something was missing, something empty in his gaze. His eyes were dull as lead. "We'd better not leave any witnesses, then."

"I've got this," said a younger guy she hadn't noticed until now. He'd hung back, silent and watchful. Metal glinted at his lip and brow. Several intricate tattoos inked his arms. He looked to be about twenty, tall and lanky, with a head of short russet-red hair. His narrow, pointy face and cunning eyes reminded her distinctly of a fox. A very handsome fox.

The fox lifted the rifle that had been slung over his shoulder and aimed it at Phil. "Get what we asked for, or you'll regret it."

"You heard Damien." Dekker's lip curled in faint amusement. He holstered his gun. "I'll have him blow your kneecaps, then your ankles, then your hands, one by one, and then we'll watch you bleed out and die like a stuck pig. Or, do what he says, and maybe you'll live to bury your ugly son."

Raven waited, every muscle taut, fear and adrenaline pumping through her veins. Phil turned without a word. Trembling, he bagged the remaining medications. A couple of bottles fell off the counter and rolled onto the floor.

"Faster!" Damien snarled, gesturing with the gun.

Dekker slapped Damien on the back, grinning. "Looky there. The young pup is coming into his own!"

Damien gave a hard little grin as if he was enjoying this. They all were. "Get the damn meds, old man."

Minutes felt like hours. Finally, the bikers got what they wanted. Phil crammed the last of the bottles and boxes into the backpack. Every step he took, he was forced to walk in Carl's blood. His whole body was shaking. His face drained of color. He looked like a ghost. "That—that's it."

Damien cursed at him. The other men laughed, jeering and mocking.

Phil cowered. "Please," he whispered. "Please don't hurt me. Please."

"You're just a pathetic old man." Damien leaned over the counter and jabbed the barrel of the rifle hard into Phil's chest.

From her hiding place, Raven cringed, half-expecting him to shoot Phil for the fun of it. Phil went rigid, closing his eyes, as if he expected the same thing. Maybe a part of him wanted it, so he wouldn't have to bear the pain of living in a shattered world without his son. Despite his fear and grief, he did not look in Raven's direction or reveal her presence.

Her free hand drifted toward the tranq gun sticking up from her pocket. It used a pressurized gas system that utilized carbon dioxide in an air-driven system to launch the darts from up to 150 feet. She could hit one of these thugs easily, take him down. Maybe she'd get two or three before they discovered her and did worse to her than to Carl.

Only tranquilizers didn't work right away, not like in the movies. The potent levels of xylazine in each dart would stop a human heart, but not necessarily before one of them strangled her to death.

She couldn't fight them all. Carl was beyond saving. Was Phil? Her hand tightened on the gun. Was she brave enough to try to save him, after his kindness toward her and her father? Could she stand by and let another innocent person die?

Her muscles tensed. She hunched even lower. No. She was a coward. She would do what her father had said. She would stay small and invisible to save herself.

Damien poked Phil again in the chest, but Phil didn't respond. He stood, still and silent, waiting for whatever would come next—death, or the next agonizing breath, the next minutes and hours in a world bereft of his son.

Raven prayed fervently, mouthing the words over and over: *Just go away, leave, and go away. Don't hurt him. Don't hurt him. Don't hurt him.*

Growing bored, Damien turned away with a dismissive sneer. "He's not worth the round. This place stinks. Let's go."

The bikers stomped from the pharmacy, knocking the few remaining items off the shelves, bulging backpacks slung over their shoulders.

Raven shrank back, heart roaring in her ears, but none of them bothered to look around. They strode through the front door. The bell jangled maniacally.

After a minute, their motorcycles roared to life. The sound of engines was almost eerie after weeks of quiet. They peeled out of the parking lot and disappeared in a glut of dust and whooping shouts.

Raven forced herself to stand, her legs wobbly, and rushed to the counter. On the other side, Phil squatted on the tile floor next to his son. He cradled his head in his hands, weeping.

It was a private moment, one she had no part of. She backed away to give him privacy. There was nothing anyone could do for Carl.

She tugged her phone from her pocket and had to punch in the numbers three different times before she finally managed to hit 911.

"Service cannot be reached," the phone chimed.

She tried again and got the same answer. She tried the local police and the county sheriff. Still nothing. She swallowed hard. What had she expected? It was one thing to hear something over and over and quite another to live it. Now, she believed.

It felt like the floor was cracking open beneath her, and she was falling, falling, falling, with no bottom in sight. It was true, then. There really was no more law, no more police. Here, at least. Maybe everywhere. Probably everywhere.

Phil rose stiffly to his feet. He wiped at his stricken face with the back of his hand. He stared dully at his streaked fingers, stained with his son's blood. "You should go home. Stay there. This is no place for a girl."

She wanted to say this was no place for anyone. What the hell did being a girl have to do with the rampant destruction of society and the mass extinction of all mankind?

Her words turned to ash in her mouth. She wanted to comfort him, but there was nothing to say, nothing that would make a differ-ence against this meaningless act of violence.

Instead, she nodded mutely, turned, and ran from the shadows of the store into the late afternoon sunlight. The street was utterly empty. Not a single living soul was in sight. A couple of torn plastic bags skittered across the sidewalk.

She reached the car and dug into her pocket for the keys, still holding the useless phone in one hand. The back of her neck prickled. Someone was watching her. She glanced down the street to the left. A block down, seven or eight motorcycles were parked in the overgrown grass in front of the bank. The bikers were inside—they'd smashed the glass doors. Except for one. Raven surreptitiously stuck her hand in her pocket and wrapped her hand around her gun.

A man stood directly to her left, half-hidden behind the stalled minivan so that she hadn't seen him when she'd exited the pharmacy. Dekker leaned against his bike, smoking a cigarette in one hand, his pistol in the other, lounging languid as a cat poised to strike. His gaze was fixed on her.

Their eyes met for a brief, electric moment. His eyes were dull, lifeless, like hollow black pits. Inhuman. A shiver of fear raced up her spine.

"Well, well," he said, "what do we have here?"

Chapter Seven

Raven's heart jackhammered against her ribs. It felt like it was about to pound right out of her chest. Her mouth went dry. "I'm not bothering you. I'm leaving. I'll leave. You'll never see me again."

Dekker smiled. "I'll determine when—and if—you leave. Where did you come from?"

"Nowhere."

His eyes narrowed. "I highly doubt that."

"Just... at the end of town. Past the river. Cherry Street." She had no clue if Cherry Street was past the river or not. Panic threatened to strangle her. She forced herself to keep it together. Predators could smell fear.

Dekker's gaze traveled up and down her body. Raven stiffened. She felt exposed, vulnerable. She wanted to punch him in his smug, handsome face, break his nose, and maybe claw out an eyeball or two.

"You look... well fed. Where are you getting all this food that gives you those nice curves?"

She swallowed. "Nowhere. I'm starving like everyone else." She was careful not to say *we*, to reveal that she had something—and someone—worth protecting.

"Hmmm." His tone was non-committal. He tapped his pistol against his thigh. "Not sure you're being honest with me, sweetheart. How about that car of yours? Not much gasoline to be found around here. The fuel trucks haven't been through town in two weeks."

"It's a hybrid."

His brows raised. "Ah, so you have a generator to charge it, then."

"It's on empty," she said quickly. "This is my last trip. Besides, it's falling apart. It's a miracle it got me here."

"I get the sense you're not being truthful with me."

"I am."

"I'll ask you again, one more time, because I'm polite and mannered. I suggest you mind your manners, too, little girl."

She said nothing.

"Where do you come from?"

"I told you, Cherry Street here in town," she said quickly. "Near the library. My parents are—are dead." She hoped he believed the genuine catch in her voice. "It's just me."

"You were inside the pharmacy."

She didn't break eye contact, kept her voice even. "No, I wasn't."

"Your car was here when we arrived. I admired your bumper stickers."

Her heart thundered in her ears. "I parked here to walk to the general store. To save on mileage because I'm almost out of battery."

His smile deepened. "I could almost believe you, Chica, except for the pharmacy bag sticking out of your pocket right there."

Her face reddened against her will. "I was in there earlier, hours ago."

"Right." He tap, tap, tapped the pistol against his leg. His finger drifted toward the trigger. "The thing is, I'm going to need that bag and its contents from you. And hell, you can throw in the car, too. I know a guy who can fix it up as good as new."

"You can't steal my car." Without it, she'd be stranded. It would take her an entire day of walking to get back home.

"I prefer the term acquisitioning. I mean, seeing as you live just around the corner, I'm sure you won't mind walking home. Everyone's taking up walking these days. Those that still breathe our rarified air, that is." He winked. "Thanks for your generosity."

Raven folded her fingers around the grip. She jerked the tranq gun from her pocket. Holding it steady with both hands, she planted her feet and aimed it at Dekker's chest.

Startled, it took him a moment to react. He started to raise his pistol.

"Don't!" she snarled.

He went still, the hand gripping the pistol hovering a few inches above his thigh. "That's not even a real gun."

"It's not a water gun, either." She kept her gaze lasered on that pistol. If he moved an inch, she would shoot him. Her hands shook. She fought to keep them steady. "This dose is loaded for a five-hundred-pound tiger. The tranquilizer dosage must be carefully calculated by a trained professional based on the target's weight, metabolism, anatomy, and medical history. The margin of error is extremely thin. Too much, and you easily kill the target. In this case, the dosage will cause imminent cardiac arrest followed by death."

"That so?" He acted nonchalant, but his eyes never wavered from the tranquilizer gun, just as hers were focused on his weapon. Insects whirred in the overgrown weeds sprouting from the cracks in the sidewalk. "I think you're still lying to me."

Raven raised the barrel a fraction. "I wouldn't test me. Sure, you can do what you want to me, but I won't miss. It's mutually assured destruction. Do you want to die today?"

There was a beat of quiet that stretched taut as a rubber band. Raven didn't dare to breathe. A bead of sweat trickled down her spine. She gestured with the tranq gun. "Toss your pistol into that sewer grate right there. Then raise your hands and walk backward to the corner beneath the stop sign. Don't move until I'm gone."

His lip curled in a sneer. "You think you've won. You haven't."

"Just do it!"

"This isn't over."

"I said move. I won't ask you again."

After a moment of hesitation, he obeyed. He must've seen something in her eyes. She would squeeze the trigger, and he knew it.

Moving with that eerie, languid ease, he sauntered to the edge of the sidewalk and dropped his pistol through the grate. A splash echoed as the gun hit the water below.

Hands raised, he backed up. When he reached the stop sign, he halted and grinned at her. "You gonna run now?"

Fumbling frantically, she jerked the Camry's driver door open. She hurled herself into her seat, keeping the gun up and awkwardly aimed in the biker's direction as she punched the start engine button and slammed into reverse.

As she peeled out of the parking lot, the Camry careening onto two wheels, she risked a glance at Dekker. He was bent over, reaching for something tucked into his right boot. Another gun.

She hit the gas and roared into the street, mashing the gas pedal, spinning the steering wheel hard to the right. A loud bang exploded behind her. A dull ping. The vehicle shuddered.

Dekker must have fired at her. The round hit something, she didn't know what. The car still drove, that's all that mattered.

Raven kept driving as fast as she could without crashing. The dial roared past 70, 80, then 90 miles an hour. She gripped the steering wheel so hard her fingers went numb. Her heart raced. Her breath felt torn from her lungs. She didn't slow, didn't pause for anything, and didn't dare look back.

Once she reached the edge of town, she checked the rearview mirror, expecting one of those awful motorcycles to pull up behind her at any moment. The road was empty.

Instead of driving straight back to the wildlife sanctuary, she took side roads, weaving around abandoned cars and giant tree limbs felled from the last storm. She didn't want to lead them straight to her hiding place, to the animals, or to her sick father.

Minutes passed. Nothing appeared behind her. Dekker hadn't followed her. The other bikers hadn't noticed her departure.

Maybe, just maybe, she'd escaped unscathed.

Her breathing slowed. Her racing heart steadied. She glanced down at the bag of painkillers bulging from her cargo pocket. She'd succeeded. She got what she came for.

As she crossed the bridge headed for the zoo, she couldn't stop shivering.

The bikers were right.

The world had gone to hell.

She could only hope that hell hadn't followed her home.

Chapter Eight

By the time Raven returned to Haven, the Camry's electric battery was completely drained. She drove through the back entrance, passing the bonobos, otters, and Leo the leopard, who was lounging on his favorite tree branch in the shade, and parked in the garage behind the lodge.

Upon examining the exterior, she discovered a tiny hole punched into the trunk just above the keyhole. The round hadn't hit anything too critical. She'd gotten lucky—this time.

She almost plugged the vehicle into the charger, then hesitated. The electrified fences in the park had automatic backup generators that would last a few more weeks. She didn't want to turn on the one for the lodge where she and her father lived, not unless she had to. If the power was out for months, maybe longer, the generators were all she had.

She brought the tranq gun into the house, locked the front door, and set the weapon on the coffee table. She didn't want it in his room or anywhere near where he might reach it.

The pills would help. The pills would take away his pain.

Raven entered the doorway to her father's bedroom. Like him, it was spartan—a lumpy mattress, a scarred desk, a nightstand, the orange armchair, and the log walls bare of pictures or sentimentality.

She held the bottle of painkillers in one hand, low near her thigh. "Dad?"

He didn't answer.

Heavy shadows drifted across the room. Dusk stained the windows. The dense air stank of sour sweat and sickness. Her stomach roiled. She slipped an N95 mask over her mouth and nose and went to his bedside, flipping on the solar lamp.

His chest rose and fell in jerky, uneven movements. Rasping breaths tore from his chest. He moaned and writhed, tangling the rumpled bedding. The sheets beneath him were damp.

A drop of blood rimmed his outer ear. Another dot of crimson stained the hollow beneath his right eye.

Hemorrhaging from multiple orifices...

This was it, then. The last stage before the end. Before death.

How had he hidden it from her for so long? How could he have been so sick and stayed on his feet? The fever stage burned through adults at over 105 degrees. She remembered that little nugget from the CDC health alerts.

Why had he purposefully kept this from her?

"Dad." She cleared her throat. "Dad. I got it. I got you medicine."

He groaned and opened his eyes. They were glassy and threaded with scarlet.

She fumbled with the bottle and spilled three pills into her palm. She added two more, to make sure. "This will help you feel better."

His reddened eyes widened slightly as if he were surprised to see her. Like he hadn't expected her to make it back. "You're here."

"I told you I'd be back. Here, take these. They'll ease the pain, I promise."

He managed to lift his head. She pressed a glass of water to his lips and helped him swallow the pills. With a groan, his head fell back against the sweat-drenched pillow.

After a beat, he said, "You start coughing, you know what to do."

She shook her head. "Don't talk like that."

"You don't want to go like this, trust me."

"Dad."

"It's a better way to go. More humane."

She pressed her lips together. Tears sparked at the backs of her eyelids. "I know."

He heaved a ragged breath. "Do the animals first. Before you do it yourself. You know where the guns are."

Her mind revolted from the thought. "You should rest."

"Don't be weak. Be brave."

"I—I will."

He stared up at her like she was a stranger, his eyes so bloodshot they looked crimson. The fever-heat emanated from him in waves.

He turned to the wall as he hacked up a bloody, phlegmy cough. She handed him a clean washcloth. He wiped his mouth. For several minutes, he didn't speak. The sound of his ragged breathing filled the room.

"Dad—"

"I was weak." His face contorted. "I was weak to let Zachariah stay. He came after you. Now you've got it, too."

"It wasn't his fault," she said, stricken. She'd never seen him like this before, never heard him talk about anything beyond lessons and instructions and orders. "And you don't know that. I might be okay."

"Don't be stupid. I saw what I saw. So did you. I should've kicked him out long ago... never should've let him stay."

"That's not fair."

"He might have killed you!" her father snarled. "That's the mistake... never trust anyone... especially the ones who call them-selves '*friend*.'"

"He *was* our friend."

"He came after you. He attacked you."

Her heart contracted. "He didn't mean it."

"I don't care!"

This wasn't how she wanted things to go. He was dying. She

should say something important. Something that meant something. But her words failed her.

Her father groaned. She forced herself to look at him, at the mask of agony that contorted his face into someone unrecognizable. But she'd never really known her father. No one had.

Her gaze strayed to the medal of valor framed on the wall above the dresser. Her mother claimed he wasn't the same man after he came back from the war. A decade ago, after the Hand of God terrorist group detonated suitcase nukes across the United States, he'd served as a peacekeeper in the Democratic Republic of Congo.

He was flying a chopper full of medical aid to wounded soldiers when he was shot down. The helicopter crashed into the Congo Basin. He survived alone in the jungle for ninety-seven days. Raven had been five years old.

Her mother insisted on displaying the medal. Her father hated it. And yet, after her mother left, he hadn't bothered to remove it, either.

Once, when Raven was ten, she'd made the mistake of admiring it out loud. She'd called her father a hero.

He'd turned away, his eyes glittering with revulsion. "It is not a heroic thing to survive."

She'd never figured out whether it was the award itself he found so repugnant, or the secret foul things he'd had to do to earn it. She knew only the barest of facts: four men survived the initial crash deep in the Congo jungle, hundreds of miles from civilization. Only one man made it out alive.

Her father returned to them thirty pounds lighter, a festering knife wound in his right bicep, and no explanation for how he'd suffered it. He came back changed. Withdrawn, reticent, and beset with nightmares and PTSD.

Within six months of his return from the war, her father bought Haven Wildlife Refuge with the family's life savings. He retreated from the world, choosing the solitude of nature and the companionship of wild animals over the noise and chaos of society.

He'd taken his family with him, whether they wanted to go or not.

"Your father thinks he's an island," her mom said once, before she left. "He *wants* to be an island. He cut everyone out of his life. He keeps everything at arm's length. He thinks it makes him stronger, but he's wrong. He's the loneliest man I've ever met."

Her insides twisted. Her mouth tasted of copper. Zachariah was dead. Her father was dying. She was about to be alone, too. Totally, completely alone.

"What am I supposed to do?" she whispered. "How am I supposed to do this?"

Her father didn't answer. His features went slack. Finally, mercifully, he drifted into a drug-induced sleep.

Raven backed away on wobbly legs and sank into the faded orange armchair about eight feet from her father's bedside. It smelled old, of dust and mothballs.

Her backpack sat in her room by her bed. The remote hunting cabin in the woods waited for her. But could she leave this place, now that her father was ill? The animals still needed to be fed. The coyotes howled hungrily in the distance. The leopard, Leo, roared his displeasure. The bonobos' night house had never been cleaned.

She would take care of them as soon as she could, but she couldn't bear to leave her father's side. Not like this. Not now.

Raven swallowed hard. Exhaustion tugged at her. Her limbs felt so incredibly heavy. She ran her fingers over the soft ridges of her face mask. It was hard to breathe the claustrophobic air. It felt like she was slowly choking to death. She could never get enough oxygen.

She thought of Juliette and Forsyth. The eerily empty streets, the abandoned shops. Of Carl's face exploding right before her eyes. The arterial spray of blood, so impossibly bright. The flinty gleam in the bikers' eyes, their casual cruelty, their absolute belief that they would get away with it.

There was no longer anyone to stop them.

Her stomach cramped. Almost out of instinct, she tugged her

phone out of her pocket. She'd been charging it with her Biolite stove, though there was little reason to do so anymore.

When she tried to search the internet, nothing came up. Google wouldn't load. Neither would Firefox nor any other browser. She gave up on the search and scrolled through the archived alerts instead.

School districts closing, state by state. Corporations shutting their doors. The Centers for Disease Control and the World Health Organization releasing health alert after health alert, warning after warning.

Thousands shut inside quarantine areas lined with fences topped with barbed wire. The sick lining up outside FEMA tent cities. Soldiers marching through the streets.

And the bodies. Bodies everywhere. By the thousands, the hundreds of thousands. Then millions.

A tremor went through her, like she was standing too close to the edge of a cliff. The sheer immensity was impossible to comprehend. Not until she'd gone to Forsyth and had seen the state of things for herself. Not until she'd met the murdering psycho bikers.

It really *was* the end of the world.

As she sat next to her dying father, it felt like the whole vast universe was crumbling, perishing right along with him.

It was too much to take in. Too much for one person to bear. She was finally, irrevocably alone. She was getting what she'd wanted. To be alone. To be a loner, solitary, surrounded by silence.

But not like this, her panicked mind whispered. *Never like this.*

She shifted in her chair, her muscles aching, but remained seated, keeping vigil long into the night.

Her father's legs thrashed. Sweat drenched his ashen face. His whole body was rigid. Tendons stood out on his neck. His eyes were deep, bruised hollows.

Blood dripped like tears down his cheeks.

Raven waited. She waited for his last words, for him to finally look at her and say something meaningful, maybe some poignant last-minute advice on surviving the apocalypse. Or what she really longed for—*I was wrong,* or *I wish things had been different,* or most of all, *I love you.*

In the end, in death, he was the same as he was in life—reticent, secretive, and unknowable.

Twelve hours later, her father was dead.

Chapter Nine

The next day, Raven buried her father in the garden by the lake across from the flamingo enclosure, next to the spot where he'd buried Zachariah three days earlier.

She had no coffin, no funeral home to call. This was the new world: a bizarre, twisted funhouse mirror version of the old world. Two hundred years of progress and invention, and technology was utterly eradicated in a few desperate, horrifying weeks.

Digging a grave was hard, tough, and exhausting. It took hours to repeatedly punch the shovel through the red Georgia clay, creating a hole large enough and deep enough to protect her father's corpse from nosy predators.

Her muscles were shaky. Sweat drenched her damp *Nine Inch Nails* T-shirt to her chest and back. Her palms stung with weeping blisters.

Once she'd wrapped his body in a tarp and dragged it out to the garden in a wheelbarrow, she put him in the ground, grunting from the effort. She took one of the carvings from her pocket and lowered it gently into the grave. It was a carving of the white wolf, his favorite.

She added a family photo she'd found stuffed in a drawer. Taken in front of the wolves' enclosure when she was six, her round face shone with joy. She was the only one who appeared happy. Her dad was looking at something off-camera, distracted and distant. Her mom's expression was tight and pinched, something closed inside her, as if she were already dreaming of somewhere else.

Happiness had never been a defining trait of her family. Her childhood consisted of three people moving around each other within the same four walls, never touching, never getting too close, always orbiting the others.

She remembered the silences. Not the vibrant quiet of nature, buzzing with insects, the soft sough of the wind, the twittering of birds, and the shuffling of small animals in the underbrush, it was an oppressive silence, weighted with words hungry to be spoken.

Raven hauled the last shovelful of red clay and patted it down, smoothing the topsoil over the grave. Her arms ached. The trees rustled above her, their crimson leaves curling at the edges, ready to die.

Raven stood over the grave. Her eyes stung. Her chest was too tight. A giant hand squeezed the breath from her lungs. She couldn't get enough oxygen. The ground kept tilting dangerously beneath her feet.

She didn't know what to say or how to say it. She didn't know any poignant poems or appropriate songs. Nothing meaningful would come. Only a dull sense of despair, a numbness spreading from the center of her being.

She resented her father. She loved him. He was dead. What was there to say? Grief encircled her chest like chains, threatening to drown her.

"I wish you were still here," she said. "I wish we'd had more time to fix things. I'm sorry."

The wolves started howling again. Last night, the wolves had howled for hours. Somehow, they sensed that her dad was gone. It was a different sound from their usual collective howling to communicate with each other.

This was a chorus of grief. They sang in haunting concert,

sending up a sorrowful keening wail that echoed across the park, eerie and beautiful.

The bonobos added their screeches to the symphony. The bobcat yowled his displeasure. The zebra brayed obnoxiously. The coyotes yipped and yowled with hunger.

Haven Wildlife Refuge housed one tiger, one leopard, two black bears, six timber wolves, two hybrid wolves, four bonobos, two porcupines, one old bobcat, three red foxes, two otters, one zebra, two ostriches, one eagle, four peacocks, two tortoises, two dozen flamingos, flocks of geese and ducks, one grumpy alligator, and a fifteen-foot boa constrictor named Winston.

Every one of those animals was hungry—with the possible exception of Winston. Most of them ate copious amounts of food. None of them had been fed yesterday or today.

No wonder they were loudly complaining. The animals demanded her attention, whether she liked it or not.

"Okay, okay," she muttered. "Hold your horses. I'm coming."

First, she made her way to the front gates and checked to ensure the wrought-iron gates were closed and locked with the padlock. Her father had drilled caution into her. Every night for the last month, her father had patrolled Haven's perimeter with his hunting rifle.

A new person hadn't shown up in weeks, but that didn't mean a stranger wouldn't appear, begging for entry. An image of Carl's face moments before the round struck him invaded her brain.

There were bad people out there.

It was now her job to keep them out.

The flagstone pathway took a serpentine route through the oblong-shaped park. An enormous walk-in enclosure, featuring the gardens surrounding the small lake with its flamingos, various feathered fowl, pens for the tortoises, and the peacocks, was sprawled in the center of the park. The peacocks regularly escaped into the general park, wandering about and pooping wherever they wished.

Near the entrance were the ancient turnstiles, the Grizzly Grill restaurant, the souvenir shop, and bathrooms, along with the six-suite lodge that her dad had converted into their living quarters.

Whoever built this place fifty years ago hadn't put much thought into it. The food storage and prep sheds, which included the meat house, were located only twenty yards behind the lodge. When the wind blew in the wrong direction, she kept her bedroom window closed.

Raven entered the concrete-block building containing the frozen meat for the carnivores—the tiger, leopard, alligator, wolves, bobcat, and bears. The walk-in freezer held several hundred pounds of meat, which Zachariah picked up from a local renderer—mostly calves, sheep, and pigs, occasionally bulls or horses.

Zachariah hadn't stocked up since he'd gotten sick. The freezers were half empty.

Her gaze swept the rest of the room, flicking over the steel table meant for chopping meat, a huge steel sink, and a wooden block stuck with gigantic butcher knives.

In the corner stood the chest freezer full of rats for the birds of prey and Winston. Her father used to call them ratsicles.

A memory struck her—her father on the floor, straddling a calf carcass, brandishing a huge bloodied knife, entrails puddling around his boots as he grinned broadly, at home in the gore.

She blinked the sudden wetness from her eyes and checked the generator. It was working but running low on fuel. It would last another week, maybe two. She added propane to her internal checklist of items to scavenge, if there was anything left to find.

In the vegetable storeroom, the wooden shelves were crammed with bins full of past their sell-by-date vegetables that Zachariah collected from several local markets to feed the herbivores. The sickly-sweet odor of overripe peaches filled her nostrils. The vegetables were beginning to rot.

The dry foods section of the storeroom held the mother lode. Bales of hay and alfalfa were stacked in the far corner. Next to them stood several one-hundred-gallon vats that stored grains.

Shelves lined the walls. Every shelf was heaped with boxes and crates of edible food: canned goods, mostly expired; plastic containers of peanut butter (Kodiak's favorite food, spread on about three dozen pancakes); commercial-sized boxes of Cheerios and Fruit Loops which the bonobos loved; special high-fiber biscuit mix for the otters and the black bears; cases of nuts and seeds, bags of popcorn, and large bottles of honey, which were used to fill the enrichment balls for the bonobos, Electra and Leo, and the black bears.

Raven stared in awe at the storage vault until her eyes blurred. Her legs turned to jelly. She sagged against the wall and sank to the concrete floor.

Her dad kept a four-week store of food supplies for the animals. Vlad ate sixty pounds of meat a day. The wolves ate a full deer or calf carcass every three days. The bonobos consumed their weight in fruits, vegetables, and biscuits. Every. Single. Day.

In less than a month, the animals would starve, Raven along with them.

A terrible thought spun through her mind. If she didn't feed everything to the animals... if she kept all this food for herself...

Supplemented with what she could hunt and harvest from the forest, this food cache could last her for up to two years, maybe longer.

If she lived.

If she wasn't infected.

A wave of vertigo washed through her. The world seemed to tilt, the floor cracking open beneath her, splintering into a gaping hole about to swallow her up.

Logically, she knew what she should do. She needed to choose herself. Choose her own survival. They were animals. Thousands had probably starved to death in zoos around the country already.

If Raven *were* sick, they'd starve without her, anyway.

Even if she fed them all this food, it wouldn't last.

They would starve.

Raven would starve.

Only three days ago, she'd been about to turn her back on them permanently. What was different now? Two freshly turned graves flashed through her mind. *Only everything.*

Before, they would have lived without her.

Now, they depended upon her utterly.

No. She wouldn't let them waste away, afraid, bewildered, in pain. That was cruel, inhumane. Her father had asked her to take care of them, to offer them the mercy of a quick, relatively painless death. She had access to the rest of the tranquilizer guns kept in the maintenance shed for emergencies. She could put them down gently.

She thought of Vlad. She thought of Suki and Loki, her favorite timber wolves. What were the deaths of a few animals in cages compared to the collapse of the civilized world? Compared to the catastrophic loss of billions of dead and dying humans?

Outside the storehouse, the bonobos were growing agitated. They hooted and screeched, their frustrated calls escalating into a cacophony of chaos.

The guns were in the maintenance shed, not fifty feet away. She could go get them now, she could—

Something inside her shriveled. Her mind recoiled from the thought. She'd just buried her father. She wasn't ready. Maybe she'd never be ready. Maybe she shouldn't care, maybe she should be cold-hearted, but she wasn't. She did care about the animals, more than she wanted to admit.

It would be better to let them go happily, peacefully, on full stomachs. Wouldn't it? Wasn't that the right thing to do in this terrible, horrific situation she found herself in?

There was another option. She could release them from their cages and give them a chance in the wild to survive. The wolves would hunt. The tiger would stalk the night, searching for prey. The bobcat and leopard would do the same. Maybe.

Or maybe they would be a danger to whatever human survivors remained out there in the world. Or perhaps they would hunt Raven herself.

She stood woodenly, frozen by indecision. She would feed them today. Tomorrow, she would figure out what to do.

Tomorrow, she would face every single animal her dad had loved, that she'd grown up with, that she knew as well as she knew herself—and offer them mercy.

Chapter Ten

Raven focused on the task at hand, on getting through this awful, endless day. The shock and grief of her father's death numbed her.

She had not coughed. She didn't burn with fever. It was early still. The virus simply hadn't made itself known yet. Her father's last moments kept flaring through her mind—his bloody tears, his rigid features, his feverish limbs contorted in pain.

If that future awaited her, there was nothing she could do to stop it.

She concentrated on putting one foot in front of the other, on the chores she'd completed hundreds of times over the years. She lugged buckets of water from the well outside the perimeter fence, cleaned each pen and enclosure, disposing of the manure, ensuring the hay was fresh without mold, and methodically checking the bottom layers.

It was past noon by the time she loaded up the wagon attached to the electric cart with hay and five-gallon buckets of grain for the herbivores: the deer, the ostriches, and Sal the zebra. She'd managed to fit in a deer carcass for the wolves and cuts of horse meat for Vlad.

At the tiger house, she whistled to call Vlad inside his chamber so she could open the gate and give him his food. One long note, two short.

Vlad rose from sunning himself on his favorite flat rock, sauntered to the fence, tail twitching, and gazed at her with a distinctly displeased expression on his furred face. With an irritated chuff, he turned his rump to her. She jumped back in time to miss the spray of urine.

Vlad's spray had a distinct stink. Zachariah used to say it smelled like hot buttered popcorn. While Raven wished she could disagree vehemently, Zachariah hadn't been wrong. He hadn't been wrong often. Not much good that did him.

"Very funny," she said to the tiger, stepping backward.

He chuffed at her again, the tigerish version of a mocking laugh. He was obliging and playful again now that he'd adequately punished her.

Even in her grief, she hadn't forgotten. After she'd lugged over his dinner, she dug in her pocket, tugged out a few pieces of his favorite venison jerky, and tossed them over the fence. He consumed them in seconds.

He was so incredibly majestic, it made her heart hurt to look at him. How unfair it was to imagine the world without this magnificent creature, without any of these beautiful wild animals in it.

She'd spent her life resenting these animals for stealing the coveted attention of her father. But she had to admit that she'd grown fond of them, too. More than fond.

Her feelings for the wild animals of Haven were a tangled, complicated mess, much like her feelings for the refuge, for her father, and her mother.

This was the dichotomy of her life—she simultaneously loved and hated the same things.

"I don't want to do it," she said.

Vlad cocked his great head and twitched an ear at her.

"If I have to do it, I hope you'll understand. That you can forgive me."

Shaking her head, she stepped back from the fence. What was she doing, seeking absolution from a tiger?

The tiger ignored her. He sauntered back to his rock, plopped down, and yawned, revealing his teeth. He licked his front fangs as if to remind her who stood atop the food chain.

"Okay, show off. I'll come back to fill your enrichment ball later, okay?"

Vlad didn't bother to answer her.

As she drove the cart up the path, she passed one of the peacocks strolling the grounds. He strutted and preened, showing off his sapphire-throated elegance and flamboyant, plumed jewel-green tail feathers.

He squawked at her in annoyance as she drove the cart around him.

"I'll get to you," she said. "Be patient."

He shimmied his feathers at her to show his irritation.

"Yeah, yeah, join the line. Everyone's pissed at me today."

She decided to cross the grounds out of order to feed the bonobos next. They'd been screeching their indignation since yesterday.

The four bonobos lounged in the roped netting strung between three trees inside their habitat. Some slept. Others combed nits from each other's fur. Pepper and Newton chased each other over a tightrope, nimble and sprightly. Their tiny hands and feet clung to the rope as they enthusiastically attempted to shake the other one free.

Cousins of the chimpanzee, bonobos were the smallest and most intelligent of the apes. They were a matriarchal society, with their leader being a female. They were mostly peaceful and far less aggressive than chimps. They'd been extinct in the wild for a decade.

Zephyr was the matriarch, the oldest and wisest. She was a patient and calm leader, looking out for the others, breaking up arguments, and protecting her small son, Gizmo, from the taunts of Pepper and Newton, both four-year-old juveniles. Pepper was particularly calculated and cunning. She would distract the other bonobos and steal their food—particularly lettuce, her favorite.

Gizmo bounced on his branch, swinging his arms and offering Raven energetic screeches and hoots. He grinned, his top lip pulled over his teeth, his leathery face relieved and joyful. *Finally*, he seemed to say, *You brought dinner!*

He reached toward her, gesturing excitedly with his fingers, his black-licorice eyes gleaming. His tufts of black hair were parted in the middle on top of his head, giving him a distinctly human look.

Despite her grief, she managed a grim smile. His exuberance made her chest constrict with a hollow ache. "Nice to see you, too, Gizmo."

After the bonobos were fed, she moved on to the red foxes. Zoe, Zelda, and Magnus were as energetic as puppies—and almost as tame. They'd let her or her father enter their pen and rub their bellies or brush the burrs from their lush red tails.

Sal wasn't nearly as obliging. Beautiful as he was, the zebra was vain about keeping his black and white coat pristine, and ornery to boot. He'd sneak up and bite her on the shoulder or butt as soon as her back was turned. He also enjoyed kicking people, so she locked him in his night house when she needed to access his pen.

The bobcat, Electra, was ancient at nine years old. She appeared cuddly as a stuffed animal with her charming bobbed tail, luxurious spotted coat, and perky, black-fringed ears, but she had fast reflexes and a predator's instincts. Cute as she was, Electra could kill a grown man with gruesome efficiency.

Raven's father went into her pen. He didn't fear Electra, who was known to flip onto her belly for him and bat playfully at his arms with her razor-sharp claws. She'd leave nasty scratches if he didn't wear his leather jacket, but he didn't seem to mind.

Or, he hadn't. Past tense. He'd never again enter this pen and play with Electra. He'd never again crawl around with the wolves or watch Vlad tear into his bull's head dinner with serene satisfaction.

Raven sucked in her breath and tossed Electra's dinner over the fence. A whole plucked chicken she loved to eat fully, bones and all. Electra growled in appreciation as she pounced on it.

By the time Raven reached the rear of the park, it was early evening. At the north end, the wolves reigned over two forested enclosures. The first enclosure was the largest and held the six timber wolves. Behind a tall chain-link fence topped with electrified wire, the wolves prowled among the cluster of beech trees in the center of their enclosure.

She knew these wolves the best. They were her father's favorites. She remembered sweltering afternoons spent outside the fence, watching her father inside the enclosure with the wolves.

He would sit with them, frolic with them, sleep with them. It had taken months of patience, but little by little, the pack had accepted him. Raven had watched it happen with a complicated mix of envy, awe, resentment, and admiration.

Normally shy and wary, the wolves typically kept to the cover of the trees during the day. They recognized her scent and the smell of food. One by one, they appeared between the trees and drifted into the clearing. Slowly, they approached the double-fence line.

Titus and Loki came the closest. Loki loped up to the first fence, tongue lolling goofily. Loki, the god of mischief, was aptly named. He was the smallest of the wolves but made up for it with abundant energy. Curious and mischievous, he had a spring to his step, always the one ready to play.

Titus stood tense, ears pricked, fur raised along his spine, and his tail stiff behind him, not induced by aggression, but rather in a protective stance. He was the beta. Four years old and in his prime, he was a bruiser: tall, thick-chested, and bulky. The beta was the bouncer of the pack, the alphas' enforcer, and the first to snap at any wolf out of line.

"I brought dinner," she said.

Suki whined eagerly and took a tentative step forward, her tail lifting. She was the shyest wolf as well as the youngest, a yearling. Suki was sweet and gentle, the peacekeeper, the one who broke up arguments before Titus had to get involved.

Suki's name was Japanese for "beloved." Her dad named her when he nursed her from a pup after a she-wolf from the Chattanooga Zoo had rejected her young. It was the only sentimental thing Raven had ever seen him do.

The last three wolves hung back.

Echo was spindly, with a straggly grey coat, a chunk bitten out of his right ear, and a perpetual slinking manner, an air of cowardice. He was the omega, the lowest wolf on the totem pole.

The other two were the alpha pair, Shika and Aspen. A brindled she-wolf, Shika had a savage, restless beauty about her. She was the fastest wolf, easily outpacing her life mate, Aspen.

Aspen boasted a magnificent shaggy ruff and a single dark stripe down the center of his muzzle. He was smart and calculating. He was utterly devoted to Shika and stood close to her. Their yellow eyes were fixed on Raven.

Alpha wolves weren't the bold, aggressive type like some people thought. Aggression was the role of the beta, the alpha's second-in-command. The alphas were the brains of the operation, the central nervous system that kept the pack together and working properly. The alphas were wary, cautious; they protected the critical knowledge and hard-won experience that kept their family alive.

The male never led alone; it was a partnership, like the parents of a family. That was the pack. Raven had always respected the hell out of wolves.

Once she'd lured the wolves to their den, she locked them in, then entered the double gates, hauled the deer carcass from the wagon, and dumped it in their enclosure.

In the wild, wolf hierarchy was established by who was allowed to eat what parts of their kill. Her father preferred to feed the wolves a whole carcass instead of joints of meat. Sometimes, they fed the wolves a calf carcass, but her dad liked to hunt deer for them instead of purchasing meat from the slaughterhouse or renderer.

Memories lay thick and heavy over every inch of this place. Everywhere she looked, she saw him: lounging beneath the sprawling oak with the wolves; striding along the flagstone pathways, trailed by a peacock or two; bent over the fences, checking for breaches; and driving the electric cart everywhere, hauling water, food, and hay.

Her chest tightened. For a moment, it was hard to breathe. She pushed the feelings away. She had too much to do to waste time feeling sorry for herself.

Raven released the wolves to their dinner.

It was bizarre to watch wolves eat. They snapped and snarled at each other, fangs bared in a frenzy of furious excitement. If one tried to take a bite from the wrong section, the other wolves growled and bit at him.

It seemed savage from the outside, but her father had explained that the higher-ranking wolves were teaching the lower-ranked wolves where and how they belonged, ensuring every wolf remembered their place in the pack.

The pack used food to maintain order. Each wolf had a spot—prized organs, neck, flank—which was earned depending on its rank and role within the pack. The parts of meat they ate affected the distinctive smell of their urine, which they used to signal identity, status, and role.

Her dad had described a pack in the wild whose natural prey had been so depleted, they'd been forced to catch salmon from the river to keep from starving. With every wolf eating the same thing, their urine lost their distinctive markers. Each wolf lost its identity. As a result, the pack descended into anarchy and collapsed.

By the time Raven moved on to the next enclosure, the sun was sinking below the tree line. Weariness tugged at her. Her muscles ached. Her belly rumbled. She forced herself to keep moving.

As long as there was work to do, she could keep the pain at bay, could ignore the darkness threatening to devour her the second she let her guard down.

The second enclosure also housed wolves, but these wolves were kept separate from the timber wolves. They were too dangerous.

There were two of them, one white, one dark. Luna and Shadow.

They were genetically modified. Though it was very illegal, a black market had sprung up around wild animals engineered with traits like meekness for wealthy bored housewives who wanted exotic pets, or for aggression, for the underground fighting pits.

To gain the advantage in the ring, their owners had illegally bred cloned wolves with modified versions to produce a genetically superior hybrid wolf featuring increased size, strength, and a cunning, human-like intelligence.

When they were rescued last year from the fighting ring, no zoos would take them, claiming they were unnatural creations, cloned intellectual property rather than wild animals. That is, until her father had agreed to bring them to Haven.

No one ventured inside this enclosure other than her father. Last summer, Zachariah's teenage nephew was sent to the hospital after he reached through the chain-link fence to scratch Luna when she rubbed her back against the fence. Luna had whipped around lightning fast and bitten off two of his fingers.

Wolves weren't dogs. And hybrids weren't even wolves. They were some nebulous *other*—beautiful, uncanny, and terrifying.

Raven stepped up to the fence, peering through the trees, searching the shifting shadows. Though she couldn't see them, she felt their presence, knew they were watching. They were always watching.

"Come out now," she said in a soothing voice. "I'm not going to hurt you. You're not going to hurt me. We can be friends, if you want."

Movement caught her eye, between two trees at the rear of the enclosure. A huge white creature appeared like a ghost. Luna was easily over two hundred pounds, her coat as pure white as driven snow. Her amber eyes fixed on Raven like she could see straight through her.

For a second, Raven forgot how to breathe. "There you are."

A moment later, a shadow separated from the deeper shadows beneath the trees, forming into the shape of an enormous wolf. His broad shoulders and chest rippled with muscles beneath his thick, ink-black fur.

The black wolf raised his regal head. His muzzle was long and narrow. His amber eyes shone with cunning. His name fit him well, for he seemed to merge with the darkness, a shadow appearing and disappearing at will.

For a long moment, the hybrid wolves stared at her. She, in turn, stared back at them with equal parts awe and fear.

Abruptly, Luna's ears flattened against her skull. Her eyes slitted. Her jowls pulled back to reveal a row of sharp white teeth.

Shadow moved to stand beside her. His hackles were raised, his tail stiff behind him.

The hairs on Raven's arms stood on end. Instinctively, she stepped back. Anxiety crackled through her. Logically, she knew there was a double fence between them, that she was safe. Still, alarm bells jangled through her mind, her primitive lizard brain screaming that two enormous predators were intent on devouring her.

"I'm not here to hurt you. I'm here to help."

The wolves growled. They snapped their jaws, backs arched, hackles bristling.

Raven took another step back. She raised her hands in supplication. "Easy now. Calm down for a second and let me—"

Then she heard it, too.

The rumble of motorcycles.

CHAPTER ELEVEN

The unmuffled roar of the motorcycles grew louder, closer.

Raven stilled, rooted in place. Her mind whirred with terrible possibility after terrible possibility, each one worse than the last. They could be looters or vandals, criminals or serial killers.

But she knew who they were—the bikers from the pharmacy in Forsyth.

What the hell were they doing here? And how had they followed her? She'd been careful, so careful.

It didn't matter how. They were here, or would be in the next few minutes. She fought off the panic that was closing her throat. What should she do? Standing out here like a sitting duck was a monumentally bad idea. She needed to hide.

Maybe she could hide in the crawl space beneath the lodge, wait it out until they left. She couldn't make a run for the car; the electric battery was dead. The bikers were too close, anyway. If they heard the engine, they'd be on her in a hot second.

She should make a run for it. Her backpack with her supplies was in her bedroom in the lodge. She needed the supplies in that pack to survive alone for days in the woods. Plus, the pack contained the map with directions to the hunting cabin.

She couldn't run away without it. And she couldn't leave it behind for these thugs to find, either.

The evening sky deepened to indigo. Bats soared and dove over her head, chasing mosquitoes. There was still enough light to see by. The engine sounds grew louder. They'd turn on the road to the refuge any second.

She had to get herself out of sight, right freaking now.

Raven dropped the bucket of meat and broke into a run. She sprinted left, abandoning the exposed flagstone path for a worn-in trail through the weeds and bric-a-brac behind the exhibits.

From the back end of the park, she raced past the wolf enclosures, the bears, the ostrich pen, then the porcupine, eagle, and otter exhibits, the bonobos' house, and finally the reptile house. She reached the storage buildings nestled behind a screen of poplar trees, out of the public's sight.

The motorcycles grew louder. She couldn't see them. They were still obscured by the trees. A five-mile gravel road brought visitors through the forest to the front entrance, which was gated and locked.

At best, the locked gate would only slow down intruders. Though electrified top wires were strung along the perimeter, the fence was intended to keep dangerous things in, rather than offering protection from threats outside the walls.

If they wanted to get inside, the gate wouldn't deter them for long.

Luckily, the many trees and lush foliage obscured her presence as she raced between the storage buildings, headed for the lodge.

The motorcycles roared into the parking lot. The engines switched off. Loud, raucous voices filled the air with shouts and jeers and curses.

Darting between two bushes, she reached the back of the lodge and pressed herself against the rear wall. Her pulse thudded against her throat. *Run.* She needed to grab her gear and escape to the woods.

Her window was located on the west side of the building, directly in the line of sight of the bikers. The ground sloped downward along the rear of the lodge, making the back windows—a bathroom, her father's room, and a guest bedroom—ten feet above the ground. There were no nearby trees to climb, no way to reach the windows.

She needed a plan B, whatever that was.

Raven eased around the corner, cautiously scanning the front of the park. She counted ten bikers gathered outside the gates. She recognized several from the pharmacy: burly blond Scorpio, Damien with the sharp fox-face, a fat short one whose name she didn't know, and Dekker, the dead-eyed one who'd shot Carl in the face. The one who'd threatened her outside the pharmacy.

Of the half-dozen bikers she didn't recognize, one stood out. He stood half a head taller than the others. He was huge, with a barrel chest and blue tattoos squirming across bulging biceps the size of footballs. She was close enough to make out his square, stubbled jaw and chestnut-brown hair shorn close to his skull.

He sauntered up to the gate with one ham-sized hand resting on the butt of his AR-15 rifle. His shrewd gaze assessed everything as he scanned his surroundings.

The others were tough, burly, and heavily tattooed. They carried various weapons—rifles, knives, and guns. Most wore gloves, with masks tugged down around their necks. They circled the tall man, waiting for his orders. He was clearly their leader. This must be Vaughn, the name Scorpio had mentioned at the pharmacy.

She strained to make out their voices, which carried in the quiet.

Ponytail glared up at the fence. "What the hell is this place?"

"A wildlife refuge." Damien read the sign affixed to the gate. Ponytail looked at him blankly. "Like a private zoo."

"The animals are probably dead," Scorpio said. "Or else those crazy Earth Liberation activists released them, like they did in Atlanta."

Kodiak chose that moment to give a half-hearted bellow, which echoed through the park.

"That a lion?" asked a bearded Black man, his eyes going wide.

"You're an idiot, Cobb," Damien said. "Don't you recognize a bear when you hear one?"

Cobb scowled in embarrassment. Dekker and Scorpio laughed at him. Damien's face flushed at the show of approval.

Vaughn threw back his head and laughed. "Guess at least one wild animal is still alive. Anybody have bear meat recently?"

"My mouth is already watering," Ponytail said. "I'll take any meat."

"I'm sure you will," Dekker drawled.

"What a pleasant surprise." Vaughn peered through the bars of the gate and took in the restaurant, the lodge, the picnic tables, and the souvenir shop. "A precious jewel hidden away in the middle of nowhere."

Vlad's roar punctuated the quiet evening air.

The bikers froze and stared at each other. Damien's mouth gaped in startled awe.

Vlad roared repeatedly, the deep bass notes ringing across the grounds. It was an impressive sound, conjuring images of enormous, vicious beasts hunting their dinner.

A savage grin spreading across his face, Vaughn slapped Damien on the back so hard he stumbled. "Gentlemen, we've just entered the jungle. Good find, Dekker. You've earned first choice for your prize."

"What about the girl?" Dekker asked, sounding bored.

Raven stiffened. Dekker had looked at her like she was prey. She still didn't know how they'd found her; she'd been so careful to ensure she wasn't followed.

"She might be here, she might not," Scorpio said. "How much time do you want to waste looking for her?"

"It's not a waste," Dekker said flatly. "She and I have unfinished business. Besides, she's premium quality. And she's here. I know she is."

Dekker scanned the trees as he prowled next to Vaughn, hand resting on his holster. He was likely Vaughn's beta, his enforcer. Dekker pointed toward the carport at the other end of the parking lot. "That's her car. With all the bumper stickers."

Icy fear poured through Raven's veins. The faded, peeling stickers. The ones advertising Haven Wildlife Refuge, which her father had been so proud to paste all over the bumper. She'd forgotten about them. Damn it! That's how he'd found her, then.

"Bring her to me," Vaughn said. "If she's as hot as you say she is, I have a particular client who will... appreciate ... her exotic flair."

The bikers laughed.

"I get first crack at her," Dekker said.

Vaughn raised his eyebrows. "We'll see."

Raven inhaled sharply. Her face flushed hot with outrage—and fear. They could go to hell. Every single one of them. They were murderers and worse.

Vaughn cocked his head, listening to Vlad's distant roars. "Let's have a look around before it gets too dark, see what we can find. We'll stay here for the night."

"How about something edible?" Ponytail asked. His voice was deep and rough, like gravel. "I'm starving."

Cobb sniggered. "Don't accidentally walk into the bear cage, Rex, or you'll be the edible one."

Cobb flashed an ingratiating smile at Vaughn, as if gauging his reaction to the insult. Vaughn ignored him. Beside him, Dekker sneered down at Cobb and waved a hand at him in dismissal. Cobb slunk several paces away.

There was a hierarchy among the bikers, with the same jostling for power and dominance as a wolf pack. In this case, she doubted the alpha treated his pack like family.

"Gentlemen, a treat just landed right in our laps, thanks to Dekker's quick thinking." Vaughn gathered the men around him. "Let's go see just how sweet it is."

Cobb grabbed the bars of the gate and rattled them. "How we gettin' inside, boss?"

Rex narrowed his eyes at the bioscan lock. "No way to hack this."

"Grab the hook," Vaughn ordered. "And the chains."

"What are you waiting for?" Dekker clapped his hands at the lower-tier men. "Get to it."

Raven watched with barely contained panic as several bikers jogged back to their motorcycles. One pulled a large metal hook and chains from a case attached to the rear of the bike. Rex grabbed a bolt cutter and went to work on the gate's hinges.

Cobb and Damien wrapped the chains around the gate, then attached them to the rear of several bikes. They revved the bikes and pulled away with a squeal of tires and roaring engines. With a sickening shriek of metal on metal, the gate wrenched off its snapped hinges and fell to the asphalt with a thud.

The bikers strode through the opening in the fence like they owned the place.

Vaughn turned to Damien, Rex, and a third guy—a slight, stoop-shouldered Latino in his forties, wearing a khaki jacket and a floppy brown fishing hat pulled low over his forehead. "Damien, find us a place to sleep. Rex and Gomez, you're on food patrol. Scrounge up something decent to eat."

Damien nodded. "We're on it."

The bikers dispersed, laughing and conversing among themselves. Three of them found the main path that circled the perimeter of the park. As dusk fell, they flicked on their flashlights.

Rex and the black-haired guy in the fishing hat—Gomez—strode up the path that circled the lodge. They would skirt the side of the lodge and reach the rear in a few moments.

Raven had to move. Now.

The growing darkness would help shield her. She knew the layout of this place like the back of her hand. The darkness gave her a slight advantage—an advantage she needed if she was going to survive the night.

Chapter Twelve

Raven rose cautiously to her feet and backed away slowly, making her footfalls quiet the way her father had taught her when they went hunting together.

Like all predators, rapid movement would attract attention and trigger their prey response. If she stayed small and still, she could creep behind the buildings, head to the back of the park, reach the rear gate, and escape into the woods.

Without her pack, she had no food, water, or shelter. She wouldn't last long. But a single night while these thugs took what they wanted before going their merry way—that was doable.

They'd take some of the food, but there were only ten of them. She prayed they wouldn't hurt Kodiak or the other animals. Either way, she had no choice.

She was out of options.

It was completely dark out now. Stars winked to life overhead. Thin clouds drifted across the moon like filmy ribbons. Without electricity, the automatic security lights strung along the path were dark.

Moving carefully within the shadows, she managed to reach the maintenance shed without detection. The air had grown chilly, temperatures dropping into the forties at night. Her adrenaline masked the cold, but she would feel it later, alone in the woods at night, exposed to the elements.

She crouched, eyeing the twenty yards of open ground she had to cross to reach the cover of trees between the shed and the food storage buildings. Once she reached the trees, she'd be invisible—

Footsteps sounded nearby. Three men rounded the corner of the lodge, not thirty yards distant. They approached from the far side. Their flashlights swept the ground along the wrought-iron fence. In the dark, their shapes were only vaguely human.

Raven cringed back against the wall, cursing silently. Panic bit at her. They were between her and the fence. As soon as they reached the shed, they'd discover her.

Still crouching, she crept along the rear of the shed and peeked around the opposite corner. She faced the park now. On her left stood the lodge, the restaurant, the souvenir shop, and the entrance. Bikers bumbled around inside the restaurant. Two shapes appeared through the windows of the lodge—her *home*.

To the right, the flagstone path led past the food storage buildings to the east exhibits: the reptile house, the bonobos, the otters, eagle, and porcupines, the ostriches, then the bears and wolves at the rear.

She had only a moment to decide. The goons behind her would discover her position within sixty seconds at most. She inched out from behind the maintenance shed and moved to the path.

Waist-high bushes lined the path, with slim birch trees interspersed every thirty feet. Other than the bushes, there wasn't much cover until she reached the reptile house, another fifty yards away.

Raven ducked behind the bushes along the path and crawled on her hands and knees. Twigs and burrs jabbed into her palms. The woodsy scent of fresh mulch filled her nostrils.

Voices rang out behind her. Harsh, braying laughter echoed. Flashlight beams swept across the darkened sky.

She crawled faster. Despite the cold, sweat beaded her forehead. Icy shock trembled her limbs. Her pulse roared in her ears. Get out of sight. Get to the rear gate. *Get out. Get out. Get out.*

After what she guessed was fifty yards, she risked a peek above the hedge. Splinters of mulch needled her kneecaps. Ahead of her, the shadowy bulk of the reptile house reared out of the night.

Dropping back down, she kept crawling. When she checked again, she'd reached the eagle house. She could just make out the shape of Hera, the American bald eagle, who was napping on a high branch within the mesh walls.

Everything felt slow and jerky simultaneously. Every movement loud as a gunshot. Her breath sounded ragged in her ears. She kept going.

After what felt like an hour, she reached the bears. The perimeter fence stood only a few yards behind the bear and wolf exhibits. She forced herself to wait in the stillness, straining her ears for strange noises over the trill of insects. A peacock squawked. Across the park, the squealing of the bonobos echoed.

Voices. Not too near yet, but closing in. A flashlight beam bobbed behind her. Danger was headed her way. Time to move.

Heart in her throat, she rose to her feet.

The bear enclosure was large. To circle to the back, she had to walk along a section of path directly in front of the enclosure, about twenty yards long. It was devoid of topiary bushes or trees, leaving her completely exposed.

Her boots scuffed the flagstone. She softened her footfalls. She craned her neck as she checked in all directions, listening hard, peering through the dim moonlight, constantly scanning, searching for danger, for anything out of place—

A shadow that didn't belong.

Directly ahead of her, maybe ten feet at most, a large shape bent over the railing of the bear habitat. It stood completely still and unmoving in the darkness.

Alarmed, she blinked. The shape was still there. Her eyes adjusted enough to determine that the shape was distinctly human.

Adrenaline crackled through her. She couldn't retreat the way she'd come. Several bikers approached from behind her. Raven did the only thing she could think of. She took off running.

She raced past the bear enclosure. The shadow moved. It jerked back, startled.

"Hey!" the figure cried. "Hey! Stop!"

His footfalls slapped the flagstone behind her. He cursed, fumbling with something, probably attempting to activate his flashlight. Or perhaps a gun.

Her pursuer was larger than she was. Stronger. Likely faster. She couldn't outrun him. Her only chance was to hide—somewhere he was least likely to look.

There weren't many options.

It was a risk. It was dangerous. Between human predators who killed for pleasure and animal predators who rarely killed humans in the wild... it wasn't a choice.

Raven wheeled sharply to the right. She fled between the enclosures. Her pursuer was somewhere behind her. She had a few precious seconds. Maybe.

The timber wolf paddock was surrounded by a double fence, with several feet of no man's land between. She pressed her right hand to the bioscanner. She was shaking so hard she had to do it twice.

Finally, the outside gate opened. She slipped inside and relocked it, then sprinted to the inside gate, opened it, and entered. Taking a deep, steadying breath, she willed herself to calm the hell down.

She couldn't show fear. Couldn't allow herself to feel it, either. Wolves could smell fear. They knew if your heart rate increased, could scent every molecule of your sour, panicked sweat.

Crouch low at their level and don't move, her dad had instructed the few times he'd brought her inside the fence. *Don't startle them. Show you're submissive. Speak in their language.*

On the path behind her, a flashlight beam flickered to life.

There was no time. She was exposed. At any second, the thug would discover her. She had to get out of the clearing into the forested area around the perimeter. She had to move, to hide— right now.

She took a hesitant step into the enclosure. Then another. Her heart hammered against her ribs.

Deeper in the enclosure, a twig cracked.

The wolves were here. They sensed her presence.

It was only then, surrounded by darkness, locked inside the enclosure, that she realized her mistake.

The deer carcass she'd fed to the timber wolves earlier in the day was missing.

It had been right here, not twenty yards in. The wolves wouldn't have finished the carcass yet. Even if they had, there would be bones, a skull, patches of fur, gristle, which she'd be able to see, even in the dark.

Her heart turned to ice in her chest.

The deer carcass wasn't here because she wasn't inside the timber wolves' enclosure. In the dark, in her panic, she'd entered the second enclosure instead.

Raven had locked herself in with the hybrid wolves.

Chapter Thirteen

Sweat beaded beneath Raven's armpits. Her breath came in sharp, shallow gasps.

These were not the timber wolves she knew and understood, still deadly, still dangerous, but at least *familiar*.

The hybrid wolves were completely *other*. Alien and terrible.

Raven nearly turned around. She almost lost her nerve and fled back to the gate.

The biker's flashlight beam swept across a thicket of trees a dozen yards to her right. Fear stuck in her throat like a hook. Her pursuer was searching for her.

Human killers or killer wolves. Either choice was horrible.

The human killers were worse. They would take their time, make it hurt. They'd use her. The animals, at least, would be quick, clean.

She'd take her chances with the animals.

Frantic, she searched for a hiding spot within the enclosure—a wide tree trunk, a thick bush, a fallen log—anything. She squinted, peering into the darkness, the darkness that held any number of monsters.

The flashlight beam swept toward her. Raven scrambled down the shallow incline, shoved brambles and underbrush aside, and dove behind the trunk of a hickory tree. The bark scraped her spine, but she hardly noticed.

She drew her arms and legs close, hunched her shoulders, and made herself as small as possible.

A second later, the flashlight skimmed over her hiding place. The light glinted off something in the brush deeper in the trees. The light stilled on a spot ahead of her, not five yards from where she huddled behind the trunk.

Two pairs of reflective eyes peered back at her.

Raven went very still.

Both wolves were less than twenty-five feet away. Every cell in her body screamed at her to flee. She couldn't. The biker stood on the path above her. He trained the flashlight beam on the pairs of glowing eyes and swore softly.

A halo of white emerged among the darkly gleaming leaves. It was Luna, the big white female. Luna's mate remained utterly camouflaged in the darkness. Only the glitter of eyes stared intently back at her.

The hairs on the back of her neck stood on end.

She was trapped inside a cage with two genetically modified wolves almost twice her weight. Each wolf was designed by nature and man to maim, to tear and destroy, to kill with impunity, endowed with a bite force of fifteen hundred pounds per square inch.

It took every ounce of self-control she possessed not to scream. She gritted her teeth against the panic, the adrenaline, the terror thrumming through her veins. Her muscles taut, she counted the eternal seconds.

Finally, the flashlight swept away.

The biker stumbled down the path away from the enclosure. The flashlight wavered wildly as he cursed and shouted for his friends. "I found her! She disappeared on me!"

"I think she's over here by the otters!" another voice shouted back.

Raven didn't have the time to sigh in relief.

The white wolf moved. She glided silently closer, her back low, hackles raised. Somehow, she was suddenly twenty feet away, then fifteen. Her ears twitched. She never took her gaze off Raven.

Raven dropped her gaze in submission. It seemed like the wolf stared at her forever. The other one was here, too. She felt him. Somehow, it was more frightening not to see him. Were they taking her measure? Did they see her as a potential threat? Or were they deciding which parts of her to eat first?

She knew the answer. Her organs. Her heart, lungs, stomach, and intestines. Alphas got the choicest bits. These two were the most alpha of any alpha wolves she'd ever seen.

Her stomach lurched. Somehow, she remained still, quiet, and submissive. She was no threat to them. Neither was she prey. Hopefully, they were smart enough to figure that out. Or else, they were about to tear out her warm, beating heart.

In an eye blink, the white wolf vanished. The black wolf, too. She could feel his presence, then she couldn't. It was that fast. One second, they were there. The next, they faded silently into the darkness.

She peered into the gloom, her gaze sweeping from left to right and back again, straining to make out a familiar predatory shape in the shadows. She'd thought it couldn't get worse, but it could. Not seeing them, not having any idea where they were, whether they were sneaking up on her right this second, preparing to pounce from any direction—this was worse.

Could she leave without being attacked? Had they grown tired of her and wandered off somewhere to sleep? Maybe she could rise quietly and sneak back to the gate.

But no. There was no sneaking. Not with wolves. They could detect her every movement by scent. They would know the second she stood.

If she made it to the fence, it was because they'd allowed it, as opposed to the other option: tearing her throat out.

It was worth a chance. Better than sitting here and waiting for death to come. Slowly, she rose from her crouch. The clouds drifted from the moon, and pale white moonlight spilled across the enclosure.

As she stood, something sharp jabbed into her thigh. Adrenaline shot through her. Images of gleaming claws and fangs flashed through her mind.

It wasn't claws or fangs.

It was her whittling knife. It was still in her pocket. She hadn't changed since yesterday, since she'd buried her dad.

Raven drew the knife from her pocket and flicked the three-inch blade open. It wasn't much, but it was better than nothing.

On her feet, she took a single, cautious step. Dead leaves crackled beneath her boot.

Ahead of her, a low growl erupted from the bushes.

Raven froze.

The black wolf materialized out of the darkness.

She forgot how to breathe.

The wolf stood between two maple trees, less than ten feet away. He was stiff-legged, tail straight out behind him. He tilted his regal head, studying her with his intense amber eyes.

He growled again. His ears flattened.

Instinctively, she backed against the tree and lowered herself, so she was smaller than he was, less of a threat. She gripped the knife but kept it low and pressed against her thigh.

"Whoa now," she said softly. "I'm not here to hurt you."

As soon as she sat back down, making herself small, the wolf's ears lifted. He gave her a piercing look, as if to say, *Now, stay there.*

She settled against the trunk of the hickory tree. Yellowed leaves rustled over her head. "You want me right here where you can keep an eye on me," she murmured, hardly daring to breathe. "Is that it?"

The black wolf prowled around her in a slow, languid circle, sniffing the ground, the air, never breaching that ten-foot radius. Ten feet or ten inches, it hardly mattered. If he wished, his jaws could snap around her throat in less than a second.

For several minutes, he circled her. Raven sat rigid, nearly passing out from lack of oxygen. Abruptly, the wolf loped away and disappeared into the underbrush.

This time, she knew better than to move. He remained present but out of sight, watching her. The white wolf, too. She could feel their presence in the prickling of her skin, the rapid beat of her heart.

This was their territory. She was the intruder. Whether she lived or died tonight was entirely up to them.

She inhaled a slow, shaky breath and glanced up. Should she try to climb the tree, escape their reach? There were no low branches. She scanned the other trees—all too slim to bear her weight. Besides, movement would attract the wolves. If they deemed her actions threatening, they'd be on her in a heartbeat.

Better not to move until they tired of her. At least she was temporarily safe from the murderous bikers. There was that.

She sat against the tree trunk and waited, the knife clenched at her side. The cold ground seeped through her pants and chilled her legs and backside. Above her head, the sickle of the moon hung in the trees, caught in a snarl of branches.

For what seemed like hours, she waited and listened to the pulse of the night, the pitter-patter of tiny nocturnal creatures, and the soughing of the wind through the trees. She stayed alert for any sound or glimpse of the wolves, but there was nothing. They moved through the darkness like ghosts.

An hour later, the black wolf returned.

Chapter Fourteen

This time, the wolf came closer.

He trotted around Raven, sniffing the ground. He circled her again and again, each time drawing closer and closer.

She waited and watched, forcing herself to breathe, to keep her heart from hammering right out of her chest. *Don't be afraid, don't be afraid. Don't give him a reason to kill you.*

His behavior was much like the timber wolves investigating some new toy or strange object in their enclosure. Almost like a dog, though he was no dog. He was enormous. This close, she had to look up at him. His high, regal head. That broad, thickly furred chest and long lean legs. Those sharp teeth.

Abruptly, he bounded close to sniff at the soles of her boots. She gasped. Her brain shrieked in alarm. Somehow, she managed to remain still.

Just as quickly, he darted away.

"Shadow," she whispered. "I'm your friend, not your enemy. I think you know that, right?"

The wolf half-turned as if to leave. Without warning, he whirled on her. He snapped his jaws and nipped her shoulder.

She flinched, stunned. *Run!* Her brain screamed at her.

But her brain was a liar. To run now would trigger his prey response. Instinct would drive him to attack, even if that wasn't his original intention.

She couldn't run. She couldn't do anything but remain statue-still and endure this. Whatever this was.

It was a test. A test she either passed and lived or failed and died. Right here, tonight.

Her shoulder smarted. Slowly, gingerly, she raised her hand and felt the wound. No blood. No missing chunks of flesh.

The wolf hadn't bitten her, not really. He wasn't trying to hurt her. Or at least, not much. Not yet.

He was interested in something else.

Shadow disappeared into the underbrush.

Again, Raven waited.

Another hour passed. The air grew colder. Slender white-trunked birch trees glowed faintly in the moonlight. Fallen branches littered the ground at her feet. She shivered, drawing her arms around her torso for warmth.

To keep herself awake, she picked up a nearby stick, thick as her forearm, about a foot long. It was a good stick for whittling.

At least she had the knife. An image of the wooden bird she'd carved at her father's bedside flitted through her mind. Her father's body, going stiff, growing cold. Even though she'd wrapped him in a tarp, she imagined the red Georgia clay filling his gaping mouth, pressing against his dead eyeballs.

She scraped off the bark in sharp, jerky movements. She inhaled a breath. *Focus.* Drive every bad thought out. She made long, sweeping cuts with the grain, carving a rough outline, breathing deep with each stroke.

Her hands fell into the familiar rhythm almost without purposeful thought. Using push and pull cuts, she gently carved the soft shape, the curve of the body, the sweep of the wings, the arc of the head, and the sharp V of the beak.

Another hour passed. Wood shavings scattered in the leaves beneath her. She smiled grimly at the carved raven, cradled it in her palm, an ache in her chest. She used to leave them around the house for her mother and father to discover, little secret gifts. Only her mother ever noticed them, tucked in her dresser drawer or nestled beneath her pillow.

How Raven missed them, both of them, even as she resented them for leaving her behind, abandoned and completely alone, trapped in a nightmare that wouldn't end.

She'd thought being alone was what she wanted.

She was wrong.

The truth was, no matter how much she'd tried to hate her mother, no matter how thick the resentment and anger had grown around her heart, Raven could not stop loving her.

The love hurt more than hate ever could.

In the end, her mother hadn't loved her enough to come back.

Raven placed the carving on the leaf-strewn ground. She blinked rapidly, fighting the stinging in her eyes. She didn't cry. She never cried. Tears were weakness, her father said—used to say.

A moan escaped her lips. She shouldn't think these things, shouldn't feel the pain twisting her gut. Not now, when she had to focus on surviving the night.

She drew her knees to her chest, shivering as she concentrated on the night sounds. A symphony of crickets. The haunting hoot of an owl. The skitter of a small creature through the leaves.

Despite the danger, exhaustion caught up with her. She'd barely slept for three days. More than once, she dozed off, jerking awake with a start at every rustle in the brush, every crack of a twig.

She felt, rather than heard, the wolf's return.

Her eyes snapped open.

Shadow stood less than four feet away. He was staring straight at her.

Before she could react, he sprang in close and nipped her knee. His fangs ripped a small hole in her pants, scraped against her skin.

She didn't move. Didn't wince at the sting of pain.

He stood so close, the damp musk of his coat filled her nostrils.

Hot breath streamed between his open jaws. His pink tongue lolled. Mud coated the bottom of his gigantic paws.

He stood over her, lowered his head, and nipped her calf.

She swallowed a whimper.

He gave her a calculating, inscrutable look. His amber gaze was penetrating as if he was staring right through her, and could see every beat of her shuddering heart. A strange, wondrous terror filled her.

Shadow stepped to the side, across her legs, and bumped hard against her shoulder as he passed. Without the trunk braced against her back, he would've knocked her over.

He circled so close he brushed against her with every turn. His body was solid, all muscle, coiled strength, and power. His fur was coarse and thick. Once again, he circled her, this time bumping her legs as he passed.

He was investigating her, making sure she wasn't a threat—but also checking to see if she was something he'd enjoy devouring. Each time he brushed against her, and she didn't act like prey or predator, it strengthened his decision to let her be.

Relief cascaded through her entire body. The hybrid wolf didn't want to hurt her. Shadow would let her go.

Her relief lasted only an instant.

The wolf spun so swiftly her brain barely registered the movement. He lunged in and snapped his jaws. His lips curled back from his teeth.

He snarled inches from her face. A spray of saliva struck her cheeks. His hot wet breath seared her skin. She smelled the stink of a carnivore's breath, the scent every creature of prey smelled before their untimely demise.

The wolf seized her neck in his jaws.

Chapter Fifteen

Raven froze. Not swallowing, not breathing, not moving a millimeter. Terror stopped her heart in her chest.

The wolf's teeth pricked the flesh over her jugular. His powerful jaws would pulverize her neck, her spine. Those jaws could crush the breath from her body.

He could kill her in a heartbeat, without even trying.

She considered stabbing him with her knife, but that would cause him to bite down on instinct. Either way, she was dead.

She was completely helpless. There was nothing she could do but remain still and count the eternal seconds in her mind, willing herself not to panic, to lock her terror somewhere deep inside.

Five seconds passed. Ten. Twenty. Forty-five. A full minute.

Finally, the wolf released her throat.

She gasped for breath. Still, she kept herself completely motionless. A single bead of blood dripped down the side of her neck.

The wolf stepped back and stared at her with his yellow eyes. He didn't growl or yelp or bare his teeth. He simply watched her, his gaze shrewd and assessing.

What was she supposed to do now? He wanted something. Expected her to do something. But what?

Her mind raced, scrolling through her conversations and observations of her father, all the things he'd taught her about wolf biology and behavior.

It was a test.

This whole night was a test, from the circling to bumping into her to nipping her shoulder and leg. By seizing her throat—one of the most vulnerable parts of the body—he displayed his power and authority as alpha. He had demonstrated his ability to kill her if he wished.

Now she had to prove that she understood him. Raven dropped the knife and rolled onto her back, exposing her belly in submission like she'd seen the lower hierarchy timber wolves do. In this way, she was showing him she knew that she was weak and defenseless. That she recognized he was the one with the power, not her.

This wasn't an attack. It was a request for trust.

"I get it," she whispered. "You're in charge. I respect you as the leader above me."

Again, he stood over her, leaned down, and took her throat in his jaws.

She lay there, every muscle taut. She stared glassy-eyed at the patches of star-spangled sky through the black branches. Her heart beat in her throat, pulsing against his jaws.

The wolf squeezed her neck harder. *You know what I'm capable of,* he seemed to say. He was purposefully choosing not to harm her, proving that she could trust him back.

"I understand," she forced out. "I... I trust you."

He let go of her neck and stepped back.

He watched as she pulled herself to a sitting position, breathing hard. She rubbed her throat. It was tender, slick with hot saliva. Apart from the shallow puncture, she was unharmed.

Relief and astonishment tangled in her stomach. He could've easily killed her, but he didn't. A true alpha wasn't the one who used unnecessary brute force. He was the one who chose not to.

"Thank you," she whispered. "Thank you, Shadow."

His ears flicked toward her, like he was listening. His tail wagged gently.

Shadow trotted away, then paused and glanced back over his shoulder. He took a few more steps, then glanced back at her again.

An invitation.

He wanted her to follow him.

She did.

Raven fumbled through the leaves, found her knife, and shoved it and the carving into her cargo pocket. She rose to her feet, not bothering to comb the leaves from her hair or brush the dirt from her pants.

A sharp, wild-edged thrill thrummed through every cell in her body. She followed Shadow through the trees and thick underbrush. He led her to the far-right side of the enclosure, where the wolf den, otherwise called the night house, was located.

She broke into the small clearing and halted.

The white she-wolf, Luna, lurked at the den entrance. Her hackles lifted, and her lips peeled back in a growl. Not fearful, but wary.

Luna was the distrustful one. That made her smart. People could whisper *I love you* and *I miss you* while they stabbed you in the back. Raven knew that better than most.

She lifted her hands, palms out in a gesture of surrender, and took a step back. Luna's growl deepened.

Of course. A wolf wouldn't understand a human gesture of surrender. Raven dropped to a hunched sitting position, making herself small and submissive. She kept her gaze on the ground. "I'm not a threat to you. I promise."

Luna turned her growl on Shadow. He wagged his tail at her. She showed her teeth, reiterating her displeasure at Raven's presence, who was an interloper who didn't belong.

Shadow loped toward Luna and licked her muzzle, his ears pricked hopefully.

She snapped at him before sashaying out of reach.

Undaunted, Shadow approached and nuzzled Luna's side. Her lips pulled back. She gave him a severe, disapproving look. She snapped at him again, her jaws closing an inch from his left ear. A punishment.

This time, Shadow backed off with a low whimper.

Luna turned and stalked into the den, her hackles raised. Growling, she abandoned Shadow and Raven to the cold.

"She's mad at you," Raven said. "I think she would have preferred to have me for dinner."

Shadow's tail drooped in disappointment. He knew rejection when he saw it. He looked like a dejected teenage boy who'd just been turned down for a date.

"You and me both," she whispered. "I get it. I do."

His ears pricked. He was listening.

"Thanks for not eating me, by the way."

He stared at her, not moving.

What did he want from her now? He was waiting for something.

Using only careful, controlled movements, Raven slowly lowered herself into a sitting position on the ground. She crossed her legs and folded her hands in her lap.

The black wolf appeared satisfied. He circled her a few times, then flopped onto the ground. He stretched out not three feet from where she sat, so close she could feel the heat radiating from his large body.

Thick clouds drifted across the moon. The night grew darker, colder. Raven barely felt it. She listened to the steady rhythm of his panting breaths. She didn't dare touch him, though she wanted to. She simply watched him, awestruck.

The whole insane night filled her with a marvelous incredulity, a reverence, along with a host of inexplicable emotions she couldn't name, let alone describe.

This was what her dad must have felt all those years, so close to the wild creatures he loved. It was like she was connected to some hidden, unseen thing greater than herself, united in this moment with the vast, unknowable universe.

Like she'd touched a dazzling star with her bare hands.

She had not forgotten the danger the bikers posed. She had not forgotten that her father was dead, that her mother had abandoned her, or that the Hydra Virus might be proliferating inside her, hijacking her cells and turning her body against her.

This moment was something else. It was a gift. She was perceptive enough to recognize it for what it was. She felt the shift like tectonic plates beneath her feet, a sharpness in the air, a lightness in her chest.

In this small, perfect moment, the dying world seemed so very far away.

This was a separate place, a thing of wonder and enchantment, of impossible dreams and stars close enough to touch.

It was magic.

Chapter Sixteen

Raven awoke to the sound of voices.

It seemed unimaginable, absurd even, to fall asleep right next to two hundred pounds of lethal predator, but she had managed it. It had been a deep sleep, too, rife with tangled dreams she could no longer recall.

The voices grew louder.

Adrenaline shot through her limbs. Instantly, she was wide awake. Her heart thumped. Her eyes sprang open. Turning her head, she searched the small clearing, scanning the empty ground on either side of her, the trees towering above her prone body.

Shadow and Luna must have smelled the bikers long before Raven heard them. The wolves had vanished into their den or had hidden themselves somewhere in the trees and heavy underbrush.

Twenty yards and a thicket of trees separated the wolf den from the public viewing area. According to her father, wolves were private creatures. He'd refused to cut down the trees, even when guests complained that they couldn't see the star attractions.

Now, Raven was grateful for the concealment. She sat up slowly, her back aching, a crick in her neck. She ran her tongue over her furry teeth. Her mouth tasted sour. What she wouldn't give for a toothbrush. Her scalp itched. She felt dirty, unwashed.

Sanitation was currently the least of her problems. She'd hoped the bikers would be gone by now. They weren't. Her stomach sank.

She strained her ears to hear the voices over the rumbling of her empty stomach. She couldn't catch more than a stray word, the murmur of low voices. There were two choices. She could remain hidden, or she could creep closer to overhear something useful.

Knowledge is power. One of her father's favorite phrases. He'd taught her to stay alert, to maintain something he called situational awareness. Assess the situation, analyze the available information, then act.

The more she knew about these thugs, the better.

As soundlessly as she could, she rolled onto her stomach and crawled beneath several pine boughs. The syrupy scent of sap filled her nostrils. The air smelled earthy and damp. Twigs, sticks, and rocks dug into her knees and the palms of her hands. Leaf litter clung to her shirt and pants.

It was past dawn. The early morning air was chilly. Her breath puffed in white swirls. Goosebumps broke out on her arms. The pinkish sky was like glass, so clear and sharp she could almost see through to heaven, or maybe the future.

After several painstaking minutes, she reached a boulder and hunched behind it. Hidden in deep shadows beneath a pine tree, she was relatively concealed but close enough for a clear view of the path and the double fence two dozen yards ahead of her.

Between the trees, she glimpsed four burly bikers leaning against the guardrail. One smoked a cigar as they gazed into the hybrid enclosure. They wore pistols holstered to their hips, with hunting rifles or AR-15s strapped across their brawny chests. She recognized Vaughn, the leader, Dekker, the psycho killer, the guy with the ponytail they called Rex, and Damien, the sharp-faced redhead.

"I don't see anything," Rex whined. "We've been standing here for ten minutes and nothing. You must be seeing things, kid."

"I saw it," Damien said.

"It was night. You certain?" asked Vaughn.

"Absolutely," Damien said. "The thing was white as a ghost and huge. The biggest wolf I've ever seen, even a genetically modified one."

Vaughn's grin widened. He patted Damien on the back in approval. "Good job, son."

Damien smiled gratefully. A faint blush of pride spread across his pale, freckled skin. "Thank you."

She shivered involuntarily. Damien was the one who'd surprised her at the bear padlock last night. She couldn't quite figure him out. He hadn't shot Phil, but he nearly did. He was much younger than the other men, barely older than she was. He looked like he belonged in the halls of high school, heading to band practice or theater or yearbook, worried about pimples and girlfriends.

Of course, age had nothing to do with psychopathology. He might be as cruel as Dekker. Or even worse.

There was a hardness in the slash of his cheekbones, the narrow jut of his chin. It was obvious he was eager to prove himself. That made him dangerous.

"Can we leave already?" Dekker asked in a bored tone. "I'm starving."

"Mickey is making breakfast," Damien said. "He found actual pancake mix. And there's more where that came from."

Next to Dekker, Rex blew out a ring of cigarette smoke. "Did you see how much food is here? This place is a gold mine."

"And mine it we shall," Vaughn said. "In due time. I'm not leaving until I see it for myself."

Dekker's expression tightened, like he wanted to roll his eyes in disgust, but he didn't. He knew who was boss, who demanded his respect. "Sure thing."

"Have a little patience. The best things come to those who wait." Vaughn leaned forward, draped his arms across the guardrail, and stared intently into the enclosure. He had a sophisticated air about him, a civilized facade, like he might strangle you with one hand while sipping expensive wine from a crystal glass with the other.

Scorpio and Rex were his guard dogs, unthinking brutes who killed on command. Dekker, though, was something else.

Dekker rubbed his goatee, his eyebrows dark slashes over eyes black as silt. Raven had seen the look on his face when he'd shot Carl. He didn't kill in self-defense or because he was following orders; he killed because he enjoyed it.

To her left, a branch quivered. A few dead leaves fluttered to the forest floor. Raven flinched. Without making a sound, she swiveled her head to the left.

Not five feet from her position, the black wolf crouched. She hadn't even heard him approach. He was so dark he blended with the shifting shadows beneath the trees. Ears back, he gazed intently at the men beyond the fence. His jowls pulled back over his teeth.

Likely, Luna was nearby as well.

Stay back, she whispered to them in her mind. *Stay hidden.*

"Enough of this," Dekker said. "You want to see a big-ass white wolf? I'll draw the beast out. It can't hide forever."

Dekker bent and chose a loose, fist-sized rock from the path. Over the years, much of the flagstone had cracked and crumbled. Her father hadn't had the time or the budget to get it fixed.

Drawing his arm back, Dekker hurled the rock into the enclosure. It struck the trunk of a nearby sugar maple with a resounding crack.

Vaughn laughed. His laugh was loud and boisterous, with a cruel edge. Damian flicked a questioning gaze at the man's face, assessing his response before deciding how to react. A second later, he laughed, too.

"Come out, come out, wherever you are," Dekker said in a sing-song voice. "Here, doggy. We've got a treat for you."

"That's one way to do it." Rex's voice was deep and rasping, like he'd been smoking for fifty years—though he couldn't have been older than thirty.

Rex seized a rock and threw it at the pine tree Raven was crouched beneath. The rock punched the center of the trunk about ten feet above her head. The branches quaked. Pine needles rained down on her hair.

Shadow growled. The low snarl rumbled from deep in his chest.

"You hear that?" Damien shouted. "It's right there in the center of those trees."

Raven wanted to shush him, but she couldn't afford to make a sound. The wolf was pure predator, 100% alpha. It wasn't in his nature to cower, to live in fear, to act the prey. She stared at Shadow as hard as she could, desperate to somehow communicate her thoughts: *Be quiet. Be still. Don't let them see you.*

"We all heard it," Rex drawled. "No need to get your panties in a wad."

"Keep going," Vaughn ordered. "Draw it out."

Rex and Dekker hurled several more rocks into the enclosure. With each crack and thud, Shadow's growls grew louder, more fierce.

She longed to touch him, to soothe him, to comfort him somehow. She didn't dare. He was no dog. And she had zero desire to lose her fingers to those teeth. Last night was something she still couldn't explain. But he was far from tame.

A rock struck the trunk of an elm less than a foot from Shadow's head.

With a snarl, the wolf sprang from the protection of the trees. He charged the fence, his tail stiff behind him. He growled deep in his throat, the ruff on his neck bristling.

He looked huge, aggressive, and menacing. His jowls stretched back, revealing every one of his forty-two teeth.

Damien whistled. "Damn! There's another one!"

"Look at the pelt on that beautiful animal, boys!" Vaughn said. "It's gorgeous!"

Rex lifted his rifle and aimed at the wolf. "What a prize, boss. Let me do the honors."

Raven tensed. Fear speared her chest. She longed to leap out after Shadow, to defend him, to *do* something, but she couldn't. Not yet. If she revealed herself, they would take her and do terrible things.

She needed to stay hidden. Her life depended on it. She could only pray these jerkwads didn't harm the wolves.

"Easy now." Vaughn put his hand on the barrel of Rex's rifle and forced him to lower it. "Not yet. We don't want to waste the meat or ruin the pelt. And that's a magnificent pelt. Prettiest I've ever seen."

"Whatever you say, boss." Rex gave a careless shrug. He fixed his gaze on Shadow, his eyes gleaming. "I call that one."

"Who says it's yours?" Damian asked.

Rex spat on the ground. "It's certainly not *yours*, kid."

Dekker rolled his eyes. "It's just an overgrown dog."

"That right there is an apex predator, my friend. You treat a prize like that with respect." Vaughn spoke with a measure of awe in his voice, awe and something like longing.

"Sure, whatever." Dekker seized another rock and heaved it at the wolf. It struck Shadow in the flank.

The wolf yelped. He leaped forward with a savage snarl. Behind him, the white wolf appeared. She plunged out of the trees and loped to a spot beside her mate. She snapped her jaws, ears flattened against her skull, and eyes blazing.

Vaughn straightened. His entire face lit with greedy, rapacious desire. "Look what we have here. There he is, in all his glory. You were right, kid. That white pelt is fit for a king."

Dread coiled in Raven's stomach. She hated the way the bikers viewed the wolves—like trophies. She dug her nails into her palms to keep from screaming. She wanted the men to just leave. Better yet, she wished she could set each one of them on fire and burn them alive.

Vaughn turned away from the fence. He glared at his men. "The white wolf is mine. No one touches him until tomorrow."

"How long are we staying here?" Dekker asked.

"Antsy already?" Vaughn dropped the stub of his cigarette and ground it out with the heel of his boot. "Everything in its time. We're in no rush. We seize opportunities as we find them, remember? This right here is a golden opportunity. And we have you to thank for it."

Dekker stepped in close to Vaughn. "We're wasting time. There's too much to do. We can't afford to waste days here and squander—"

Vaughn's expression went hard. "When I want your opinion, I'll ask for it."

Dekker scowled. For a second, he looked almost mutinous. After a tense moment, his face cleared, and he smiled lazily. "Sure thing, boss."

Vaughn turned his back on Dekker. "Let's go."

Dekker stayed behind as the others followed Vaughn along the path back toward the lodge. Damien glanced back at Dekker, a question on his face. "You coming?"

Dekker didn't bother to answer him. He stood staring into the pen with his hands folded behind his back, his legs spread wide. Damien shrugged, then left with the others.

Once he was alone, Dekker bent to the grass, felt around for more stones in the dirt, and chucked them one by one at the wolves. One struck Luna on her right foreleg. The second one hit Shadow's flank.

"How you like them apples?"

The wolves snarled.

Dekker smiled, an eerie, oily smile that set Raven's teeth on edge. "Don't like me, do you? The feeling's mutual."

The wolves fell back, growling and snapping in impotent fury.

"I hate dogs. Nothing to do but put you down in the dirt where you belong." His expression was scornful, malignant. He made the shape of a gun with his fingers and pointed it first at Shadow, then Luna. "Bang, bang. You're dead."

Chapter Seventeen

After Dekker left, Raven didn't move from beneath the pine tree for several long minutes. Anger sizzled through her like an electrical current. Anger and fear, knotted and jagged, and not just for herself.

Shaking, she gritted her teeth. How dare they mock the wolves? How dare they hurt such marvelous creatures? She wanted to hit something, to pound her fists against the nearest tree and scream her frustration.

Or better yet, take out her anger on the bikers. Maybe throw some rocks at Dekker's face, give him a taste of his own medicine. The thought gave her a moment of grim satisfaction.

Finally, she forced herself to sit up and brushed needles, dirt, and leaves from her hair and clothes. The wolves had retreated to the safety of their den. Cautiously, she stood and followed them.

Raven stepped into the clearing.

The white wolf stood sentry at the entrance to the den. Luna whirled on her, lips curling back from her fangs.

Her heart racing, Raven dropped to a submissive sitting position, her head down, staring at the ground.

It wasn't enough for Luna. She growled and lunged at Raven.

The wolf reared up and struck both great paws against Raven's shoulders.

Raven was knocked backward onto the ground. The back of her head smacked the ground hard. Pain jarred her spine. She sucked in air that wouldn't come. The force of the blow knocked the breath out of her. She stared up at the wolf in dumb shock.

The wolf's huge paws dug into her shoulders, pressing her down. Luna lowered her head inches from Raven's face, opened her jaws, and snarled. Hot breath spewed against Raven's cheeks. Dank saliva splattered her chin, cheeks, and lips.

Teeth bared, Luna snapped her jaws inches from Raven's nose. Her vision filled with gaping jaws, a raw red throat, and needle-sharp fangs. Her heart shuddered inside her chest. The she-wolf was about to tear her face from her skull. She was certain of it.

Luna had been pummeled with rocks. Of course, she'd be enraged. Of course, she'd take revenge on the nearest human. It made sense. If Raven were a wolf, she'd feel the same way.

She had her whittling knife in her pocket. Not like it would do much good. Luna's jaws could crush bone, shred ligaments and tendons, and pulverize flesh. Fighting back would only enrage the wolf further. She could do nothing. She was utterly helpless.

Raven forced herself to remain limp and pliant. Hopefully, Luna was only posturing. Otherwise, Raven would die in a few seconds.

From inside the den, Shadow growled.

Luna snapped her head up.

Raven took the moment of diversion to shield her exposed face with her hands. She tried to curl herself into a ball to protect her vulnerable internal organs, but Luna remained standing on Raven's shoulders, pinning her to the ground.

Shadow growled another warning. He loped toward them, shouldered into Luna, and shoved her off Raven. He nipped at Luna's flank as if to order her away from Raven.

Luna came back snarling and snapping, this time at Shadow. The black wolf stood his ground between Raven and Luna. Raven scrambled backward on her elbows, gasping for breath, her pulse a roar in her ears.

The wolves stared at each other. They stood stiff, ears back, their stances combative, aggressive even. Raven lay absolutely still, afraid to move, to breathe, to draw a shred of attention her way. Her heart caught in her throat. Her pulse was a dull roar in her ears. She watched the wolves, only feet apart, teeth bared.

Luna growled. Shadow growled back. He didn't move from his position directly in front of Raven's prone, shaking body.

For whatever reason, Shadow had picked Raven for something.

It was clear that Luna had not. Luna didn't trust humans. She considered Raven an outsider, an interloper, which was true.

Humans had trapped Luna, beat her with whips, and forced her to battle to the death in a fighting ring. Humans had jeered at her, thrown rocks, caged her. Humans had hunted and murdered her kind for sport and entertainment.

It was a miracle that Luna hadn't already crushed Raven's windpipe with a single bite.

Luna gave a belligerent growl, her head lowered. Shadow growled right back in irritation. Neither gave way. Neither submitted. It was a standoff.

Raven recalled something her father had taught her about pack behavior when one wolf challenged another. For a lesser-ranked wolf, a battle of domination and submission would ensue, sometimes to the exclusion of the losing wolf from the pack. Sometimes even to death.

Not with these two. They were alphas, partners, and equals.

Shadow gave a low whine in the back of his throat. He loped to Luna, pressed in and nuzzled his mate's side, as if in apology, an attempt to make amends. She nipped at him angrily, but she didn't bite or shy away.

He licked her muzzle. She snorted, still truculent.

He licked her again with affection, his tail lifting hopefully.

This time, she didn't nip at him. Conceding, she lowered her head and tucked it beneath his head, tenderly rubbing her muzzle against his shoulders and neck.

Perhaps this meant Raven would be spared. Perhaps she was reading too much into their behaviors, attaching human emotions to animals whose instincts had driven their nature for thousands of years.

Raven held her breath. Sticks and twigs and rocks dug into her spine. A spider crawled up her forearm. Still, she dared not move.

Luna snorted and trotted away from Raven, toward the far side of the clearing. Seeming to ignore Raven altogether, Luna turned in a tight circle and settled onto the ground.

The fight seemed to be over. For now, at least.

Shadow also ignored Raven. He sank down beside Luna and buried his muzzle in the soft fur of her neck. She, in turn, rested her head on his back.

Raven wasn't sure what she should do now. Not move for hours, until the wolves retired to their den? Or could she safely get up now? Did they want her out of their territory, or would her movement activate their prey drive?

Cautiously, her gaze on the wolves, she raised one hand and flicked the spider from her upper arm.

The white wolf fixed her unblinking amber eyes on Raven. *I'm watching you*, her wolfish expression said. *And I don't like what I see.*

Raven stayed on the ground. She wrapped her arms around her rib cage, unable to stop shivering. Hunger gnawed at her empty stomach. Her mouth was so dry it felt caked in sand. She coughed.

The wolves didn't move. They didn't react.

Raven, however, was flushed with fear. A single cough didn't mean anything. Did it? She wasn't getting sick. She didn't have it. She was just nervous after the scare with the bikers and then the wolves. People coughed all the time. She needed to clear her throat. That's all. Nothing more. *Please, please be nothing more.*

She closed her eyes for a moment, mentally counting the days. Four days since exposure to the Hydra Virus. The cold symptoms should've started yesterday. If she were infected, she would know soon.

Raven opened her eyes and stared up at the sky through the tangle of branches overhead. A bird drifted high, some kind of raptor. Maybe a hawk.

Dread sprouted in the pit of her stomach, an ugly fear spreading black roots. She couldn't waste energy on worrying about whether she was sick or not. Worrying wasn't going to stop it or hurry it along, either way.

She had more pressing concerns. The bikers would be back soon. She had to figure out a plan.

Beyond the nature preserve, there were too many towns, too many people. What were the towns like right now? Macon. Atlanta, the suburbs? All of Georgia? The country? What about the world?

Were most people sick or dead? Had law and order truly fallen? And if it had, then anyone not sick would be either desperately out for themselves or actively preying upon others to take whatever they could.

She only knew that Forsyth had been an incredibly dangerous mistake. She had to be smart. She might not outlive another mistake like that.

Anywhere people were located was dangerous. So, if she was supposed to avoid towns and cities, then what could she possibly do? Where could she go that was safe?

The cabin. Her grandfather's hunting cabin was located somewhere about a hundred or so miles north of here, well past Atlanta, Marietta, Alpharetta, Canton, Cumming, and Gainesville.

The map to the cabin was folded safely in the inside zippered pocket of her backpack. She couldn't find the cabin without the map. The Chattahoochee National Forest alone encompassed over 750,000 acres. The Blue Ridge Mountains stretched over 34,000 miles of dense wilderness, of mountains, forests, valleys, streams and rivers, and ravines.

That was after she navigated the hostile highways and dangerous cities between here and there. And she would have to keep well east of Atlanta and the surrounding suburban sprawl, as well as Gainesville.

The threat of roving gangs, thieves and raiders, terrified locals, and of course, Raven being a lone young woman made things even more dangerous.

Before her mother left, they had visited the cabin every summer with her family. She closed her eyes, envisioned the rough-hewn walls, the worn pine floor, the peeling cabinets in the kitchen, and the farmer's sink with the gingham curtains she'd sewn herself when she was twelve.

It was a safe place. The cabin had a fresh creek running through the forty-acre property for fishing, solar panels for electricity, a hand-pump for the well, plus a stocked larder. Nestled in a small valley surrounded by looming hills, it was as isolated as it was beautiful.

She would have food, water, and shelter. Most importantly, it would be worlds away from the dangerous bikers and the virus.

But that also meant leaving the animals behind. The thought made her sick. The cabin was her eventual destination, but she couldn't leave the area completely, not while the Headhunters were still here and the animals weren't safe.

But she needed to escape the zoo for now. If she had to, she could hide out for days in the woods of the Piedmont National Wildlife Refuge and nature preserve. They wouldn't find her. She would be safe while she waited for them to get bored and leave.

Once they were gone, she could return to the zoo. This was temporary. She promised herself it was only temporary. She would return, and the animals would still be okay. Hungry and grumpy, but okay.

There was one big problem, though. Her backpack was still in the lodge.

She had to retrieve the pack, and not just for the map.

She needed her snares for catching small game, the lures and wire for fishing, the water filtration kit to keep her drinking water free of contaminants, the flint to make fire, her compass for direction, the tarp and rope, and a sleeping bag for warmth and shelter.

Without the contents of her pack, she wouldn't last long in the harsh elements, exposed to the cold, the rain, cut off from shelter, heat, and running water.

Her father had drilled the facts of survival into her long ago. Without survival supplies, she would succumb quickly to exposure.

Tonight, under the cover of darkness, she would creep back to the lodge and retrieve the pack from her bedroom. Much as she loathed the thought of going anywhere near the bikers, she had to risk it. There wasn't another option.

She couldn't remain inside the zoo any longer. She had to run for her life.

In the distance, the bonobos screeched grumpily. The bears growled at each other. The foxes and coyotes yipped and howled their discontent.

The animals were hungry. They were upset, anxious. Maybe they just wanted to be fed. Maybe their keen primal senses recognized the threat infiltrating their sanctuary.

Raven turned her head. Luna's piercing, judgmental eyes stared straight into hers, as if the wolf knew what she was thinking. That she planned to leave, to flee, abandoning the animals to their fates.

Guilt speared her ribs. A sickening sensation in her stomach made her nauseous.

She dropped her gaze from the wolf's. What could she possibly do? She was one teenage girl against an army. She hated the idea of running away with every fiber of her being, but she was out of options. Wasn't she?

"It's only for a little while," she whispered. "I'll be back. I promise. It'll be okay. It has to be okay."

Once the bikers left, she would come back. The next thought came unbidden: what if it was too late for the animals? They couldn't survive without her, not in their cages, not without a steady supply of food. They needed her.

She told herself this was the right move. The animals would be fine. The dangerous thugs would leave. She would come back. They could live off the food in the storage sheds for a month, and then make a plan from there. It was going to be okay.

But no matter how many times she repeated it like a mantra, she couldn't make it true.

CHAPTER EIGHTEEN

Raven hid in the wolf pen for the rest of the day.

Hours passed in agonizing slowness. Eventually, morning gave way to afternoon and afternoon to evening. Eventually, she dared to rise into a sitting position and huddled beneath an aspen tree, her spine scraping the bark, her arms wrapped around her shins, her chin resting on her knees.

At one point, she gave in and found a spot to squat and pee. At first, she feared the wolves would think it an act of aggression, of marking territory, but they recognized that hers was merely human and ignored it completely.

She spent the hours thinking and planning, playing out the various options, potential strategies and pitfalls, and the most plausible method of escape.

Every plan led straight to disaster. But she had no choice. If she stayed, she'd certainly be found and killed. If she fled to the woods, she'd probably be found and killed.

She'd take her chances.

She ignored the cold, ignored her fuzzy teeth, ignored the hunger gnawing at her belly, her aching back, her thirst. The sun descended second by endless second, until finally the sky darkened to night.

The trill of crickets and cicadas filled the air. Stars spattered the glossy black of the sky. Fog drifted over the trees like ribbons of tulle. Only when darkness had well and truly fallen did Raven risk standing up.

Every muscle ached and squealed in protest. She ignored the pain and squinted, barely able to make out the shapes of the wolves resting near the den. Tensing, she waited.

Nothing lunged out of the fog at her. No menacing growls echoed through the trees.

Cautiously, she moved back through the trees toward the fence line. Her thigh muscles cramped, and her sore back ached. She kept walking. Each step felt like a mile.

Shadow and Luna remained close to the den. They watched her go in silence.

Reaching the fence, she paused to listen for footsteps. The fog thickened, making it harder to see. After checking to make sure the coast was clear, she opened and then shut each gate of the double fence, using her prints to lock them.

She pulled out her whittling knife and gripped it in one hand as she crept along the path, passing several enclosures. She passed the porcupine pen. Duke and Duchess waddled out of their night house, quills bristling. They hissed at her in outrage for daring to interrupt their nocturnal habits—whatever those might be.

Hera ruffled her feathers from the aptly named eagle's nest, a two-story wire-mesh enclosure with a tree in the center. The raptor sat serenely on her perch, talons gripping the wooden pole. Her beady eyes tracked Raven's movements as she crept past.

The otters chirped in greeting when she inched past their glass-front habitat. She could barely make out the shapes of Whiskers and Mo lounging on their favorite heat rock.

Raven reached the cinderblock maintenance shed and hesitated. The tranquilizer guns and the emergency rifles were stored inside. Though she felt exposed and vulnerable standing out in the open, she couldn't justify leaving them behind. The bikers were dangerous. She might need to protect herself.

Quietly, she unlocked the rusted metal door with her handprint.

The corrugated roof leaked. Junk cluttered every corner—coils of rusting wire, broken power tools, buckets of old batteries, shelves of solar lamps, hammers, and wrenches.

A filmy layer of grease and grime coated everything. Dust swirled in the panels of milky moonlight filtering through the single, high window.

A tickling sensation irritated her throat. She swallowed a cough, forcing it down. *Only dust,* she told herself. It wasn't the first sign of a lethal disease. *It's only dust.*

She maneuvered around the metal workbench, grabbed a burlap sack hanging from a hook next to the shovels, and sidestepped two large containers of jugs of gasoline for the lawn mower shoved against the wall below the gun rack. In front of her, two tranquilizer guns and one hunting rifle hung on the wall.

She shoved the guns into the sack, stuffed her cargo pockets with a handful of ammo and extra tranquilizer darts encased in metal cylinders, then hooked the strap of her father's hunting rifle over her shoulder. She attached the burlap sack to a loop in the rifle strap.

As she exited the shed, she locked it behind her, then moved on. The rifle banged against her ribs. The heavy sack dug into her shoulders. She straightened her spine and kept walking. Her footfalls echoed strangely in the fog. She strained her ears for any sound that might signal danger, for the thud of footsteps stalking her every move.

A minute later, she reached the lodge.

Voices boomed from inside, raucous laughter and boisterous shouts echoing into the night. The bikers must've found the Grizzly Grill's alcoholic-beverage supply. The front windows glowed with the light of several solar lamps.

Her bedroom window was dark.

Raven scanned the area, searching for something to aid her plan. Her gaze caught a row of cinderblocks lying beneath the oak tree behind the woodshed. Her father had intended to build a fire pit, but it never happened. They would serve her now.

Raven crept across the lawn, hauled one of the cinderblocks in her arms, and moved awkwardly toward the lodge, huffing as quietly as she could. Dropping it beneath her window, she removed the burlap sack and set it next to the concrete block.

Using the block as a stool, Raven stepped on it and peered inside her bedroom window. Shadows drenched the darkened room. The bedroom door was closed. She grasped the window frame and carefully inched it up. The lock had broken years ago. No one had bothered to fix it.

The window scraped against the wood.

Her heart hammered against her ribs. Every sound was impossibly loud. Balanced on the cinderblock, she craned her neck from side to side, searching for movement, for a man-shaped shadow slipping through the fog.

She paused for another long moment, listening hard. No strange or out-of-place sounds. The loud voices continued. Nothing moved inside. Nothing moved outside.

Raven pushed the window up, her muscles straining. She braced her elbows on the sill and pushed off from the cinderblock, using momentum to push herself up. She clambered inside, careful not to kick or bump anything on her dresser located directly to the left of the window.

Lowering herself soundlessly to the floor, she stood in her bedroom and let her eyes adjust to the darkness.

The bikers had been in her room. A few drawers were left open. The rumpled bed had been slept in, her pillow on the floor next to a pile of her clothes. Her dresser was cluttered with dusty wooden figurines and spilled wood shavings. She caught a whiff of her green apple body lotion.

The faded army-green backpack leaned against her dresser, ready and waiting. Raven took a dark-colored raincoat from her closet. With her undershirt, a sweater, and her raincoat, which boasted an inner synthetic lining for warmth, she had enough layers to withstand frigid October nights in the woods, when the temperatures dropped into the 30s, sometimes colder.

Quietly, she pulled her good hiking boots from the closet and packed extra socks. Her stomach growled loudly. She froze, half-expecting the bikers to hear it on the other side of the lodge. They didn't.

She had granola bars in her pack; she could eat later, but her thirst was overwhelming. Her throat felt dry as a desert. Her whole body ached for water.

Fumbling for her water bottle, she took a long swig, water dribbling down her chin. She wiped her mouth with the back of her hand, then took another drink. She could have cried from gratitude.

Her body needed sustenance and fuel. It made her feel weak and needy, but also alive. So afraid, but alive.

Before leaving, she paused, scanning the bedroom for anything else she might need. Something glinted in the back of her closet. The hoverboard her mother had bought for her seventeenth birthday. The one Raven had refused to use on principle, as if her mother would have even known whether her daughter used it or not.

Maybe it would come in useful. She could travel faster, without leaving footprints. She grabbed the hoverboard and the solar charger, too.

She unzipped her pack, shoved the board halfway in, and dragged it over to the window. She had no way to lower the pack silently. She'd just have to dump it and hope no one heard. She hefted it, her sore muscles groaning in protest, and pushed it out the window. It hit the ground with a thud.

The raucous voices down the hall covered the sound of her movements. They were so loud she could almost make out the individual words. They were getting louder, drunker.

She turned away from the window, listening hard. A single word came through clearly: *wolf.*

Torn, she glanced at the window, then the door.

They were discussing the wolves. *Her* wolves. Shadow and Luna.

Her stomach twisted. What were they going to do to the animals? Was there a chance they would just let the animals be? Or would they kill them for sport? For meat? Burn them alive in their pens?

Raven turned back toward the window. She should leave. She should get out. Right now.

She hesitated. She turned back toward her bedroom door.

She had to know. She couldn't leave. Not yet.

She crept across the carpet toward her bedroom door. Instinct screamed at her to run. Another part of her whispered that she couldn't live with herself if she fled now. Maybe it was stupid, but she could take this small risk. Guilt ate at her. She needed to know to what fate she was leaving her beloved animals.

As if that would make it better. As if it would make any of this terrible situation any easier. She knew it didn't make sense. And yet. Perhaps learning more about their plan would allow her to learn when they would leave, so she could know when it was safe to return.

She grasped the door handle, twisted, and pulled the door open about six inches.

The long hallway was dark. The doors to the two guest bedrooms on the left were open, but no light filtered out. There were three more guest bedrooms on the other side of the kitchen. Her father's door was closed.

At the end of the hallway, she crouched and cautiously peered around the corner. The lanterns in the kitchen gave off a warm glow. Thick tendrils of smoke hung in the air. In the center of the kitchen, a half-dozen men hunched around the scarred wooden table where she'd eaten breakfast a thousand times.

They were playing some sort of card game, drinking and smoking, placing bets and yelling insults, roaring with laughter, all drunk.

She could make out a thread of conversation over the ruckus— the sound was coming from somewhere closer than the kitchen table. She turned her head to the left and glimpsed a man's shoulder jutting from the opposite wall into the space at the end of the hallway.

The man wore a leather vest, his hair slicked back in a long greasy ponytail. It was Rex. The others were likely sitting at the bar chairs at the counter peninsula, just around the corner from her line of sight.

"When are the others coming?" She recognized Rex's low, gravelly voice.

"Phillips went to get them." Vaughn's ringing baritone was unmistakable. "He left yesterday afternoon. By the time they gather their supplies, get the truck, and make it back... I'd reckon sometime tomorrow night."

"I'd kill for a working phone." Damien's voice spoke into the silence. "This lack of communication blows."

"Wouldn't we all, kid." Vaughn chuckled. "But look on the bright side. Instead of focusing on what's been destroyed, focus on what we can build from the rubble. A new world. A new society, with order and rules that make sense—even better than the last one."

"How many men is he bringing?" Rex asked.

"I told him thirty. We'll need that many to load all that food."

"There aren't enough beds for them," Damien said.

"They can sleep on the floor, or out in the tiger's cage for all I care." Dekker's voice was smooth as honey, hiding the poison beneath.

"We'll make do," Vaughn said. "We always do. This was a lucky break. We need to make sure we transfer every last piece of this treasure."

"And then we head back home?" Dekker asked.

"Why are you so eager to get out of here?" Rex asked. "You scared of a little tiger or two?"

"This place is creepy. Don't you feel it? All those savage beasts screaming and howling all night long? It's haunted. There's something off here. I don't like it. We should go back."

Vaughn let out a booming laugh. "You going all sissy on me now?"

"Nah, of course not," Dekker said quickly. "I just hate all these damn animals. They're loud and disgusting."

Rex sniggered. "Thought you wanted that girl. The wolf girl."

The hairs on Raven's neck stood on end. Her stomach lurched. She gripped the door with whitened knuckles.

Dekker swore. "She's mine."

"Don't you worry," Vaughn said. "She can't hide forever. You can have her. After we load up our goodies and I get that wolf pelt, you can burn this place to the ground for all I care."

"Do we all get a pelt?" Rex asked.

"Sure." Vaughn was quiet for a moment. "That's a damn fine idea. Imagine us all dressed out in wolf and leopard pelts like ancient Viking warriors. What terror and awe that would inflict on the hearts of our adversaries."

"Great idea, boss," Rex said.

"Let me guess, Damien wants the tiger," Dekker said. He snorted in derision. "You'll have to grow into that one, boy. You still have to earn your chops. If you've got them, that is. Unless you're too much of a pussy." His tone was teasing, but something was mocking in the way he spoke.

"Go screw yourself." Damien sounded petulant. "I can take care of myself."

"Enough sitting around," Vaughn said. "The night is young! We've got work to do. Dekker, get my gun. Damien, get me some more of this beer, and be quick about it." A chair pushed back, scraping against the tile. Vaughn's broad back appeared as he shoved the chair into place, tattoos squirming across his neck and bulging arms. "Remember, the white one is mine."

Heart hammering in her throat, Raven crept back down the hallway to her bedroom, snuck back inside, and shut the door. She stumbled backward. Her stomach roiled in shock and fear. More of them were coming. They were going to take all the food in the storage buildings—the food she was depending on to stay alive.

She should have guessed what they would want. Some part of her had known, but to hear it spoken aloud made it horrifyingly real. And Vaughn was going to kill Luna. He was going to kill her right now, tonight.

She had to get out of there. She needed to think things through somewhere else, somewhere safe. She lurched for the window—

The bedroom door swung open.

CHAPTER NINETEEN

Liquid fear shot through her veins. Raven dove into the shadows between her dresser and the bed. Hunkering down beneath the window, she made herself as small as possible.

It was a pathetic hiding spot. But without light to illuminate her tiny, shadowy form, she might have the barest chance. As long as she didn't give herself away, didn't move or breathe.

Silently, she reached into her pocket for the knife. She had to shift her thighs for access, leaning into the wooden side of the dresser, her body squished. She pulled it out but didn't dare flick it open. It would make a small snicking sound that might give her away. She grasped the handle with both hands and held it to her chest, her knuckles white, and every muscle taut.

The intruder strode into her bedroom. He was a murky shape among murkier shadows. He shut the door behind him. A *click* sounded as the lock turned. There was a soft thumping sound. Then, silence.

Her lungs burned for oxygen. Her body screamed at her to suck in deep, ragged breaths. But she couldn't. She breathed shallowly through her nose, fighting against the panic slithering up her throat, squeezing her windpipe.

The intruder was completely silent, except for the sound of

breathing. It wasn't normal steady breaths, but ragged and uneven, like a runner gulping for air. Raucous laughter from the kitchen filtered through the shut door, dim and far away.

What was the intruder doing? Had he spotted her? Did he know she was there? Was it a trap? Perhaps he was waiting for her to make the first move before he pounced. Maybe a gun was pointed at her location right now, just waiting for her to peek her head around the corner.

The anxiety of not knowing wound tighter and tighter inside her ribcage. Her heart felt like it was about to crack wide open.

Seconds that felt like hours stretched longer and longer. From the sound of his rasping breaths, he remained near the door of her bedroom. He hadn't moved closer to her position.

Anxiety thrummed through her entire body. If death was coming for her, she wasn't going to die cowering. She wasn't a coward. Not like her mother.

Gathering every ounce of her courage, she leaned forward a few precious inches and peered past the edge of the dresser.

She blinked, adjusting her eyes. In the dimness of the room, she could just make out a tall, lanky shape on the opposite side of the room. It was Damien. He slumped against the door, head back, his chest heaving. His arms hung loose at his sides, his hands clenched into fists. She couldn't make out his expression. It looked like his eyes were closed. It was hard to tell.

At any rate, he hadn't appeared to have spotted her. He wasn't hunting her. He didn't have a weapon. A sliver of relief pricked her.

Outside the window, the fog thinned for a moment. The pale shine of moonlight poured through the window, bathing the room in a silvery glow.

Maybe she should have ducked back behind the dresser, stayed hidden. She didn't.

Damien was just standing there. His chest rose and fell rapidly. There was something haggard and grim in his face. His piercings glinted. As he breathed, his fists gradually unclenched. His tense expression relaxed, and he suddenly looked younger. Young and unburdened, like a caged animal newly released. Like he'd just escaped something terrible.

He was as handsome as she remembered. He didn't seem dangerous at this moment. She knew better. The rattlesnake lay coiled in the sun, appearing harmless until it struck. The hippopotamus looked fat and lazy but was responsible for more human deaths than crocodiles. The furry slow loris was adorable, but it released toxins from its elbow, one of the only venomous mammals.

She tightened her grip on the knife handle. Her palms were damp. Her pulse thudded in her throat.

She'd never attacked anyone before, animal or human. She didn't want to start now. What did she know about fighting? She wanted to live, she knew that much.

She wished he would turn around and leave. He'd never know she had been crouched just feet away. *Just go, just go.*

Damien opened his eyes and looked straight at her.

For an infinite second, she stared back at him, frozen.

He looked at her blankly, as if she were a ghost he didn't quite believe was real. His gaze lowered and fixed on the small knife in her hands.

Raven exploded into motion. She leaped to her feet and lunged at him. She flicked the blade open as she ran. Panic clawed at her throat. Her only thought was to stop him from warning the others, the hardened criminals less than twenty feet away.

She thrust the knife to his throat before his face had even registered surprise.

He grunted and let out a curse. "What—"

"Shut up!" she hissed. "Do or say anything to alert your friends, and I swear to you, I'll slit your throat."

He raised both hands in a gesture of surrender. "And if you do that, they'll come looking for me, find me dead, and then they'll know you're here." He kept his voice low. It was the only thing that kept him alive.

Adrenaline spiked through her veins. Her hands shook as she

pressed the blade against his Adam's Apple. Despite her fear, she kept her tone firm. "They already know I'm here."

He gave the faintest shake of his head. She pressed the blade deeper. "I said, don't move!"

He winced. "Sorry, sorry. I won't scream. I'll tell you whatever you want. Just—just don't stab me, okay? I'm not going to hurt you."

"I'm the one with the knife. I'll decide who gets hurt."

"Fair enough."

"And I'm the one asking the questions. Tell me the truth, or you'll regret it."

"Okay, okay. I got it." The whites of his eyes shone in the dim shadows. He looked as terrified as she was. "Whatever—whatever you want."

She let up on the pressure, just slightly. "How did you follow me here?"

His words ran together in a breathless rush. "At the pharmacy, Dekker saw the Haven bumper stickers on your car. He found a pamphlet for the wildlife refuge in one of the gas stations, you know, the touristy ones for visitors."

Raven's heart sank. She knew exactly what he meant. Of course, the pamphlets had Haven's address on them, as well as cute photos of Vlad and Electra and the bonobos, the entry fees, and hours of operation.

"He was pissed. He wanted you real bad. He doesn't take an insult easily, and you got the best of him. He doesn't let things like that go. Plus, you looked like you might have some loot we would want. So, he insisted we come here. Dekker wants you, and he recognized the car you drove in the parking lot, so he knows you're here. I think Vaughn could be convinced to leave without finding you. But if you kill me, what do you think is going to happen when they find out what you did? They'll hunt you down in earnest."

"You're insane if you think I'm just gonna let you go."

Moonlight limned the hard planes of his face. He attempted a smile, but it came out like a grimace. "You can let me go. I won't say anything, I swear. I told them I was going for a piss. But really, I just needed... I wanted a minute to myself, you know? Look, I'll just go back and say nothing. None of them'll be the wiser."

"Yeah, right. I have no reason to trust you."

"You don't know us, but we're not bad people. We look tough, but—"

"Liar."

"I'm not a bad person, I swear it—"

She shot him a scathing look. "I know what you did. I saw what happened to Carl. I saw you point your gun at Phil's face."

His eyes widened. "You were inside the pharmacy, then? Dekker didn't tell us."

"That's right. I was there. Your pretty face and your pretty lies won't work on me. I know what you are."

He swallowed. "You don't know what things are like out there, how bad it's gotten."

"I've watched the news. I saw the state of the town. I—" She almost mentioned Zachariah and her father, but this traitor didn't deserve to see her grief. Her mouth shut hard.

Damian shook his head. He stiffened as the blade sliced through a layer of his skin. A droplet of dark red blood dribbled down his neck. "The country is in chaos. Everything is... everything is gone. It's over. The world has ended."

"Maybe. Maybe not. That doesn't give you the right to steal from others. That doesn't give you the right to kill people."

"There's no more law. No police. No rules. It's kill or be killed, eat or be eaten."

"Carl was unarmed."

He blinked. "I—I didn't want to kill him. I wouldn't have."

"I call B.S. You people didn't have to kill them. You did it because you wanted to."

"I didn't! I swear it! It wasn't me. I didn't want any of that to happen."

"Whether you pulled the trigger or not doesn't matter. You're *with* those monsters. That makes you just as bad. Worse, maybe."

"Okay." His gaze flickered desperately around the room, searching for something, probably a weapon, but there was nothing for him. He pursed his lips, trying a different tactic. "Listen. Dekker is a psychopath. I know that, okay? I know what it looks like to you. I get it. I'm not a moron. And I'm not a monster, okay? I'm not like them. But you've got to understand. I don't have a place like this, out here in the boonies, away from all the sick people, with lots of food to hold me over. I didn't have anything like this. It's been six weeks since this crazy disease started killing everyone. The national supply chain broke down over a month ago, longer maybe. Do you know how much surplus food stores hold? Three days. After the panic started, store shelves were empty within days. Days! There's been nothing to buy for weeks. What are we supposed to do? Everyone not sick is so hungry they're going mad. People murdering each other for a can of green beans. It's not just us. We're not even the worst of the gangs, okay? There's worse out there. What was I supposed to do?"

"Not join a murderous gang, for one."

"If you don't align yourself with the type of people who can protect you, then you're already dead."

"And just who *are* the people you're with?"

"They call themselves the Headhunters. They're a group of organized criminals, operating in Georgia and parts of North Carolina, specializing in weapons smuggling, drug trafficking, stuff like that. But once the virus started destroying everything, they saw an opportunity. They're traders and service providers.

"The Headhunters travel around scavenging, searching for anything of value. They can get people whatever they want or need—illegal weapons, drugs, expensive, rare medications. Pretty much anything. Communities exchange their resources in trade for services rendered, like offering protection from thieves and marauders."

She caught how Damien spoke of the Headhunters as "they" and not "we," trying to distance himself from their brutality, trying to make her believe he was somehow different from Dekker and his ilk.

She scowled. "What other kinds of services?" She suspected, but she needed to know. She needed to hear him confirm it.

"I'm not sure. I'm just a low-level guy. I don't know everything—"

She tilted the curved razor-edge of the blade enough to draw another trickle of blood. "Tell me."

He swallowed. The edge of the knife bobbed along with his Adam's apple. "Sometimes, they trade in... people."

Her blood went cold.

"Like I said, there's no law anymore. No one to stop those with certain... appetites. They pay for people. Mostly girls. Young, pretty ones that can be subdued and... trained." His lips pressed together, as if he were embarrassed. Good. He should be.

"That's why they want me. To sell me to the highest bidder."

"I'm not a part of any of that, I swear. Mostly it's trading in good things, helping people survive, to get medicine and food, and other stuff they need. I've—I've never even killed anyone." He said it like a confession, like it shamed him.

Me neither, she almost said. But that would've defeated the purpose of the knife—and the threat behind it. Just because she hadn't killed before didn't mean she wouldn't, if she had to. All creatures would fight to the death to defend themselves. It was instinctive.

"Let me go," Damien said. "Please."

"No way."

He sighed. "Then we're at a standstill. Either you kill me, or you don't. Eventually, Dekker is going to come looking for me, and then what are you going to do?"

She had no idea, but she wasn't going to tell him that. "Then I'll kill you now and take whatever head start I can get."

"I won't say anything." His voice was steady. He didn't sound afraid anymore. "Isn't that worth the risk? If you kill me, they will hunt you down. Whether you have ten seconds or ten minutes, they will find you. If you let me go, there's a chance I'm true to my word, and they won't know where to look for you, or that you were even here tonight."

She despised his logic, but it rang true. An image of Shadow's jaws closing around her throat flashed through her mind. *An alpha was the one with the power to kill, but who chose not to.*

She didn't want to kill this guy, even though she was fairly certain he was lying through his pretty teeth. She didn't want blood on her hands. Not yet, anyway.

He looked down at her, his expression unreadable. "Are you going to let me go now?"

Abruptly, she was aware of how close she was to him, his breath rustling her hair, the hardness of his body pressed against hers, his muscles spare and wiry. His piercings shone in the dim light when he tilted his head slightly. She could make out the individual lashes brushing his cheeks when he blinked.

Her breath caught in her throat. "No. I can't."

"Yes," he said. "You can. Because you know I'm right."

"You're the bad guy."

"That's a matter of perspective."

"Tell that to Carl. Or Phil. That was on you. You nearly killed him."

"I was *saving* him—from Dekker. Dekker would have killed him, too, if I hadn't stepped in. Better to be knocked out than shot in the head. That wound is pretty hard to heal from. I never would have murdered that old man."

She stared at him in the dark, trying to wrap her mind around his words. They made a terrible sort of sense.

"Damien!" a muffled voice shouted from down the hall.

"You're running out of time," he said, his voice infuriatingly calm. But his frequent swallows betrayed his nervousness. He might not sound afraid, but deep down, he was. He didn't want to die, either.

She watched the blade ride up and down his throat. Damn it. She hated that he was right. She hated that she didn't trust this guy as far as she could throw him. But in the end, she had little choice. Only one option made sense. These men would come barreling into this room in a minute; she had to be gone when they did.

"Fine," she said grudgingly. Inhaling sharply, she stepped back, removing the knife from his neck but keeping it up and ready, half-expecting him to scream. Or attack her.

He did neither. He stood, hands loose at his sides, his head tilted. The way he looked at her—wary but curious, fascinated even—it was jarring. She didn't like it. She wasn't one of the captive animals meant to be stared at, examined with impunity.

"What's your name?"

"None of your damn business."

A ghost of a smile flickered across his face. He took a small step toward her. "Tell me your name."

Fear jolted her heart. She pointed her knife at him. "Stay back!"

That cunning look was back on his face. Like she was the chicken in the hen house, and he was the fox in search of dinner. But that wasn't quite right, either. "You've stayed alive all this time. I've seen so many people die. Strong, capable people. How did you do it?"

From the kitchen, someone shouted. "Damien! Hurry the hell up! Let's go!"

Raven and Damien froze. They were four feet apart. He had the room to shout before she could reach him. Would he yell now? Betray his promise and reveal her presence? How many seconds did she have? Five, ten? Not enough.

"Run," he said. "Run, and don't look back."

She ran. Feeling far too exposed and vulnerable with her back to the enemy. Sprinting to the window, she clambered up and out awkwardly with the small knife still in her right hand.

Her heart raced, waiting for a bullet to the back. None came.

She nearly stabbed herself as she shoved her body over the sill and tumbled to the ground. Scrambling to her feet, she flipped the pocketknife closed and shoved it in her pocket, then hoisted her backpack and the rifle with the burlap sack over her shoulders. She fled without a backward glance.

The fog had thickened. It drifted between the exhibits in hazy white ribbons, making visibility poor. Ahead and fifty yards to the right, a few lights bobbed like spotlights in the murky gloom.

She swerved sharply, her legs pumping, and sprinted behind the meat storage building. Pressing her back against the concrete block wall, she peered around the corner. The fog both helped and hindered her. What hid Raven also hid any potential skulking Headhunters. She could barely see forty feet ahead or behind her.

The bobbing flashlights drew nearer. She held her breath, waiting for the cries of alarm. Had Damien told them she'd just escaped out the window? Were they hunting her down right now?

Agonizing seconds passed. Then minutes. No shouting. No Headhunters running toward her, guns blazing.

Perhaps Damien had kept his word after all. Relief flooded her, along with another emotion she couldn't quite name or understand. Now was not the time to examine her feelings. It was time to stay the hell alive.

Raven eased around the far corner of the building, keeping it between her and the group of Headhunters as they drew closer. They weren't hunting, though. They strolled along the path with their flashlights aimed at the flagstone at their feet.

Heart in her throat, she waited for their voices to dim, for their footfalls to fade into silence.

In her frazzled state, she didn't remember the hoverboard until she'd started running again. She was too scared to stop. She stayed off the main path and kept to the rear of the exhibits.

Weeds and thorns snagged her pant legs. She ran and ran, legs pumping, adrenaline shooting through her veins, cold breath searing her throat.

She raced past the reptile house, the bonobos, the otters, the eagle, the porcupines, and the ostriches. Then she circled back onto the flagstone path, rounding the bear enclosure where Kodiak and Sage slept soundly. The rear gate loomed in the fog, forty yards away. She reached the narrow space between the bear and hybrid wolf paddocks. Almost there, almost out of the sanctuary and to the woods—

Sudden voices to her right. Flashlights wavered wildly. Echoing laughter. To her right, several human figures clustered by the timber wolf enclosure forty yards ahead of her.

Instinctively, Raven dropped to the ground to make herself small and invisible. She'd been out in the open, clearly visible if they'd been looking in her direction, if the fog hadn't obscured her approach.

Grass damp with frost dampened the front of her jacket, seeped through her pants. Cold wetness kissed her cheek. With her face pressed to the grass, she could barely make out their shapes, moving in the mist.

The Headhunters stood between Raven and the rear gate, between her and freedom.

The first gunshot cracked through the air.

CHAPTER TWENTY

One of the timber wolves let out a cry that sounded eerily human, a cross between a pained whimper and an agonized howl. A terrible thump of a wolf's body hitting the ground.

The men laughed, hooting and yelling in celebration.

The Headhunters were shooting the wolves. For sport. For fun.

Five men leaned over the timber wolves' paddock, their rifles tucked against their shoulders. They aimed their weapons into the enclosure.

Their backs were turned to her. They didn't see her lying rigid, numb and horrified on the grass next to the bear enclosure. Though fog swirled thick and dense, she was still too exposed if anyone took a close look in her direction.

She recognized the vague figures of Vaughn, Rex, Dekker, and Scorpio. The fifth Headhunter was half-turned in the other direction. When he swung back toward the enclosure, a flashlight beam caught his face—angled cheekbones, narrow chin, spiky fox-red hair, the gleam of metal piercings.

A sharp bitterness welled in the back of her throat. Damien may not have ratted her out, but he was one of them. A Headhunter. A thug and a killer. Cruel and malicious. Despite his pretty face and pretty words, he was no different than the rest of these repugnant thugs.

Another gunshot rang through the air.

The timber wolves fled into the protection of the trees, desperate to evade the thunderous noise and explosions of pain. Aspen and Titus snarled and growled fiercely. Loki and Suki whimpered. Shika let out a long, mournful howl of despair. She recognized their distinctive howls. The missing wolf was Echo. He was the one they'd shot and killed.

The Headhunters moved around the fence. They shouted insults and laughed gleefully. When they couldn't spot the wolves, they shot randomly into the underbrush.

Titus burst out of the trees, charging at the Headhunters in a desperate bid to protect his pack. Dekker aimed and fired.

Titus took two staggering steps and fell with a moan. His tail fluttered weakly. He lay limp in the dirt. He didn't get up.

Vaughn and Dekker jeered in triumph. Rex slapped Dekker on the back. Damien's expression was impossible to read from this distance. He stood with the others. He didn't cheer or shoot at the wolves. He stood silently and watched.

Run! Raven's brain screamed at her. Get up and *RUN!* But she couldn't. Her legs were lead. They wouldn't work properly. She felt dizzy, disconnected, her brain stuffed with cotton.

Where to go? The Headhunters had trapped her. She couldn't escape out the back now. And she couldn't head back into the sanctuary, where even more Headhunters prowled among the various enclosures.

She was trapped.

Finally, her muscles started to work properly. She crawled backward, her pack cumbersome, the grass slick against her palms. Creeping between the enclosures, she slithered on her stomach until she reached the gate for the hybrid wolves' enclosure.

Rising onto her knees, she opened the outer gate with cold fumbling fingers, slipped inside, and locked it. Crossing the no man's-land barrier, she repeated the same motions on autopilot, hardly realizing what she was doing. Her mind was numb, frozen with horror.

Mist curled around her legs. Everything had taken on an eerie, silvery glow. The fog crept closer and closer, swirling and shifting, almost like it was a living thing. Like it would take everything she cared about and devour it, one murky, malignant mouthful at a time.

More gunshots split the air. She flinched.

Another wolf screamed in agony. She wasn't sure which one. Suki or Shika? Her mind churned with revulsion and helpless fury.

She had to keep moving. She couldn't think about what was happening to the timber wolves. She couldn't focus on the horror, or it would destroy her. She managed to stagger inside the hybrid enclosure. Her thoughts came frantic and furious. Panic turned her brain to mush. Was she safer? Or was she putting herself in even more danger? The frog jumping out of the frying pan into the fire. The hybrids might be so frantic at the gunshots, they could tear her to pieces where she stood.

Still on her hands and knees, she crawled into the enclosure, through the trees and underbrush, and entered the clearing near the den. Shadow's great head appeared. He whimpered, his beautiful amber eyes brimming with apprehension and bewilderment.

Head down, Raven crawled to the edge of the den. She shrugged off her pack and the rifle and collapsed on the cold damp ground, shivering uncontrollably.

Shadow stood over her. He nosed her trembling shoulder with his muzzle. He licked her cheek. Luna appeared at his side.

She'd heard them discussing pelts, but it hadn't truly registered through her fear and panic. Now it did. Now she truly understood the horror of what they meant to do with the animals she'd resented and loved her entire life, the creatures her father had so adored. The Headhunters would slaughter them, one by one, butcher each animal for their own sick entertainment.

A terrible sense of helplessness overwhelmed her. Shame and regret burned bitter in the back of her throat. Surely, she should have done something to stop this, to prevent it.

You planned to do the same thing, a wretched voice whispered in her mind. But it wasn't the same thing. Hers was an act of mercy, tranquilizing the animals first so they'd never feel the sting of the bullet, so they'd pass in peace, not with violence, terror, and suffering.

The way her father had spared Zachariah days of anguish. The way he'd wanted her to spare him.

And besides, she wasn't convinced she would have gone through with it, anyway.

The white wolf stepped over Raven's body like she wasn't there and paused in the center of the small clearing. She tilted her head, ears pricked as if listening to the horrible things happening in the next enclosure.

She growled. Her lips peeled back from her fangs, and her ears flattened against her skull. Instinctively, she understood something terrible was happening, and she was angry. Luna wanted to fight.

Raven sat up. She wiped dirt from her cheek and brushed pine needles from her clothes. Her bones vibrated beneath her skin. She tasted her heart in her mouth. A chill crept over her, filling her veins with a cold, crystallized anger.

She desperately wanted to live. For as many days or weeks or years as she had left. Even if the Hydra Virus had breached her immune system. An insidious invasion replicating itself, ravaging her organs, plundering her bones, her flesh, assaulting her from the inside out, cell by infected cell. Even if she was sick, she would fight to her last breath.

At the same time, Raven was done hiding. Done allowing fear to rule her.

She couldn't run, not from this. Refused to run.

She was all alone in the whole wide broken world. It was up to her. The only one who could do something. The only one who could try to stop this.

Haven was *her* home. The wildlife sanctuary was *her* refuge.

It was her job to protect it, to defend it.

There were nine Headhunters to her one. And tomorrow night,

an additional thirty men would arrive to further desecrate her sanctuary.

She couldn't take the Headhunters on by herself.

She couldn't defeat them, but neither could she let the Headhunters win.

They would take Haven from her, but they couldn't have the animals, too. Raven wouldn't let them.

There was only one option left. One chance to save what she could.

The choice she should have made from the beginning.

She wouldn't leave the animals behind to be slaughtered. Animals she'd known since childhood. Vlad, Kodiak and Sage, Suki and Aspen, Electra, Mo, Gizmo, and all the others. Animals she'd spent so much time resenting, she'd forgotten she also loved them dearly.

She never would have gone through with ending their lives, not even as a mercy. The animals might die anyway. They were half-tamed, zoo-raised captives unused to fending for themselves in the wild.

They deserved a chance.

She owed them that much.

It was dangerous. Maybe reckless. Certainly stupid.

Raven would free the animals.

All of them. Every last one.

Chapter Twenty-One

It was after midnight when the Headhunters' cacophony died down to silence. Raven waited another hour, crouched at the foot of the wolves' den. Every muscle tensed, her heart burning. Anger zapped through her like a live wire.

Fog drifted, snaking between the trees. Luna had finally succumbed to restless sleep inside the den. Shadow stretched out a few feet from Raven. He was awake, alert, though his head rested upon his paws. His ears flicked this way and that as he listened to the animals express their anxiety and confusion.

The bonobos screeched and hooted, pleading and begging for food. Kodiak bellowed hungrily. The remaining timber wolves howled in grief, their keening wail rising toward the sliver of the moon and the hard uncaring stars.

Raven could make out three distinct voices. Three still alive. That meant three of the timber wolves were dead.

She clenched one of the tranquilizer guns in one hand. The hunting rifle was slung over her shoulder. It was fully loaded. She was not completely weaponless.

She would do her best to make sure the rest of Haven's creatures lived through the night. After that, she didn't know.

With the world outside dead and dying, maybe there would be

enough food for the animals. Without the humans encroaching on their habitats or hunting them to extinction, perhaps the captive zoo animals could survive out there, could finally live in freedom.

Of course, they might eat each other. Or go after the few surviving humans.

There were probably better plans. Smarter ideas. But she was out of time. And she was on her own.

Her dad would have known what to do. Whatever his flaws, he would've stood beside her and defended their home. He would've done a far better job than she could on her own.

The sudden ache in her chest stole her breath. She missed him with every beat of her heart. The pain of her loss felt like her soul being ripped out of her chest.

Only a few days ago, she couldn't wait to get away from her father. Now she missed him with an urgent desperation she couldn't put into adequate words.

She'd be thrilled to see her mother, too. *I'll forgive you. I'll forgive you if you just come back. Please come back.*

But neither of them would ever come back. She was completely alone.

Raven blinked hard and glanced at the big black wolf. No, not completely alone. Not anymore. Whatever the terms of this strange new relationship, the wolf gave a measure of comfort. She would take whatever scraps she could get.

With the wolves nearby, she felt stronger, more courageous.

It was time to be brave.

Raven unbuttoned her raincoat but didn't remove it. Still crouched, she tugged the hood over her head and hoisted her backpack and the hunting rifle to her shoulders.

"Come with me, Shadow. I want you to live. I want you to be safe. If you stay here, you'll die like the other wolves that I couldn't save. Please, follow me and be free."

His ears twitched, like he was listening. In some strange way, she felt like he could understand her, or at least that he realized she was attempting to help him, that they were on the same side in this battle.

She kept her voice calm and soothing, breathing deeply to settle her heart rate. "Come with me. I'm going to set you and Luna free. This is the only way I can think of to help you, the way you helped me when I needed to hide. Okay? Come with me."

She rose to her feet and moved for the trees, headed for the gate. She didn't hear Shadow move, but when she reached the gate, he was right behind her.

Warily, she scanned the grounds outside the enclosure. The fog lay white and dense as a stifling blanket, deadening sound. She could see less than thirty feet in any direction. Her pulse rushed in her ears.

No lights were bobbing through the fog. No murky figures darting in the shadows. An oppressive silence had settled dense and heavy over the sanctuary. She heard no night sounds, not even crickets or the rustle of leaves.

When she was sure the coast was clear, she unlocked the gate with a press of her palm and opened it wide for the hybrids. She stepped through to the second gate and opened that one as well. She turned back to the wolf.

Shadow remained inside the enclosure. He regarded her curiously, his tail half-raised.

She gestured to him to follow her. "You're free now."

He made up his mind quickly. He trotted through the gates, sniffing the ground eagerly, taking in all the new, strange scents. His ears pricked, and he turned back toward the enclosure before letting out a series of low yips.

A moment later, Luna appeared out of the mist like a white ghost. She paused at the first gate, hesitating. Shadow yipped to her again as if in encouragement, tail low and gently waving.

Luna whined. Her ears flattened. She certainly didn't care for this crazy idea.

"I know, I get it. We have to take the risk. It's the only way."

Shadow loped over to the white wolf and nuzzled her neck with his muzzle, as if to offer reassurance. He strode a few yards past the gate and turned, looking over his shoulder with that same encouraging gaze he'd given to Raven.

Luna's tail lifted. She took a hesitant step outside the enclosure. She raised her head, sniffing, her ears lifting tentatively.

"It's okay," Raven whispered.

Luna jerked her head in Raven's direction and growled.

Raven raised her hands in surrender. "Okay, okay. I won't talk to you or look at you. I get it."

Seemingly reassured that Luna would follow in her own time, Shadow bounded off toward the bears with great enthusiasm. Luna moved slowly, warily, investigating every scent and object before moving on.

They loped toward the center of the park, headed toward the walk-in enclosure with the lake and the flamingos.

"That's the wrong way," she whispered as loud as she dared. "Shadow! Luna! Come back. The woods are this way."

They didn't listen, didn't even bother with an ear twitch or tail wag. They were wolves, after all. The alpha pair. They obeyed no one, especially not a teenage girl.

Raven watched them go, a sinking sensation in the pit of her stomach. She hadn't actually believed they would follow her around like faithful companions, had she?

They weren't dogs. They were wild creatures. The king and queen of the forest.

She knew that. Yet she'd somehow expected that they would willingly follow her to safety, that she would save them, and miraculously, they would understand and appreciate what she'd done.

Instead, they'd loped off in the opposite direction of safety. She had no way to call them back or redirect them. She could only pray they'd make it out on their own.

She wasn't a praying type of girl, but she prayed then. Fervently, with her whole heart and soul.

A mournful howl split the silence. A second and then a third joined the chorus. The hairs on Raven's arms stood on end. The surviving timber wolves needed her now, too.

No time to waste on self-pity and worry. There was too much to do.

First, she made for the back gate of the wildlife refuge to open it for the animals to escape. Using the bioscanner to unlock it, she swung the gates wide and disengaged the electrified wires along the entire exterior perimeter fence. Without the electrified top wires, the tiger, zebra, and wolves could leap the wrought-iron fence at any point along the perimeter.

The bears and bonobos could clamber over it, while the foxes—Zoe, Zelda, and Magnus—and the otters could squeeze through the bars.

The remaining animals would have to find the open gate to get out.

After propping open the rear gate with a rock, Raven moved stealthily back to the timber wolves' paddock. On a normal night, they'd be locked in their night house. This was no normal night.

Even through the mist, she could see their filmy shapes in the center of their clearing. They sat on their haunches, heads thrown back as they howled their sorrow at the sky. It was a beautiful, tragic, haunting song that filled her heart with grief.

Moving quickly, her eyes stinging, she unlocked the gates and flung them open. Suki, Loki, and Aspen were the only ones left. She scanned the grounds for the bodies of the other three. Several patches of blood gleamed in the moonlight. The bodies were gone.

The Headhunters must have shorted out the electrified top wires of the fence with a branch or something similar, then climbed inside to retrieve the carcasses of the dead wolves, since they couldn't open the gates. Sour-sick nausea sloshed in her stomach.

"The gate is open," she whispered. She pushed the heartache somewhere down deep. She couldn't think about the dead. She had to focus on the living. "Come on, Suki. Let's go, Loki. I'm sorry for your pack. I'm so sorry I couldn't save them. It's time to go."

The wolves' howls ceased abruptly. They rose to their feet and padded toward her on silent paws, their heads and tails low.

Her brain told her she should feel fear, but she didn't. Not after her terrifying night with the hybrids. Compared to them, the timber wolves seemed practically tame. They knew her. They had known her father.

Still, caution was needed. *Stupid gets you killed every time,* her dad used to say.

Raven pulled the gate back against the fence so that it made a triangular shape with her body safely inside it, the gate between her and the timber wolves. It wasn't much protection, but the wolves had more important matters on their minds than bothering with her —like escape.

Escape they did. Loki and Aspen galloped out of the enclosure. They took off in the direction of the lodge. Perhaps they scented the meat left in the rendering shed. Or the lingering scents of the Headhunters who'd slaughtered their pack.

Only shy, meek Suki remained inside. She whimpered, lowering her furry belly inches from the ground, her tail curled beneath her.

"It's okay, Suki," Raven murmured.

Suki had been brought to Haven as a young pup after the mother had abandoned her lone surviving offspring. The long nights cradling Suki's tiny, shivering form against her chest for warmth. The hours spent bottle-feeding her. Sometimes, Suki had suckled the milk from her fingers, her tiny teeth pricking Raven's skin.

Suki inched closer to Raven. She whined unhappily. Something dark stained her muzzle. Raven couldn't see clearly in the night, but she knew what it was. Blood. Suki must have nuzzled Echo or Titus as they lay wounded and dying.

"Come on, girl," Raven said. "You have to come out now. You have to run away. We both do. I know this is your home. It's mine, too. But this is the only way."

Suki wouldn't come. Her whine deepened into a frantic, bewildered growl. The hackles on her spine raised in alarm. The wolf was confused and petrified. She responded to her terror with aggression.

No matter what Raven tried, she couldn't coax Suki from the enclosure. After more time than she could afford to lose, she gave up. She had too many tasks tonight. She couldn't force Suki to leave her paddock. She could only hope the wolf would work up the courage to escape.

Raven left with the gate propped open with a stick.

As the bleak mist continued to envelop everything in its path, she crept to the bear habitat. Kodiak and Sage were napping. They looked like great black humps in the gray murk.

Quietly, she opened the service door and then the night house drop gate, careful not to wake them. Unlike the wolves, she wasn't dumb enough to think they might listen to her. Hopefully, they'd figure it out on their own when they awoke in an hour or so.

After the bears, she went to the bonobos. When they spotted her, they hooted and hollered, swinging frantically from their rope netting. Gizmo puffed up his chest, grabbed a handful of excrement, and threw it at her. It struck the viewing window with a splat and oozed down the glass.

He huffed a hoarse, goofy laugh, then grinned in delight.

"That was so classy, Gizmo." She opened the metal door inside their night house. "You're pissed you haven't been fed in a while. I get it, buddy."

Bonobos weren't as strong or as aggressive as chimps, but they could be dangerous without meaning to be, though the two female bonobos had never shown any inclination toward violence, and Newton was the calmest of the bunch.

Gizmo, though, was the excitable one. She wasn't sure what he was capable of when he was agitated, or if she could adequately keep him calm. In the same way as with the timber wolves, she opened the gate fully while backing herself into the space between the wall and the door, using the gate as a shield.

Like the wolves, the bonobos were much more interested in escape than in pestering a boring human. Gizmo was the first to leave. He whooped to the others as he scampered out of the enclosure onto the flagstone path. Pepper and Newton followed, with Zephyr, who was older and slower, taking up the rear.

The four bonobos immediately charged the snack house, hooting joyously. They'd spent years watching humans relish delectable treats. Now they were determined to obtain those treats for themselves.

Next, Raven opened Hera's cage. Her wings were clipped, but Raven freed her anyway, because she had to. Then she opened the door to the otters' habitat, too. There was a river less than three miles away, though she doubted the otters would be able to find it.

But she couldn't worry about the next steps, only the here and now.

She freed the tortoises and the ostriches. Maybe it made her an awful person, but she left Winston the boa constrictor in his glass aquarium. He might outlive them all.

When she invaded the porcupines' paddock, the porcupines, Duke and Duchess, waddled toward her in outraged fury. They turned their backsides toward her in warning, wiggling their sharpened quills. She exited swiftly with the door left open and left them to their own devices.

After pausing to check for danger, Raven kept moving. She circled to the western side of the park. She freed Sal, the zebra, and the leopard, who was conveniently napping, so she could slip away silently. Then the foxes, who scurried between her legs and streaked to freedom. Electra the bobcat gave her a moody stare from her perch atop a faux-rock outcropping, her black-fringed ears flicking grumpily.

Finally, there was only one animal left.

Chapter Twenty-Two

The fog shrouded the buildings in a funeral veil. Like death, drifting closer and closer. Raven shook her head to clear her thoughts. The eerie fog was getting to her. Her imagination was starting to run wild. She braced herself, then took a deep breath.

She'd reached the tiger house.

She approached Vlad's enclosure with trepidation. Doubt and indecision roared through her mind. Was she seriously going to let a tiger loose? Five hundred pounds of coiled muscle and brute strength. Two-inch fangs. Four-inch claws like blades, built for eviscerating prey.

Was she insane?

Vlad stretched out on his favorite rock, gazing at her with his sharp eyes. His tail twitched. The sleek dark shape of him rose as she approached. His eyes gleamed in the darkness.

She stood and stared at him through the fence. If she left him in his cage, he would die of thirst and starvation, if he wasn't brutalized by the Headhunters first. If she released him, she'd be freeing a lethal apex predator into the world, a predator blessed with a fierce, formidable intelligence.

But perhaps a lethal predator was what she needed. A predator who would hunt the Headhunters.

At least, a tiger unleashed might distract them enough so the other animals—and Raven—could escape.

The battle in her mind warred back and forth. The risks were great. But also... if Vlad attacked a few of the Headhunters, was that worth it?

In countries where the people respected tigers and kept their distance, tiger attacks were extremely rare. It was humans who hunted the tigers, taunted them, wounded them, and then reacted with stunned outrage when a tiger pushed to the limit responded with violence.

She knew the studies and research her father had shown her. Tigers were naturally wary of humans and usually showed no preference for human meat. Although humans were relatively easy prey, they were not a desired source of food.

Most man-eating tigers were old, infirm, or had missing teeth. They chose human victims out of desperation.

Raven bit her lip, conflicted to her core. If she freed him, would Vlad attack her? Would he hunt down the wolves or the bonobos? Would he head toward the towns and hunt the few remaining humans struggling to survive?

Or would he live out his days in the miles of forest surrounding Haven, hunting deer and rabbits and raccoons, never harming anyone?

She didn't know. She couldn't know.

She thought of Vaughn. She thought of Dekker. There were humans more dangerous than any tiger.

"I need help," she said aloud. "I can't do this alone. Can you help me?"

Vlad's gleaming eyes tracked her. She felt him watching her. *Well?* He seemed to say. *Get on with it.*

"This might be the stupidest thing I've ever done. The second I open this door, you might just slice my bowels open. Please don't, okay?"

Once she'd decided, there was no going back.

First, she tossed him a few pieces of deer jerky so he'd remember how much he liked her—and who brought him the treats he loved. Then, she made sure the sliding gate Vlad used to enter his chamber from the enclosure was closed. She swung the service door wide and pocketed the remote control for the sliding gate before exiting.

Lowering her pack, she kept the tranquilizer gun strapped to her waist in case of trouble. She climbed the branches of the maple tree next to the tiger house. When she was parallel to the roof of the tiger house, she leaned out, grasped the top edge of the roof, and hauled herself over and up, as she'd done a hundred times before.

Everything was harder at night, with the fog, the darkness, with the barely contained panic churning her insides.

From the safety of the tiger house roof, she knelt and looked down at Vlad. "Please don't make me regret this."

He chuffed in response.

She removed the remote from her pocket and flicked the manual override. The gate creaked as it slid open.

Vlad stared up at her. In the darkness, she could make out his form, those intently glowing eyes. Could he understand what was happening? What was going through that predatory mind?

Hopefully, he remembered that she was the one who'd fed him every day. She was the one who'd hung out here for hours, keeping him company. As if tigers got lonely like teenage girls.

Twisting, she scanned the park again. Still no lights, no human noises, no Headhunters. It was 3 a.m. No one was out searching for her.

Whoever Damien truly was, he'd kept his word. He hadn't betrayed her.

She whistled one long note, two short. The signal for food. Vlad rose languidly, leaped from his rock, and stalked to his chamber. How long would it take him to figure out the service door was open?

She didn't have long to wait. Within seconds, Vlad sauntered out of the service door like he was embarking on a regular evening stroll.

He raised his great head and stared straight up at her. Their gazes locked.

He was magnificent. He was absolutely terrifying.

She stopped breathing. Adrenaline spiked through her veins. Every hair on her body prickled. From the park side, the roof of the tiger house was only ten feet from the ground. A tiger could leap twelve feet straight up from a dead standstill.

If he wanted to, Vlad could be on her in less than three seconds. No tranquilizer dart in the world took effect that fast.

He shook his huge head and sniffed the air. His tail twitched, as if deciding how hungry he was. As if he, too, was considering just how far he could jump for his dinner.

"You know me," she said, trying to keep her voice calm. "Who else gives you your favorite jerky snacks? Who else hangs out with you for hours atop your tiger house? I've told you my deepest, darkest, most embarrassing secrets. That alone means you owe me. Besides, I'm scrawny. I'd barely serve as a snack, while several delicious Headhunter jerkwads would taste fabulous to a tiger. You don't want to eat me. You like me. You *know* me."

His ears pricked. He was listening to her. He gave a loud chuff, turned, and stalked along the path as if he owned it.

The enormous tiger vanished into the fog like a specter in the night.

Raven couldn't shake the disconcerting feeling that twisted her stomach. She'd either saved them all or made the gravest error of her life.

Chapter Twenty-Three

After Vlad was gone, Raven slipped from the tiger house and headed toward the grassy fenced enclosure at the center of Haven, where the flamingos preened in the pond. She'd forgotten about the flamingos and needed to release them, too, as well as the peacocks.

The fog drifted and slithered around her legs. It was impossibly sluggish, an opaque white haze. She knew every loose flagstone in every path of Haven by heart. Yet in the misty darkness, the wildlife sanctuary took on an eerie otherworldliness that prickled the hairs on the back of her neck.

Walking through the fog gave her the strange sensation of sinking into a strange world, into a deep, impenetrable substance, alien and unknown.

A scuffling sound came from behind her.

She swung around, peering into the fog. To her right, the reptile house loomed. To her left rose the snack shack. A birch tree stood beside it, its leaves almost gone, bare branches raking the sky.

If someone was out prowling the park and had a light, they'd turned it off. She could see nothing amiss, could hear nothing out of place, other than the bonobos calling to each other from the roof of the snack shack.

She turned back and kept walking, her footfalls muffled.

She stilled. Her heart jolted in her chest. Had she heard another footfall, just after hers?

She spun around again, searching the fog to the left, then the right. She couldn't see more than fifteen feet in any direction. Distance was impossible to measure. The world outside her circle of visibility might have vanished entirely, and she wouldn't know. She listened for sounds, heard only her own ragged breathing.

She'd never escape at this rate. She had to get moving. She couldn't let her fear of the unseen control her, damn it.

Raven braced herself, straightened her shoulders. She tucked her tranq gun in her waistband and grasped her hunting rifle, shifting it into both hands. Her finger curled around the trigger. She resumed walking.

Something dropped to the ground directly in front of her.

Alarm flared through her body. Raven resisted the urge to leap back in terror. She clamped her mouth shut to keep from screaming and raised the rifle.

A blurred shape leered out of the murky shadows. A bonobo materialized. It hooted at her. It jumped in glee. Its lips peeled back from its teeth as it smiled. Its licorice-black eyes glittered eagerly up at her.

Relieved, she lowered the rifle. Her hands trembled from the adrenaline.

"Gizmo," she said. "You about gave me a heart attack, and I about shot you in your smug little face. Go terrorize someone else, would you?"

Gizmo reached out his leathery fingers and took her hand. For a moment, he clasped her fingers gently in his. Startled, for a moment she didn't move.

She stroked the black fur on the back of his hand. "Thank you," she said, not sure what for. Abruptly, she felt like weeping. It was the middle of the night. She was exhausted, sore, and frightened. Her home was under attack. Three of her wolves had been killed. And her own safety was in jeopardy, her risk increasing every moment that she remained here.

And here was a captive ape, giving her a moment of reprieve, the smallest act of kindness. It almost shattered her fragile heart.

Gizmo hopped on one foot, hooted softly, and gave her that hoarse, goofy laugh of his.

Her eyes pricked. She blinked rapidly. "You're free now. Go. Find your troop. Live a good life."

Gizmo rose on his hind legs. His smile changed—his lip curled up, revealing his top teeth. To the untrained eye, Gizmo still looked like he was smiling. Raven knew better. He wasn't smiling because he was happy.

It was a fear grin.

Urgency crackled through her veins. She pivoted, lifting her rifle, finger already tracking toward the trigger. Too late.

Footsteps sounded behind her.

A gunshot shattered the air.

Gizmo let out a tortured shriek.

Before she could orient herself to the danger, to find her target and squeeze the trigger, a hand clamped around her mouth.

Something knocked the rifle out of her grip. Rough hands seized her arms. Her backpack was torn from her shoulders and tossed onto the ground.

Her spine was shoved violently against something hard—a man's chest. The cold muzzle of a gun kissed her temple.

"Don't scream," Rex said into her right ear. Hot breath scalded her cheek. He stank of sweat and beer. The sour stench of him clogged her nostrils. "Or go ahead and scream. I love it when they pretend they don't like this."

Her heart bucked against her ribcage. Her chest filled with molten panic. She tried to wrench free. His grip was iron.

At her feet, Gizmo writhed in agony. His furry hands clutched his stomach. Blood oozed between his fingers. He looked up at Raven. His small black face contorted in pain and confusion. In his entire life, a human had never hurt him.

Hot outraged tears streamed down her cheeks. "You monster!"

"It turns me on when you whisper sweet nothings to me, you know."

"You didn't have to do that!" she cried in a strangled voice. "He wouldn't have hurt anybody!"

"You got her," a second voice said. A figure materialized out of the fog a few yards to her right, carrying a flashlight in one hand, a pistol in the other. A semi-automatic rifle was slung across his shoulder. "I knew you'd find her."

"You bastard," she hissed.

Damien smiled tightly, his eyes in shadow. "That's me."

"Shut that thing up already," Rex ordered.

Damien glanced at the shrieking ape, aimed his gun, and shot the bonobo in the head. Gizmo's furred body slumped and went still.

A cold fury rose within Raven. Gizmo was only here because he wanted to greet her, to perform his usual antics, to show off, to say thank you and goodbye in his way.

Instead, Rex and Damien killed him.

Rex toed the dead ape with his boot. His gun was still pressed to the side of her head. "Too bad we can't get a pelt out of this thing."

Somewhere to the east, invisible in the heavy fog, another bonobo wailed in grief. It was Zephyr, Gizmo's mother. Bonobo mother-son pairs were closely bonded for life. She must have seen what happened from a perch on the reptile house roof or one of the elms lining the path.

Zephyr wailed again. She knew what it meant—her son's body lying limp and still. Raven felt the bonobo's pain like her own. Grief stitched into her bones.

"Kill that one, too," Rex ordered. "I can't stand their damn screeching."

Damien swung the handgun and pointed into the fog, firing off several random shots. The sound thundered in her ears.

"Stop it!" She tried again to wrestle from Rex's grip. She kicked backward at his shins and clawed at his skinny forearm with all her might. It was no use. "Leave her be! You don't have to kill them!"

Rex gave a guttural laugh. "They're glorified rodents. Filthy beasts. We're doing them a favor."

She choked on helpless anger, unable to speak.

Damien lowered his gun and peered into the murk, shining the flashlight from tree to tree, from building to building. He frowned at the sound of tiny nails scrabbling over a metal roof.

Unseen, Zephyr scurried to safety, still shrieking in anguish.

"We've been looking for you," Rex said. "And to think, the others almost gave up on finding you. Dekker and Vaughn will both be thrilled."

"Screw you! I hope you die!"

Rex only laughed. "Now, let's get down to business," he said in her ear, his breath hot on her cheek. "You're the one who let the damn monkeys out, aren't you?"

"They're not monkeys, they're apes, you moron," she spat.

His fingers dug painfully into her shoulders. "Now, I like a bit of spunk, little girl. Too much and you'll see a side of me you wish you hadn't."

He wanted to see her afraid. She'd rather die than give in to him. "Go to hell."

"You'll be sorry for that, you little—"

An ear-splitting yowl echoed through the night. It sounded both close and directionless, like it could be ten feet away or a mile. A harsh, guttural bark answered from somewhere nearby.

Rex went rigid. In shock, his right arm dropped. The gun slipped a few inches from her temple. "What the hell was that?"

A smile spread across Raven's face.

Damien spun, gun up, sighting nebulous shapes in the shifting fog. "Which animals did you let out?"

Her smile widened. "All of them."

He shot Raven a horrified look. "What do you mean, all of them?"

"Just what I said." She let the tremble creep into her voice, let the panic clawing up her throat escape. "That yowl you heard? That's

Vlad, the man-eating tiger. It's the sound he makes right before he attacks."

It was a lie. The grating yowl came from Electra the bobcat, not Vlad. And the dog-like bark belonged to the zebra. Neither animal would attack three full-grown adults.

But Rex and Damien didn't know that.

Their faces drained of color. Rex's attention strayed from Raven to the menacing fog, which hid any number of clawed, fanged, and deadly creatures who desired nothing more than to eat him alive.

"Where is it?" he cried. "Shoot, damn it, shoot!"

Damien crouched, his gaze sweeping in a slow circle. "I don't see anything!"

Rex gestured with his gun. "Shoot anyway! Scare it off, damn it!"

This was her chance. Raven jerked her head backward. The back of her skull slammed into Rex's chin. Simultaneously, she stomped on the top of his foot.

He grunted. His one-armed grip loosened. She jerked free.

Whirling, she shoved her hand into her pocket and seized the whittling knife. She yanked it out, fumbling to flip it open.

She didn't think. She simply acted on instinct. Carnivores always went for the most vulnerable points of the body—the belly, the neck. So did she.

Angrily, Rex lunged for her.

Raven plunged the blade deep into his throat.

Chapter Twenty-Four

Hot blood drenched Raven's hands. It slicked her fingers. The knife slipped out of her hands and clattered to the flagstone.

Rex staggered backward. His face went slack with astonishment. He dropped his gun. His eyes were sunken in his gaunt face, his pallor ashen. He clutched his neck with both hands, frantically attempting to staunch the dark red blood gushing from the wound.

Damien's flashlight swung in a wild panicked arc, throwing garish shadows everywhere. His wide gaze darted from Rex to Raven and back again. "What the hell? What'd you do?"

"Shoot her!" Rex croaked.

In the darkness and harsh light, Damien's expression was grim, unreadable. He dropped the flashlight and swung the barrel of the gun toward her. The gun barrel was pointed at her chest. "Raise your hands."

Fear surged through her chest. The whittling knife lay on the path a yard from her feet. The blade glistened dark with blood. Rex's gun lay even further away. Her hunting rifle was on the ground somewhere behind her, and the tranq gun couldn't help her.

By the time she went for it, Damien could shoot her a dozen times.

"Raise your hands!" Damien ordered. His flat voice was terrifying.

Raven went very still. She lifted her blood-drenched hands into the air and fixed her gaze on Damien. "You don't have to do this." Her voice trembled. Her body felt numb, disconnected from her brain.

"You little—I'll kill you—!" Rex took a step toward her and stumbled. He gasped, half-choking, still clutching at his throat. "What're you waiting for, Damien! Kill her!"

"You have a choice, Damien," Raven said. Her voice sounded high and distant, strange, like it belonged to someone else. "Please don't do this."

Rex plucked at the spurting hole in his neck. He sank to his knees. His breath came in shallow, rapid pants. "Kill her and get me to Gomez! He's got the med kit—shoot her, damn it!"

Damien hesitated. His rifle wavered. His body was taut, his face hard as stone. Once again, his gaze flitted from Rex to Raven and back again. Something flashed in his eyes—uncertainty.

Raven waited for the bullet to the chest. This was it. This was how it would end, how she would die here, alone in the fog and the cold and the darkness.

No. She would not give up. Not until her last breath. Maybe if Damien's rifle wavered just a bit more. Maybe she could dive for the knife, or dart for the trees.

Her gaze never left that gun.

Blood bubbled from Rex's lips. His skin had lost all color. He attempted to stand but toppled to the ground with a groan.

Rex's hands tightened over his throat. A thick dark puddle of blood spread beneath him on the flagstone. "I'll kill... kill her myself... you stupid, worthless—"

"No," Damien said. His voice was firm. His expression cleared like he'd decided something. He shifted and aimed his rifle at Rex. "You won't."

Rex sputtered incoherently. A look of betrayed shock crossed his agonized face. He made several choking, gurgling noises as he tried to speak, but no coherent words came out.

Damien didn't pull the trigger. He didn't need to.

Rex's eyes rolled back in his head. Within a minute, he ceased moving. He stopped breathing, stopped everything.

Damien lowered the gun barrel several inches, but he kept his finger on the trigger guard. He let out a soft curse and sucked in his breath. "Is he dead?"

"Yeah, he's dead." Raven's legs turned to jelly. Dizziness washed through her, but she fought to remain standing.

Her mind took several seconds to process the rapid change in circumstances. Damien still held the gun, but he wasn't acting like he was going to shoot her with it—probably.

She wanted nothing more than to sink to the ground, curl up into a ball, and weep with relief and horror simultaneously. She couldn't. Not yet. She was still in danger.

Damien had a weapon. She didn't.

She took an unsteady step backward, toward the hunting rifle lying where it had landed when Rex knocked it from her hands. Her backpack lay crumpled on the flagstone beside the gun.

In one swift move, she crouched, seized the rifle, and leaped to her feet.

Damien tightened his grip on the handgun. He started to swing it in her direction, wariness and apprehension on his face.

She lifted the rifle slowly but kept the barrel aimed downward. "I'm picking it up. That's all."

He nodded tightly. "You were supposed to run," he said, his voice accusatory. "You weren't supposed to still be here!"

She trembled all over. Her voice shook. "I *was* running. Until *you* caught me."

"That was out of my control. I thought you were already gone, so it wouldn't matter how hard we looked. You were supposed to be gone. That's not my fault."

A fresh jolt of anger gave her the strength to keep standing. She bared her teeth. "You were there. I saw you. You were shooting at the wolves. Shika, Echo, and Titus are dead."

His face darkened. "I had no choice."

She gave a furious, disbelieving snort.

"I shot *at* them—I didn't hurt any of them myself. I swear it."

"Once again, you were there and did nothing. You might as well have killed them with your bare hands." At the mention of hands, she remembered her own. Dismayed, she stared down at the blood staining her fingers, her fingers clutching the gun.

The blood of the man she'd just killed. In self-defense, but still. She was a killer now. Like an animal caught in a trap, willing to gnaw its own paw off. Willing to do anything to stay alive.

Acid burned the back of her throat. She wiped her hands fiercely on her cargo pants. Dark streaks marred the cloth. She let the anger rise up, let it drown out the grief and fear and revulsion. "And Gizmo? What's your pathetic excuse for murdering him?"

"Rex shot him first. He was suffering. There was no way he would have survived that. I put him out of his misery, and you know it."

In some small part of her brain, she knew Damien's shot was a mercy killing. He'd ended Gizmo's suffering. All the same, she hated him with a blazing intensity. Seeing him standing there next to Dekker and Vaughn while they killed Shika and Titus and Echo—it had felt like a betrayal.

She barely knew this guy, and yet, in this bewildering, hostile new reality, she'd thought she had an ally. She'd been desperate for a friend.

He ran a hand through his hair and sighed. "Look, I can't act weak, okay? I have to play a part. If I don't, they'll abandon me—or kill me."

"So what? Just leave."

"It's not that easy."

"Looks that easy from where I'm standing."

His gaze dropped to Rex's body, then swiftly snapped up again. He met her eyes. "Ivan Vaughn is my uncle."

She stared at him.

"My dad's brother."

"Your last name is Vaughn," she said dully. "Damien Vaughn."

"He came for me." His voice was strained, his eyes hooded. "Please, you have to understand. I lived in Alpharetta, a suburb of Atlanta, with my parents and two little sisters. I am—was a sophomore at Emory University, studying engineering. I... I wanted to design cars. Atlanta was one of the first cities to fall. It was hit hard and fast because of Hartsfield-Jackson International Airport.

"Almost three hundred thousand passengers a day passed through that airport, spreading the virus with every cough and sniffle and sneeze. People masked up immediately, they did the usual social distancing stuff, schools and businesses shut down, just like the other pandemics. This one was different. It is different. It's a super-virus like no one has ever seen before. It took out just about anyone and everyone."

"I know."

He continued like she hadn't spoken. "Early on, we sequestered ourselves, even when we ran out of food, even when the water turned off. We heard sirens all day long. And then we didn't. My mom made us separate into our bedrooms, into different parts of the house. She divided the food, water bottles, and toilet paper, and she had bought tarps and duct tape and sealed up the ductwork, and all around our doors and windows. She said if one of us had already contracted the virus, maybe the rest would survive. We didn't want to do it like that, but she insisted. My mom was small but fierce. It was awful. Hearing them getting sick, one by one. The vomiting. The moaning in pain. The weeping. I was in that house with my dead parents and my dead little sisters for days."

He didn't look at her, didn't meet her gaze. He stared off into the mist, eyes glazed and distant, recalling the horror. "I thought I was going to die, too, just like them, the fevers, the coughing up blood, writhing in agony, my insides melting like jelly. But I didn't. I guess my mom's actions saved my life." His voice went hollow. "Lucky me."

"I'm sorry," she said. It was genuine. What a useless word. The most useless word ever invented. She could see the grief etched on his face, sharpening his features.

"I was trapped in that death house for five days, three days after I'd run out of anything edible. I was afraid to leave, afraid to contract the virus, obviously, but also because of everything else that was happening, with all the rioting and the mobs. People were so scared, they panicked. Some of them had watched their entire families suffer and die within days. They were out of their minds with panic and grief. In some places, especially the big cities like Atlanta, people started killing other people. By then, the cops were dead or had fled. There was no one to stop anyone from doing whatever they wanted. They were robbing their neighbors for their food, shooting them if they fought back. They killed anyone who coughed or breathed wrong. Everyone was so afraid. It was like... like everyone went crazy, all at once."

Raven shuddered. "That's awful."

"It was... apocalyptic. And then my uncle came," Damien said. "He fought his way through a riot and dragged me out of that house, and he saved me. I'm alive because of him. I owe him everything."

Damien wanted her to sympathize with him. A part of her did. Another part remained hard as stone. "He sounds like a real winner, your uncle."

"He's a criminal. I know that. I get that. But—he's not as bad as you think. He has a code. He doesn't usually kill women and children."

Incredulous, her eyebrows shot toward her hairline. "Usually?"

"Trust me. There are worse alternatives."

She remembered the look on Dekker's face back at the pharmacy. His flat black eyes as he blew Carl's face off for no reason at all. How he'd looked at her like she was a meal to be consumed, or trash to be disposed of.

"Do you think any of that matters to Carl? To all the other people he's killed?"

Damian's jaw pulsed. Emotions flitted across his face—anger, resignation, something like sadness. "I'm not your enemy."

"Hard to believe from where I'm standing."

"I could've shot you just now, but I didn't, did I?"

"Why didn't you?"

"I told you. I'm not a killer."

But I am. She pressed her trembling hands against her thighs. They wouldn't stop shaking. "And yet I still find that hard to believe."

"I'm just trying to survive like everybody else. That doesn't mean I like what I have to do."

She regarded him with narrowed eyes, still wary. "I don't understand you."

He gave a helpless shrug. "I do what I can to help, when I can."

"As long as it doesn't cost you anything. Right?"

He glanced away, stiffening, that muscle in his jaw pulsing. He turned and met her gaze. There was an odd look in his eyes. Part angry. Part ashamed. "You're right. I'm a coward."

"Then we agree on something."

"Maybe." There was no sarcasm or defensiveness in his voice. Only a weary resignation. That shadow of shame again. "I guess so."

Something squeezed in her chest.

"I didn't want to hurt you," he said. "I don't want to hurt you."

"Then prove it."

"Okay. I will." He holstered his gun, then lifted both hands, palms out as if beseeching her to trust him. "I am, see? Like I said, I don't want to hurt you."

Yeah, right. She didn't believe it for a second. She couldn't allow herself to believe it, believe him. Could she? Her weapon lowered a fraction.

"I'm not going to hurt you."

"Unless your Uncle Ivan is around, you mean."

"No, I won't. I swear it. Not even then."

"How noble of you."

He winced. "Touché."

"I don't trust you."

"I get that, but you can. I swear it, I'm on your side."

She didn't trust him. She despised him. Didn't she? Shouldn't she? He was one of the murderous Headhunters. Yet he'd been true to his word. He hadn't ratted her out back at the lodge.

He'd also stood by and watched his friends shoot the wolves. He'd done nothing when Rex took her hostage. And yet. He'd refused to shoot her, had turned his gun on Rex instead.

Conflicting emotions roiled inside her. It made no sense. She didn't understand it, didn't understand him. His very presence was disorienting, discomfiting.

He was a Headhunter. He was dangerous.

She should kill him right now, while she had the chance.

His weapon was holstered. She held the rifle in her bloodied hands. If she was quick enough, she might get off a shot before he did.

It was the smart move. The right move.

Raven lifted the rifle and pointed it at Damien.

Chapter Twenty-Five

Damien tensed, but he didn't move, didn't go for his weapon. He kept his hands up, palms out. "Go ahead, if that's what you feel like you need to do."

She should do it. Her father would have. It was too risky not to do it. An image of Zachariah flashed through her brain. Her dad wasn't wrong. But the right thing wasn't always the right thing.

There was something in Damien's eyes, though. A softness, a vulnerability that was hard to fake. She saw it. Even in the fog, the darkness shimmering around the flashlight, still shining a wide spotlight from its position on the ground between them.

Her gut twisted. He was the enemy. He'd also spared her life. Twice.

She could hate him, but she couldn't kill him. She wasn't her father.

With a sigh, she lowered the hunting rifle.

For a long moment, they stared at each other without moving or speaking.

"Can I get the flashlight without you trying to shoot me?" he asked.

She nodded.

He bent and retrieved the flashlight, then straightened. "Thanks. You won't regret this, I swear it."

"I'd better not."

He grinned. "Now, we need to—"

A scratching, shuffling sound came from somewhere behind them.

Damien went rigid. Raven tensed. She held up one finger for absolute quiet.

Eyes wide, Damien nodded. He shifted slightly and unholstered his handgun with his right hand, shifting the flashlight to his left. He pointed the beam aimlessly into the fog, swinging it from left to right.

She strained her ears, trying to make out the source of the sounds. The mist was thick as soup around them. The beam of the flashlight barely penetrated ten yards. For a panicked instant, she imagined Vlad stalking them, prowling closer, unsheathed claws clicking the flagstone.

But no. The sounds were wrong.

Several heavy, shuffling steps. A loud snuffling sound.

A larger dark shape reared out of the murk behind Damien.

Damien whirled in alarm. His gun hand rose.

"Don't shoot!" Raven lunged forward. With her free hand, she grasped the barrel of Damien's gun and slapped it down.

Damien shot her a horrified look. "What are you doing—!"

"Stay still, and he won't hurt you."

"What—?" And then Damien saw it, too.

An enormous black bear emerged from the thick fog, not twenty feet away.

Damien made a strangled sound in the back of his throat.

Kodiak lumbered toward them, his huge head low. He sniffed hungrily at the bushes along the path, searching for potential dinner. His fur was thick and black but for the white star-shaped patch between his eyes.

About ten feet away, the big bear hesitated. He looked at them curiously, his head swinging from Damien to Raven.

"Don't move," she murmured. "He's more curious than anything."

To Damien's credit, he didn't move a single muscle. He probably stopped breathing, too. His face was so pale, his freckles stood out like drops of blood.

Haven's black bears were big, lazy oafs. They could cause harm, sure. They weighed three hundred pounds and had teeth and claws, but they were not aggressive. Not if you knew what you were doing.

"There's no food here for you, Kodiak," she said calmly. "The exit you want is back the way you came. The woods are full of the food you want."

Kodiak snuffled. He lumbered straight at them. The huge black shape passed not five feet from where she and Damien stood. The sour dankness of his fur filled her nostrils. He was so close, she could've counted the thick coarse hairs of his pelt.

The bear ambled past them. His mouth agape, Damien turned and stared after the black bear until he vanished into the fog. Damien turned back to Raven with a look of absolute awe. "I thought for sure he was gonna eat us."

"Most animals aren't a threat to humans unless the humans are a threat first."

He ran his hands through his hair and took a steadying breath. His gaze fell to Rex's body. "I have to go back and alert Vaughn and Dekker."

Of course. His first loyalty was still to his uncle. Raven had her loyalties, too. Her responsibilities. She'd dallied here for far too long. Every second she stood here with him increased the chance of discovery.

Squatting, she set down the rifle just long enough to shoulder her backpack and seize the whittling knife. Retrieving the rifle with one hand, she stood and wiped the knife clean on her pants with her other hand, then closed it and stuffed it in her pocket.

Part of her never wanted to lay eyes on the blade again. Part of her couldn't bear to leave it behind. The whittling knife was her mother's last gift to her.

Besides, it had saved her life. Perhaps, it might again. She started up the flagstone path. "I need to go."

Damien swiftly crossed the space between them and seized her arm. "Wait."

His touch shuddered up her arm. Alarm buzzed through her blood. But also, something else. Something she couldn't name. It turned her stomach inside out. Her skin felt too tight, the air too dense. "Let go!"

He was stronger than she was. He could have forced her to do whatever he wanted, but he didn't. Frowning, he released her arm. "Sorry."

"I just—I don't like to be touched."

He shrugged. "Okay. Just don't go yet."

"What do you want?" Her voice came out harsh. She rubbed her arm with her free hand. His touch had surprised her, set her even further on edge.

"There's something you need to know."

The fog enveloped them in a murky white soup. They stood facing each other, tension sizzling between them like electricity. Her muscles tensed, ready to flee at the slightest provocation.

If he touched her again, she was gone.

"They'll hunt you now," he said hoarsely. "They were losing interest, getting bored since they didn't find you right away, but not now. Dekker won't stop now that Rex is dead. When it comes to vengeance, he's like a dog with a bone."

She stared at him, numb. "It was self-defense."

"Do you think they care about that? Do you think Dekker will care? This isn't just anybody." He took a sharp breath. "Rex is—was —Dekker's brother."

A frisson of dread zapped down her spine. All the blood rushed to her head. Dekker was dangerous. The terrible images flooded her brain. Carl's face imploding. All that blood. Dekker's flat, dead-fish eyes seeking hers.

Before, she'd been a plaything, an object he could use and then discard. Nothing special or very important. A passing interest.

Before Rex's death, she could have left like she'd planned. None of the Headhunters would've been the wiser for it. They wouldn't have bothered to search for her outside of the wildlife sanctuary.

Now, she would be pursued. She would be hunted.

Damien's mouth thinned. "You need to understand. Vaughn wanted to take you in alive before this. To... to sell you, like I told you. It wouldn't matter what Dekker wanted—he'd have to obey. But now Dekker has a blood debt against you. Vaughn won't stop him. Dekker will kill you."

"I got that part."

"It won't be pleasant. He'll... he'll want to torture you first. I've seen it before. It's how he gets."

She swallowed hard. Fear pressed up against her throat, making it difficult to breathe.

"You gonna tell me your name yet?"

She gave a sharp shake of her head. "Haven't earned it."

"I will." He shot her a grim smile. For a tense moment, they just stared at each other. Damien cleared his throat. "Want to know why I was hiding in that back bedroom when I first saw you?"

"Why?"

"Because I'm afraid. Okay? I'm afraid, too. Every time Dekker looks at me, I don't know if he's gonna smile that slick smile or slide a blade between my ribs. Or maybe both at the same time. He sees me as a threat because of who I am to Vaughn. He'd take over the Headhunters if he thought he could get away with it. He's dangerous."

She nodded and licked her dry lips. Her scalp prickled with cold sweat. "I'll hide the body. They won't know what happened to him, not until I'm far enough away where they can't find me."

"There's blood all over the flagstone. No way we can get it all out before sunrise."

"They'll think it was one of the wild animals. The tiger or one of the bears."

"Even I know animals don't kill with a knife." He grimaced. "Vaughn knows hunting. We wouldn't be able to make it look convincing that an animal did it. He'd know. I have no choice. I have to tell Dekker what happened—or a version of it. If I don't, they'll discover the body anyway, and he'll suspect me, too. He knows Rex and me went out together. Vaughn won't be able to stop him. He'll start cutting off my fingers one by one until he gets the truth."

There were no good choices. Only terrible ones.

Impotent rage burned through her veins. At Damien, at the Headhunters, at her dead father, at her mother who'd left her all alone, at this whole stupid dying world.

"You have to get out of here," Damien said. "I'll wait as long as I can, but I can't wait too long. It will be dawn soon. I'll try to divert the search, send them in the wrong direction. It won't work long-term, but I can give you time. Use it wisely."

Fear roiled through her stomach. So did something else, something sick and dark. Raven straightened her shoulders, bracing herself. "I'm not running. Not yet, anyway."

Damien stared at her, aghast. "What do you mean? No, you have to run. Run as far away as you can, and never come back. Dekker will kill you. They'll all try to kill you."

"I understand that. They're hunting the animals, too."

"But—"

"Haven is my home. I released the animals, but they're still here, wandering around in confusion inside the refuge or the nearby woods. They're not free yet. They're not safe. I can't leave them, and this place, in the hands of the Headhunters. Not until I give the animals a better chance to get away."

And not while Luna and Shadow were still here, too. She didn't say that part out loud. He wouldn't understand.

"No, you don't get it—"

"I get it," she said. "There are some things I can live with, and some things I can't. My whole life, I thought I couldn't wait to get away from this place. It turns out, my heart is here. It was here all along. My dad, he dedicated his whole life to the Haven, to these animals. I—I can't just leave them defenseless. I have to at least give them a chance."

She didn't say that she was probably infected and likely to die anyway. It wasn't any of his business. Besides, she didn't want to voice it into existence. Not yet.

Raven waited for him to say that they were just animals. That they didn't matter. That they weren't as valuable as her human life. But he didn't.

Instead, he handed her his flashlight. "Hide out in the woods for the night, at least. Find a safe place if you can. There's nowhere for you to hide here. I'll do what I can to help you from this side. If—If I can do something to help, I will."

For the first time in what felt like months, warmth filled her chest. She had a flashlight in her pack, but she wasn't about to tell him that.

She accepted the flashlight. "I'll hold you to that."

"Good luck," Damien said. "You'll need it."

Chapter Twenty-Six

Raven headed for the woods.

She ran as fast as she dared in the dark, too afraid to use the flashlight Damien had given her. Her legs pumped. Her pack thumped against her spine. Her pulse was a roar in her ears. Tears burned her vision. She blinked them away fiercely.

Reaching the back of the park, she sprinted between the bear and hybrid paddocks. One of the peacocks veered into her path. She nearly tripped over the damn bird but managed to keep her footing. Finally, she reached the wide double gates, still propped open with the rocks she'd placed earlier.

The forest loomed, rising before her like an immense black wall —bleak, foreboding, bristling with unknown terrors.

She hesitated for an instant, glancing back over her shoulder. She peered through the fog. The faintest shine of moonlight pierced the haziness. It would be morning in a few short hours. This was the longest night of her life.

Come on, Shadow. Come on, Luna. And Vlad, Suki, Kodiak, all the others. She couldn't wait for them. She had to trust that they could find their way out.

She turned and sprinted into the woods. She'd played in this forest her entire childhood. She knew it well, though not so much at night. She'd once had a favorite fort she'd built herself, and it was there that she headed now.

Burrs and brambles clung to her clothing. Thorns snagged her hands. The underbrush was thick and dense. The woods smelled of crushed pine needles and damp, dank earth. The skeletons of the trees stretched long bony fingers to scrape the sky.

The darkness closed around her like a fist.

She kept her eyes open wide, wary of every flicker of movement, every sigh of the leaves, every pulsing shadow in the underbrush. A second of inattention might determine the difference between living and dying. A single wrong move—tripping on a tree root or stepping wrong on a felled branch—would alert predators to her presence.

She moved as swiftly but quietly as she could. Shadows spilled all around her like ink.

In the dark, she lost her way a few times and had to backtrack. The deer path was incredibly difficult to follow, though she'd explored these woods a thousand times.

Sweat beaded her forehead and dripped between her shoulder blades. Every footfall seemed to announce her presence to the night, to all the creatures that called this wild forest their home—and possibly to some that did not.

Raven searched the darkness for shifting shadows, for the gleam of predatory eyes. She strained for the sound of padded paws slinking through the forest. Or worse, human footsteps pursuing her.

Thirty minutes later, she finally stumbled upon the familiar ring of stones surrounding her childhood firepit. A few yards behind it stood the lean-to fort she'd built herself seven years ago. Several of the branches had fallen, though most still stood, creating the small shelter in the crook of a boulder and a giant spreading oak.

The moss roof she'd worked so hard on had crumbled long ago, but it didn't matter. This place was comforting and familiar. She needed that.

Her legs shaky from exhaustion, she sank onto one of the log seats that surrounded the firepit. Above her, hints of starlight glimmered between the black tangles of branches.

She looked down at her trembling hands. Blood stained her fingers. Blood from a dead man. A dead man who'd tried to kill her.

Strangely, she felt no guilt. Like every wild creature, she'd instinctively protected herself. The drive for self-preservation was innate.

But now the dead man's brother and his entire gang would soon be hunting her in earnest.

The weight of it struck her then. Unbearably heavy, like a thousand bricks pressed against her chest. Her loneliness threatened to overwhelm her. The impossibility of the task that lay before her.

Would she live to see another day? Was she about to lose everything that she loved?

She could still run. She still could.

She leaned over and vomited.

Shaking, she wiped her mouth with the back of her hand.

A flash of silver streaked through the trees on her right. A twig cracked on her left. Adrenaline thrummed through her veins. Swiftly, she reached for the hunting rifle, unslinging it.

Ten yards away, a great white wolf stepped between two trees. A black wolf glided beside the white one, a shadow among shadows.

Raven released a tense breath. Relief flooded every cell of her body. Wetness blurred her eyes. She choked back the flood of tears that threatened to overwhelm her. This was no time to lose it.

"You came back for me," she whispered. "You came back."

Luna lurked at the tree line, but Shadow trotted right up to her. The black wolf brushed his powerful shoulder against hers, nearly knocking her off the log. She took several steadying breaths and glanced at Shadow.

His ears pricked. His tail swished slowly, expectantly.

She managed a grim smile. "You have no idea how happy I am to see you."

Gradually, the mind-numbing terror faded. Her heart rate slowed. Now that the wolves were here, she felt immeasurably better.

She had never been afraid of the dark or of these woods. But tonight, surrounded by predators of all kinds, the last thing she wanted to be was alone.

Would the wolves stay with her? She almost didn't dare to hope. She wasn't sure she could bear the profound disappointment if they left her again. She felt stronger in their presence. Braver.

Raven unzipped one of the outside compartments of her pack and withdrew three strips of dried venison. She gnawed on a strip herself and tossed a piece to the wolves. Shadow sniffed at the venison, unconvinced that this strange object was food.

She took a swallow from her water bottle and wiped her mouth. "It's good, I promise."

Shadow licked it, gave a little whine, then gulped it down. Luna sniffed hers daintily and lifted her nose in disdain. Shadow happily ate her share.

A wave of dizziness washed over her. Her eyes were gritty. She could barely stand, she was so exhausted. The adrenaline from the fight was wearing off.

She was incredibly weary. Her eyes burned. She couldn't remember the last time she'd slept. Not last night, and not the night before, either.

Luna and Shadow regarded her, their heads tilted, ears pricked as if asking, *What now?*

"Rest," she said, climbing to her feet. "I need to get some rest. I don't know yet what comes next, but I have to get some sleep. Can you stay here with me? Will you warn me if someone or something gets close?"

The wolves just looked at her.

"Well, good night then."

Exhausted, she crawled into the lean-to on her hands and knees, dragging the pack and rifle behind her. Quickly, she swept handfuls of leaves over the ground and tossed aside several twigs and rocks. She was too tired to do much else.

Night sounds filled the air: crackling branches, the hoot of an owl, the raspy song of crickets and cicadas. With the pack as a pillow and the rifle clutched in both hands, she closed her eyes and tried not to dream of blood and death.

Chapter Twenty-Seven

A low growl woke Raven from a dead sleep.

Instantly wide awake, she tightened her grip on the rifle, staying still and quiet, ears straining. At first, she heard nothing. Blearily, she blinked to clear her vision. The predawn light was dim and gray, but she could make out the thick branches above her, the brown leaves beneath her, and the details of her backpack.

Cautiously, she peeked her head out of the lean-to, pushing aside a pile of dead leaves. She crawled out and stood. Her muscles ached. Her teeth felt furry, her tongue thick and gunky. She rubbed her gritty eyes.

At the edge of the small clearing, both wolves stood side by side, facing the trees to the west. Shadow's ears flattened. Luna growled low in her throat.

Raven froze, her hands going to the rifle.

Simultaneously, both wolves whirled and bolted into the forest.

She shivered against the chilly morning air. She was alone again. They would come back. They'd found her once. They could do it again.

Something rustled behind her.

She spun, raising the rifle, heart clenched. "Shadow?"

The hairs on Raven's arms lifted, her scalp prickling. Something —or someone—was close. She could feel it.

Then she heard them. The distant sound of something large crashing awkwardly through the underbrush. Distinctly human noises reached her. Grunting and swearing. A gunshot went off. Then another.

The Headhunters.

They must have found Rex's body. And now they were coming for her.

Returning to the lean-to, she seized her pack and shouldered it, then found a pine branch and attempted to smooth the ground around the lean-to and the fire pit. Most of the ground was covered in a film of fallen leaves, obscuring her footprints. That was good.

She headed deeper into the forest. Last night, it had been too dark to find a better hiding spot. Heart in her throat, she scanned the forest, looking for a place to disappear.

The Headhunters blundered through the woods somewhere behind her. They were big and clumsy in the forest. They were also strong, angry, and well-armed. They were drawing closer.

Near the roots of a fallen tree, a sliver of space gapped between trunk and earth, no taller than a foot. A huge, dense hydrangea bush nearly covered it completely. It would have to be good enough.

She shoved her pack into a space between the roots and covered it with handfuls of dead leaves, then scrambled over the side of the log and burrowed in the deep underbrush growing along its flank.

She managed to jam most of her body beneath the log. The rifle butt jammed against her shoulder. The barrel dug into her thigh. Reaching up, she bent several low branches of an oak leaf hydrangea, covering herself with its reddish-purple leaves.

The gnarled roots of the tree rose in pale and tangled knots above her. A centipede crawled beneath the sleeve of her jacket onto her bare arm. Something else crawled along her ankle. She stilled, inhaling the decaying scent of dead leaves, the sharp scent of pine.

If the Headhunters took the deer path that meandered nearby, they would bypass the fallen log and her childhood fort. She prayed fervently that they would walk right past her.

Nearby, another twig cracked. A bush rustled. Something large moved close to her location. Her pulse roared in her ears. She steadied her breathing, desperate to quiet her pounding heart. It felt like it would pound right out of her chest.

For several minutes, the forest seemed still and quiet. Small creatures rustled through the underbrush. The wind whispered through the pines as the sun rose and the deep darkness lightened to shades of gray.

More noises broke through the stillness. Footsteps approached. Raven held her breath. She closed her eyes, as if they couldn't see her if she couldn't see them.

Then the Headhunters were upon her. They crashed into the small clearing, breathing hard and cursing.

"You find anything, Dekker?" Vaughn asked.

"Found some footprints a ways back," Dekker said, his voice so close she strained not to flinch. "If it hadn't been so dark and damn foggy, I could have tracked her more easily."

"We'll find her," Scorpio said. "She can't have gone far."

Dekker's voice sparked with raw fury. "No one touches her but me."

"Don't worry," Vaughn said. "You'll avenge your brother. I'll make sure of it."

"You positive you don't have any idea which way she went?" Scorpio asked gruffly.

She could hear him stomping around the underbrush a few yards from where she hid. Heavy footfalls, angry grunting steps.

"Like I told you," Damien said. "As soon as I went to help Rex, she took off. I didn't see anything. It was dark and foggy as hell. You know that as well as I do." He sounded frustrated and defensive.

Raven's heart squeezed. Damien was putting himself on the line for her. How long would they believe him? How much danger was he really in?

"I found blood on a leaf forty yards back." Dekker's voice was low and furious, sharp-edged as a knife. "My brother's blood."

"We'll keep looking," Vaughn said. "We won't stop until we have her."

"What about the zoo animals?" said a voice she didn't recognize. "She released them all."

"Scorpio already got one of the foxes," Vaughn said. "We want these pelts. We need to get them now, before they scatter. It's hunting season, boys."

"And the tiger?" Damien asked, a hint of unease in his tone. "The bears?"

Vaughn snorted in derision. "We have semi-automatic weapons. They're stupid caged beasts trained to bask on fake rocks all day. It'll be like shooting fish in a barrel. Only a hell of a lot more fun."

"Just get me that damn girl," Dekker said.

"You're angry," Vaughn said. "You want blood for Rex. He was one of us. I swear to you, he will not go unavenged. I'll give you that blood! We'll bathe this rotten forest in blood. Every single beast, we bring it down. For Rex!"

Several Headhunters growled their agreement.

"Find the girl," Dekker ordered. "Kill everything that moves."

Raven waited, hardly breathing, every muscle tensed. Eventually, Headhunters broke off and headed deeper into the woods to hunt.

Her stomach roiled. Outrage boiled through her veins at the thought of Shadow and Luna being hunted like rats. And Zephyr, Vlad, Suki, and the rest.

Vaughn was right. The sanctuary's animals had spent most of their lives in captivity. They didn't know to fear humans. Kodiak would lumber right up to their outstretched guns if they offered him food. So would Loki and the foxes. Even grumpy Electra was a sucker for a treat.

She hadn't freed the animals so the Headhunters could hunt them down and brutalize them. She wouldn't. She couldn't. Besides, if she were infected, death was coming for her anyway. She wasn't going to take it lying down. No way in hell.

She rose to her feet, wincing as her muscles ached in protest. She tightened her grip on the rifle. A steely determination settled in her gut. The fear was there, but so was an unwavering sense of purpose, of conviction. She knew what she had to do.

The Headhunters weren't the only human predators in these woods.

Raven was a hunter, too.

CHAPTER TWENTY-EIGHT

Raven went on the hunt.

The chilly air stung her exposed cheeks. Her hands were red and chapped. She shivered as she caked her face and hands with dirt and smeared the bottom of her boots with red clay and mashed leaves and twigs into the mud to mar her footprints.

She strapped the rifle across her chest with the sling, adjusted her pouch of ammunition, and rechecked the tranq gun, still tucked into her waistband. The second tranquilizer gun was tucked into her backpack. She kept the whittling knife folded in her pocket.

While she worked, she remained alert to the sounds of the woods, to the intruders who had so savagely invaded her sanctuary.

Every few minutes, gunshots shattered the early morning air. The Headhunters were loud. They stumbled and thrashed through the underbrush. The men shouted to each other through the trees, followed by the *rat-a-tat* of semi-automatic weapons.

If they were pursuing wild creatures, they would never have found them. But the captive animals were confused, anxious, and frightened. The alien scents and strange sounds were alarming and disorienting.

They wandered through a foreign land they no longer recalled, frantically searching for a familiar sense of safety that eluded them.

One by one, the Headhunters began to pick them off.

The retort of another rifle cracked. Raven cringed. Another shot. Another animal she loved was being chased down. With every boom and crack of a gun, her heart broke a little more.

This wasn't hunting.

It was barbaric. It was a massacre.

It needed to stop.

Raven placed the hood of the jacket over her head. With the black jacket and hood, with her dark-colored pants and dirt-smeared skin, she hoped she would fade into the shadows, just like the black wolf.

She knew this forest like the back of her hand, knew the ravines and meadows and streams of the Piedmont Wildlife Refuge, 35,000 acres of woods and hills and trails.

The Headhunters didn't.

With a deep breath, she set off in the direction of the nearest gunshots. Moving quietly, darting from tree to tree to shield herself, she made her way westward, heading in the direction of the Ocmulgee River, which ran parallel to the wildlife sanctuary, about a mile west of the rear gates of the zoo.

Shuffling footsteps and a muffled curse alerted her to a nearby threat. Raven took cover behind the thick trunk of a poplar, and eased cautiously around the trunk. Brilliant yellow leaves cascaded over her head.

She glimpsed a human shape about thirty yards to the south. A man knelt with his back to her. He wore a puffy silver jacket and a red baseball cap. His rifle was up, and he peered through his scope at something up in the trees to his left.

The branches of an elm tree shook. A handful of orange-yellow leaves fluttered to the forest floor. A flash of inky fur caught her attention.

It was Newton, one of the bonobos. He perched on a lower branch about twenty feet off the ground. He seemed to be alone, intent on seizing leaves and tearing them to shreds.

The Headhunter was searching for a decent angle before he fired.

Raven steadied herself against the poplar tree, widened her stance, fit the stock against her shoulder, and found the target in her sight. She aimed at the back of the man's red baseball cap.

Time seemed to slow. She breathed in, breathed out. She'd killed a man already tonight. Some soul-deep, bone-weary part of herself dreaded doing it again. But she couldn't allow this killing spree to continue.

She had the tranq gun, but this was a Headhunter. He was a bad guy.

Raven steeled herself. Her frantic heartbeat calmed as she lowered the barrel slightly. She inhaled, exhaled, and squeezed the trigger. A loud boom sounded. The round struck the Headhunter in his right shoulder.

The man shrieked in shock and pain. He dropped his gun. Twisting, he clutched at his shoulder, screaming. He fell to his knees.

Alarmed, Newton screeched. He scooted up the tree limb and leaped to another tree, scampered along a branch, and disappeared deeper into the woods.

Raven blew out a calming breath, aimed, and fired again. This time her round struck him lower, in the back. He dropped to the ground, screaming.

A male voice shouted to her left. Someone ran toward their position, footsteps thudding loud and frantic.

Lowering her rifle, Raven slunk back between the trees. As soon as she was out of earshot, she broke into a run to get a safe distance between herself and the fallen Headhunter.

Every few minutes, she paused to catch her breath, straining her ears to listen to the warnings of the forest surrounding her. A bluebird twittered overhead. The wind sighed through the softly swaying trees. Through the crisscrossed branches above her, patches of sky brightened in shades of grapefruit pink and burnt orange.

Raven slunk through the woods, a shadow among shadows. She found another Headhunter alone, his pants down, pissing against a tree trunk. He'd been loud, unused to the forest and its ways, and she'd had no problem discreetly following him until he'd lowered his gun—and his pants.

Sinking to her knees, she nestled the stock against her cheek, let out her breath, and fired. The round struck him in the left thigh. He moaned in pain, attempting to spin, but his feet tangled in his pants, and he collapsed.

She disappeared before he could find his weapon.

An hour later, she spotted Kodiak near the creek. The big black bear lumbered along the bank, snuffling huckleberry and elderberry bushes, searching for berries to quench his hunger.

She watched him for several minutes until she heard the inconspicuous noises of two Headhunters hot on Kodiak's trail. Warily, she circled back on the Headhunters and stalked them from behind as they stalked Kodiak.

Before either of them got off a shot, she dropped to one knee behind a wide stump for cover, aimed and fired several rounds in quick succession. Two found their mark. The first Headhunter collapsed with a bullet in his lower back. The second took a hit to the right side of his head.

They went down screaming. Neither would be shooting a gun again anytime soon. Without prompt and intensive medical intervention, they'd probably die.

Startled by the sudden screaming, Kodiak took off in the opposite direction.

Raven backed away swiftly and did the same.

More screams mingled with the shouts and jeers echoing through the trees. Confusion and fear were taking hold. Maybe the Headhunters would give up now.

To save their lives, all they had to do was leave.

She hadn't made it half a mile from the creek when a sound startled her. A few yards to her right, something large growled.

It was close, very close.

A shiver raced up her spine. Raven darted for the cover of the nearest tree. A small clearing lay ahead of her, a break in the trees where bunches of ferns grew in abundance.

The woods grew abruptly silent. The birds stopped singing.

A male voice broke the eerie quiet: "Stay back, now. No closer!"

Maintaining her cover behind the trunk of a massive oak tree, Raven cautiously peered around the corner. Her heart beat rapidly against her throat. Her palms were clammy.

In the center of the grove of ferns, one of the Headhunters stood with a rifle aimed at something she couldn't quite make out. In his thirties, he wore a khaki jacket, jeans, and work boots, and a floppy brown fishing hat over his short black hair. She recognized him—the one they called Gomez.

Three yards from him, crouched in the ferns at the base of a massive boulder, was a timber wolf. The wolf gave a menacing snarl. Its back was arched, hackles raised.

For a moment, Raven didn't recognize the wolf, so alien was the ferocious snarl. Meek Suki faced down the Headhunter with amber eyes blazing, fangs bared.

"Go on now! Get out of here!" Gomez's hands visibly shook. He was terrified. "I said scram!"

Before Raven had the time to get her own weapon up, he could have shot the wolf. Instead, he shifted his aim and fired wide.

The loud *boom* trembled the leaves. The round struck a tree somewhere off to the right.

Suki skittered to the side. Raven expected her to flee. She didn't. Instead, she crouched down low, ears flattened, and snarled louder.

Raven hesitated, her weapon raised but her finger on the trigger guard, not the trigger. Gomez wasn't aiming directly at Suki. He didn't want to shoot the wolf. He was attempting to scare her away instead.

Damien was right. They weren't all bloodthirsty killers.

The Headhunter fired again, another wide shot. Bark splintered several feet above Suki's head. Still, she refused to run. She gave a ferocious growl and crept closer to Gomez. The wolf was the aggressor, not the Headhunter.

Darkened blood matted the fur along Suki's jaw, mingled with a sickly yellowish saliva. It glistened from her fangs and dripped down her muzzle. It stained the white hairs on her chest.

Dread pooled in Raven's stomach. Something was off.

Wolves rarely attacked humans. They were wary, cautious creatures. If a human invaded a wolf's territory or went after one of the pack's pups, a wolf would defend its pack, but Suki hadn't been backed into a corner.

She could escape. She could turn and run. Why didn't she?

Raven stared at the wolf in bewildered horror. She'd never seen foamy, yellowed saliva like that.

Something was wrong with Suki.

The Headhunter seemed to come to the same conclusion. "Damn it!" Gomez swore. "You're infected."

Shock flared through Raven. Animals could carry the virus, too. And if they carried it, they could spread it.

But how could the wolf have gotten infected? Zachariah didn't go inside the enclosure. But her father had. Had he somehow passed the virus on to Suki in the days before he died?

With a vicious growl, Suki sprang at the Headhunter. He dodged and attempted to aim his rifle. The wolf hurtled toward him, jaws snapping. She darted swiftly to the side, only to fling herself at him from another angle. She dodged back and attacked again and again.

Gomez cursed. Abject fear contorted his features. He stumbled back, his rifle flailing wildly. Wherever he aimed, Suki moved quicker.

Then Suki was on him in a flash. It happened in a fraction of a second. The timber wolf pounced. Eighty pounds of fury and fangs struck Gomez in the chest.

He fell backward. The rifle was knocked from his hands. He threw his arms up to protect his face and throat.

Suki's jaws closed over his forearm.

Gomez howled in pain.

Wolf and man wrestled in a death-lock. Gomez punched at Suki's muzzle with his free hand. The wolf's powerful jaws sank deeper into his flesh. With a sickening snap, Suki's teeth pulverized bone, muscle, and tendons. Gomez shrieked in agony.

Raven shifted her aim between Gomez and Suki, searching for a good shot. There wasn't one. Man and wolf wrestled in the ferns.

Her finger massaged the trigger, but she didn't fire yet. Both man and wolf were dangerous. She didn't want to kill Suki, sick or not. And because Gomez had attempted to spare the timber wolf, she wasn't certain she wanted to kill him, either.

With his uninjured arm, Gomez fumbled frantically for the holster at his hip. He managed to reach his handgun. He yanked it out and jammed it against Suki's furred chest.

Before Raven could fire a shot, Gomez pulled the trigger. Once, twice, three times.

Suki never even whimpered. The wolf dropped on top of Gomez's chest like a sack of grain, instantly dead.

Chapter Twenty-Nine

"Gomez!" a Headhunter shouted. Several sets of footsteps pounded through the woods toward the clearing. The thrashing of heavy bodies tearing through underbrush filled the silent forest. "Where are you? What's wrong? Gomez! Answer, damn it!"

"I'm fine!" Gomez yelled. "I'm okay. I think, anyway."

Raven shrank back into the shadows, hiding deeper among the trees, ensuring she was well hidden. She lowered her rifle. Much as she wanted to attempt it, she couldn't take out several Headhunters at once. Her best ploy was to remain undetected.

As Raven peered between branches, Gomez shoved the dead wolf from atop his body and climbed weakly to his feet. With a pained shudder, he shrugged off his jacket and slung it over his injured arm, hiding the bite.

He stepped forward, so the bent, matted, blood-slick ferns lay behind him, along with Suki's corpse.

Two Headhunters emerged into the clearing. The first one was Cobb. The burly man gripped a semi-automatic in both hands. "Did it get you?"

"Nah, man," Gomez said shakily. "I'm good."

Raven recognized the second Headhunter, too. Scorpio, the one with the tattooed neck. He nudged Suki's body with his boot and gave a contemptuous snort. "It's infected. You're lucky. One bite is all it takes. Just like those damn infected feral dogs."

"I shot it before it got near me." Gomez leaned against the nearest tree, feigning nonchalance. The Headhunters didn't appear to notice the tremor in his legs or the faint, red stain seeping through his jacket. Raven saw it all.

Scorpio turned slowly, scanning the wood, his eyes glittering with a cunning intelligence. He was one of the dangerous ones.

"Good thing," he drawled. "Seeing as Diaz and Cooper both got themselves shot."

"That girl got them?" Gomez's face was growing pale. Sweat beaded his forehead. He swiped at his face with a surreptitious movement, knocking his brown fishing hat askew. "That little girl really got them?"

Cobb nodded. "Diaz is dead. Cooper might as well be. Martin took one to the shoulder, and O'Reilly got nailed just below his ass."

"Their own stupidity, if you ask me. Only pansy-ass wusses let a little girl get the best of 'em." Scorpio turned his back on the woods. He stood less than five yards from Raven's hidden location. "Dekker be damned. If I find her first, I'll kill her myself."

"To hell with Dekker." Cobb slapped at a mosquito and cursed. "And to hell with that damn girl. Enough of those damned woods! I'm starving. There's plenty of loot back at the zoo, and we've barely enjoyed a thing. Dekker wants this chick so bad? Let him freeze his balls off out here. I'm out."

"I'm with you," Scorpio said. "I could eat one of those monkeys raw right about now. Or hell, this damn wolf."

"Vaughn ordered everyone back to the zoo," Cobb said. "For food and to bandage up the idiots who got themselves shot. And to bury Diaz."

Cobb and Scorpio headed for the perimeter of the clearing. Scorpio paused over the wolf's body. He glanced at Gomez. "You gonna pitch a tent out here or what?"

"Nah—I'll stay out a bit longer." Gomez lifted his gun with a trembling hand. "Found some more tracks. Gonna bag me that lynx."

"Suit yourself," Cobb said. "No one's saving grub for you."

Gomez nodded shakily. "I'm good."

Scorpio gestured at Suki's body. "I'm claiming this one. It'll make a damn fine pelt."

"It's yours," Gomez said, though Raven doubted he had a choice. If Scorpio wanted something, he seemed the type to take it.

Scorpio bent, hefted the limp body of the wolf, and slung the corpse over his shoulders. Cobb followed at his heels. Gomez watched the Headhunters depart with glazed eyes. Sweat soaked his hairline. His face was waxen.

Once his companions were out of sight, Gomez sank to the ground. His breath came in loud pants. Still crouched within the trees, Raven watched as he unwrapped his bloody jacket and examined his arm.

Fresh blood oozed from several ugly gashes across his forearm. Suki's jaws had torn his flesh to shreds.

Gomez bowed his head. He let out a raw, guttural sob.

Raven's fingers tightened on the rifle, but she didn't lift it. *One bite is all it takes*, Cobb had said. Gomez must be infected, now. He was a dead man walking, and he knew it.

The Hydra Virus could spread between animals and humans. It affected animals differently, making them more aggressive, like rabies. An image of Zachariah seizing her arm flashed through her mind. At the end stages, humans became combative and threatening, too.

Would it happen to her, too? It had been four days since she'd been exposed. There was a disconcerting scratch in the back of her throat, though she'd had far too little to drink, and thirst made her parched. She'd coughed a few times. With her free hand, she felt her forehead. Her skin was warm, but not hot. No fever had set in. Yet.

The Headhunters were gathering their wounded and regrouping at the lodge. They'd be back on the hunt soon.

For now, she had a short reprieve. She needed a place to rest and regroup, to make her next move, whatever that might be, whether it was time to run or to fight again.

Gomez remained in the clearing, stained with blood and quietly sobbing. She considered shooting him but decided to save her ammunition instead. He still held his pistol in his lap. Perhaps he'd take care of things himself.

Stealthily, Raven rose and backed away. Her stomach roiled. She was sick and tired of everything, of disease and death and violence. Sick of the constant fear, of the grief always hot on her heels, ready to sink claws of despair into her the moment she stopped running.

The unfairness of it all made her want to destroy something. Suki had been meek and gentle. She hadn't deserved that kind of death. She should have lived.

The late afternoon sun was slanting into evening as she entered a thick copse of birch trees. The back of her neck prickled. A sigh in the wind, a flicker in the shadows. Instinct made her pause and look down.

Sunken into the dirt, surrounded by scattered leaves, was a single, perfect paw print. A pad and four toes, spanning over five inches wide.

Only one animal could make that large, distinctive mark.

The tiger.

CHAPTER THIRTY

As the sun sank in the sky, Raven knew she needed shelter. Her throat burned with thirst. Though she took judicious sips of water, her water bottle was running low. She could filter drinking water with the purification tablets in her pack and refill her water bottle, which was less than half full, but the river was a few miles away.

She wasn't sure what to do next. Run or keep fighting? She'd done some damage. Was it enough? She wasn't sure.

Right now, she had to figure out how to survive the night.

Her legs could barely move. A great weariness overtook her. Her steps became sloppy, breaking twigs and bending leaves with every step, leaving a trail for the Headhunters to follow.

It would be night soon enough. She had her tarp, rope, and sleeping bag in her backpack. She could bed down anywhere. Still, the thought of Vlad close by, prowling amongst the shadows, made her think twice about napping on the ground.

Maybe a tree? Tigers could climb, but they didn't particularly like to do so. A tree was probably her safest bet.

She had a rope. She could find a large oak with a thick branch twenty-five feet off the ground. She could tie herself to the branch to keep from falling and breaking her neck in her sleep. It would keep her safe from the Headhunters, also. Safer, anyway.

There was no such thing as safety.

Ten minutes later, she'd found a suitable oak tree with low, thick branches she could easily climb. She shrugged off her pack, unzipped it, and dug around for her coiled rope.

The sensation of being watched raised the hairs on the back of her neck.

Her pulse raced. Outwardly, she remained calm. Keeping her movements steady, she slowly reached for the rifle lying beside her backpack. With clammy hands, she seized the rifle, stood, and spun around to face a new threat.

The white wolf watched her. The wolf stood ten feet away, in between two tall pine trees. Raven hadn't heard her silent approach. The wolf moved as a ghost, drifting like the otherworldly fog from last night.

Raven lowered the gun and dropped to her knees on the leaf-strewn ground. Instinctively, she bowed her head. It made her feel a bit ridiculous. She didn't care. Overwhelming relief flooded her entire body.

She took a breath and raised her head. "I can't tell you how happy I am to see you, Luna."

The wolf's lips pulled back. Just enough to show a sliver of teeth. She pivoted and trotted away. She glided between a gnarled pine tree and a thicket of huckleberry bushes.

Before she slipped out of sight, she paused, looking back over her shoulder. Her yellow eyes stared at Raven.

An invitation. She wanted Raven to follow her.

Raven rose to her feet. She zipped and re-shouldered her pack, then grabbed her rifle. Exhausted as she was, she didn't want to be alone. She would go wherever the wolves wanted to take her. "Please don't go far, or my feet will fall off."

The sun sank behind the trees. As dusk fell, she trailed the wolf, winding through dense thickets of mountain laurel and sumac, traipsing through copses of yellowwood, maple, and white oak trees.

Luna disappeared often, her loping gait too swift for Raven to keep up. When she was lost, Raven would stop and wait. Within a few minutes, Luna reappeared. Her jowls pulled back, not in a snarl necessarily, but perhaps an irritated grimace, her wolfish expression like a mother irked at her troublesome, too-slow children.

"I'm trying, I promise." Her legs ached. Her eyes burned. Exhaustion pressed down on her like a thousand bricks. Still, she followed the wolf.

It was nearly dark by the time Luna led her up a steep hill, then around several moss-covered boulders the size of trucks. Eventually, the wolf paused before a massive rock jutting at least twenty feet high and thirty feet across. At its base opened a narrow, dark crevice about five feet wide and three feet tall.

The wolf ducked inside the crevice and disappeared. The crevice appeared to be a cave.

A series of yips and whines echoed from inside the cave. A moment later, the large black wolf emerged. Shadow trotted up to Raven and pushed his shoulder against her hip, like a greeting, or a sign of grudging affection, perhaps.

"Hello to you, too." She dared to stretch out her fingers. Gently, ever so gently, her fingertips grazed the ruff of his neck.

The wolf didn't growl or react at all.

Growing bolder, she cautiously stroked the fur along his spine. Though his guard hairs were coarse, the thick black fur underneath was incredibly soft.

Shadow circled her. He rubbed against her thighs as she petted him. He was so powerful that when he bumped her, he nearly knocked her off her feet.

After a few minutes of this, he abruptly departed. He trotted to the cave entrance and slipped inside.

For a long moment, Raven stood outside the cave, conflicted. In the wild, adult wolves didn't use dens unless they had pups. Wolf packs preferred to sleep outside beneath the stars.

Was it possible they had chosen this cave for her? Did they want her to come inside with them? Was that why they'd invited her here?

If she dared to invade such a tight, intimate space, and the wolves didn't accept her presence, it might trigger a defensive attack.

She had two options: find another tree and spend an exhausted, restless few hours feeling cold and incredibly uncomfortable, or she could accept the invitation of these strange, wild creatures and willingly enter a wolves' den.

Raven chose the wolves.

Removing her pack, she retrieved some of her beef jerky and a bag of nuts, then hid the pack behind a nearby boulder. Though her throat felt dry as a desert, she took only a few swallows from her water bottle. She needed to conserve what remained and find a fresh water source first thing tomorrow.

Using her whittling knife, she cut several slender branches from a nearby pine tree to brush the dirt near the cave of her footprints and then covered the pack.

She crept to the crevice, careful to keep her balance on the sharp edges of the rocky shelf. Taking a breath, steeling herself, she dropped to her hands and knees.

She crawled inside the cave, dragging the rifle with her in one hand, the flashlight in the other. Dense darkness washed over her. The smell of earth, pine, and rotting leaves filled her nostrils.

Once inside, she flicked on the flashlight and shone it across the walls. The cave was around six feet across and four feet high. At the back, it narrowed into a small tunnel that led who knew where.

On the left, Shadow and Luna lay tangled in a furry pile. Shadow licked Luna's muzzle while she nuzzled her head against his neck. The wolves lifted their heads as she entered.

Luna yawned, showing her gleaming white teeth, as if to remind Raven who was in charge.

Her heart thudded in her chest. "Trust me, I know."

They did not appear threatening. Still, to be in close quarters with such powerful, lethal creatures was disconcerting.

Raven curled up on the rocky ground on the far-right side of the cave to give the wolves their space. She lay facing the entrance, the rifle next to her.

The cold hardness of the rock seeped through her clothes. Though the dank air within the cave was significantly warmer than it was outside, it was still frigid. Her breath expelled in white clouds. She shivered.

Feeling cold was a good thing, wasn't it? She pressed the back of her hand to her forehead. Still no fever. But her throat was dry and hurt when she swallowed. She was so tired. Every muscle hurt. Was that a symptom of the Hydra Virus? She couldn't remember. She was too tired to think about anything.

Which was a good thing. Her eyes stung with a fountain of unshed tears. Grief was always there, crouched deep inside her. Her heart was a mangled wreck. Zachariah was gone. Her father, dead. Everything she loved, in peril. She was being hunted, forced to take shelter with huge furry predators who could devour her if they so wished.

No use thinking about any of that now. She could worry and mourn in the morning, if she lived through the night. And if she did live, she needed a plan.

After a few hours of sleep, she could think clearly enough to figure something out. For now, she desperately needed sleep.

Raven flicked off the flashlight to conserve the battery. She fought to keep her eyes open, determined to remain alert.

While she wasn't afraid of the wolves—well, maybe a little—Vlad was still out there. So were the Headhunters. She couldn't afford to let her guard down.

Despite her best efforts, her eyelids grew heavier and heavier. She breathed in the sweetly dank scent of wolf and watched the narrow sliver of daylight beyond the cave entrance blur and fade to darkness.

CHAPTER THIRTY-ONE

Raven awoke with a start.

For an instant, she had no idea where she was or why. Complete darkness enveloped her. Her limbs were stiff. Her muscles ached. The ground beneath her was hard and cold.

Something huge, hot, and hairy pressed against her right side. Something equally warm and incredibly heavy lay across her legs.

Bewildered, her heart rate spiked. She reached tentative fingers into the dark. Her palm skimmed a dense pelt of fur. Beneath the fur, the rise and fall of steady breathing.

She blinked rapidly, her eyes adjusting to the darkness. The palest hint of starlight trickled in from the cave entrance.

Gradually, she made out Luna's pale silvery shape sleeping beside her. The dark form of Shadow sprawled across her shins. His head was lowered, his muzzle resting on his forelegs.

His eyes gleamed faintly. He was awake, keeping watch. Protecting Raven and Luna. Protecting his pack.

Powerful emotions surged in her chest. Astonishment. Wonder. A deep, incredible awe. It was extraordinary. These feral creatures. Accepting her as one of their own.

The world was unbearably broken. This was true. The world also held a profound and fragile beauty. An unknowable magic, the unexpected and unexplainable.

Little by little, she became aware of another feeling expanding within her ribcage: a deep sense of contentment. Even amid the grief and the fear and the horror. In that moment, she felt at peace.

She was somehow a part of the wolves, and they were a part of her. Her soul connected to the universe, connected to the great whirling galaxy of stars and planets and suns, to God, to everything.

It was like nothing she'd ever felt.

It was belonging. It was comfort. It was connection.

Memories flooded her mind. The times she and her father had spent together: deep in the forest, crouched in a blind, waiting to spot a deer; shoveling bonobo dung and cracking poop jokes; lugging great hunks of meat to the wolves; field dressing a snared rabbit.

In all those years, he had never hugged her. He'd never put his hand on her shoulder in approval or tugged affectionately on her hair. He had never once said, "I love you."

Before her mother left, she used to tell Raven, "You know he loves you."

That was not true, though. Raven hadn't known. And neither had her mother, drowning in her unhappiness and misery until it drove her to despair. Until, finally, it drove her to abandon her daughter, too.

Raven remembered that day. The day she wished she could erase, take back, that she'd buried so deep, she hoped the guilt could never hurt her. It could, though. It could and it did.

The image flared in her mind, unbidden. Her mother, sitting at the kitchen table, clutching a cup of coffee, the light streaming from the window haloing her dark hair. And her words: "Do you want to come with me?"

While her heart cried, *Please, don't leave me*, Raven had answered with her anger and resentment instead. "I hate you!" she'd yelled. "Go ahead and leave. We don't want you anyway. Leave and don't ever come back!"

That day, something crucial had fractured inside her mother. A critical, irreparable fault line. Raven had wished she could take it back, but her stubbornness hadn't let her.

In that moment, her anger obliterated her love.

She'd unleashed her words like a weapon. She'd intended to hurt, to wound, just like she was hurting. Only now did Raven understand how her mother, already unloved by her husband, hadn't been strong enough to cope with another bitter rejection, not from her daughter.

Right or wrong, that's how it happened.

The next day, while Raven was at school and her father was busy fixing a broken fence post in the zebra's enclosure, her mother had packed her meager belongings in a single suitcase, called a cab, and disappeared.

Raven had come home to an empty lodge. A paper note was folded on her pillow with Raven's name printed in her mother's dainty handwriting.

Her mother needed to leave before this place killed her. She had no choice, she wrote over and over. The letter was full of empty apologies, line after line of *I'm sorry, I'm sorry, I'm sorry.* The ink was blurred with splotches that might have been tears.

When her father returned that evening, sweating and dirty, Raven handed him the letter. His mouth thinned to a grim bloodless slash. He crumpled the letter in his fist and tossed it into the nearest trash can.

"Your mother is weak," he said.

"What are we going to do?" Raven asked, fighting back a sob. A gaping hole had opened up inside her, and she was drowning in it. She didn't know how to climb out or how to ask her father to pull her up. She didn't have the language.

Her father must have known that his young daughter would be devastated. How could he not have seen that she was drowning right in front of him?

He hadn't pulled her into his arms. He hadn't hugged her. He hadn't attempted to comfort her.

His expression hardened. "It's best you learn this lesson early, I suppose. There's only one person you can depend on. Yourself."

As if to hammer home his point, he'd left her in the lodge by herself. He'd escaped to the comfort and distraction of his wolves. He'd abandoned her as surely as her mother had, leaving her to deal with her overwhelming grief completely alone.

Her father never brought up her mother again. One moment, she was there. The next moment, she wasn't. They went on without her. End of story.

Over the months that followed, a few letters came in the mail, a few packages. Raven kept them in her room, hidden in her closet. She knew he didn't want to see them. Raven never spoke of her mother aloud again, either.

The truth was, she knew that it was her fault. Not that her mother had chosen to leave, but that her mother had left without her. That she never came back for Raven.

Because Raven had told her not to bother. Raven had told her to go. And so, she did.

Raven buried the words she should've said somewhere deep inside her. She buried a lot of things. Thoughts she didn't want to think. Feelings she didn't want to feel. Tears she couldn't bear to cry.

She learned to stop pining for what she couldn't have. She learned to stop dreaming, to stop wishing, to stop wanting her family back. To stop feeling anything that might hurt her.

Now, lying on the rocky floor of a cave, nestled among wolves three times her size, she breathed in their raw animal scent while their large furred bodies kept her warm—warm and safe and wanted.

Despite everything, she found herself wanting this and all it entailed, longing for this moment to never end.

Because she understood. She knew the magnitude of this development, what it signified for her, and for them.

The wolves had made her their pack.

They'd made her family.

CHAPTER THIRTY-TWO

Raven woke before dawn. The black wolf stood tall over her. He bent his head and nudged her neck with his cool, wet nose.

Luna stood by the cave entrance, nearly blocking the gray pre-dawn light with her enormous form. Her tail swished with impatience.

The wolves seemed to know it was time to get up and do something. She just had to figure out what that was—and do it.

Her stomach rumbled. She had to go to the bathroom. Her mouth was dry and gritty with thirst, her teeth fuzzy. With a groan, she rolled onto her stomach and crawled out of the cave.

The charcoal sky loomed over the black outline of the trees. Dark shadows cloaked the land, dew clinging to the leaves.

Clambering over several rocks, she found a spot to relieve herself. She returned to the mouth of the cave, removed the pine boughs, dug out her backpack, and tore open a self-heating chicken-flavored meal packet.

The wolves watched her with interest. Adult wolves ate five to fourteen pounds of meat per day on average, though in the wild, sometimes twelve days or more could pass between feedings.

Though they were incredibly intelligent and lethal, a wolf's typical hunt was successful less than ten percent of the time. They survived on a feast-or-famine diet.

Shadow and Luna could last a few days without a meal. Still, she threw them several strips of dried venison. Shadow gulped down his share with an eager wave of his tail. Luna growled grumpily, but she ate them, if begrudgingly, as if she disliked owing Raven a favor.

Raven had successfully driven the Headhunters from the woods for a while, giving the animals a chance to flee further from the zoo. She'd killed one Headhunter and injured three others. Gomez wasn't a threat anymore, either.

That was five fewer Headhunters.

Her luck would run out eventually. The Headhunters would be back, and in larger numbers. They wouldn't leave until they got the blood they sought.

Raven had done what she could for the animals. She had Shadow and Luna at her side. It was time to run.

Time to head north for the cabin. She'd have supplies, water, and food. Solitude and safety.

She could stay there for months, years, even longer. She could fish, hunt deer, and snare small game. She had the map. She could get there.

The cabin would be her salvation.

It had to be.

"This time, you follow me," Raven instructed the wolves.

She had no idea if they would obey her. They were an alpha pair. They were the leaders, not followers. She hated the thought of the wolves leaving her again. It threatened to crack something deep inside her.

She didn't want to do this alone.

After eating and checking her compass, she shouldered her pack and retrieved her rifle. The air was brisk, the temperature in the low forties. It would be a chilly, sunny day.

Dawn rose over the trees. Shards of golden light pierced the canopy and gilded the forest floor. The wolves ran ahead and behind her, appearing and disappearing regularly.

When they entered the tree line, the leaf canopy blotted out much of the light. The air around her grew darker, colder. Raven lifted her hood and drew her coat tighter around herself.

Her scalp prickled. She felt rather than saw pairs of eyes peering at her from the shadows. She half-expected five hundred pounds of muscle, claws, and fangs to pounce at any moment.

Vlad was somewhere close. She could feel his menacing presence.

Her heart jolted at every rustle in the brush, every cracking twig. She strained her ears, listening for the rustling of the trees, the scrabble of squirrels, the chirp of a bird or fluff of its wings.

A loud cawing drew her attention. She gazed up at a patch of sky through the trees, shielding her face with her hand. A dozen crows soared in low circles to the northwest, the direction they were headed.

In the wild, crows would follow a tiger the same way ravens followed wolves. It significantly upped the crows' odds of getting fed, shifting from *if* to *when*.

Ten minutes later, she found the first tracks.

Pausing, Raven knelt on the ground. Crisp brown leaves crackled beneath her knees. She brushed away crumbling leaves, clumps of pine needles, and a spider's web.

It was the same deep imprint as before. The thick palmar pad, four smaller digit pads fanned around the larger print.

She studied the ground. More tracks. The closely spaced indentations indicated a slow, sedate pace. The tiger was taking a stroll, or perhaps stalking something—or someone.

How long ago had Vlad made these tracks? Hours? Minutes?

Despite the impressive size and the rich russet and black stripes of its fur, a tiger could make itself quite invisible when it so desired. Tigers moved in absolute silence. They cloaked themselves in shadows.

Vlad would sense her long before she laid eyes on him.

She wouldn't see him until he wanted to be seen. Until it was too late.

He might have doubled back from these tracks and could be tracking her even now. Tigers were ambush hunters, masters of stealth and surprise.

Her heartbeat quickened. Her palms went damp. Anxiety hummed through her.

If Vlad was stalking her, she needed to know. She needed to follow the tracks for a while to see where they headed, whether they doubled back, whether a tiger was perhaps lying in wait for her even now.

Her father had taught her basic tracking skills. Hopefully, it would be enough. Head bent, alert to every sound, she traced the tiger tracks through clusters of yellowwood, beech, and white ash trees along the base of a steep slope to her right.

The forest was alive with brilliant fall colors. Golden yellow spice bushes and crimson sumac grew everywhere.

After several hundred feet, the tracks changed abruptly. Ahead of her, the dense forest broke into a clearing about forty feet wide and twice as deep. Vivid green ferns swished in the breeze.

Just before the clearing, at the base of two poplar trees, she spotted something odd. Cautiously, she approached. Beneath the tree, the underbrush was matted down like a heavy log had smashed the long grasses. A log, or a massive predator.

Vlad had been here. The tiger had lain in wait for something.

Her gut tightened. She paused, hesitating.

Wild tigers were nocturnal hunters, but Vlad was a captive tiger. Having just escaped said captivity, typical tiger behavior would likely not apply.

Plus, if she accidentally invaded the territory of his kill, he'd be more inclined to attack.

Vlad was capable of anything, at any time, against anyone.

Her pack felt like it weighed a thousand pounds against her spine. Cold tingled in her fingers. She felt exposed, vulnerable. She wanted to call the wolves to her, but making a sound was a dangerous and stupid thing to do.

Raven scanned the clearing again, searching for any sign of imminent danger. Her gaze snagged on something several feet into the clearing. A mountain laurel bush. Red droplets stained a clutch of green leaves.

Fresh blood.

CHAPTER THIRTY-THREE

Each droplet of blood was perfectly shaped. Not a smudge or a smear. Like beads of water, only thick and crimson.

More bloody droplets formed a grisly trail behind the bush and kept going.

Raven stared at the blood. Her breath caught in her throat. Her brain screamed at her to run. She didn't run.

When she was ten years old, Zachariah had told her that it took less than a hundred pounds of pressure to crush a man's windpipe. It took five pounds of pressure to block the carotid artery. A tiger's jaws exerted a thousand pounds of pressure per square inch.

Humans were soft-skinned and thin-boned, as easy to break as snapping a twig.

She'd never forgotten it.

The trail of blood led to a spot a few yards beyond an aspen tree. On high alert, the rifle gripped in her hands, Raven crept closer, stepping softly among the ferns.

The stench of blood and death grew stronger. Gradually, the gruesome scene revealed itself.

Long red streaks in the trampled ferns and churned-up dirt. An empty shoe, turned on its side. A set of keys, glinting between two tree roots. A bloodied piece of khaki fabric that may have once been a shirt or pair of pants.

Her gaze followed the blood-soaked drag marks. Thirty yards into the clearing lay a wide circle of horror. A single arm, without a hand or shoulder attached. Bones, gnawed white. Blood drenched the ground in a ten-foot radius. So much blood.

Her belly heaved. Her guts churned. She felt sick, flushed and dizzy. Horror, shock, and revulsion flooded her senses.

Aghast, she turned abruptly and retched into the bushes. Retreating a step, she wiped her mouth with the back of her hand. She was shaking, trembling all over.

Something else caught her eye. A semi-automatic rifle lay in the center of the bloodied circle. Blood stained the stock, the pistol grip, the barrel. It hadn't helped the Headhunter.

Instinctively, she tightened her grip on her rifle. As if that could save her.

A floppy brown fishing hat lay less than a yard from the semi-automatic. She stared at the hat until her eyes blurred. Acid burned the back of her throat. It was the only recognizable thing left of Gomez.

He hadn't returned to the lodge with the rest. He'd stayed out in the woods, unaware that he was being hunted until it was too late.

Perhaps some part of him wanted to die quickly. He was doomed, the Hydra Virus already ravaging his body. His death might have been quick, but it certainly hadn't been painless, or free of terror.

Gomez was a Headhunter. Still, he'd shown mercy to Suki. She couldn't help the rush of pity at his fate.

Raven took a step back, and then another. Urgency thrummed through her.

In the wild, tigers would stay with their kill or bury it to return and dine over a period of several days.

The tiger was likely very close.

She needed to get out of here as quickly as possible.

A twig cracked behind her.

Raven spun, rifle up, and flicked off the safety. Her heart raced. Panic clawed at her throat. Alarm bells screamed in her head, warning of imminent danger. Her primitive brain went haywire, begging her to *run*.

Her primitive brain was going to get her killed.

Fleeing a tiger was all but inviting death. Inciting a chase would provoke an uncertain tiger into attacking.

Back away, step by step. Move slowly and calmly. Don't show fear. Her father had taught her how to act around predators to minimize the chance of attack. *No sudden movements.*

Even in her terror, she recalled her father's instructions. *Stay upright. Stand tall. Look like a human.* A brave, fearless, bland and tasteless human.

She forced herself to straighten to her full height, resisting the urge to cringe and cower. It made her look stronger, bigger, and less like a helpless prey animal. Crouched down, a person appeared weak and small, which increased the chances of an attack.

Turning, she sighted more trees, more empty shadows. The forest was impossibly still. She heard no birds. Even the crows had fallen silent.

Her frantic gaze flicked from tree to tree, scanning bushes, shadows, scrubby underbrush. She saw nothing. But that didn't mean he wasn't there, prowling silent as a held breath, waiting to pounce.

Most likely, she wouldn't see it coming.

Tigers surprised victims from the side or from behind, either approaching upwind or lying in wait downwind. They rarely pressed an attack if they were seen before they'd mounted their ambush. Of course, a captive tiger might attack anyway.

How many shots could she fire in the second or two it took for the tiger to cross thirty yards? How many rounds would it take to bring him down? Could she even aim accurately with a monstrous beast hurtling toward her at speed?

Abruptly, Shadow appeared to her right. He bounded past her in a blur of teeth and black fur. He halted, stiff-legged, and stared past the cluster of bushes at something in the shadows she couldn't see.

His hackles bristled. Agitated, he growled low in his throat, his tail curled beneath him.

Luna appeared from the woods to Raven's right and loped to Shadow's side. The two wolves stood several feet in front of Raven. They alternately growled and whined, tails curled beneath them, backs arched, jowls pulled back from their teeth.

They smelled death. They smelled danger.

And then she smelled it, too. Faint, and then stronger.

The strangely disconcerting smell of buttered popcorn.

Raven froze.

The wolves howled. They whirled and lunged at phantoms. The palpable, sickly-sweet stench of the tiger's spray was nearly unbearable. They snarled frantically at tiger musk thick in their nostrils.

The hairs on the back of her neck lifted. He was close. He must be close. They needed to get out of here, right now—

A thunderous roar split the air. It seemed to come from everywhere at once.

The deafening sound slammed into her. Paralyzing her muscles. Constricting her heart in utter terror.

The tiger erupted out of nowhere, as though out of the earth itself. Thirty yards away. He sprang from the wooded shadows. A blur of yellow eyes, orange fur, and gleaming fangs.

Raven screamed.

Chapter Thirty-Four

Raven froze. Deep primal terror surged through her veins. Her hands were on the rifle. Fingers numb. Her muscles no longer remembered how to move, how to pull the trigger. Her heart refused to beat.

The tiger leaped toward her. Thirty yards away. Twenty. Ten.

One thought seared her panicked mind—she was going to die. She was going to die a hideously painful death. Not a damn thing she could do about it—

Five yards from her trembling form, the tiger halted. Instead of pouncing, Vlad crouched and stared at her.

Raven stood, stricken. Rooted to the earth, unable to move.

The snarling wolves sounded dim and far away. Everything disappeared but the tiger. Her brain registered only the lethal predator crouched before her.

His massive head was larger than a basketball. His paws were the size of pot lids. Fangs the length of a finger. Claws like meat hooks.

Every inch of him radiated spectacular brute strength. Power. Virility. Cunning.

He was the apex predator. The undisputed king of his domain.

His ears flattened. His tail lashed. Vlad glared at her with his piercing yellow eyes. Eyes hypersensitive to movement, designed to track prey.

If the prey response was triggered, even a fully sated big cat would pounce.

To move now meant certain death, gun or no gun.

Raven remained utterly motionless.

Vlad unhinged his jaws and roared.

A tiger's full-throated roar was an impressive display she'd rarely experienced, and never this close. It was a savage, ferocious, terrifying noise. An explosion of aggression, dominance.

Loud as a jet engine and directionless, everywhere at once, expanding inside her skull, scrambling her brain, rendering her immobile with fear.

It was a roar that shook the earth, trembled the bones encased in her flesh. It rumbled over and through her like an avalanche.

Think! Her mind screamed.

The wolves snarled and growled, circling Raven and the tiger, darting in and skittering away. Not even the wolves could stop a tiger intent on ripping apart its prey.

Vlad hadn't killed her yet. She clung to that thought. She had a chance, slim as spider's silk perhaps, but still a chance. She wouldn't waste it.

She couldn't move, but she could speak. Remind Vlad who she was.

Tigers were incredibly smart. They boasted the second-largest brain of all carnivores and had a phenomenal memory. She knew he remembered her.

It took a supreme act of will to open her mouth, to form words on her tongue, and force them out.

"You know me, Vlad." Her voice sounded shaky and high-pitched. She cleared her throat. "You don't want to kill me."

The tiger snarled and bared his fangs. His tail snapped. He remained crouched, with his right paw lifted. His right foreleg was streaked with blood. He was wounded.

Gomez must have gotten off a single shot before the tiger tore his limbs from his body. A wounded tiger was an extremely dangerous creature.

She attempted his favorite whistle to remind him of who she was. It didn't work.

Vlad slunk closer to Raven. He growled at her, deep and guttural. He was angry, acting aggressive and threatening. It was terrifying.

Though he hadn't attacked yet, he was upset and getting more agitated by the second. Something she was doing was riling the tiger further.

She'd remained completely still and non-threatening, so then what—?

The gun. Her father once explained how tigers were intelligent enough to connect gunshots—the thunderous noise, a flash of pain —with the black stick in the hands of a human fifty yards away.

Vlad despised tranq guns from every vet visit he'd ever known. Then Gomez used a gun to shoot him in the leg. Vlad recognized the rifle—and its intended purpose.

As long as she held it, he viewed her as a threat.

Contrary to every primal instinct screaming inside her brain, she needed to disarm herself to stay alive.

This close, the rifle was unlikely to stop the tiger before he slaughtered her, anyway.

"Here goes nothing." Slowly, very slowly, her hands shaking, she lifted the rifle strap over her head.

Mere feet away, the enormous tiger snarled his displeasure.

Fear thumped in her chest. One wrong move, one inadvertent motion. That was all it would take. Crouching cautiously, Raven lowered the rifle to the ground and set it down in the ferns.

She risked an additional movement. She put her hand in her pocket and pulled out a strip of venison. She'd kept some jerky, just in case she and the tiger met again.

Raven tossed the treat at his paws.

Vlad roared in her face. Tiger spittle struck her cheeks. The ground shook. Her bones rattled.

Her stomach churned with sour-sick panic. Her plan hadn't worked. He was angrier now. Any second, he'd pounce. His four-inch claws would sink into her belly and eviscerate her bowels.

"You don't have to do this, Vlad," she said. "I know you don't really want to. Please. We know each other, remember? You know me. Who fed you treats all those years? Me. It was me."

Vlad tilted his great head, as if listening to the cadence of her voice. His long tail twitched behind him. He lowered his head, sniffed at the jerky, and swallowed the venison whole.

Out of nowhere, Shadow plunged in close. Snarling, he bit Vlad on his flank.

The tiger whirled and swiped at him. Vlad's razor claws missed the wolf's muzzle by a hair's breadth.

Shadow galloped out of harm's way. Vlad didn't chase him. He hissed in the wolf's direction, then crawled a few steps backward, limping as he went.

The tiger swung his massive head back toward Raven. His piercing eyes fixed on her. His posturing was still angry, though slightly less threatening now that she no longer held the gun.

Shadow and Luna snarled as they continuously circled the tiger. Shadow on Vlad's left, Luna on his right. The wolves darted in, snapping their jaws at the tiger, then springing away.

His ears laid back against his skull. His yellow eyes blazed with irritation.

Vlad spun toward them, slashing with his claws. They danced out of reach.

While the tiger was momentarily distracted, Raven straightened, steeled herself. Forced the panic down. She focused on lifting her foot and taking a slow step backward. Then another, and another.

The tiger whirled toward Luna and swiped at her flank. The wolf yelped and scrambled backward.

He might've pounced then, taking her down with a single leap, but he didn't. He spun in the opposite direction, hissing at Shadow, who prowled at the tiger's exposed backside.

Raven's gaze darted past the tiger, where the corpse of Gomez lay in the bloodied grass. Since he'd appeared, Vlad had remained between her and the wolves and his next meal. The tiger was defending his kill.

If they left him alone, hopefully, he would do the same.

Raven moved silently, carefully backward. Ten yards, fifteen, twenty. Her pulse roared in her ears. Finally, she reached the perimeter of the clearing.

Thirty yards away, Vlad faced down the wolves. If he wished, the tiger could still reach her in two seconds.

At the moment, he seemed more surly than enraged. His roars had become growls. He batted at the wolves like irksome flies, snarling at them to let him be.

She slipped between a sugar maple and a dogwood tree, thorns snagging her pants as she stumbled backward, unwilling to take her eyes off Vlad for a second.

The wolves seemed to have come to a similar conclusion as Raven, because a moment later, Shadow and Luna retreated from the clearing, backs arched, their hackles bristling.

Vlad snarled at them half-heartedly. Rather than chase after them, he hunkered down in front of his kill, protecting it. The tiger gave a deep-throated moan as he licked his wounded paw in peace.

For whatever reason, he'd spared them. She wanted to believe it was because Vlad knew her, recognized her smell, associated her with affection and kindness, all those years of jerky treats and back-scratches against the chain-link fence.

More likely, he simply wasn't hungry. Or he'd been more interested in protecting his kill and wanted them out of his domain. Maybe it was a mixture of multiple things. She'd never know for sure.

Whatever the reason, she was still alive.

Once out of Vlad's sight, Raven whistled to Shadow and Luna. Then she turned and ran north, ducking branches, weaving between trees, leaping over roots and fallen logs. Branches and thorns snagging at her clothes and skin. Feet pounding, breath panting, heart whooshing against her ribs.

The wolves trotted with her for a while and then disappeared deeper into the forest. She ran until her stomach cramped. The pain seared her side and bent her double. Her throat burned. Gasping, sucking in precious oxygen, she kept going until it felt like her legs would collapse beneath her.

Finally, she took a moment to rest. Pausing beneath a spreading oak, she retrieved her last water bottle from her pack and drank several mouthfuls until the bottle was empty, then she shoved it back into its pouch.

The damp, earthy scent of the woods filled her nostrils. Sparrows, finches, and swallows chirped. A red-tailed hawk soared in the patches of sky through the leafy canopy.

The trees were bursting with vivid color, their crowns tinged in fiery shades of burnt orange, crimson red, and canary yellow. Squirrels chased each other from trunk to trunk, branch to branch. Chipmunks scurried across the leaf-littered ground ribbed with gnarled roots.

Raven wiped the back of her mouth with her jacket sleeve. Her legs trembled. Her sides heaved. None of that mattered. She was alive. Gloriously, miraculously alive.

Shadow appeared through the trees and stalked to her side. He rubbed against her side as if to make sure she was okay, to reconnect. Luna was nowhere in sight.

"We survived," she said, her throat raw. "We faced the king of beasts and lived."

She buried her hands in the thick ruff of his neck. The cool fall air chilled her skin. The wooden wing of the bird carving in her pocket dug into her thigh. The stitch in her side burned. Dead leaves and twigs crunched beneath her feet.

She felt everything, every beautiful, glorious thing.

Shadow gave a low yip. He bolted into the forest ahead of her. On her left, she glimpsed Luna slinking through the shadows. A moment later, she too vanished through the trees.

They were off to hunt or explore or do whatever it was that

wolves did in the woods. They'd come back. She was certain of that. She trusted them. The wolves hadn't abandoned her to Vlad.

Together, they'd escaped the jaws of death.

Raven knew how lucky she was.

She'd lost her gun, though. No way could she risk going back for it. Vlad would stay with his kill for another two or three days at least. She couldn't afford to wait for it—not with the Headhunters stalking her through the woods. Not with Dekker bent on vengeance.

She withdrew her tattered paper map from the inner zippered pouch of her backpack, unfolded it, and dragged a finger along the faded line drawn from Haven Wildlife Refuge across the expanse of green through the Piedmont nature preserve, north through the Oconee National Forest to avoid people as much as possible, and to circumvent the sprawling metropolis of Atlanta and the city of Athens.

She'd keep north until she hit I-75 at the small town of Monticello, up through Mansfield, then 78 to Monroe, 11 to Winder and Braselton, 85 to 441 up to Baldwin and Clarksville to circumvent the larger city of Gainesville.

From Clarksville, she'd head northwest to the place called Scorpion Hollow. From there, the trail was marked to the cabin's exact location. Detailed coordinates were scrawled above the spot on the map.

If her calculations were correct, she needed to travel approximately one hundred and forty-seven miles if she took the roads, or only a hundred miles as the crow flies if she could circumvent most of the main roads.

If she pushed herself, she could reach the cabin in a week or a few days more, if she could hike fifteen miles a day. Of course, that pace depended on how many towns and cities she'd have to skirt between her current location and the Blue Ridge Mountains.

A week or so. It felt like a lifetime. If she had the Hydra Virus, she'd be dead by then. If she wasn't sick, she still had to figure out how to travel long distances within proximity to other humans and not die.

One thing she did know for certain: days of heavy exertion without water would be impossible. Her water bottle was bone dry. No clouds in the sky promised rain, either.

Frowning, she scanned the map again. The closest body of water by several miles was the Ocmulgee River, which was located approximately two miles to the west of her current location. Entirely the wrong direction.

Despite how far it felt like she'd fled, she was still within three miles of Haven. Not far enough to feel safe from the threat of the Headhunters. The dense underbrush had slowed her down considerably. Every instinct urged her to get as far from the Headhunters as she could, as fast as she could.

Thirst parched her throat. Her tongue felt gummy in her mouth.

She had no choice. She couldn't survive without water.

She had to reach the river first and fill her water bottles before heading north toward the mountains. Raven checked her compass and reoriented her direction to the west.

She set out toward the river. Shadow and Luna were off somewhere, but they could track her scent—they'd find her when they wanted to. The first spark of hope flared to life somewhere deep inside her chest. Maybe she could actually make it.

Maybe she would survive the end of the world, after all.

Chapter Thirty-Five

An hour later, the midday sun burned bright in the sky, which revealed itself in patches between the canopy of the forest. The day had warmed considerably, into the low fifties.

Raven wore her jacket around her waist, sweating and thirsty as she followed the narrow deer trail that she'd discovered an hour ago, which meandered in the direction of the river.

The burble of the river reached her over the birdsong and breeze rustling the branches overhead. She was almost there.

A loud yip sounded from somewhere ahead of her. Shadow or Luna? Or one of the timber wolves? Pausing, she listened hard but heard nothing else over the rustling leaves.

Pushing through heavy underbrush, she moved off the deer trail and headed in the direction of the sound. She eased through a thicket of sumac and mountain laurel. The rush of the river grew louder.

Just before she stepped out of the woods onto the pebble-strewn riverbank, she paused, moving aside a branch to take a look before she revealed herself. The long winding river was thirty feet at its widest point. Rushing brown water splashed over smooth stones and slick fallen logs.

At the edge of the water, about fifty or sixty yards downstream, a car-sized boulder loomed next to a copse of shagbark hickory trees. The shaggy bark peeled from the trunks in great swaths like wood shavings.

Beneath the shagbark trees, the white wolf stood over something on the ground. Luna bent her head, sniffing at the object. Her black lips curled back from her teeth eagerly, hungrily.

Squinting, Raven took a step closer. The object on the ground took shape. It was a calf carcass, lying on the ground beneath the tree along the riverbank.

Alarm shot through her veins. Something was wrong. The calf carcass belonged in the wildlife refuge, stored in the walk-in freezer of the meat house. It did not belong out here in the woods. A carpet of pine needles spread across the ground beneath the trees. Too flat, too even. No pine trees, either.

She opened her mouth to shout a warning.

Too late. Luna sank her jaws into the carcass. The movement triggered the trap. A roped log dropped from the tree above the wolf, a counterweight to the hidden net spread beneath the wolf's paws. Simultaneously, the net snapped up and closed over Luna's body. The net rose into the air, hauling the wolf seven feet above the ground.

Luna thrashed fiercely, her paws tangling in the netted rope. She yelped in mingled fury and fear. The net swung but held the wolf fast.

Raven shrank back. Instinctively, she crouched low behind the cluster of bushes. Rage burned through her veins. Every fiber of her body longed to burst from the trees and rush to save Luna, to cut her down with the whittling knife in her pocket, yet she resisted the urge. Forced herself to wait and watch, to surveil the scene first.

Her caution was warranted. A moment later, a man stepped out from behind the huge boulder downriver. One of the Headhunters. A second man soon joined the first. Cobb and Dekker. And then three more burly men she didn't recognize emerged from the trees.

The Headhunters carried rifles. They wore wolf pelts slung across their shoulders like capes. The pelts still raw and oozing blood.

Raven's chest constricted. Aghast, she recognized the distinctive markings on the pelts: Titus' streaks of black and Shika's beautiful, brindled coat.

A surge of grief burned the back of her throat. Cold rage iced her veins. How dare they mutilate such beautiful creatures for their own craven benefit. She loathed them with every part of her. She wanted the Headhunters to die horribly and painfully.

"Look what we have here," Cobb shouted. "We bagged one! Told you it would work. Look what a beauty she is, too."

Luna growled ferociously. She snapped and snarled, but it was no good. She was caught fast.

Dekker laughed. "Those teeth won't do it much good, now."

He stalked along the riverbank toward the sprung trap. The angles of his face sharpened in the dappled sunlight. He lifted his rifle and aimed at Luna. "What a pelt this one will make."

Hidden behind the bushes, Raven reached for the tranquilizer gun, but the men were out of range, too far downriver. Helpless, she despised herself for her impotence. What she wouldn't give for her rifle. With a gun, she would've had a chance to nail several of them, at least.

Her empty hands curled into fists. She didn't have a weapon worth anything. Her whittling knife was worse than useless. Silently, she prayed that Shadow, off hunting somewhere, remained far away, hidden and safe.

"You can't shoot it," Cobb said, almost apologetic.

Dekker swung around and glared at him. "Like hell I can't."

"Vaughn wants to kill the white wolf himself."

Dekker cursed. "You gotta be joking."

Cobb shrugged. "You know how he is."

"And how does he propose we bring it to him? On a leash?"

Cobb pulled a tranq gun from his waistband. He must have stolen it from the lodge, where Raven's father kept a backup for emergencies. Cobb shot Luna in the flank. She yelped in pain.

For an agonizing minute, the animal thrashed and twisted within the net, but she was helpless. Raven watched in horror as Luna's desperate movements slowed.

Recrimination burned in her chest. Without Raven, the wolves might be far from here. They'd remained close to Haven and the Headhunters because of Raven. This was her fault.

A minute later, the wolf stilled, unconscious.

"You gonna help me here or what?" Cobb asked.

Dekker leaned lazily against one of the hickory trees, arms crossed over his chest. "I pass. You want the glory, you do the heavy lifting, man. If you can hack it."

Cobb grimaced but shrugged in resignation. He gestured to the other men to help him. They cut the wolf down, untangled the net, and tied her fore and hind paws together with rope.

Raven hated them all. She wanted to kill them. She wanted to run from the trees and attack them, stop them somehow.

They would kill her. She knew that. So, instead, she crouched, hiding, tears slick on her cheeks.

Cobb squatted and slung the wolf's limp body over his broad shoulders with a pained grunt. "Damn, this thing weighs a metric ton."

"Let's go," Dekker growled. "Every second we're not hunting that damn girl, we're just wasting time. I can't wait to burn this place to the ground."

Dekker headed back into the woods, along the path that led the few miles back to Haven, with Cobb at his heels and the other men following close behind. The beautiful gray and brindled fur pelts on their backs rippled in the breeze.

The Headhunters crashed through the forest. For several minutes after the last sounds faded, Raven crouched, her thighs aching, hands trembling, her pulse a roar in her ears.

They were going to kill Luna. Slaughter her like a pig. Butcher her wild beauty and reduce her to a flat, dead thing—a rug, a stupid cape for some cruel thug to wear. And Raven could do nothing to stop it.

A low, despairing moan escaped her lips. She'd needed water, but

She should've done things differently. She shouldn't have risked the river. Shouldn't have believed she was far enough from Haven to take the risk.

She should have driven Shadow and Luna away from here, away from her somehow. She'd be alone, but they'd be safe—and alive.

She forced herself to stand on shaky legs.

The breeze rustled through the trees. Grasshoppers trilled. Birds chirped. Tiny creatures scurried across crackling leaves. She staggered to the riverbank, sank to her knees, and shrugged out of her pack.

Pebbles dug into her kneecaps. She barely felt the pain. Numbly, she retrieved her water bottles and filled them with automatic movements, adding the disinfectant tablets, then stuffed them back inside her backpack.

Raven stared unseeing at the rushing water.

At least they didn't have Shadow, too. Shadow had been with Luna the last time she'd seen them, but luckily, he hadn't been at the river, or they would've taken him, too. She didn't know where he was. Off hunting for rabbit or deer, no doubt. He didn't know the Headhunters had taken his mate. How would he react when he returned to find Luna gone?

Would he smell the Headhunters' scent mingled with Luna's beneath the cluster of hickory trees and understand what had happened? Would the wolf comprehend that this was Raven's fault?

She'd been forced to watch helplessly as the Headhunters killed Shika, Echo, and Titus. Suki and Gizmo. How many more innocent creatures had they slaughtered last night? Was Zephyr still alive? Kodiak and Sage? Electra?

She could still run and save herself. She should run. It was the smart thing to do. She had water. She could make it to the cabin in a week or so. She could survive there, alone.

Wasn't that what she'd wanted all along? From the beginning, hadn't she longed to leave the world behind? Hadn't she planned to abandon all this? The animals, the refuge, the responsibility. Everything.

She was a loner. Solitary, isolated. A recluse, just like her father.

But that was before. Before Zachariah died. Before her father died. Before the Headhunters came and started killing anything that moved. Before Shadow and Luna made her part of their pack.

She sank to her hands and knees. Her palms pressed against the smooth pebbles and mud at the water's edge. Her fingers sank into the sludge. The mud smelled dank and sulfurous. Like something dead and rotting.

She was only one girl.

She'd done everything she could. She'd released the animals from their cages. She'd stalked and killed one Headhunter and wounded three others, driving them from the woods for a few precious hours so the surviving animals could flee.

She'd murdered Rex.

Hadn't she tried her best? Hadn't she done enough?

No one would even know if she ran. The world was dead. Everyone she'd ever cared about was dead. Except perhaps her mother. Did she even count?

Her mother had left. Her mother ran. Wasn't that what Nakamura women did best? They left when the going got tough.

The frigid water numbed her hands. She yanked them from the river and drew back, wiping them on her pant legs. She drew her legs up to her chest and wrapped her arms around herself. She lowered her head to her knee and moaned.

Luna was just a wolf.

But that wasn't true, and she knew it, felt it in the deepest parts of herself.

Her mother used to say it was a mistake to ascribe human emotions to animals. They were just genetics and instinct, her mother had claimed. But she was wrong.

It wasn't *human* emotion. It was simply emotion. And some emotions—joy, anger, fear, grief—transcended species. Animals could feel, could think, could store and retrieve memories. They could show and receive affection.

They were sentient beings. Their lives held value, connection, and beauty.

Luna's life held value, connection, and beauty.

What are you going to do?

If Raven did nothing, the Headhunters won.

The outside world was destroyed. Everything had shattered into a million pieces. She might die of the Hydra Virus. Her hand strayed to her throat, then to her forehead. Still not hot.

What was left but this? But here?

The Headhunters had destroyed Raven's world. The Headhunters had stolen her home, her food, her safety. The Headhunters killed the animals she loved.

To go back to the lodge now... they would most certainly capture her. Torture her. Abuse her. Then kill her.

It was ludicrous to consider it. Insane. Dangerous.

But not impossible.

If she were smart. If she were careful.

What are you going to do?

Only a short while ago, she'd sat on the roof of the tiger house and planned to flee, to escape her problems, to run from the things she loved. That was a lifetime ago.

She was someone else now. Someone new. Someone better.

It was a reckless decision. Stupid, most certainly. The wrong move. It would probably get her killed.

She was going to do it anyway.

The river rushed and gurgled. Sunlight sparkled on the surface of the water. The trees swayed in vibrant colors.

Raven unfolded her legs and stood. Her feet were steady.

She turned and headed into the woods toward Haven.

CHAPTER THIRTY-SIX

It was dusk by the time Raven reached the outskirts of Haven wildlife refuge.

She skirted the perimeter of the park outside the fence until she neared the front gates of the refuge, then crouched in the underbrush near the front of the lodge. Her pack weighed heavily against her spine, but she feared going anywhere without it.

Cautiously, from her position hidden in the bushes outside the fence, she listened and waited. Crickets whirred in the long grass. An owl hooted from somewhere nearby. The air smelled of smoke.

A few dozen motorcycles were parked along the drive at the park entrance. The semi-truck had arrived. The rear of the truck was backed up to the food storage buildings, the rear doors hanging open, the interior empty. The men hadn't begun loading yet.

About forty Headhunters crowded around the ten picnic tables in front of the Grizzly Grill. All were men except for one or two hard-looking women. They mostly did the cooking and cleaning, it seemed.

Loud voices drew her attention. She forced her anger down and shifted her focus to the group of Headhunters. Scorpio wore a collection of three fox pelts across his broad shoulders. The lush red tails rippled down his back. He stood in front of the large grill, turning slabs of meat. Damien stood next to him, his back to Raven.

The delicious scent reached her nostrils. She could guess the meat.

Beside the grill, Vaughn held a chunk of grilled meat in his bare hands, ripping out chunks with his teeth. Juices dribbled down his chin. Scorpio laughed and took another swig of bourbon. Cobb slumped at a picnic table, picking at his teeth with a twig.

Dekker wasn't eating. He wasn't smiling or laughing or swearing with the others. He paced in front of the picnic tables, his movements languid but his shoulders tense, his body coiled as if ready to spring, alert as any predator. His eyes blazed with bloodlust.

She spotted the men she'd wounded yesterday hunched at one of the picnic tables. Their wounds were bandaged, probably from the first aid kit in the lodge. They nursed bottles of bourbon they'd stolen from the restaurant's bar.

Would the Headhunters search for a hospital after they left the refuge? Were there any functioning hospitals left?

Right now, she didn't care. She hoped their wounds developed gangrene. She prayed they died horrific, agonizing, slow deaths, screaming for their mamas.

One of the picnic tables was loaded with piles of guns—mostly semi-automatic rifles, handguns, revolvers, and a few hunting knives sheathed in leather.

On the last picnic table, several raw pelts were stretched to dry. Timber wolf pelts. She recognized Echo, Loki, and Suki's dark gray fur.

Anger scorched through her, turning her veins to ash. The foxes had never hurt anyone. The wolves were primal beauty and grace in motion.

They were all beautiful. The Headhunters had slaughtered them.

Her stomach lurched with grief and anger. She forced herself to stay focused, to tamp down her rage. At least Kodiak and Sage's pelts were missing. As were Electra's and many of the other animals. Hopefully, they'd made it far enough away to be safe.

Luna's mournful howls echoed from the direction of the tiger house. The Headhunters must have locked her in Vlad's chamber.

Raven couldn't wait any longer. Though the sky was darkening into twilight, it wasn't completely dark yet. The Headhunters would finish eating and drinking shortly.

They'd soon be in the mood for killing.

They'd butcher Luna. Then they'd come for Raven.

Raven shifted her position, moving to her hands and knees, and crept along the fence line, cautious with each movement.

If they heard her, it was all over. Luckily, their raucous voices were loud enough to cover any accidental sounds she made.

Keeping low to the ground, she traced the perimeter fence line back to the location of the maintenance shed. After checking to make sure the electrified wires were still disabled, she clambered back over the fence and raced low across open ground until she reached the shed.

Slipping inside, she rose to her feet as she strained her ears for any change in the noise coming from the picnic area. The loud, boisterous voices continued.

She fumbled for a lighter from the dusty top shelf, stuffed it in her cargo pocket, and wiped her grimy fingers on her pants. She grabbed two containers of gasoline and backed out of the shed.

Ignoring the meat house, she made her way to the food storage building. She drenched the weathered wooden siding in gasoline, then peeked in the single window to make sure no one was inside before entering.

The stench of rotting fruit filled her nostrils. Undaunted, she poured gasoline over the pallets and shelves, the bags and boxes and containers full of precious, life-sustaining food.

Food that could feed her for over a year. It was also food the Headhunters desperately wanted. If she couldn't save it, then she would take it from them. They wouldn't have a reason to stay with the food destroyed.

Even more importantly, burning the food also served the crucial purpose of a much-needed distraction. If the Headhunters were drawn to the fire, they wouldn't be paying attention to the tiger house.

The oily stench of the gas churned her stomach. Dizziness wavered through her. She fought it off. After she'd finished, Raven backed out, splashing a trail with the last of the gasoline. She tossed the container aside and pulled the lighter out of her pocket.

Twilight had fallen in earnest. The sky deepened to rich indigo. Bats whirled and darted above the treetops. The first stars winked to life. The wind picked up, carrying with it the tang of ozone. Dark clouds glowered thick and low over the horizon.

Raven glanced upward. A storm was headed their way, after all. In a couple of hours, the rain would come. The storm would ensure the fire didn't spread further than the refuge.

She didn't hesitate. She lit the lighter, dropped it onto the saturated grass, and leaped back.

Flames whooshed to life.

The fire raced along the trail of gasoline straight into the food storage building. The fire licked the walls hungrily. Swiftly, it flared into a blaze, consuming the old wood, eating through the boards, burning through the gas-soaked interior with startling fury.

Raven watched the fire for a moment. Heat seared her face. Her eyes watered. She blinked and coughed. An acrid stench stung her nostrils, her eyes.

The air went blurry with the intensity of the heat. Crackling and popping sounds filled the air. Wood splintered and heaved. Everything bathed in a flickering orange light.

Thick black smoke rose in a billowing column. A signal, a warning.

Panicked shouts rose over the crackling roar of the fire.

Time to go.

CHAPTER THIRTY-SEVEN

In the dark, Raven ran for the tiger house, following the sounds of Luna's growls and howls, furtively darting from building to building, passing the lodge, the restaurant, the souvenir shop, the entrance, and the parking lot, staying low to the ground and keeping buildings or trees between herself and the Headhunters as much as she could.

Behind her, smoke spiraled into the dark sky, blotting out the stars. Orange flames leaped and sparked along the storage building.

The Headhunters shouted in alarm. Several dark figures sprinted for the blazing building. The ruckus obscured her noise as she rounded the rear of the tiger enclosure, climbed over the perimeter fence, and dashed through the overgrown grass to the tiger house.

As if sensing her presence, the white wolf's howls grew louder.

From somewhere outside the refuge came an answering howl—long and low and desperate. Shadow had found them. He was out there in the woods beyond the refuge, searching for his mate.

"I've got this," Raven said under her breath, though the black wolf couldn't hear her. "I'm going to save her, I promise."

She hoped the Headhunters wouldn't go after him, that they were too distracted by their food supply going up in flames. She had to focus on saving Luna. Shadow was safer outside the refuge—she could only pray he stayed that way.

The service door hung open. Raven ran inside and collapsed onto her knees beside the mesh gate. Luna lay on her side. Knotted ropes bound her paws. Other than the rope shackles, she appeared unharmed.

The wolf raised her head and pressed her nose against the mesh, whimpering frantically.

"I'm getting you out." Raven slapped the button to raise the sliding gate, pulled her whittling knife from her pocket, and flicked it open. She climbed awkwardly inside to reach the wolf.

Luna writhed on the cement floor, so agitated that Raven had difficulty cutting the rope without accidentally hurting the animal.

"Hold still!" she hissed. "I'm trying to help you!"

Luna snapped. Her jaws closed an inch from Raven's wrist. Adrenaline shot through her veins, but she held her ground.

"No," Raven said firmly. She met the wolf's frantic amber gaze and held it. "I said enough!"

Luna was frightened, bewildered, and furious. She was the alpha; she'd never needed to be submissive a day of her adult life. Until now.

"Let me help you," Raven said. "I'm going to help you, but damn it, you need to do what I say for a change."

They stared at each other for a moment. Luna wild, panicked, and distrustful. Raven fighting down her own desperation.

She kept her eyes fixed on Luna's, willing her to understand. "We're going to have to trust each other, you and I. You're not going to bite me, and I'm not going to cut you. Understand?"

Luna's ears pricked. She whined low in her throat. Her lips remained peeled back from her fangs, but she didn't growl. She didn't snap.

It was a good sign. At least, Raven chose to take it as one.

She held Luna's foreleg down with one hand, sawing at the rope with the whittling knife. She worked quickly but carefully. If she accidentally cut Luna, she'd lose whatever fragile trust they'd built between them.

Each second passed with incredible slowness. She felt every beat of her heart, every panicked breath as she worked through the first rope.

In the distance, Shadow's howls intensified. He sounded as desperate as she felt.

After an endless minute, the frayed rope finally snapped.

Luna attempted to scramble up with just her forelegs. Her hind legs, still bound, collapsed. She yelped in surprised pain.

Raven pressed her down again. "Not yet. Let me work, damn you."

Pausing for half a second, she listened for the Headhunters. Their shouts and yells echoed in the distance. It was fully dark outside. The shadows inside the tiger house were so deep she could hardly make out Luna's pale form.

With one hand, she felt along the wolf's muscled flank for the rope, fumbling to Luna's hind legs. As she sawed through the rope, the blade rasped through the thick fibers with agonizing slowness.

"Come on, come on. Hurry the hell up!" Beads of sweat gathered at her hairline. Her heart hammered against her ribs. "Almost there, I promise."

The last rope fell away. Luna was free. In a blink, the wolf leaped up and shot out of the chamber, through the service door, and out into the park.

"Run to Shadow!" Raven whispered as she rose to her feet and sheathed the blade. "Run!"

She exited the tiger house, blinking to readjust her eyes to the night.

The sky was a glossy black. The bank of towering thunderclouds roiled closer. Not yet masked by the incoming cloud cover, the moon was a bright sliver, casting a luminous glow over everything—the trees, the buildings, the habitats, the flagstone pathway.

Then she saw them. Her heart stopped.

On the path, forty or fifty yards away. Three Headhunters sprinted toward them. Whooping and hollering. Their faces hungry, drunk on blood and vengeance. Scorpio was shouting, pointing at the white wolf.

Vaughn and Dekker held rifles.

Dekker aimed his rifle at Raven's chest. Vaughn swung his gun toward Luna.

Raven didn't think. She sprinted straight at the Headhunters. They were going to kill Luna. She had to stop them.

"Go!" she screamed at Luna. "Run!"

Luna made a sharp right, off the path, and streaked across the grounds.

Vaughn fired at her. The gunshot boomed.

Luna kept going. A pale white streak in a sea of black shadows.

Vaughn shifted his weight, planted his feet, and leveled the rifle, about to fire again.

Raven ran faster. She lowered her shoulder and slammed into his side. It was like smashing into a brick wall.

The rifle went off. The sound of the gunshot exploded in her ears. Vaughn had barely moved, but she'd struck his arm, shoving the rifle aside as he'd fired. Vaughn cursed loudly.

Raven staggered, dazed. Pain radiated up and down her shoulder, her right hip.

Luna loped north, headed between the enclosures, for the rear gates. She vanished into the darkness. Unharmed. Still alive. She'd made it. Outside the refuge, Shadow gave a long, high-pitched howl, followed by a swift yip of excitement. They'd found each other. Luna had reached Shadow.

Raven turned to flee. Her legs wouldn't work properly. She wasn't fast enough.

Another gunshot exploded. The round whizzed past her ear and struck the wall of the tiger house in front of her with a dull *thunk*. The sound thundered in her ears. Everything went distant and tinny.

"Next time, I won't miss," Dekker said. His voice sounded like it was underwater. "Stop right there!"

Raven kept going. Her only chance was to escape. Her pulse

roared in her ears. She stumbled, righted herself, and ran again. It felt like running through Jello.

Footsteps pounded behind her. Angry shouting voices.

Someone seized her arm and jerked her backward. Hauled her off her feet. She nearly collapsed, but the hand on her bicep dragged her upright.

Scorpio spun her around to face the others. Vaughn slung his rifle over his shoulder and held a flashlight, pointing it at Raven's face. Scorpio tightened his grip, cutting off circulation.

Black soot filmed his enraged features. "You set fire to our food!"

"You owe me a wolf," Vaughn growled. "Not just any wolf. *That* one."

Raven lifted her chin. She said nothing. Tears stung her eyes. The fear was a winged black thing beating frantically against her chest, her ribs, her throat.

Dekker got right in her face. His eyes flat and dangerous. "You killed my brother. You stabbed him and left him to die like an animal. Admit it. You did it."

She refused to give them the dignity of an answer.

Scorpio shook her hard. Her brain felt like it was rattling around in her skull. "You dumb as well as stupid?"

She clenched her jaw, bit back the scream of terror clawing at her throat.

Dekker sneered. "Tiger got your tongue? I can get you to talk. Give me five minutes, and I'll get you to squeal like a stuck pig."

Treacherous tears burned the backs of her eyes. She blinked them back furiously. She wouldn't give him the satisfaction. She wouldn't give them anything.

Dekker leaned in close and spoke softly, his breath in her ear. She could smell his sour sweat, could see the pores in her skin, the knife-sharp angles of his face. "When I'm through with you, you'll be begging me for mercy."

Raven repressed a shudder. She raised her chin, afraid but defiant.

Dekker smiled. It was an ugly, dead thing. His eyes held no mercy. He gestured for Scorpio to release her arm.

As soon as Scorpio let her go, Dekker punched her in the mouth.

Pain ruptured throughout her jaw. Her lower lip split. Blood trickled down her chin. She tried to keep her balance, but the force of his blow knocked her to her knees. Scorpio ripped the backpack from her shoulders and tossed it onto the ground at his feet.

"You came to us, you stupid little whore." Dekker bent over her. "We didn't even have to hunt you down. What a shame. I was looking forward to that."

Dekker struck her across the side of her face with the back of his hand. Lights exploded across her vision. Her ears rang. Dizziness washed over her in waves. She felt like she was going to vomit.

Dekker kicked her in the stomach. She toppled, falling backward. Flagstone cracked against her skull. She shuddered, gasping, crying. She clawed at the ground, trying to rise to her hands and knees, to crawl away. Pain gnawed at the edges of her mind.

Dekker delivered a savage kick to her ribs. He knocked her down again. Agony lanced her ribs like a razor-tipped spear. She groaned, rising again to her hands and knees.

She licked blood from her split lip. No use. It ran down her chin. She attempted to stand.

Vaughn and Scorpio watched impassively, their faces in shadow beyond the beams of their flashlights.

Dekker pushed her over easily, as if she were nothing more than a sack of grain. He nudged her onto her back, then lifted his steel-toed boot and slammed it down on her ribs.

Something gave with a sickening crunch.

Raven writhed, groaning. White-hot pain blinded her. Pain so deep and wide it engulfed her whole body. Pain without beginning, without end.

The world glimmered in and out of focus. Blackness hovered at the corners of her vision. The moon and stars were hidden now. The sky a mass of dark clouds. A gust of wind swept over her.

She tasted ozone mingled with blood. The storm was almost here.

Distantly, she heard footsteps.

"Is this necessary?" Damien's voice, sharp with disgust. "She's no threat."

"After what she did?" Scorpio scoffed. "She'll be lucky if we don't flay her alive."

"But she's a—"

"A what?" Dekker asked coldly. "A girl? Or a cold-blooded murderer?"

"You're the murderers!" Raven spat between clenched teeth. She could barely force the words out through the agony spearing through every part of her body. It was like a gaping maw of pain swallowing her whole.

Scorpio sneered. "So, she can speak."

"Haven't you done enough already?" Damien asked. "Looks like you've gotten your pound of flesh, Dekker."

"I haven't even started."

Her entire body hurt. Her ribs like molten lava, knives prying apart her bones. She clung to consciousness with every fiber of her being. The darkness yawned at the corners of her vision, rising beneath her bones.

"I thought we didn't torture women and children." Damien's tone was beseeching. "Come on, Uncle. Stop this."

Dimly, she saw Vaughn shrug. "Doesn't count when they murder one of our own, son."

Damien fell silent. His silence said everything. In the end, when it counted, he would fail her, like everyone else. She'd get no help from him. Or anyone.

No one was coming to save her. There was no one to call for help. She had no parents. No police anymore. No 911. No soldiers keeping the peace.

There was no one. No one and nothing.

This was it, then.

This was the end.

Her eyes burned. She didn't cry. She refused to cry, refused to give these monsters an ounce of satisfaction.

Dekker bent over her, leaned in close. Above his looming form, lightning clawed the sky. The white pulse sharpened his cheekbones to blades, hollowed his eyes to deep black pits.

"You killed my brother." He seized a handful of her hair and yanked her head painfully. A jolt like a live wire zipped up her neck. His fleshy lips touched her ear. "For that, you're going to die."

CHAPTER THIRTY-EIGHT

Raven awoke to a darkness so complete that for several dreadful seconds, she thought she was dead. She didn't know where she was or why she wasn't safe in her comfortable bed. Why the bonobos weren't calling to each other in the distance. Why her father wasn't snoring down the hall.

Reality crashed into her with the force of a charging bull. With the horrific memories slamming into her brain came the fresh assault of pain—and the fear.

Raven gasped. The hurt radiated from every muscle and bone in her body. The sweet release of unconsciousness faded quickly. The pain took center stage.

The pain was immense. Everything ached. Her right ribs throbbed. The sickening pain pulsed like a second ragged heartbeat. She wasn't sure if it was cracked or broken or simply deeply bruised. It hurt, and badly.

At least she had saved Luna. At least the wolves were free.

Forcing her head to clear, she took careful stock of her surroundings. She opened her eyes wide and blinked. Wherever she was, it was nearly pitch black. She lay on something hard, unforgiving.

Somewhere above her, thunder rumbled ominously. Rain pelted

the metal roof. Tree branches scraped against the exterior walls like fingernails.

Lightning pulsed and flickered, wavering across slick steel walls. Painfully, Raven turned her head. She lay on a concrete floor inside a square concrete box.

Another pulse of lightning flared through an open service door a few feet to her right. The bars in the sliding gate glimmered faintly. The sliding gate led to another gate with a reinforced mesh screen. Beyond that lay the animal enclosure.

A creeping dread stole over her. She knew where she was: the tiger house.

The gates were closed, locked, and chained.

The Headhunters had locked her inside. She was caged like an animal.

They'd trapped her in here until they decided to kill her, or perhaps they would torture her some more, play with her the way a cat plays with its dinner.

Dekker wanted her to suffer. He'd promised that in the end, she would be the one begging them for death.

Sheer animal panic rose within her like a deep, dark sea, threatening to consume her, to swallow her whole. She'd asked for this. She'd put herself at risk. This was her fault.

Raven fought down the rising terror. If she had any chance of getting out of this alive, she needed to think, to be smart. Stretching her arms out, she patted down her body, searching for her weapons.

Her backpack was gone. Her tranquilizer gun was gone. But the little whittling knife stuffed deep in her cargo pocket—it was still there. They hadn't searched her as thoroughly as they should have. She was just a nuisance to them. A pretty prize.

Little good the tiny blade would do her now.

A strange scraping sound to her left drew her attention.

Outside the tiger house gates, the shadows shifted, coalesced into a thick dark shape. A monstrous thing loomed above her. A terrible demon. A monster more dangerous than any tiger.

Her lungs constricted in fear. The walls of the small square room blurred. She blinked rapidly. The shadows solidified into the shape of a man.

Damien.

No. The dark shape was too bulky, too huge to be Damien. The dark figure leaned forward to peer at her. She caught the gleam of the whites of his eyes. She smelled smoke and the burned stench of charred meat.

Outside, lightning streaked the sky. The pulse of light highlighted the hard planes of his face, the square stubbled jaw. The tattoo snaking up his thick neck. The shine of his teeth.

Vaughn smiled that cruel, familiar smile. "It doesn't have to be this way, you know."

She wanted to hurt him. To smash in his smug evil face with a brick. To stab him in the throat with the whittling knife hidden in her pocket.

But she was caught in a cage. Helpless, trapped, impotent. She could do nothing, and he knew it.

She licked her swollen lip and spat out the blood caked between her teeth. "Go to hell."

Vaughn sat against the wall outside the tiger's cage. He held a hunting knife. The long sleek blade gleamed as he flicked it back and forth between his large hands. "I'm a reasonable man, you'll find. One of the more reasonable ones left in this world."

She tried to move. Her stomach lurched, a surge of acid burning the back of her throat. She sucked in her breath, her jaw stiff as a rusted hinge.

As her eyes adjusted to the flickering dark, she made out more distinctive details. Vaughn stretched his legs languidly out in front of him. Next to him, on his right side, lay a familiar shape. Her backpack. The top rim of the hoverboard stuck out slightly.

"That's mine."

A flash of white teeth. "Not anymore, it's not. To the victors go the spoils, though you threw a wrench in that when you burned the storage shed and all that food." He set the knife in his lap and unfolded something she hadn't noticed before. "What's this map for?"

"None of your business."

"Hmmm. This leads to somewhere important. Doesn't it?"

Acrid rage stung the back of her throat. She wanted to vomit. He'd stolen her map, too. "It's nothing. It was my father's. I just wanted something of his, that's all."

"You'll tell me in time."

"Don't count on it."

"I'd wager this is where you were headed before we took your wolf. Somewhere with more food, I'd bet, if I were a betting man."

"Go to hell."

"You said that already," Vaughn said. "You know, when it all goes to hell, it's not necessarily the strong who survive. It's not the prepared. Not even the ones who saw it coming. The ones who survive are the ones willing to do anything, to anyone, at any time, to keep breathing. There is no moral code in the jungle. No mercy on the savanna. There are only predators and prey."

Even rolling her eyes hurt. "Sounds like a steaming pile of B.S. you tell yourself in the middle of the night when you miss your mommy."

Vaughn chuckled.

Cautiously, Raven eased herself into a sitting position. She felt her face, wincing at the swelling around her left eye, the split lip, the blood dried in a thin line on her chin. She lowered her hands and gingerly pressed her ribs. A spasm jolted through her ribcage. Throbbing, fiery needles stabbed and sliced through flesh and muscle and bone.

She hissed through the pain. But she could move, at least. There was that.

"We are going to break you in ways you cannot even imagine," Vaughn said.

"I won't break."

"I assure you, everyone breaks with the right pressure applied. It will take time. And it will be horrific for you." He paused, as if to let his words sink in, let the horrors of her imagination take root, dig in deep.

She dug her dirty fingernails into her palms to keep from screaming. She refused to let him see her fear.

"The gentleman in me would rather not contemplate such a fate for you, considering you are of the weaker sex."

Raven snorted.

Vaughn continued like she hadn't made a sound. "It is out of my hands, you see. You killed Dekker's brother. He has the right to retribution, however he sees fit. It is our code. Our law."

"Kill or be killed, right? That's the new law, according to you. Because there are no more laws. Because there is no one left to enforce them."

"The old ways are for the weak. In this new world, the only law is the law of nature. And nature survives. Nature kills. It is the natural state of things."

People have killed each other since the beginning of time. It wasn't anything new. But now... now there was nothing to stop men like this from killing and killing and killing again. To kill anyone and everyone, according to their whims.

There were myriad ways a person could hurt and kill another person. Other species killed their own kind—in battles for dominance, territory, and the right to mate.

When Raven was seven, the refuge had taken in several chimpanzees. Six months later, two of the chimps conspired to assassinate their alpha.

They waited until Zachariah and the other keepers had gone for the night, then they viciously attacked their leader. The two chimps bit off their victim's fingers and testicles, then left him to bleed to death on the enclosure floor.

The next morning, when she went with her father to clean out their night house, it was Raven who discovered the dead, mutilated chimp.

She could still recall vividly the damp chill of horror. The way her father had stepped back with an involuntary gasp, shielding her eyes with his hand, though she'd already seen enough. She'd seen everything.

Her father had believed that animals were elevated, evolved, and honorable, somehow above the horrors and atrocities of humankind.

Perhaps for the most part, they were. But not always.

Animals weren't free of the stigma of brutality.

In the wild, groups of chimpanzees waged war on other troops. A group of chimps would hold down an enemy while the others dismembered him, tearing the enemy apart, limb by limb.

When a male lion joined a new pride, he would kill the cubs sired by another lion. Juvenile foxes, owls, and hyenas sometimes killed and then ate their siblings. Orcas had been known to sadistically torture and kill other living creatures simply for their entertainment.

But it was humans who had turned the murder of other humans into an art form—en masse, by the hundreds of millions, by the billions. One man butchered another for greed, jealousy, or power. Or for no other reason than perverse pleasure. Because they could.

"We are not slaves to our natures," Raven said. "We can choose."

"I doubt that."

She closed her eyes, saw again the blood slick on her hands. To survive, she would kill. But not for nothing. Not like these vicious bastards. "You can choose not to kill me."

"Perhaps." Vaughn shifted slightly in the dark. "You may be right. Perhaps we can come to an agreement. There is an alternative. If you will consider it."

Thunder crashed. The rain pounded harder against the roof. She swallowed and stared blindly up at the ceiling until her vision blurred. She was parched. Her mouth caked with sand. She hadn't had anything to drink for hours.

The silence grew thick between them. He waited for her to respond. He wanted to dangle a bit of hope, then wrench it away.

This was part of the enjoyment for him. The way wolves ran a bison to exhaustion before attacking, wearing down its hope, draining its will to live, step by despairing step.

She should ignore him. She shouldn't give him anything. If it was her fate to die, she was determined to do it on her terms. Not by begging. Not by losing herself.

With every minute that ticked past, with every painful breath, her resolve eroded. Hope, after all, was the very last thing to relinquish itself. Even in the face of catastrophe, of devastation, of despair, hope was the thing that stubbornly held on.

The wind shrieked around the tiger house, beating the maple's branches against the walls and roof. Thunder boomed and crashed. Nature itself shrieked its outrage.

Raven said, "What is it? Your proposal?"

Vaughn grunted. "Finally seeing reason, are you?"

"Just spit it out."

The sharpened edge of the knife glittered. He dragged it along the folded edges of the paper map. "The white wolf. You came back for it, to save it. A few of the men claimed they saw you in the woods with the white wolf and the black wolf. I must admit, I am intrigued by you. A girl and a wolf, together. And not one wolf, but two. How fascinating."

Raven said nothing. Her stomach curdled.

"You have a relationship with them. They trust you. You know where they go."

She thought of the wolves. Of the night spent sleeping between them in the den. The steady, comforting warmth of their bodies. The coarseness of their fur against her skin, the dank feral smell of them in her nostrils. The awe and wonder and astonishment of it.

"What do you want?"

"You can take me to the wolves. The white wolf in particular."

She closed her eyes. "You want their pelts."

"Those wolves are like nothing I've ever seen. Like the modified ones. Genetically engineered, but not like the piss-poor substitutes the labs create. These hybrids are truly something special. Larger than regular wolves. Stronger. Smarter, too. You can see it in their eyes. Pure cunning. The white one is... marvelous. He's the alpha, there's no doubt. I'm an alpha. He's an alpha." She could sense him grinning in the dark. His eyes shone greedily. "We're meant for each other."

"Luna is indeed an alpha," she said with grim satisfaction. "But *he* is a she."

Vaughn was silent for a moment. When he spoke, his voice darkened. "What are you talking about?"

"Alpha doesn't mean what you think it means." She smiled in the dark, despite the pain in her split lip, her swollen eye socket, as she recalled yet another lecture from her father. "Wolf packs are families. The alphas are paired, male and female. They care for the pack together. In some ways, the female makes more decisions than the male. She chooses who to hunt, she picks a specific prey animal out of the herd. She instructs the other wolves when and where to strike."

Vaughn snorted dismissively. "Enough with the silly stories. You're talking gibberish. The white one is the male. The leader, the alpha. I want the alpha. You are wasting my time with your pathetic lies."

He rose to his feet, stuffed her map into his jacket pocket, and sheathed his hunting knife. His gaze raked over her, lingering on her face. "There is a place for you in the world that remains. You are quite the specimen. Beneath the dirt and rudeness and that ugly scowl, your delicate Asian features could serve you well. You could be taught to be a proper woman. A respectful, dutiful woman. *If* you learn to hold that tongue and respect those empowered to rule over you."

"Sounds like hell on earth."

He laughed mirthlessly. "If you bring me to the wolves, to the white wolf, I will spare your life. You can join us, and one of the men will choose you. Dekker will accept it because I tell him to do so. He will have no other option. If you do not do as I've ordered, I'll allow Dekker to do as he wishes with you. And that, my dear, will not be pretty."

"You're lying. I'm dead either way."

His eyes flashed in the dark. He raised his voice over the crash of thunder. "I am a man of my word. If I say it's going to happen, then it will. You've been watching us these last few days, I presume. Then you know my men respect me. They will obey me, whether they like it or not. It's a generous offer. You should accept it."

"You can shove that offer right up your ass."

"The choice is yours. Do as I say, and live. Or don't, and die in agony."

A crushing sense of powerlessness pressed against her chest like a thousand bricks. Insurmountable, hopeless. Beneath her debilitating fear, there was a low thrum like a heartbeat. Insistent, urgent, that fierce, unfaltering will to live.

I will survive this.

That powerful instinct for survival as ingrained within her as in any wild animal. That primal drive for self-preservation above all else. Above honor and goodness and even love.

Damien was right, after all. Her father was right. Even Vaughn. Humans would do anything to survive. It was their nature. It was her nature, too, in the end.

Life or death.

Death or life.

His shadow loomed over her, blocking out everything else. "Decide now."

The wolves would come to her. She knew they would. Vaughn wasn't wrong when he said they trusted her. They'd made her pack.

It was her only choice. Her only chance. She stared bleakly at the darkness above her. A blackness that was all-consuming, absolute.

"Well? What say you, girl? I won't ask you again."

The words were barbed wire on her tongue. "I'll do it."

"I knew you were smart." Vaughn bent and hefted her backpack over his shoulder, shoved her tranq gun into his waistband, and turned for the door as he stood to his full height. Before ducking out into the pouring rain, he glanced back at her. "We leave at dawn."

Chapter Thirty-Nine

The storm raged for hours. Early the next morning, the thunder dissipated, but the rain remained. The sky was gray as a bowl of ashes. The air was cold and wet as dawn broke over the horizon.

Raven ached all over. Exhausted, she could barely stand, let alone walk. But walk she did, because she had no other choice. Her hands were bound in front of her with zip ties. She hobbled between Damien and Vaughn, with Dekker right behind her.

Scorpio, Cobb, and a few others took up the rear as they entered the forest at the north end of the refuge. The men carried semi-automatic rifles slung over their shoulders.

They wore camouflaged pants and hunter green raincoats. A few carried packs on their backs. She recognized the familiar camo-green pack Damien wore strapped to his shoulders.

She was too exhausted to be angry at yet another thing they'd taken from her. The map in Vaughn's possession might as well be on Mars, for how inaccessible it was now.

She'd never see it again. She'd never see the hunting cabin again, either.

The Headhunters glowered and cursed as they hacked their way through the dense undergrowth. Rain pounded their heads and shoulders, dripping from branches, streaming in rivulets from the bushes. In minutes, they were soaked, their clothing sodden. Their boots sloshed through the mud.

They followed the narrow deer path that Raven had traversed earlier, which felt like months ago. They hiked for almost two hours. Raven's wet pants clung to her body, though her arms and torso beneath her jacket were dry—still freezing, but dry.

She lifted her head and drank the rain, soothing her parched throat.

"Hurry up!" Dekker prodded the small of her back so hard she stumbled over a tree root. Pain stabbed her ribs with every step. She pushed it down somewhere deep inside.

Damien tightened his grip on her arm, holding her up. "Lay off. She's doing the best she can."

"This better be worth it, wolf girl," Dekker said.

Raven summoned a flat smile. "It will be."

Damien quickened his pace to create some distance between them and Dekker. He squeezed Raven's arm and pulled her along. She hated that she needed his help, but she did.

He kept shooting her tense, worried glances. His brows knitted in concern. "You okay?"

"Do I look okay?"

"I know, stupid question."

She said nothing. What was there to say? Her nerves were stretched taut. It was difficult to breathe from the fear and anxiety churning in her belly.

"I came to see you last night." Damien lowered his voice. "I brought you medicine, but Vaughn wouldn't let me give it to you. He wouldn't let me inside the tiger house to talk to you, either. I'm sorry. I tried."

"Try harder," she muttered.

"I am, I promise you. I've been talking with my uncle nonstop, advocating for you. I'm the one who suggested you could find the white wolf for him, in exchange for your life, okay? It's good he went for it. You'll be okay now. Everything will be okay."

She shook her head. How stupid was this guy? Things were as far from okay as she could imagine. "Dekker will just murder me anyway."

"No, he won't. He knows Vaughn will kill him for disobedience. He'll do what Vaughn says. If my uncle says you live, you get to live."

"Okay, sure." She still didn't believe it. Not that it mattered.

Vaughn marched on ahead. He paused, twisting to stare back at her. "You'd better know where we're going."

"I do."

She'd been studying the tell-tale signs. A paw print here and there, not quite smeared by the rain. Mostly hare, raccoon, badger, and deer tracks. But there were a few other prints, larger ones. She noted bent and broken twigs, a torn spider's web, a crushed leaf, a snarl of her own black hair snagged on a bramble.

Though she had no GPS or compass to guide her, her father had taught her how to find her bearings in the middle of the woods, how to track the creatures of the forest—even if that creature was herself.

"Keep north," she said. "It's not long now."

"You know what will happen if you mislead us," Vaughn warned.

As if she could forget. She didn't need the threats. She was well aware of the predicament she'd found herself in. "I know."

They trudged through the dank, miserable wetness, heads ducked against the rain. Her hamstrings tight, her ribs aching. Rain sluiced off her hood. Her skin was chilled, clammy. Dread and horror tangled inside her, growing heavier with every step.

"You shouldn't have come back." Damien's voice was low enough that only she could hear him beneath the blur of the rain. "You were free."

"I don't expect you to understand. I couldn't just leave her."

He looked at her, eyes bleak. "I tried to do something. It wasn't enough."

"No," she said. "It wasn't."

"I didn't want this to happen. What Dekker did to you…"

"You stood there and watched."

"There was nothing I could do. I wanted to kill him, trust me."

"Is that what you tell yourself?" There was no venom in her words, no blame. Not anymore. She understood the feeling of being trapped between two impossible choices, each with terrible consequences.

"I can keep you safe now."

She glanced at him. His expression was solemn, pensive. Rain trickled down his narrow face, plastered his russet hair to his scalp, and beaded on the silver ring piercing his lip. His cunning features still sharply handsome.

"As safe as I am right now?"

He frowned. "After you give them the white wolf. You keep your end of the bargain, and Vaughn will protect you. I'll protect you."

She made a noncommittal, disbelieving sound in the back of her throat.

"I swear it. I'll ask my uncle for you. I can keep you safe."

She raised her cuffed hands, emphasizing the cuffs. "Right."

"I'll take those damn things off as soon as you take Vaughn to the wolf. That's all you have to do, okay? Just take us there, and everything can be different. It'll be better, I swear it."

She saw guilt swimming in his eyes. Remorse. He wasn't a monster, though he lived among them.

In his own way, Damien had found himself caught in a life he hadn't chosen. He'd done what he had to do to survive. She couldn't blame him for it, even if she disagreed with his choices.

"And if I want to leave? After you've supposedly saved me?"

"Then I'll help you."

"Yeah, right."

"I will, I swear it. Even if... even if it kills me."

Survival was about more than keeping yourself breathing. It was about choices and sacrifices, choosing what you could live with. And what you couldn't.

Everyone had to make that decision for themselves.

Her anger dissipated. She didn't have the energy for it anymore. Not against him. "I'm sorry."

"For what?"

She shook her head, blinked water from her eyes. "I can't expect you to risk your life for me, a stranger. I shouldn't have. It isn't fair. That's what I'm sorry for."

"I'm choosing to. I want to."

"Why, Damien? Why are you risking anything for me?"

"You were brave," he said after a moment. "Back at the lodge. And now. Hell, every time I've met you. You're doing something brave. Stupid, but brave. Or good. I... maybe I admire that."

"Maybe?"

"Yeah. I do. I really do."

She said nothing. There was nothing to say. Bravery wouldn't help her now. It was too late for that.

They trudged on. A few minutes later, her exhausted feet tripped over themselves. Damien caught her. His hands were strong. His nearness was strangely comforting.

He wouldn't save her, but at least he was here. At least he was on her side, sort of. It was something.

"Move faster," Dekker spat from behind them. "You need better motivation? How about a bullet through your hand? Or your shoulder? You don't need your arms to walk."

Raven gritted her teeth and pushed away the pain, forced it into a box, and locked it up somewhere deep inside her. She had to keep walking, keep going, just a little while longer.

She focused on reading the signs of the forest. Three yards to the northwest, a gnarled trunk of an oak with knots in the shape of a triangle. Ahead to the east, an outcropping of rock beside a spruce with its top half sheared off. Familiar signposts.

They were getting close.

The wind howled through the empty trees, rattling the bare branches. The storm last night had shorn nearly every tree bare.

The men cursed occasionally. Thorns raked at their clothing. They tripped over roots and rocks hidden beneath the damp, matted leaves filming the forest floor.

Scorpio hunched inside his coat, glowering at the wet gleaming tree trunks surrounding them on every side. "How much longer? I'm freezing. My balls are colder than a witch's tit in a brass bra."

"We're wasting time," Dekker said. "Just give me the girl and we'll be done with this mess. We could be warm by the fire with hot food in our bellies, not out here wandering around the wilderness like damn fools. Hell, she's probably got us lost."

"We're not lost," Raven said. "I know exactly where we're going."

"We're done when I say we're done." Vaughn's voice was sharp with warning. Scorpio and Dekker fell silent.

They reached a steep incline. Raven shuffled past the stump of a great oak as tall as her shoulder, the broken shards of trunk jutting like teeth. On her right lay a cluster of boulders. Mountain Laurel bushes creaked wetly in the wind.

She stepped into the clearing and lifted her head. The sky was dark and chaotic, though it couldn't be past 10 a.m. yet. Turbulent clouds churned overhead. The meadow of ferns glistened in the rain.

"What the hell are you doing?" Dekker stepped into the clearing behind her. He gripped her arm and yanked her around to face him. "If you've tricked us, so help me—"

"We're here."

Raven whistled. One long note, two short ones.

Chapter Forty

"The white wolf's den is here," Raven said. "Across the clearing."

Dekker sneered. "You better not be lying, you little—"

"I'm not lying." She pointed straight ahead, into the shadows of the trees on the other side of the clearing.

The Headhunters moved around her and entered the clearing, their legs swishing through the thick damp ferns. They spread out, rifles up, scanning to the left and right.

Thunder rumbled in the distance. Lightning splintered the sky. Raindrops splattered her face, soaking her hair.

It was a huge risk to bring the Headhunters here. She didn't know what else to do. She was out of options. No other moves to play but this one.

It was a desperate move—a rash, reckless, foolhardy choice in an array of awful choices, each worse than the last.

There was one slim chance to get out of this alive.

If it didn't work, at least she would die on her terms.

Adrenaline flared through her veins. Her tense gaze swept the tree line. She strained her ears, listening hard for any sounds over the drum of the rain.

There was nothing to hear.

There was nothing to see.

There wouldn't be. Not until it was too late.

"Over here!" Scorpio called. His voice was unusually high and shaky. He'd wandered across the clearing and now stood behind the Mountain Laurel bush.

Something lay crumpled beneath the large bush near the opposite edge of the clearing. The sodden fishing hat, brown as dirt, barely visible through the sheeting rain.

Scorpio pointed at something on the other side.

Raven knew what it was.

He'd found the body. Or what was left of it.

And there, a few yards from the bush, beneath the shagbark hickory trees—something else glinted wetly. The rifle she'd been forced to leave behind.

Dekker, Vaughn, and Cobb crossed the clearing to join Scorpio. Dekker and Vaughn swore. Cobb stumbled backward, hand over his mouth in disgust and horror. His face went ashen beneath his beard. He turned his head and retched.

"So that's what happened to Gomez," Dekker said.

"Those damn wolves tore him to pieces," Vaughn said in awe. Like he was impressed rather than horrified.

Raven clenched her jaw and said nothing.

The Headhunters milled around the wide matted circle of the kill.

"Here's an arm," Scorpio said.

"I found a leg," Cobb called.

If she ran now, she wouldn't get far. They'd hunt her down easily.

Raven eyed her rifle beneath the trees, lying in the underbrush. It was visible only if you knew where to look. Twenty yards, if that.

She would have to run straight across the clearing, grab the rifle, and start shooting before the Headhunters could reach her.

Even then, she might take down one or two, perhaps three if she were lucky, but there were ten of them. Too many.

Unless, of course, they were otherwise engaged.

She yanked at the plastic bindings digging painfully into her wrists. The rifle was a moot point without her hands free. It wouldn't be easy to get to the whittling knife stuffed into her pocket, and she needed the knife to cut the zip ties.

Approaching footsteps commanded her attention. She glanced up. Vaughn and Dekker strode toward her. Vaughn's face was a mask of rage in the rain. "Bring her here!"

Beside her, Damien tensed. He stepped in front of her. "For what?"

Dekker's flinty eyes shone with sadistic anticipation. They were dark as beetle shells. "Time for this little slut to make good on her promises. If she can."

"I told you," Raven said. "The den is just past the hickory trees on the other side of the clearing. I swear it."

"We looked over there. No den," Dekker said.

Damien's jaw pulsed. He tightened his grip on her arm. "Leave her alone."

"Where's the den?" Vaughn kept his gaze laser-focused on Raven. He barely glanced at Damien. "I'm only going to ask you once."

Raven's heart hammered against her bruised ribs. "It's here, just through the trees—"

Dekker's eyes narrowed. "Liar."

"I told you what would happen if you played me." Vaughn's tone flattened. He nodded at Dekker. "She's all yours."

Dekker's smile bristled with sharp white teeth. "With pleasure."

"Stop it!" Damien cried. "Don't touch her. You can't hurt her."

Dekker snorted. "You going soft on us, boy?"

"This isn't part of the deal—"

Vaughn said, "There is no deal."

Damien looked shocked. "But you said—"

Dekker shot him a contemptuous look. "Don't you get it? She's trash. She's a whore. She's nothing. She's not one of us. Now shut the hell up and give her to me."

Fear flashed in Damien's eyes. He didn't shrink back. He opened his mouth, closed it. His jaw clenched. Every word he spoke seemed to cost him something. "And if I don't?"

Dekker sneered. "How about I gut you both? That what you want? To die with this trashy little whore?"

"Watch yourself, Dekker." Vaughn's voice went cold and hard. He cared nothing for Raven, but Dekker had insulted his nephew. He didn't like that. "Damien, give him the girl."

Damien hesitated. His sharp eyes flicked uncertainly between Vaughn and Raven.

The rest of the Headhunters stood silent and unmoving. The rain beat down on them all.

Damien reached for the gun at his hip. "No."

"Damien!" Vaughn said. "Put that thing away before you get hurt and step aside. Last warning."

Dekker didn't give Damien a chance to obey. He sprang at Damien and shoved him, tearing the gun from Damien's grasp in one fluid movement and tossing it away.

Damien went sprawling. He landed hard on his butt, flattening several ferns.

Before Raven could react, Dekker unsheathed his hunting knife, grabbed the back of her head, and pressed the blade to her throat.

"Stop!" Damien pulled himself to his feet, wiping the mud from his pants. He frantically searched for his pistol, hidden in the tall ferns. "Leave her alone!"

Scorpio drew his pistol and aimed it at Damien's chest. "Don't move!"

"Don't hurt her!"

"Enough!" Vaughn held up a hand to stop his nephew. His other hand rested on the strap of his hunting rifle. "Think, now. Don't do something you'll regret, son."

Damien went still. He stood silent, muddy and rain-slicked, his face anguished. He was weaponless, as helpless as Raven in Dekker's grasp.

Lightning lit the underbelly of the clouds. Torrents of rain poured down.

The edge of the blade scraped Raven's throat with every swallow. Terror clawed at her with cold, frantic fingers.

She'd miscalculated. Vlad wasn't here. For whatever reason, the tiger had abandoned his kill early and moved on to greener pastures.

It was over.

She'd gambled and lost.

Vaughn glared at her. "For the last time, where is the damned wolf?"

The knife blade jabbed into her throat. She blinked wetness from her eyes and raised her chin in defiance. She was going to die, but she hadn't given them everything.

They hadn't won. She'd made sure of that.

"The wolves aren't here. They got away. You'll never find them. You failed."

Vaughn's face darkened in outrage. "Kill her."

Dekker seized her hair and dragged her back against his chest.

She couldn't help it. She screamed. She tried to pull herself free. The knife bit into her throat, drawing blood.

"Now," he said in her ear, "where were we?"

At least she would be in the woods when death came for her. At least she would die with rain on her face, dirt beneath her feet, the gray mouth of the sky swallowing her up.

The blade pressed deeper. Pain and dizziness exploded in front of her vision. At least—

Out of the corner of her eye, she saw it.

A streak of motion bolted into the clearing. Then another. One white, one black. Twin demons of snarling fury.

CHAPTER FORTY-ONE

The black wolf launched at Vaughn.

With a ferocious snarl, the white wolf charged Dekker.

The clearing exploded into chaos. Shouts of confusion and fear. Screams of pain and terror.

Dekker's knife slipped an inch from Raven's neck. His body went rigid against hers. "What the hell—!"

Raven took her opportunity. She raised her foot and kicked backward with all her strength, aiming for Dekker's kneecap.

He had time to scream.

Then the white wolf was on him.

Luna sprang at Dekker just as Raven dropped and twisted sideways. The wolf's paws struck Dekker in the chest. She closed her powerful jaws around Dekker's forearm. The wolf's teeth sank into flesh, muscle, and bone.

Dekker screamed and fell backward. The knife slipped from Raven's neck. A line of fire seared her throat.

They collapsed to the ground, entangled in flailing limbs. As she fell, Raven twisted free of the wolf's scrabbling paws. Landing on top of Dekker, Luna kept her iron grip on Dekker's arm with her teeth.

Raven rolled on the ground, flattening a swath of soaked ferns. Shakily, she clambered to her hands and knees. Scratches covered her arms and face. Blood dripped steadily from the cut across her throat. The zip ties dug into the flesh of her wrists. Rain slicked her face, soaked her body.

She didn't care about herself. Scrambling awkwardly to her feet, she scanned frantically for the wolves.

Raven shouted, "Run, Luna! You have to run!"

They shouldn't be here. The wolves were supposed to be far from here, running free. Safe and alive. They weren't supposed to come back.

They weren't supposed to save her.

Twenty yards away, in the center of the open clearing, Shadow battled Vaughn. Vaughn managed to slam the butt of his rifle against Shadow's muzzle. Shadow let out a pained whimper and darted out of harm's way.

Three Headhunters armed with pistols sprinted toward Vaughn. Scorpio and Cobb ran toward Dekker. They shouted, their rifles drawn, aiming wildly. They didn't shoot for fear of hitting Dekker.

Dekker writhed beneath the wolf. Screaming in pain, shrieking curses. Snarling, Luna crouched atop him. She snapped viciously at his throat. Dekker attempted to shield his neck and face with his arms. Punching at her snout, striking at her head.

Run! Raven's brain screamed at her. This was her chance to escape. But she couldn't run.

She couldn't leave the wolves in the hands of the Headhunters.

Not when they had come back for her. Not when they were in such danger.

The wolves had made her pack. They'd made her family.

She had to *do* something.

Time slowed. Her heart battered against her ribs. Rain pelted her exposed head. The world was gray and hazy, blurred by the raindrops clinging to her eyelashes.

Across the clearing, Shadow kept Vaughn at bay. Circling and darting, leaping and snarling and biting.

Vaughn fired several times but couldn't aim fast enough. Shadow was a black ghost, dissolving in the rain to mist before reappearing to tear a gash in Vaughn's arm, to nip viciously at his leg.

Raven needed a weapon, a better one than her tiny whittling blade. She was helpless without one. She scanned the slick wet grass, searching desperately for Dekker's serrated hunting knife or Damien's pistol—

There. Among the bent ferns, a glint of steel.

Before she could seize the large hunting knife, Damien appeared. He picked it up and turned toward her. His face a rictus of fear, confusion, indecision.

Raven thrust out her bound arms. "Help me!"

Damien sliced through the zip ties with the knife and freed her wrists. The plastic pieces slipped to the grass. Raven grabbed the knife from Damien's hands. Her fingers were slick with her blood. It soaked into her shirt.

"You need to go!" His voice was frantic. "Quickly, while they're distracted. Go. Run!"

"I can't. Not without—"

Another gunshot sounded. Much closer. Louder.

Raven's heart stopped. Her ears rang. She whirled to the right.

Scorpio had fired at Luna and missed. On the ground, Dekker wrestled Luna to the death. Scorpio and Cobb circled them warily, searching for an opening.

Luna snarled and snapped at Dekker's throat. Dekker's clothes were shredded. His arms and chest were bloodied and tattered. Luna lunged for his throat, closing her jaws a hair's breadth from his Adam's Apple. She was ferocious, unrelenting in her attack.

Cobb lifted his rifle, finger on the trigger.

Raven raised the knife and lunged at him. "No!"

Sensing her attack, Cobb dodged to the side. Her knife scraped harmlessly across the arm of his leather jacket.

Cobb whirled and struck her in the side of the head with the rifle.

Pain exploded inside her head. Stars danced across her vision. She staggered, momentarily stunned. The knife slipped from her hand.

Cobb fired. The round nicked the white wolf's left ear, drawing blood. He cursed.

Before he could fire again, the wolf plunged her jaws into Dekker's throat. Her teeth closed deep. She clamped her jaws and shook her head fiercely, ripping and tearing and shredding through the man's jugular. Blood arced from his throat in a wide red spray.

Dekker shuddered. His mouth opened in a gurgling scream. His eyes bulged in horror. His body twitched, convulsed, and then stilled. Blood soaked the ground, the ferns, his torn throat.

Luna had killed him.

The Headhunters shouted in alarm. They couldn't help him now. Their rifles swiveled toward the wolf.

"Kill it!" Cobb shouted. "Hurry! Don't let it get away!"

"Luna!" Raven cried. "Run! Go!"

As if comprehending her words, Luna leaped from Dekker's limp form before the Headhunters could regroup and shoot her. The wolf streaked across the clearing.

But Luna didn't flee into the safety of the woods. Instead, she swerved toward Vaughn and Shadow, coming to her mate's aid.

She was ten yards from Shadow, then five.

Everything moved in a terrible, languid slow motion. Raven tried to take a step and stumbled, still dizzy. She could only watch in breathless dread.

Cobb swung around, planted his feet, and raised his rifle. He was too far for Raven to stop him. He aimed and fired at the white wolf.

Luna yelped in pain. Her right hind leg dragged on the ground. Blood bloomed across her hindquarters.

Raven screamed. "No!"

Before she could run at Cobb again, Damien wrapped his arms around her waist and pulled her back. Raven fought him, twisting to get away. He was strong and held her fast. "It's not safe! Stay back."

Her legs buckled. Pain speared her ribs, her skull, the bleeding cut on her neck. "Let me go! Luna!"

Too late.

Cobb fired again.

Luna staggered. She took a faltering step, then another. With a whimper, she slumped to the ground.

"Get up!" Raven cried. "Get up! Run!"

Luna did not get up. A scarlet stain spread through the thick fur of her throat. Her legs twitched like she was chasing a deer through the woods on a beautiful moonlit night. Only she wasn't. She couldn't. She would never run again.

Raven shoved at Damien, trying to break free, to get to Luna. "Let me go! Luna!"

Damien tightened his grip. "They'll kill you. Raven, stop—"

"Luna, get up! Get up!"

Luna's sinewy body shuddered. Her great chest heaved with the effort of each panting breath. Her regal head lifted once, as if searching for her mate, for Shadow, then it sagged limply to the ground. The wolf let out a faint, pained moan. Then she went still.

Thunder boomed overhead. Lightning flashed. The sky split into jagged pieces.

"NO!" Raven stared at the fallen wolf, bereft. Damien tightened his grip, holding her upright. "No, no, no!"

Rain pelted the wolf's body. It mingled with the blood and ran in reddish rivulets through the matted fur like small bright rivers. She didn't move. Her chest did not rise and fall.

The white wolf was dead.

Chapter Forty-Two

Luna was dead.

Raven cried out in horror. Her grief clenched tight as a giant fist inside her.

She could do nothing but watch in numb despair as Cobb stalked across the clearing and stood triumphantly over the dead wolf. He punched the air in victory with his fist.

He kicked the limp body savagely, mercilessly. Then he laughed.

Raven felt flayed. "Stop! Stop it!"

Shadow howled. High and plaintive, full of grief. Abandoning Vaughn, he darted across the clearing to Luna's side. With a bewildered whine, he nudged her head with his muzzle, as if begging her to open her eyes, to leap to her paws.

She didn't. She wouldn't, ever again.

Shadow crouched over her fallen body, raised his great head, and snarled at the Headhunters. He was protecting her, even in death. But his honor would get him killed, too.

"Run!" Raven screamed at him. "Run, damn it!"

Cobb had retreated several feet at the black wolf's approach. Several Headhunters formed a loose half circle several yards back from Luna's fallen body and from Shadow, a growling, snarling demon of hate and rage.

Cobb raised his rifle at the wolf.

"Don't shoot!" Vaughn roared. He cradled his left arm against his chest, which was tattered and streaked with blood where Shadow had gotten in a few bites. He'd lost his rifle somehow in his fight with the wolf. "That wolf is mine! I get the kill shot. Bring me a gun."

The men looked at him like he was insane, but they obeyed. They kept their rifles up and ready, but no one fired a shot.

One of the Headhunters handed Vaughn a pistol. He gripped it in his uninjured hand.

"Let me go!" Finally, Raven tore free of Damien's grasp and ran toward the wolves. Slip-sliding in the slick ferns. Staggering, stumbling, dizziness washing through her, panic burning in her chest.

She lunged in front of Shadow. Placing herself between the wolves and Vaughn, she raised her arms, shielding Shadow as best she could. "NO! Don't you dare hurt him!"

"You," Vaughn said through gritted teeth. "You did this."

She had no weapons, not even the knife now. She didn't stand a chance. She knew it, but still, she didn't move. Behind her, Shadow crouched, snarling. She would protect him to the end, just as Luna had protected her.

Vaughn's eyes glinted with cold anger. "You're going to pay for this."

His right finger curled over the trigger. The barrel began to rise. Slowly. So slowly. Rain pattered off the gun. Rain pouring in a thick gray sheet. Each drop splattered as loud as a cannon blast in her ears.

The barrel settled on a spot between her eyes.

Damien shouted something she couldn't make out clearly. Sound drained away. Everything disappeared but the muzzle of the gun aimed at her face.

Everything but the smell. The hairs on the back of her neck stood on end. It was muted in the pouring rain. Faint but unmistakable, that smell: the sickly-sweet aroma of buttered popcorn.

Vaughn flicked off the safety. His finger massaged the trigger, started to squeeze. "I'm going to enjoy killing you and your wolf."

The roar was loud as a freight train. The deafening sound trembled the ground beneath their feet.

Raven's brain formed a single frantic thought—*tiger*.

CHAPTER FORTY-THREE

The tiger exploded from the underbrush. He launched at the Headhunters in a ferocious orange blur, crossing twenty feet in a single bound, spanning the distance to his prey in under a second. An arcing missile of death.

Screaming, Cobb spun and fired a wild burst of shots. In his sheer panic, the gun veered wide. He had no time to correct his aim. The tiger was on him.

Vlad collided with his target at full speed. His claws extended. Jaws gaping.

Man and beast went down together. A writhing ball of teeth and fangs and vulnerable exposed flesh.

The tiger struck Cobb in the side of the head with a paw like a sledgehammer. The man's skull snapped back. The blow might've broken his neck.

In the next instant, Vlad plunged his fangs into Cobb's throat and crushed his jugular.

Cobb's scream was abruptly truncated. He gurgled. His mouth hung open strangely. His hands fluttered uselessly. His eyes rolled wild and frantic. His blood gushed in a torrent, drenching the bent and matted ferns beneath him.

Mere seconds had passed. Three, perhaps four. Everyone stood frozen in shock and terror.

Including Raven. Even Shadow, standing guard over Luna, went stiff-legged, half turned toward this new insidious threat.

They watched in horror as Cobb's face contorted into a grotesque caricature. Blood burbled like a fountain from his lips, from his opened throat. The guttural sounds faint in the drumming rain.

The tiger rose to his full height. He cut an astonishing figure, terrible in his enormous size, his immense strength, his dreadful beauty. The vibrant burnt orange of his coat, the thick snowy white fur of his broad chest and belly, the rich oiled black of the bands striping his sleek back. A quarter ton of coiled muscle and sinew.

Vlad's muscular shoulders rippled as he stood over Cobb's body. His yellow eyes narrowed to slits. His ears flattened against his skull. He bared his fangs. His four-inch claws were unsheathed and razor-sharp.

With shaking hands, one of the Headhunters raised his rifle. "Shoot it!"

The tiger swung his great head. His intent gaze riveted on the man and that hated rifle. It happened so fast. One second to the next.

With an enraged snarl, Vlad sprang.

Airborne, he arced fifteen feet through the rain.

Vaughn attempted to track the tiger with his gun, but the beast was too quick. He fired a few impotent rounds that struck the trees somewhere above their heads.

The tiger pounced on his victim. With a single savage swipe of his paw, he slashed the man in the face. The blow knocked the Head-hunter to the ground and stripped the rifle from his useless hands.

Vlad seized the man's head in his enormous jaws. He shook the Headhunter like a rag doll. Then he bit down.

A terrible tearing sound echoed through the clearing. A sickening crunch of bone cracking, breaking, the skull caving in on itself. Vlad's jaws crushed the man's cranium. The man didn't even scream. In an instant, it was over.

The tiger crouched over the body. His tail lashed. His back arched. His great head swung back and forth, seeking his next prey. Something thick and dark dripped from his jowls. Then he roared.

Chaos erupted. Shaken from their shocked stupor, the Headhunters burst into motion. They fled for the supposed safety of the trees.

Vaughn shouted directions to his men, screaming at them to regroup and hunt the tiger down. His men ran, too scared to face down a five-hundred-pound monster.

Raven had to run, too. Get Shadow and flee. If Vlad went after the Headhunters, she could escape—

A sinister growl stopped her in her tracks.

The tiger had moved from the Headhunter's body. He stalked toward Raven. Only ten yards away, his belly low, slinking closer.

Terror clamped her throat. She stood absolutely still. A thousand times, she'd been this close to Vlad, but always with a fence between them.

Now, there was nothing but ferns, rain, and empty air.

The whittling knife lay snug in her pocket. Damien's pistol was nearby, the rifle further away, the knife somewhere in the ferns. She didn't make a move for them, didn't want to activate the tiger's prey response. A knife would do little against a tiger, anyway.

"I'm not your enemy," she whispered. "Remember?"

Vlad stared straight at Raven with fixed yellow eyes, his pupils slitted, unblinking. His jaws hung strangely, hinging open and closed, in a way she'd never seen before.

But then, she'd never seen him crush a man's skull with his teeth before, either.

Even through her terror, something niggled at the back of her brain. Something was off. Something *wrong*.

In the frantic seconds of the attack, in the blur of the rain, she'd missed it: a thick, yellowish slobber clung to the tiger's black lips. His jowls dripped with red-streaked foam. The yellowed slurry of blood, pus, and foamy slobber matted his furred throat, chest, his forelegs.

The realization jolted through her like a lightning strike. Vlad had killed and eaten Gomez. Gomez was sick. Vlad had consumed diseased flesh.

The tiger was no longer a tiger. No longer a captive beast nor a wild one. Not if the virus had infiltrated his body. His diseased brain would seek to bite and infect everything within sight. Including her.

The tiger was infected.

And she was his next target.

Chapter Forty-Four

Five hundred pounds of apex predator sprang at Raven.

The world stopped spinning. Rain droplets froze in midair. The chaos of screaming and shouting went dim. It was as if Raven were trapped underwater. Everything went distant and blurry, everything except the tiger.

Vlad bounded toward her. A streak of orange and black terror with claws. She had a single second. She did the only thing she could. She whistled. One long note. Two short ones.

Ten feet away, his powerful hind legs crouched for a final spring, the tiger hesitated. His ears rotated toward her.

Did he recognize her whistle? Deep in his diseased predator's brain, did some part of him recall an affinity for a certain familiar human?

Whatever the reason, he paused.

"You know me!" She took a slow step backward, still facing him. Then another step. "You know me."

His head tilted. He snarled at her, baring his bloodied, foaming fangs.

"I'm so sorry, Vlad." She took another step. Twenty yards from the edge of the clearing. "This isn't your fault. I'm sorry."

Vlad made a low hissing, spitting sound. His ears twitched, and he swung his head away from her. As if searching for new prey.

He had spared her. Even sick, he remembered—

Then Vaughn shot him.

The round struck Vlad's right hindquarter. With a pained roar, the tiger spun and sprang at Vaughn with outstretched claws.

Raven didn't waste a second.

She had to move. Move right now.

Grieve later. Mourn later. Think later.

Now, she had to live. Had to protect Shadow.

Time to run.

"Shadow!" she screamed. "Go!"

Shadow had remained at Luna's side. Alternatively whining and snarling. Howling his grief.

Raven ran to him. Dared a glance at Luna's bedraggled form, dragged her gaze away. The dizziness was fading, the pain a dull throbbing.

Behind her, the tiger roared. Another gun went off.

They didn't have much time.

She dared to put her hands on Shadow. She grabbed the thick ruff of guard hairs at the back of his neck and tugged. Her feet slipped in the slick ferns. She pulled at him. "Run! We have to run!"

Shadow flicked his ears toward her. He shook his huge head, as if coming out of a mournful fugue. He bolted across the clearing.

The wolf dodged between the boulders at the edge of the clearing and disappeared between the trees. Rain obscured his dark shape among darker shadows.

Raven sprinted after him. Her pulse thundered in her ears. She fixed her gaze on the rifle lying in the ferns. The rifle she'd left behind what felt like years ago.

Dimly, she heard the shouts of the Headhunters, Vlad's roar, the blasts of guns. Her ribs on fire, her back throbbing. Still, she ran. Her back felt like an exposed target.

She reached the hickory trees, squatted and grasped her rifle, slick with rain, rose and kept running, deeper into the shelter of the trees. Smears of mud crusted her soaked clothes. Cold rain pelted her face.

Behind her echoed the roars and screams and gunshots. Eventually, they'd realize she'd escaped and come hunting for her.

In her panic, she tripped over a rock she hadn't seen in the rain and went down hard, barely getting her arms up to protect her face. The rifle went flying. Her body struck mud.

Spasms of pain ripped through her ribs. Her skull pulsed with red and white stars. Her vision went blurry.

Rapid footsteps sounded behind her.

Someone seized her arm.

Terror spiked through her veins. She reared back, about to head-butt her assailant, rip out a chunk of his cheek with her teeth, whatever she had to do—

"Hey!" Damien's voice pierced through her fear. "It's me! It's me!"

Raven staggered to her feet, chest heaving. She spun, searching for a weapon.

Damien's face was ashen, his eyes wide and stricken. "Let me help you. I'm here to help."

She nodded, too terrified to argue. "The gun. I need the gun."

He bent, grasped the rifle, straightened and slipped the rifle strap over her shoulder and across her chest. He took her elbow and helped her shuffle haltingly to the edge of the clearing.

They were still just inside the tree line, sheltered beneath the broad trunks of the hickories. Damien paused. He shot a nervous look across the clearing. Numbly, she followed his gaze.

She could just make out a blur of movement and color in the clearing. So much red. The tiger had brought down another Head-hunter. The body lay bloodied and unmoving.

A fourth man screamed and crawled through the ferns, his shredded leg dragging behind him.

Vlad had disappeared into the forest on the other side of the clearing. Headhunters screamed and shouted, their panicked voices flat and thin in the rain.

She knew what would happen next. The tiger would hunt them down one by one in silence, then attack from behind when they least expected it. They'd never see him coming.

A terrible pride filled her chest. "I hope he kills them all."

Damien shrugged her pack from his shoulders and held it out to her by the straps. "I brought it for you, just in case. It has your LifeStraws, filtration tabs, the wire for snares, a compass, binoculars, filled water bottles, and some food. I added granola bars and nuts I found in the lodge. I couldn't get your map back, though. I'm sorry."

She touched the hoverboard sticking out of the top zipper with trembling fingers. Her whole body was shaking so hard, he had to help her shoulder the straps of the pack.

"Here." Damien pulled something out of his pocket. Two small bottles, one filled with antibiotics, the second, prescription-strength painkillers. "It's not much."

He handed her the bottles. She took two of each, swallowing them dry, and shoved the bottles into the backpack and zipped it. "It will help. Thank you."

"Your throat. It's bleeding."

She touched it gingerly. Her fingers came away red. "A flesh wound."

Behind them, a gunshot exploded. Then another. Vlad roared. Someone screamed in fear and pain. The agonized sound cut off abruptly.

Damien flinched.

Raven met his gaze. Rain plastered his hair to his forehead and dripped down his face. It softened his features. He was still sharply handsome, all hard angles, but he looked younger, more vulnerable.

She felt a pull, deep inside her. He had tried to do the right thing despite his circumstances. He could've done nothing. He should have left her to the Headhunters, but he hadn't.

She was still alive because of him. The words slipped out before she could stop them. "Come with us."

The briefest smile creased his mouth. It brightened his face for a moment. Then resignation darkened his expression. "I want to. I wish I could. But I can't."

"You aren't like them. You don't belong with them."

He shook his head. His mouth pressed into a grim line. His gaze darted toward the clearing again. "I owe Vaughn my life. I can't just—"

"Yes, you can."

"He's family. He protected me."

"You don't owe him your life. You don't owe him your soul."

Damien shook his head. "It's not that simple."

"It is that simple. You know who they are. What they are."

"Dekker and Rex are dead now. They were the worst."

"They're all bad." She stared at him, at his anguished features. "You're just afraid."

He blinked, wiped the rain from his face. He sighed heavily. His shoulders slumped. "Maybe you're right. Maybe I am afraid. Maybe I'm terrified every second of every day. Maybe I know deep down I'd never make it on my own."

"You can—"

He shook his head again, resolute. "No. I know myself, I'm not like you."

"Damien." With every beat of her heart, she wanted him to come with her, to make the right choice, the right sacrifice.

She couldn't force him. She couldn't decide for him.

He dropped his gaze, ashamed. "I know what you think. You think I'm a coward for choosing to stay with people who keep me safe by killing other people."

"That's up to you."

Another roar echoed from behind them. More gunshots in the distance. Raven scanned the woods over Damien's shoulder, searching for danger, but there was nothing. The trees, the sodden bushes, the muddy ground. The rain blurred everything.

The violence had moved away from them, for the moment.

Damien took a step toward her. He stood less than a foot away.

He looked at her intently, as if begging her to understand with his eyes, pleading for her absolution.

"They'll come after you," he said urgently. "Whoever survives this massacre. If Vaughn lives through this, he will hunt you. You'll be caught unless I stay."

She started to protest. "Come anyway. We'll figure something out—"

He cut her off. "There's no time. You know it's true. I can cover some of your tracks after you go. I can tell them I followed you in a different direction. With all the rain obscuring your footprints, it'll work. It'll give you the head start you need."

Her heart sank into her stomach. She was shaking all over from adrenaline. Her belly churned, sick with fear and panic. The image of Luna's dead body flashed through her brain. She didn't want to be alone. She wanted to curl into a ball and weep forever.

Finally, she nodded mutely. She resented him for it, but he wasn't wrong. By staying, he doomed himself. But it would help her and Shadow escape. "Fine."

His eyes darkened with emotions she couldn't quite read— doubt, regret, longing. "I'll do everything I can to help you. I swear it."

Another gunshot sounded in the distance.

Deeper in the woods, Shadow whined impatiently.

It wouldn't be long before Vaughn turned his attention toward Raven, seeking revenge for the death of his men. He was a man of his word. She didn't doubt he would hunt her down.

She had to make sure he didn't find her. Or Shadow. Not ever.

"Vlad—the tiger—he'll kill other people, after the Headhunters. He's sick. He has the virus. He's a danger now to every creature he comes across, human or otherwise."

Grief threatened to strangle her. Her love for the tiger swelled in her chest, squeezed her bruised and tattered heart. All those years she'd hung out on the tiger house roof, chatting to Vlad, pretending he was listening, that he understood her like no one else in her life did.

"Will you make sure that—" She swallowed the lump in her throat and gazed at him imploringly. "Make sure he doesn't suffer. Don't let those monsters torture him. Please."

His eyes widened. "How?"

"Deer jerky. He loves it. He can smell the venison a mile away. I have a couple of packages hidden in my room, in the bottom drawer of my dresser. Leave a trail and he'll follow it. Just—make it fast."

"I will," Damien promised.

She believed him. "You should leave them. The Headhunters. When you're strong enough, brave enough."

The muscle in his cheek jumped. "Someday, I will."

Raven wasn't sure if he was lying to her or himself, or if perhaps someday, he would gather the courage to leave everything and everyone he knew for the faint promise of something better.

She thrust her hand into her pants pocket and withdrew one of her carved wood ravens. She thrust it into his palm and closed her hand over his. "To remember me by."

His palm was warm and rough against her own despite the chill of the rain. His fingers tightened over hers. "As if I could ever forget you."

"My name... my name is Raven."

He smiled at her. "Until we meet again, Raven."

Their gazes locked. For a moment, for an instant, they were connected by something larger than themselves. Two humans at the end of the world. Two survivors. Two friends.

She longed to hold on, to never let go.

He'd made his choice. And she'd made hers.

She pulled away. He clutched the small carving in his fist.

Shouldering her pack, Raven ran for her life.

Chapter Forty-Five

For hours, Raven ran. Shadow ran with her.

They did not stop to eat. They did not stop to drink.

They ran on and on, terror and grief chasing at their heels.

Shadow could have outpaced her easily. He could've been miles away by now. He stayed with her anyway. Sometimes beside her, sometimes ahead of her. Sometimes visible, sometimes not.

At times, he loped at her side, head down, ears and tail drooping in sorrow. At other times, he disappeared for an hour or more, scouting ahead.

The woods were grim, dark, and wild. Branches slapped and stung her face. The air was dense and close and smelled of wet earth and ozone. Her fear chased her, close as an expelled breath on the back of her neck.

Every muscle in her body ached. Every cut and bruise pulsed with pain. Her throat throbbed. Like knives scraping flesh, but she could move, she could run through the hurting.

That's what mattered. The only thing that mattered.

The only thing she was certain of—if she fell, she wouldn't get up again.

The thought flared through her mind: the map. The cabin nestled deep in the forest. The cabin she could never find without the map Vaughn had stolen.

It was lost. All of it, lost.

As she ran, her stricken mind drifted away from her body. The cabin faded in her mind with every step she took. So did Haven.

She couldn't think of her lost home, of her dead father, or the animals she loved left behind.

She shut it all out of her mind lest the immense weight of it crush her.

She thought only of escape. The single-minded focus of survival. Staying alive for one more minute. One more hour, one more day.

Every so often, she checked her compass to ensure they were traveling in a general northerly direction, but she kept slightly northeast to remain within the relative safety of the woods of the Oconee National Forest.

Eventually, the thunder dissipated. The rain ceased. The towering black clouds shrank and diminished. The sky remained gray as ash, gray as death, as if the heavens were in mourning with them.

It was late afternoon when white flashes popped before her eyes. Heat flushed through her, then icy cold like lead in her veins. She felt like she was going to faint. Her legs turned to jelly, her bones melting to a puddle of nothing.

She faltered, nearly collapsing.

Shadow loped up to her and whined in concern. He nosed her thigh urgently.

"I'm okay," she said. "I'm okay."

Though she wasn't okay. She wasn't okay at all.

She paused to pee beside a hickory tree, using a branch for balance, and then drank what felt like a gallon of water before pulling out the first aid kit and tending to the cut on her neck. With trembling fingers, she disinfected it and bandaged it as best she could. It had stopped bleeding. That was a good sign.

Raven continued onward. After a while, Shadow ran off and disappeared into the darkening shadows of the forest.

She forced herself to put one foot in front of the other. On and on and on. Through woods into meadows and farmland and rolling pastures. A few houses dotted the horizon in the distance. She avoided them, passing several two-lane roads, blank and silent and emptied of all forms of human life.

The hours passed. The day began to die slowly and then all at once. Twilight descended. She veered off the dirt road she'd been following and headed back into the safety of the woods.

Eventually, Shadow appeared from behind a rocky outcropping and trotted to her side. He halted. His ears pricked, his head turned to the side.

She stopped, her hand pressed against her ribcage, like that could reduce the fiery pain. Her legs felt like rubber, her thighs were trembling. Blisters had formed and then burst on her heels and toes. Fluid oozed in her hiking boots.

She looked around blearily. Trees, trees, and more trees. Still, the forest was somehow comforting, not threatening, not like the men who hunted within it. The woods closed in, hiding her. Protecting her and the black wolf.

"What is it, boy?"

His tail drooped, his head bent. He whined. Then, he turned and loped off, headed up the steep ridge to the east.

As night fell, the shadows deepened into a bruised purple-black. The trees grew taller, darker. Night creatures scurried and slithered in the underbrush.

She withdrew the flashlight from her pack. The beam cut through the dark creeping shadows as she shuffled up the hill after Shadow.

Near the top of the ridge, the wolf yipped softly. He looked back at her over his shoulder, beckoning her to follow. His form silhouetted against the rising moon.

He led her along the ridgeline to a tiny clearing in the center of a ring of spruce trees. A sheer rock face towered at least forty feet above her head. At its base was a jagged crevice, with a narrow, mossy opening about three feet high and ten feet deep. Several bushes clustered at the entrance, concealing the crevice from the casual observer.

Her throat thickened with unshed tears. She was so tired she could barely stand. Her legs trembled. The painkillers had worn off hours ago. Her face was one big bruise. Her ribs throbbed with white-hot flame.

"Thank you," she said. Shadow watched her intently.

Grimacing, she lowered herself to her hands and feet and crawled between the bushes beneath the ledge of stone. Shucking off her rifle and backpack, she drank more water and adjusted the pack beneath her head as a makeshift pillow. She kept the rifle next to her, within easy reach.

The rock was hard beneath her. The air was chilly and smelled of earth and dust. A spider crawled along a ridge of stone near her face.

Still, the ledge would shelter her from rain and wind and the worst of the cold, as well as conceal her from whatever might be lurking in the woods.

Her eyelids drooped. She felt like she could sleep for a thousand hours.

Dimly, she realized that Shadow had not entered the shelter with her.

"Shadow!" she called hoarsely.

She waited. He didn't come.

Despite the protests of her exhausted body, she crawled out of the crevice, switched on her flashlight, and searched for the wolf. She couldn't bear to be alone. Not tonight.

A few hundred yards along the ridge, she came to a long shale outcropping that jutted from the top of the ridge. Far above, the stars glittered like hard diamonds flung across the cold black canvas of the sky.

Beyond the outcropping of rock lay eternal darkness. No lights glimmered from the multitude of towns she knew were sprawled somewhere below her. No tiny orange glow from vehicles crawling along winding highways.

There was only the night. The night and Raven and the wolf.

The black wolf stood at the edge of the outcropping. He threw back his head, raising his muzzle toward the vast star-studded sky, and howled.

It was a haunting, mournful sound. A sorrowful song, clear and pure as a bow drawn across a violin.

It was a requiem. An elegy. A howl of grief for the lost mate who wasn't coming back. Shadow howled his sorrow and pain and loss for Luna.

Raven turned off the flashlight. She stood still in the dark and listened. Her heart felt like it was cracking wide open. The pieces of herself splintering, shattering. The hard shell of her soul, broken wide open to reveal the raw, pulsing center of her heartache.

The grief and pain and loss of her own, which she'd buried deep since her father died. Since long before then. Since her mother had abandoned her. Since she'd first realized her father couldn't love her like she needed to be loved.

Since she'd started to believe that perhaps that was what she deserved—to be alone. To be utterly lonely, forever.

The pain flowed through her. A dark river of sorrow drowning her from the inside. She grieved for Zachariah. She grieved for her father, whom she'd loved desperately, resentfully, bitterly. But still, she'd loved him.

She grieved for her mother. For the broken woman she'd rejected without understanding that brokenness came from a monstrous darkness deep inside her mother that couldn't be fixed. She understood it now.

In that grief, in her understanding, lay something like forgiveness.

She grieved for the animals. How she hadn't realized how much she'd needed them until they were gone. For Gizmo. For Shika, Titus, Echo, and sweet Suki. For regal Vlad, who didn't deserve the disease or the death coming for him.

And for Luna, beautiful, loyal, honorable Luna. Who'd made a human part of her pack. Who'd sacrificed her own life to save Raven's.

Her eyes burned. Tears glittered in her eyes.

For the first time in three years, she let them fall.

Standing there in the center of the dark, unknowable, empty universe, Raven wept.

CHAPTER FORTY-SIX

A long time later, minutes or hours, Raven shuffled back to the crevice. She crawled beneath the ledge and collapsed on the rocky ground, exhausted, weary to the core. Completely emptied out.

In the cold darkness, Shadow stood over her and nuzzled her neck. His breath was warm against her cheeks. The musky scent of his damp fur filled her nostrils.

She held out her hand and ran her fingers through the thick guard hairs of his ruff. With a sad snort, he flopped down beside her, his flank pressed against her side.

"It's you and me, now," she said.

He gave a mournful whine as if in response. The faintest hint of starlight limned everything in a pale glow. The wolf's eyes glimmered in the darkness. Awake and alert, keeping watch over what remained of his pack.

"I can't do this alone, okay? I need you. We need each other."

Raven curled into Shadow. She nestled her cheek against his fur and breathed in the precious, comforting scent of wolf—of earth and grass and wind, of things wild and primal, of fierce love and pack and family.

Chapter Forty-Seven

In the morning, Raven awoke before dawn. Shadow was already up and outside somewhere. Her lower back spasmed as she crawled out from beneath the mossy ledge, brushing a few crawling bugs from her legs.

She was sore and achy all over, dirty and thirsty. She ran her tongue over her fuzzy teeth, longing for a hot shower. How she'd taken things like a soft mattress and running water and electricity for granted.

The rising sun transformed the sky above the trees in vivid shades of sherbet orange and cotton candy pink. Shivering against the chill, Raven drank from her water bottle and ate one of the granola bars.

Gingerly, she raised her shirt and took stock of the damage. A garish watercolor painting of blue, purple, and yellowish green bruised the right side of her ribcage from her bra line to her hip. She sucked in her breath. It hurt to look at it.

Lowering her shirt, she changed the bandage on her neck, then checked her rifle and zipped her pack. Once she was ready, she headed through the trees across the rocky ground toward the outcropping.

Last night, it had been too dark to see anything. Now, as rays of golden sunlight speared the cottony clouds, she stood at the tip of the outcropping and looked across the great expanse of forest, split by roads and trails with a few buildings clustered here and there.

From here, she couldn't make out any signs of life. All was silent, still. The ravages of the Hydra Virus invisible from this height, from this distance.

Somewhere out there was the small town of Elijay, her mother's last known location. Was her mother still out there? Was anyone?

So much nothingness. Far beyond the bounds of the wilderness, the mountains, the small towns and the larger cities. All lightless now, and perhaps lifeless. Peaceful, finally, in death.

And beyond the towns and cities of Georgia, the other states sprawled outward—Tennessee, Kentucky, the Carolinas, Illinois, and Ohio. The boundaries of the United States, of Canada and Mexico, and then the world beyond North America, other countries and continents, once brimming with billions.

Now empty. Now quiet and still. No one busy working or commuting to work or going to high school or college, attending classes or buying things or eating out or playing or laughing.

There were the dead, the dying, and those fighting not to die.

Was that it? Was that all? Had this virus truly taken hold of the whole world and crushed it beneath its vile, diseased jaws?

For days, she had focused solely on survival, on keeping herself and then the animals alive. No time or thought was spared for what came after.

This was the after. She felt like weeping. She felt like crumpling into a heap and never getting up again. You could know something logically in your head without feeling the truth of it in your bones, without understanding how it could break you.

The world out there was a void of emptiness so enormous, so vast, so endless, it took her breath away. It was too much. Too big to take in.

It was over. History. Civilization. The human race. All of it. The tattered remnants of the whole world left to scavengers and vultures, the worst of the worst.

Her brain throbbed dully. Her thoughts skittered over the oily black hole of a reality too bleak to comprehend in all its horrors.

She could only accept it gradually. Piece by piece. Day by day. Hour by hour.

That was the only way she knew how to make it.

You survived. With every breath, with every stumbling step, you survived. No matter what they took from you. No matter the devastation, the grief, the death, the travesties happening all around you, every second of every day.

You breathed. You walked. You kept going. You survived.

And she wasn't completely alone. She still had Shadow.

Raven whistled for the wolf. Through the trees, he responded with a single sharp yip. He bounded through the trees and trotted to her side. She petted his huge head.

"We're going to follow the river," she told him. "It'll take us where we need to go."

While she no longer had the map, the wilderness of the Blue Ridge Mountains still seemed like a safe bet. Fewer people. The protection of the forest. Rivers and streams for fishing, cleaning, and drinking. She'd figure it out as she went.

For a few days, Raven and Shadow traveled from dawn to dusk, resting when they needed to do so, leaving the empty roads and seeking the shelter of the woods at night.

Each night, Shadow howled his sorrow and grief. Each night, Raven wept with him. She mourned everything and everyone she'd lost.

The world was broken. It felt empty, forsaken. Bleak and hopeless.

But within the suffering, their shared loss, she felt the connection —silvery, thin as a spider's web, but strong—threaded between herself and the wolf howling his misery into the sky.

Each morning, they rose and walked again. As they traveled, she kept roughly parallel to the road, tracking north with her compass and using her LifeStraw to filter drinking water from any streams or creeks they passed. She foraged for food, gathering fallen hazelnuts, hickory nuts, and black walnuts to boil over a fire for dinner.

While there wasn't as much food to find in the fall, when it was spring and summer, she could forage for highbush blueberries, elder-berries, and sawtooth blackberries, wild sweet potato and wild ginger roots, cattails and clover, and of course, dandelions. The entire plant —flower, leaves, and roots—was edible, if a bit bitter.

Her father had taken her on numerous trips to the hunting cabin. Each visit, he'd shown her edible plants, made her memorize them, and then had her forage for them on her own.

"You can't depend on anyone but yourself," he'd said.

Her heart ached at the memory. In some ways, he'd been right. But in other ways, he was wrong.

Because of the things he'd taught her, she could survive.

The awareness came upon her gradually and then all at once: she wasn't sick. She wasn't dying. She hadn't suffered so much as a cough since Zachariah had splattered infected blood in her face.

That was three weeks ago.

There were two possible reasons she wasn't dead.

The infected blood had missed her eyes, her mouth, her nostrils. Or it hadn't, and she was one of the few immune. Either way, she'd gotten lucky as hell.

But she didn't just want to survive. She wanted to live.

She understood the difference now.

Isolation wasn't the answer. It couldn't be. Not anymore.

She didn't want to be her father, with his small limited life, his clenched fist of a heart.

She wanted more.

There had to be more.

Even with Shadow at her side, that deep, abiding loneliness never left her. The grief, always like an open wound. All the things she had believed she could leave behind were the things she needed most.

Gradually, as they made their way further north, the pain that haunted her every step lessened. Her swollen eye and split lip healed. The ugly yellowish-green bruises marring her ribs faded.

Dekker had beaten her badly. But she was alive, and he wasn't. She thought of Vlad and hoped he was at peace. The tiger had saved her life, after all.

In the evening, she set her snares, searching the underbrush until she discovered a well-used trail leading to a rabbit burrow. After three days of empty snares, she finally caught dinner.

She skinned and dressed the rabbit. She built a fire the way her father had taught her. The first time, she worried she wouldn't remember the steps correctly, but she did.

Her chest ached, that urge to weep stinging her throat as she dug two holes, each eight inches across, and a couple of feet deep. She made a tunnel between the two at the base to connect them and filled one with twigs, bark, and small sticks.

The second hole acted as a chimney to suck oxygen down to feed the fire. The fire was nearly smokeless, and the flames couldn't be seen from afar.

There were others like the Headhunters out there. She had to remain vigilant at all times. The forest would protect her, but only if she was smart and cautious.

Raven crouched over the small ball of tinder she'd gathered, mostly dried moss and pine needles, struck the flint with the edge of the steel with a glancing motion, and gently fanned the sparks into a tiny flame.

While she waited for the rabbit to roast, and during moments of rest, she whittled. She carved little birds, wolves, bears, and a small, fierce tiger. How she loved the feel of the wood beneath her fingers, the shape of something hidden within waiting for her to bring it out into the open, fully formed.

She'd allowed her bitterness and resentment to take something precious from her. Not only her carvings, but also the good memories of her parents. Not anymore. She held onto every memory—the good and the bad. They were all she had left.

She left the wooden figures on stumps, in nooks between branches, or nestled in the hollow of a tree. Maybe someone would find them. Maybe it would make them smile, give them a tiny sliver of hope. Sometimes that was enough to keep going, to keep trying.

Perhaps one day Damien would find another one to join the wooden raven she'd given him. She thought often of Damien, wondered what he was doing, if he was thinking of her, if he would one day leave the Headhunters.

She didn't know. It probably didn't matter. How could he find her in this empty, ruined, perilous world? How could anyone find anything—?

The forest echoed with a loud, eerie howl.

At first, Raven thought it was Shadow. But the black wolf lounged across the fire, not twenty feet away. The howl had not come from him.

Shadow leaped to his paws. His coat bristled, ears up. He raised his snout and sniffed the air. A warning growl started low in his throat.

Raven rose to her feet, tensing, her gaze searching the clearing, the woods.

Across the clearing, in the purple-gray of twilight, a large canine shape appeared through the tall grasses. Its muzzle was narrow, its coat a tawny mix of brown, gray, and black, with reddish fur along the creature's ears, face, and legs. Its bushy, black-tipped tail lowered to the ground.

It was a red wolf.

CHAPTER FORTY-EIGHT

Raven watched in mounting alarm as another wolf appeared beside the first.

And then a third and a fourth wolf. Then two more, then three more, until nine wolves were ranging around them, perhaps thirty yards away, no less.

Red wolves were not native to Georgia, though she remembered her father telling her that a few wild packs survived further north in the Chattahoochee National Forest. A wolf pack wouldn't normally travel so near to humans, but everything had changed. There were far fewer humans now.

For a split second, she'd hoped it was Loki or Aspen, but these were not the wolves of Haven Wildlife Refuge.

They were smaller than Shadow at sixty to eighty pounds, but the wolves were lean and long and lethal. Two of the wolves bared their teeth.

Raven went rigid. The whittling knife in one hand, the half-carved bear in the other hand. She kept still and quiet so they wouldn't see her as a threat.

Shadow raised his hackles. His ears laid back against his skull. He snarled another warning. Aggressive, dominant.

There were nine of them against the black wolf, if they decided to attack. They could circle him, come at him from multiple angles, tear into him, piece by piece. Wolves regularly took down much larger prey. They could take down Shadow.

Raven shuddered. Fear caught like a hook in her chest. Her rifle lay at her feet next to her pack. She didn't want to kill any of them, but she'd shoot as many as she could to protect Shadow. She didn't like their odds, though, two against nine.

The red wolves remained at the fringe of the clearing. They didn't slink closer. Neither did they back down or disappear. One of the wolves, the largest one and the closest, raised its head and howled. The other wolves joined in.

Their howling joined in a lilting chorus. It was a high, plaintive sound. Beautiful and haunting. The hairs raised on the back of Raven's neck.

The wolves weren't threatening to attack. Something else was happening here. Her heart thudded harder against her bruised ribs. The coppery taste of dread settled in her throat.

Shadow's ears pricked forward. She waited, not daring to breathe, to see what he would do. To see if he would howl back.

Sometimes a pack would announce a vacancy, putting out a call to any nearby lone wolves who wished to fill it. Potential candidates would be challenged by the pack to ensure the chosen one was strong, smart, and capable enough to defend and protect their new family. Then, they would welcome the new wolf as one of their own.

Shadow was the lone wolf.

They must have heard his mournful, solitary howling over the last several nights, and they had come to find him, to feel him out, to allow him to audition, if he so desired.

Did Shadow feel like a lone wolf? Did he want to join his own kind? Though he was a hybrid, they still seemed willing to accept him. Their howls increased in volume, mingling with yips and yelps, filling the clearing with their symphony.

Shadow looked over his broad shoulder at her. His amber eyes were steady as he stared at her. As if he were asking her for permission.

Her gut tightened. She felt like she was balanced on the edge of a cliff, about to fall into a bottomless black pit of nothingness.

"Do you want to go?" she asked.

His tail swished once, twice, three times. His hackles had lowered. He stared at the wolves with great interest. More than curious, he seemed fascinated by them.

Three of the red wolves loped eagerly back and forth along the edge of the clearing. The biggest wolf lifted its head again and howled, long and loud and high.

Shadow gave a low yip. It wasn't a howl of acceptance. Not yet. Not quite.

He glanced back at Raven again, whined low in his throat, plaintive and woeful.

Did she detect yearning in that whine? Longing in that amber gaze?

The words hurt to speak aloud. They were like boulders in her throat. But she knew this if she knew nothing else: love always gave the choice.

"I understand," she said, barbed wire in her throat. "You lost Luna. It's only me, now. You deserve a family, too. You and Luna saved me. You have my blessing, my loyal friend." It felt like dying. The thought of losing Shadow like losing a part of her soul. Still, she spoke the words aloud. "You can go. You can go to them if that's what you need."

Shadow did not go. He did not bound off into the meadow and join the waiting wolves as she expected, as she dreaded with every fiber of her being.

Instead, he turned and loped back to her side. He pressed lightly against her thighs. She rested her hand on the ruff of his neck. The feel of the fur beneath her fingers, the taut strong muscles bunched beneath his skin.

He whined softly, as if in reassurance.

The howling settled into silence. Slowly, one by one, the red wolves drifted back into the tree line. One by one, they disappeared into the night.

Shadow stayed.

Another piece of her shattered heart fit back together.

CHAPTER FORTY-NINE

Raven trudged through the trees, her thighs burning, breathing hard. Breaking from the tree line, she found herself at the summit of a wooded hill overlooking a small town.

The sky glowered a miserable gunmetal gray. The chilly morning air reddened her cheeks. She exhaled white puffs as she stood staring down at the small crisscrossed streets and buildings. They seemed like toys from this distance.

Her heart thumped against her ribcage. A mix of dread and excitement surged in her veins. A town meant supplies. A town meant people.

Instinctively wary, Shadow hung back. He gave an urgent, plaintive whine, as if he knew exactly what Raven was thinking and wanted her to know he disapproved.

Since the altercation with the wild wolves two nights ago, Shadow had stayed close by. His presence was a balm to her broken heart.

"What do you think? Should we check it out?"

Raven couldn't tear her gaze from the town. She hadn't set foot in a real town since the altercation at the pharmacy in Forsyth. That felt like years ago.

She was in desperate need of a physical map to figure out where she was and how to navigate the perilous terrain to get where she needed to go. She also needed a winter coat, better gloves, and a knit hat. It was downright frigid at night. Winter would be here soon.

Some canned or packaged food items, especially fruits and vegetables, would be excellent. And some new socks to replace her tattered ones. Band-Aids for her blisters. Toothpaste and a toothbrush for her fuzzy teeth. Shampoo for her itchy scalp.

She needed supplies to survive.

From her vantage point, everything appeared quiet and peaceful. That didn't mean it was. Worry gnawed at her.

"Not all people are bad," she said as much to reassure herself as the wolf.

Shadow laid his ears back against his skull as if in disagreement.

"I know last time didn't work out so well. It's dangerous, I get it. But also, I could freeze to death tonight. Winter is coming."

She had no idea what day of the week it was, or even if it was still October. Judging by the chilly weather, the frost on the grass in the mornings, and the barren trees, it was probably well into November by now.

"Five minutes," she said. "I'll be careful."

Shadow whined his reservations.

"I said I'll be careful."

She couldn't just stride into town and announce her presence to anyone who might be still alive, lurking about with ill intentions. She closed her eyes and thought of Dekker and Vaughn and Rex. Those types would be the norm now, not the exception.

Her father had taught her to be vigilant and cautious. Though her stomach was growling so loud even Shadow could hear it, she made herself wait.

Raven found a spot on the hill that gave her the best view, rummaged in the pack until she found the binoculars, and settled down to do some surveillance. With a long-suffering huff, the wolf sank to his haunches beside her.

Through the binoculars, Raven studied the town. The side roads were clustered with ranch houses. Several stores lined the main street, along with a gas station, a barber shop, a couple of mom-and-pop restaurants, and a Victorian-style bed and breakfast with a sign that read, "Shady Dale Retreat".

It was eerily quiet. There was no movement, no life.

An hour passed. Then another. Still no signs of life. After scanning the streets for another thirty minutes, her hunger and need got the best of her. It was late afternoon, though she couldn't see the sun through the dour gray clouds. She didn't want to be caught anywhere near dangerous humans after dark.

She rose to her feet. "Come on, slowpoke. Let's go. We'll be quick, I promise."

Shouldering her pack, she gripped her rifle in both hands, making sure the safety was off in case she needed to fire quickly. Cautiously, she descended the hill, darting from tree to tree, until she reached the main road leading to the town.

Shadow whined his unhappiness, but he loped obediently after her.

Dozens of abandoned cars blocked the road on both sides of the meridian. She walked in the center of the road, zigzagging between the gutted vehicles. Some vehicles had crumpled fenders or bent bumpers. Others slumped with their doors sagging open.

A mud-spattered teddy bear lay next to the flattened tire of a gray SUV. A yellow leather purse had been left behind in the center of the road. A crumpled sweater. Inexplicably, a single sneaker.

A little further along, three abandoned suitcases lay on their sides, opened and emptied. Two squirrels chased each other across the road, darting in between the tire wheels.

Raven stifled the shudder that zapped up her spine. She tightened her grip on the rifle and kept going. The air was clear and still and utterly silent. Her footfalls and ragged breathing were the only sounds other than the buzzing of insects, the occasional trill of a bird.

Ten minutes later, she passed a large sign that welcomed visitors to Shady Dale, home of the state's best fried okra. Population: 947. Not anymore.

As she drew closer, her stomach knotted in apprehension. This town was worse than empty. It had been ransacked, looted, and turned inside out.

Trash, crumpled leaves, and broken glass littered the sidewalks. Potholes pitted the streets. Discarded face masks blew across the weed-infested parking lots like tumbleweeds.

She sidestepped towers of trash bags left to rot when no one came to retrieve them, some split open with greasy bags, empty tin cans, sodden tissue paper, balled up plastic gloves strewn everywhere, blown by the wind across silent streets and into overgrown yards, the weedy grass knee-high in places, nearly to her thighs in others.

Strips of colorful paper carpeted the streets like a ticker tape parade, the paper rain-sodden now, the ink blurred and weeping. She could only make out the occasional word: warning, shelter, spreading, disease, danger, death.

Broken windows leered from most of the buildings, their interiors scraped clean of anything but trash and glittering shards of glass. Graffiti covered the boards hammered over a boutique shop's windows and doors. *Death becomes us. Kill the elites. We're all in hell.* And worse.

It was the same with the barber shop and hardware store, the gourmet café on the corner, the restaurant with the teal- and white-striped awning half-fallen over the caved-in front door.

Raven stepped gingerly over the *Welcome to Josie's* sign lying on the sidewalk, spattered with something dark-colored, and headed for the gas station.

Small holes punctured the driver's side of a blue Jeep parked in front of the gas station. The same with a gold minivan and a few SUVs crowded around the defunct gas pumps, like the owners had fought each other desperately for the last dregs of fuel.

On the side of the road sat the burned husk of a GM pickup truck, which looked like it had been torched with a Molotov cocktail.

The glass from the gas station's front door had been knocked out. Shards thrust from the frame like jagged teeth. She yanked open the door and cringed at the tinkling ring of a bell, loud as a trumpet blast in the eerie silence.

Inside, deep shadows crouched in every corner. She blinked to adjust her eyes. The hackles bristled along Shadow's spine. He kept close to her side, growling low in his throat.

She kept her voice quiet. "I know what you're thinking. It feels haunted. Everything feels wrong here. I get it. I feel it, too."

Quickly, she searched the gas station. The shelves were picked clean. Several racks were tipped over. The air smelled foul, like rancid milk and rotten meat. Flies buzzed everywhere.

Beneath an empty shelf, she discovered a single can of SpaghettiOs. Her mouth watered as she tucked the can into her pack for dinner later tonight. Nothing had ever looked so delicious.

There were no maps to be found, however. The racks were empty except for some postcards that had been spilled across the floor.

Only a few months ago, she could've found whatever info she needed in two seconds on the internet. Like electricity, the internet appeared to be long gone.

All that knowledge, the collected advancement of the human race, utterly erased in a few short devastating weeks.

It was a disturbing thought. Disconcerting. So much of this catastrophe still seemed unreal, like some terrible nightmare she might wake up from even now, even as she stared at the devastation right in front of her.

Raven tugged one of her carved wooden birds from one of the zippered pouches on her pack and placed it on the rack. She wasn't sure why exactly, she just did it.

Maybe she wanted someone like her to find it and know they were not alone out in this devastated world. Maybe some small idealistic part of her hoped Damien would leave his uncle after all and would follow her north, discovering little breadcrumbs like her carvings, knowing she was out there, somewhere, and would search until he found her.

However stupid, however unrealistic. But still.

She left the gas station and strode down the sidewalk with wobbly legs. Shadow trailed warily several yards behind her. She kicked aside a gas mask like the kind you saw in movies. The right eye lens was shattered. It must not have protected whoever had once worn it.

Down the road at the corner was a sign for Manfield's Grocery. She glanced both ways, scouring the buildings lining either side of the main street. A hardware store, a hair salon, a diner that smelled like rotten eggs.

Each store had been thoroughly pilfered. No movement anywhere, no sounds. No signs of life—or danger.

Next to the grocery store was a pre-owned clothing store. Unlike the other businesses, the store had been ransacked but wasn't completely emptied.

Sweaters and hoodies had been yanked from the shelves. Racks of pants and dresses were knocked over. Clothing spilled in puddles of colorful fabric mixed with crushed cardboard boxes and other detritus.

Raven scavenged an oversized *Beastie Boys* hoodie, a wool vest to wear beneath her raincoat, a knit navy cap, and a pair of oversized gloves, as well as a few pairs of dingy socks.

She wouldn't be winning any fashion shows, but she'd be warmer at night.

Shadow sniffed disdainfully at everything she touched.

She rolled her eyes. "Tough crowd tonight. Like you care what I look like. I bet you like my smelly breath about as much as I like yours."

Shadow turned his butt toward her and pawed at a pair of blue rubber-ducky swim shorts on the floor next to a torn sleeping bag. Someone had been hiding out here recently.

The final stop was the grocery store. The parking lot overflowed with vehicles parked haphazardly, as if in great haste. Cars were parked on the overgrown grassy berm. Near the front entrance, a dusty gray hatchback had crashed into the passenger side of a black sedan. Shards of glass and chunks of twisted metal and plastic littered the walkway.

Raven skirted the crashed vehicles and slipped through the double front doors, bending to enter through the shattered glass. The doors had once been barred with wooden boards. The two-by-fours remained stacked in a pile next to the entrance.

Someone had attempted to protect the contents of this place, or perhaps they'd tried to hoard the food from other survivors. Someone else had forced their way inside anyway.

Inside the entrance, Raven halted, blinking to allow her eyes to adjust. With few windows, the darkness huddled deeper, the shadows stretched darker beyond the row of cash registers to her left.

The smell hit her first. The stench of death. Of coppery blood and rotting gristle, of putrid, bloated flesh and feces.

Covering her mouth and nose with the hem of her new hoodie, she kept both hands on the rifle as she stepped further into the grocery store. Shadow padded reluctantly at her side, his hackles bristling, teeth bared.

She could see enough to discern the rows of barren shelves. Opened cans and crushed empty packages and split bags of rice and beans scattered across the floors, each grain of rice and individual bean long since scavenged.

The bodies lay side by side in what used to be the deli and bakery aisle. At least twenty of them. Men, women, and a few teenagers. One kid around ten years old.

Rust-colored stains marred the tile floor beneath them. The same rust-brown blotches spread across the N95 masks covering their mouths. Dried blood leaked from their eyes. The bodies were bloated and discolored, their swollen limbs locked in rigid agony even in death.

Raven jerked back, breathing hard. This was how her father had died. How ninety-five percent of the world had died. Probably her mother, too, though she didn't know that, not for certain.

Raven hadn't gotten sick like this. She'd been spared the Hydra Virus. Was she immune, or had she simply gotten lucky?

Right now, it didn't matter. She longed for the protection of the trees, the comfort of the woods. Anything to escape all this death.

She imagined every town and city in America like this. Every city in the world. Ravaged by the virus. And those who hadn't been ravaged by the virus had been left to fight over what little remained.

She saw then what she hadn't noticed at first. Each of the diseased corpses was riddled with holes. A tiny round hole was drilled into each forehead. They'd been lined up and shot to death.

Raven backed up a step. Then another. "I think I've seen enough. How about you, pal?"

Shadow growled in agreement.

She desperately wanted to skirt any other towns and highways, but the vast sprawling metropolis of Atlanta loomed to the west, and the sizable city of Athens lay somewhere directly to the north, with a population of 100,000, at least. Augusta was 80 or 90 miles to the east.

To get to the mountains and the Chattahoochee National Forest, she'd have to approach several population zones. There was no other option.

Plus, soon she would need more supplies, more food. And she couldn't wander aimlessly forever. She needed a specific destination.

Raven retreated from the gruesome scene within the grocery store and headed back down Main Street. The beginnings of an idea needled at the back of her mind, but she ignored it. For now.

"Let's go," she said. "There's nothing for us here."

The wolf loped at her side. Together, they left Shady Dale behind.

<h1 style="text-align:center">Chapter Fifty</h1>

Three days later, they came across the first living people they'd seen in a week.

It was mid-afternoon. The sun shone high in the cobalt blue sky that revealed itself in patches above the tangles of branches overhead. The air was full of the usual forest noises, the sigh of the breeze, the thrum of insects, the rustle and scurry of squirrels and chipmunks, and other small creatures.

A child's voice rang out. Startled, Raven stiffened. She leaped from the hoverboard she'd been riding along the overgrown trail she'd come across yesterday morning, and had been following north ever since.

She seized the hoverboard, darted off the trail, and pushed into a thicket of underbrush. Crouching, she clutched the board to her chest and held her breath.

Shadow's hackles raised along his spine. Silently, he vanished into the trees and disappeared. She knew he wouldn't venture far. He'd be lurking nearby, alert and watchful. If she needed him, he'd make his presence known.

Raven remained hidden, straining her ears as the noises grew louder. Three figures appeared around a bend in the trail. Stomping loud as a herd of elephants. She peeked around the edge of the trunk.

A young woman and a guy her age walked side by side, heading north toward Raven's hidden position. A younger boy straggled after them.

The two older people looked about Raven's age. The girl was Filipina, maybe seventeen or eighteen. Short and plump, with shiny black hair that fell to her shoulders and choppy bangs.

The younger boy looked about eight, also Filipino, and likely the girl's brother. His thicket of unruly dark hair fell into his black eyes.

The guy looked about twenty. He was tall and big, with warm brown skin, broad shoulders, a barrel chest, and tree-trunk arms and thighs. He looked intimidating as hell. Until he smiled at the boy, and his brown eyes crinkled affectionately. His smile seemed kind.

Like Raven, they carried packs and rifles and looked like they'd been on the road for a while. Their clothes were wrinkled, their hair matted, their eyes circled with dark shadows of fatigue.

She noted the sleek handgun holstered at the girl's hip. The girl held the boy's hand, but he was giggling and trying to escape, to pull free from her grasp.

"Benjie!" she admonished in exasperation. "You think I'm letting go of you for even a second? You have to stay right with me so I can keep you safe."

"I can take care of myself, Willow," the boy muttered.

"Like hell you can," the sister said. "What do you need to remember?"

"Stay together, stay safe," the boy repeated, his face solemn.

"Do not forget that. We stick together. We take care of each other. Got it?"

"Got it," the kid muttered, rolling his eyes.

"I mean it," the girl—Willow—said.

"I said I got it!" The boy half-turned, his eyes narrowed as he gazed back along the trail. His gaze seemed to come to rest on Raven for a moment.

Her heart stopped in her chest. Then his gaze darted past her as his sister tugged his hand, and they kept walking.

It was then that she saw it, clutched tight in the boy's left hand—

a small, rough wooden object in the shape of a bird with outstretched wings. One of Raven's own carvings.

This boy had found one somewhere. He'd kept it, held it close, perhaps treasured it the way she'd hoped someone would.

Her heart thudded against her ribs. Was it a sign? Should she show herself to them?

Still, Raven didn't move. The strangers trudged past Raven's hiding spot. The older guy made a joke, and the boy laughed. It was a high, sweet, beautiful sound that made her chest ache with loneliness.

Raven watched them go until they'd passed out of sight, until she couldn't see the wood carving held tight in the little boy's hand.

These people seemed so normal. Regular people, just like her. Did that make them safe? Or even more dangerous?

She remembered her mother's last letter. The letter she'd read while sitting on the tiger house roof, on her birthday, while Vlad lounged lazily below her feet. A lifetime ago. An entire world ago. *Find good people. Don't be alone.*

It was a risk. People were a risk. Trust in anyone but yourself was a risk.

She thought of Zachariah, his generosity and kindness. Of Damien and his choice to offer her mercy, so she could live. And of her parents, their frailties and their virtues.

The world was ugly. It was cruel and broken, savage and unfair. And yet. There was grace, too. And beauty.

She understood now in a way she never had before: a few good people made all the difference. Between isolation and connection, between despair and hope, between death and life.

Raven knew her purpose, now. She was going to search the whole shattered world if she had to, she was going to find her mother.

But first, she needed to find a tribe of good people. She and Shadow needed a pack of their own. They couldn't survive alone, not on the perilous journey that lay before them.

Perhaps she might find Damien again someday, too.

Either way, she would start right here, right now, with these three strangers. Maybe they were the ones, maybe they weren't.

There was only one way to find out.

She would follow them at a distance until she was certain of the right moment.

And then they would rejoin the world together, Raven and her wolf.

Acknowledgments

Thank you to my awesome beta readers. Your thoughtful critiques and enthusiasm are invaluable, as always: Lauren Nikkel, Michelle Browne, Kimberley Tremblay, Jessica Burland, Sally Shupe, Lia Riccio, Jeremy Steinkraus, and Barry and Derise Marden.

A special thank you to Jen Avery for her fantastic eye and detailed, thorough feedback and suggestions that made this a better story. And to Donna Lewis for being a great developmental and line editor. You both make my words shine.

To my husband, who always helps with deadlines and plot holes and listens patiently to problems about imaginary people.

And to my kids, who I love more than anything. You are my everything.

About the Author

Kyla Stone is the *USA Today* Bestselling author of over 25 novels. With over two million copies sold worldwide, her books have been translated into several languages, and her *Edge of Collapse* series has been optioned by Sony Studios for television.

She lives in Michigan with her family and spends her days writing apocalyptic, survival, and psychological thrillers. Her favorite treats while writing include dark chocolate and coffee.

When she's not writing, she enjoys reading, hiking, playing board games, and traveling around the world. She loves adventures, including rappelling down waterfalls in Costa Rica, off-roading on the dunes of Lake Michigan in her blue Jeep, parasailing in the Dominican Republic, and scuba diving in Roatan and Belize.

She loves to hear from her readers.

Email her at Contact@KylaStone.com

ALSO BY KYLA STONE

Lost Light:

The Light We Lost

The Dark We Seek

The Hope We Keep

The World We Burn

Edge of Collapse:

Edge of Collapse

Edge of Madness

Edge of Darkness

Edge of Anarchy

Edge of Defiance

Edge of Survival

Edge of Valor

Nuclear Dawn:

Point of Impact

From the Ashes

Into the Fire

Darkest Night

The Last Sanctuary:

The Last Sanctuary

Rising Storm

Falling Stars

Burning Skies

Breaking World

Raging Light

Stand Alones:

Queen of Fate and Fury

Beneath the Skin

Before You Break

9 781962 251457